Also by David Mitchell

Ghostwritten: A Novel

Number9Dream

Random House
New York

Number9Dream

a novel

David Mitchell

The author would like to thank Scott Moyers, Elena Schneider, Benjamin Dreyer, Kapo Ng, Richard Elman, Mercedes Everett, Janet Wygal, John McGhee, Evan Stone, and Evan Camfield.

RANDOM HOUSE and colophon are registered trademarks of Random House, Inc.

This work was originally published in the United Kingdom by Hodder and Stoughton, a division of Hodder Headline, in 2001.

Library of Congress Cataloging-in-Publication Data

Mitchell, David (David Stephen)
    Number9dream : a novel / David Mitchell.
        p.   cm.
    ISBN 0-375-50726-4
        1. Young men—Fiction. 2. Children of prostitutes—Fiction. 3. Fathers and sons—Fiction. 4. Tokyo (Japan)—Fiction. 5. Birthfathers—Fiction. I. Title: Number 9 dream. II. Title: Number nine dream. III. Title.

PR6063.I785 N86 2002
823'.92—dc21   2001041910

Random House website address: www.atrandom.com

Printed in the United States of America on acid-free paper

98765432

First U.S. Edition

Book design by Mercedes Everett

It is so much simpler to bury reality than it is to dispose of dreams.

Don DeLillo, *Americana*

Contents

one

□

PanOpticon

"We are both busy people, so let's cut the small talk. You already know my name, or at least you knew it, once upon a time. Eiji Miyake. Yes, Ms. Kato, *that* Eiji Miyake. Why am I here in Tokyo? Think about it. I am here to find out who my father is. And why you, Ms. Kato? You know his name and you know his address. I never threaten anyone. But I am telling you that you are going to give me the information I want. Right now."

Or something like that. A galaxy of cream unribbons in my coffee cup, and the background chatter pulls into focus. My very first morning in Tokyo, and already I am getting ahead of myself. Jupiter Cafe sloshes with lunch-hour laughter, Friday plottings, clinking saucers. Drones bark into cell phones, she-drones hitch up sagging voices to sound more feminine. Steam bears coffee, seafood rolls, detergent. I have a fine across-the-street view of PanOpticon's main entrance. Quite a sight, this zirconium gothic skyscraper. Its upper floors are hidden by cloud, and so is the real Akiko Kato. City weather is a mystery. Under its tight lid, Tokyo swelters at 34°C in 86 percent humidity—a big PANASONIC display says so. Tokyo is too close up to see, sometimes. There are no distances and everything is above your head—dentists, kindergartens, dance studios. Even the roads and walkways are up on murky stilts. An evil-twin Venice with all the water drained away. Reflected airplanes climb over mirrored buildings. I always thought Kagoshima was huge, but you could lose it down a single side alley in Shinjuku. I light a cigarette—I am smoking Kools today, the brand chosen by a biker with hair dyed blackcurrant in the line ahead of me—and watch the traffic and passersby on the intersection between Omekaido Avenue and Kita Street. City office drones, lip-pierced hairdressers, midday drunks. Nobody is standing still. Rivers, snowstorms, traffic, bytes, generations, a thousand faces per minute. Back on Yakushima you might get a thousand minutes per face. Crowds make me thoughtful. All these people have boxes of memories labeled "Father," "Dad," "Pa." Whatever. Photogenic pix, shots in poor light, scary figures, tender poses, fuzzy angles, scratched negatives—it makes no difference. Unlike me, they know who it was who ushered them into the world. Crowds make me too thoughtful.

Ms. Kato! Come down to Jupiter Cafe! It would be so much simpler. You drop by for a seafood roll and a coffee; I recognize you instantly, of course, introduce myself, admit coyly that I was hoping to bump into you here; we discuss the matter at hand—we are two grown-ups now—and you will see that natural justice is on my side. I sigh aloud, and sense my neighbor hide him-or-herself deeper behind his-or-her barrier of newspaper. How do you smuggle daydreams into reality? My careful plan seems far-fetched. A building as vast as PanOpticon surely has many other exits. It must have its own restaurants, to spare its employees the hassle of descending to ground level. Who says you even eat lunch, Ms. Kato? Maybe your slaves bring you a human heart to tide you over until suppertime. I entomb my Kool in the innards of its ancestors and resolve to end my stakeout when I finish this coffee. Hear that, Akiko Kato? I am coming in to get you.

Three waitresses staff Jupiter Cafe this lunchtime. Waitress One—the boss—is a brittle imperial dowager who poisoned her husband. Waitress Two, a corn-on-the-cob face with a braying donkey voice, is Waitress One thirty years ago. Waitress Three is turned away right now, but her hair is up and I can see she has the most perfect neck on Earth. I mean it. A syndicate of love poets could not describe how smooth and curved this neck is. Soft as a peeled egg. Dowager is telling Donkey—and half Jupiter Cafe by default—about her hairdresser's latest failed marriage. "When his wives don't measure up to his fantasies, that's when he tosses them overboard." She has an industrial-diamond voice.

The waitress with the perfect neck is serving a life sentence at the sink with a scrubber and sponge in lieu of a ball and chain. The atmosphere is hostile in here. Are Dowager and Donkey cold-shouldering her, or is she cold-shouldering them?

Hot fog is now down to the ninth story of PanOpticon. I decide to calculate the number of days I have lived. It comes to 7,286. I add four leap years. The clock says 12:51. Suddenly most of the drones in the cafe get to their feet and flock away. Are they afraid that if one o'clock finds them anywhere except their fluorescent-lit cubicles, their companies will have an ideal excuse to Restructure them? I watch lots of them enter PanOpticon, and toy with the idea of coming back tomorrow and stealing an ID tag. No. Simple is good. I strike PanOpticon today. At the stroke of one o'clock. My coffee cup stands empty in its moat of slops. I admit I am nervous. Nervous is cool. A recruitment officer for the Self-Defense Forces came to my high school—my old high school, I should say—and said that no worthwhile fighting unit wants members who are immune to fear. In combat, soldiers who are blind and brave inevitably get their platoon wiped out. An effective soldier controls his fear, and uses it to sharpen his senses. It sounded so easy. Another coffee, Eiji? No, thanks, Eiji, but I will smoke one final Kool. To sharpen my senses.

I catch the clock changing from 13:31 to 13:32. Yeah, I know, my deadline died. My ashtray brimmeth over. I shake my box of Kools. Only two left. The fog is down to the sixth story. I imagine Akiko Kato gazing through her air-conned executive-office-suite window—it is high, high up, above the fog even, maybe. The sunshine is stellar up there. Can she sense me, as I sense her? Did she wake up this morning knowing that today is one of those life-altering days? One final, final, final cigarette before "nervous" becomes "spineless." The only other customer in Jupiter Cafe who has stayed as long as me is an old man. He is plugged into a vidboy. His fingers twitch as he fires plasma bolts into the digital distance. He is identical to the ink-brush portrait of Lao Tzu in my classics textbook. I mean it. Bald, nutty, bearded. Other customers arrive, order, pay, drink, eat, use the bathroom, and go. Decades' worth every quarter-hour. Only Lao Tzu and I endure. The waitresses must be thinking my girlfriend has stood me up. Or that I am a psycho on the prowl for a female to stalk. A Muzak version of "Imagine" comes on and John Lennon wakes up in his tomb, appalled. It is sugary beyond belief, full of flowery flutes. Even the musical prostitutes who recorded this horror hated it. Two pregnant women enter, order lemon tea, and discuss what kinds of fathers their husbands will become. "Not ideal, maybe," I want to lean over and tell them, "but it could be worse. Want to hear my life story?" Lao Tzu coughs a cough of no return, and dabs the phlegm off his vidboy screen. I drag smoke down deep and trickle it out through my nostrils. I never expected Tokyo to be this dirty. It needs a good flooding to clean it up. Mandolineering gondoliers punting down Ginza. "Mind you," continues Dowager to Donkey, "his wives are such grasping, mincing creatures! They want to play the la-di-da company president's wife. I tell my hairdresser this: When you search for a spouse, pick somebody whose dreams are exactly the same size as yours. But does he listen, the brainless ape? Of course not! What would an old woman know about these things?" I inhale the foam from my new coffee. My cup has lipstick traces. I construct a legal case to prove that touching the lipstick with my own lips constitutes a kiss. That would increase my tally of kissed girls to three. Surely, less than the national average for a young male of my years. I think I want to forget the first two girls. I know they have already forgotten me. So I look around Jupiter Cafe for a suitable owner of painted lips. I settle on the waitress with the living, wise, moonlit, viola neck. She is still working through the mountain range of dirty cups and dishes. A tendril of hair has fallen loose. It tickles her nape. Lucky hair! I try to compare the fuchsia color on the cup to her lips, but I cannot see her face properly. My case is shaky. Besides, this lipstick is half-fused with the porcelain atoms. It might have been washed many times. Jupiter Cafe is not the last word in luxury teahouses. My imagination is my worst enemy—no, that is not true, but the comfort it gives is never warmer than tepid. The waitress is a sophisticated Tokyoite. She has enough rich, fashion-conscious, virile admirers to fill a laptop computer. Case dismissed. Lao Tzu growls at his vidboy. "Damn, damn, *damn* bioborgs! Every damn time!" I drink my dregs, put on my baseball cap, and stare at PanOpticon. Time to locate my maker.

□

PanOpticon's lobby is as cavernous as the belly of some futuristic robo-behemoth. Which is a fair description of the whole PanOpticon organism, only Tokyo moves around it instead of it needing to move around Tokyo. Arrows in the floorpads sense my feet and guide me to a vacant reception booth. I fake boredom. Changes in heart rate may trigger suspicion. A door hisses shut behind me. The blackness is subterranean. A tracer scans me from head to toe, blipping over the bar code on my ID tag. An amber spotlight flicks on, and my reflection stares back from the black glass. I certainly look the part. Overalls, baseball cap, toolbox, clipboard. I adjust my hair and pretend to admire myself. "State your name and business," intones an ice-maiden voice. I wonder how human she is. These days computers humanize and humans computerize and you never know. I pretend to lose my cool slightly, stare at the ceiling, and act the overawed yokel. "Uh . . . Afternoon, madam. Ran Sogabe is my name. I came to do the fish, see."

"Company?"

"No, I came quite alone."

"What is the name of your company? Your employer?" I hear irritation—excellent, my interviewer is only a human.

"Finny Friends, Inc."

"Finny Friends?"

"Inc. Haven't you seen our vidscreen ad? 'If your finny friends are feeling down, don't despair, don't you frown! A brand-new service is in town! If your—'"

"Why are you requesting access to PanOpticon?"

I act puzzled. "I service fish for the Ministry of Law."

"Which partners?"

"Osugi and Kosugi."

"Osugi and *Bo*sugi."

She is inexperienced. I check my clipboard. "Right." Let me in, Ice Maiden. Someone as dumb as me can't be a threat to anyone.

"I am scanning some curious objects in your toolbox."

Now I act proud. "Newly imported from Germany, madam, or might it be mademoiselle? May I present to you the ionic fluorocarb popper!

Doubtless a lady of your education is already well aware that the key to a successful marine environment is pH stability. Finny Friends, Inc., is the first aquaculturist practice in Japan to utilize this little wonder. If time permits, perhaps you would allow me to—"

"Place your right hand on the pad in front of you."

"I hope this is going to tickle."

"That is your left hand."

"Beg your pardon."

A brief eternity passes before a green AUTHORIZED light blinks.

"And your access code?"

Ice Maiden is thorough. I scrunch my eyes. "Let me see: 313-636-969."

"Your access code is valid . . ." So it should be—I paid the finest freelance hacker in the city three months' salary for those nine digits. ". . . for the month of July. We are now in August."

That scuzzy bum hacker. "Uh . . . weird." I scratch my crotch to buy time. "That was the access number encoded and received from"— I glance at my clipboard—"Ms. Akiko Kato. They don't come much higher up than her."

"Your access code is invalid."

I puff out my cheeks. "If you say so, if you say so. Pity, though. When Ms. Kato wants to know why her Okinawan silverspines— priceless, for all intents and purposes, now they are on the near-extinct list—are belly-up dead on the surface, I'll just have to refer her to you. Oh, well. What did you say your name was?" I pose with my pen.

Ice Maiden hardens. "Check your access codes and return tomorrow."

I shake my head, amused. "If only saving silverspines from asphyxia- tion were that simple! Do you have any idea how many finny friends I got on my turf? Obviously not. In the old days, we had more give and take, but now we run to an hour-by-hour time frame. Even as I stand here I got ninety angelfish at the Metropolitan gasping for a gill scour. Now. Your name? This is just so we don't get sued and I am not the one who loses my job."

Ice Maiden hesitates.

"Look," I say, "why not call Ms. Kato's secretary?"

"I already did. You are expected tomorrow. Not today."

"Tomorrow?" I will electrocute my freelance hacker, very slowly. "Of course I was *expected* tomorrow. But the Minister for Fish issued an industry-wide warning last night. Aquatic gill-and-mouth ebola has entered the country. The Cubans are to blame, apparently. The spores, traveling down air ducts, enter tanks, lodge in brain tissue, and puff up the fish until they literally explode. Innards everywhere. The scientists are working on a cure, but until then—"

Ice Maiden finally cracks. "Ancillary authorization granted, Mr. Sogabe. From this booth proceed to the elevator, which will take you to the eighty-first floor. You must leave PanOpticon within sixty minutes, and follow the sensor arrows at all times, or Security will not be held responsible for any injuries."

"Level eighty-one, Mr. Sogabe," announces the elevator. "I look forward to serving you again." The doors open and for a moment I think I am in a virtual rainforest. Pots, ferns, and plants half-conceal the reception desk. An aviary of vidphones trills. A woman puts down a spray mister and peers at me from behind a hyacinth as high as herself. "Security told me Mr. Sogabe was coming. Who are you?"

"Let me guess! Kazuyo? Kazuyo. Am I right?"

"No. I'm Fubuki. But who—"

"Ms. Fubuki! Of course! No wonder Ran calls you his PanOpticon Delight!"

"Who are you and what do you want?"

I act a young man driven by flattery failure into digging a deeper pit. "Uh, I'm Ran's—I mean Mr. Sogabe's—apprentice. Joji. Don't tell me he never mentioned me! I do Harajuku normally, but I'm covering Mr. Sogabe's Shinjuku clients too this month on account of his, uh . . ." I look left and right, and whisper, ". . . genital malaria."

Her face falls. "I beg your pardon?"

"Well, you can't blame him for not mentioning it, can you? Ongoing condition, I'm afraid. It flared up again last night. The boss thinks it's just a heavy cold, which is why Ran didn't cancel his appointments. All hush-hush!" I smile gingerly and glance around for obvious monitor-cams. None visible. I kneel, open my toolbox with the lid blocking her view, and begin assembling my secret weapon. I have it down to nine seconds. "Had a hell of a time getting in here, y'know. Computers have such suspicious minds. Artificial intelligence? Artificial stupidity. Ms. Kato's office is down this corridor, I believe?"

"Yes, but I have to ask you for a retinal scan. Standard procedure."

"I hope it tickles." Finished. I approach her desk with my hands behind my back and a stupid grin. "Where do I look?"

She rotates the eyescan at me. "Into this eyepiece."

"Ms. Fubuki. Is it true about the . . ." I nod at her feet. ". . . y'know . . ."

She replies crisply. "Is what true?"

"Your eleventh toe."

"My eleventh *what?*" The moment she looks at her feet I pepper her neck with enough instant-action tranquilizer microdarts to knock out the entire United Korean Army. Her knees give and she slumps conveniently into her chair, and forward onto her blotter. I make a witty pun in the manner of James Bond for my own amusement.

I knock three times. "Finny Friends, Inc., for Ms. Kato?"

A theatrical pause. A complex lock retracts. "Enter!" Checking that the corridor is free of witnesses, I slip in. The actual lair of Akiko Kato matches the imagined one, except I was wrong about her view being above the clouds. A checkered carpet, a wall of old-fashioned filing cabinets—haven't seen those in a while. Of course, a filing cabinet cannot be hacked however ingenious your hacker. A wall of paintings too tasteful to trap the eye, a curved window of troubled fog. Between twin half-moon sofas stands a spherical tank in which a cloud of Okinawan silverspines haunts a coral-encrusted sunken battleship. Nine years have passed since I last saw Akiko Kato, but she has not aged a single day. Doubtless she can afford the latest DNA reravelers from certain Chinese labs. She glances up from her desk. Yes, her beauty is as cold and callous as ever. "You are not the little fish man who usually comes."

I close the door, and with my left hand turn the old-fashioned key— retained on the same security theory as the filing cabinets—and pull out my gun with my right. "No, Ms. Kato." I have her full attention. "I am not a little fish man at all."

"So what in hell's name do you—"

"We are both busy people, so why not cut the small talk? It is a simple-enough matter. You already know my name, or at least you knew it, once upon a time. Eiji Miyake. Yes, Ms. Kato, *that* Eiji Miyake. Why am I here in Tokyo? Think about it. I am here to find out who my father is. And why you, Ms. Kato? You know his name and you know his address. What? No, I never threaten anyone. But I am telling you that you are going to give me the information I want, and right *now*—"

Akiko Kato blinks once. An abrupt laugh. "Eiji Miyake?"

"I fail to see the funny side."

"Not Luke Skywalker? Not Zax Omega? Did you compose that spiel yourself, to reduce me to awed obedience? Or did you steal it from a movie? *One island boy embarks on a perilous mission to discover the father he has never met.* Well, Eiji Miyake, I'm afraid you are going to discover what happens to island boys who leave their fantasies." She shakes her head in mock pity. "Even my closest friends call me the most poisonous lawyer in Tokyo. What makes you think you can scare me into handing confidential client information over to a child with a popgun?"

"Give me your file on my father or you will see how dangerous a child with a popgun can be."

"Are you threatening me?"

I release the safety catch and move away from the door. "I certainly hope so. Hands up where I can see them. Stand back from the desk. You don't want to make me jumpy. Not at this range."

"This nonsense has gone on too—"

I fire, and her intercomscreen explodes in a plastic supernova. The bullet ricochets off the assassin-proof window and slashes into a picture of lurid sunflowers. Akiko Kato's complexion finally turns ashen, the way I want it. She walks over to the painting and hisses: "You gutter-bred, urine-blooded infidel! My van Gogh! You are going to pay for that!"

"More than you ever did, I am quite sure. The file. Now."

"Security will be here in thirty seconds."

I allow myself a smile. "I have the blueprints to your office. Spyproofed, soundproofed. No messages in, none out, except via your intercomscreen, which is currently out of order. So stop blustering and give"—I level the gun at her head—"me . . . the . . . file."

She is alarmingly unconcerned. "You should have spent your youth on your island picking oranges with your granny and your uncles."

"I won't ask you again."

"It isn't going to happen. Your father has too much to lose. And so do I. If news of his whored brat—you, that is—leaked out, red faces would be caused in higher places than you could ever dream of. This is why we have a modest secrecy retainer agreement."

"So you are blackmailing your own client."

"*Blackmail* is a strong word for someone still in search of the perfect zit cream. My position as your father's lawyer calls for discretion. Discretion is a precious commodity in this city, and like all precious commodities—"

"I am not leaving this office without the file."

"Then you shall be here for a very, very long time. I would order us some coffee but you put a bullet through my vidcom."

I don't have time for this. I flick the switch from handgun mode back to tranquilizer. Her forearm is exposed to the elbow—the long-dreaded Akiko Kato barely has time to register the sting of the darts before she collapses where she stands, unconscious as the deep blue sea.

Speed is everything. I peel the Akiko Kato fingerpads over the Ran Sogabe ones, and access her computer. The deeper computer files will be heavily passworded, but overriding the locks on the filing cabinets is simple. MI for MIYAKE. I doubleclick: my name appears on the menu. EIJI. Doubleclick. I hear a promising mechanical *clunk* and a drawer telescopes open halfway down the wall, blocked by Akiko Kato's prostrate body. I drag her onto one of the sofas—not a pleasant task; I keep thinking she might come back to life. I put down my gun, pull out the drawer as far as it will go, and leaf through the slim metallic carrier cases. MIYAKE—EIJI—PATERNITY. The case shines pure gold.

"Put that back."

Akiko Kato closes the door with her ankle and levels a Zuvre .441 Lone Eagle at the spot between my eyebrows. Dumbly, I look at the Akiko Kato still slumped on the sofa. The doorway Kato permits herself a satanic chuckle. Rubies are set in the enamel of her teeth. "I see you have already met my bioborg. Well, I hope you feel stupid. Because you are. Very. Our spy in Jupiter Cafe picked you up—the old man next to you. His vidboy is an eyecam linked to PanOpticon's combrain. I saw you coming. Tracked your every tediously predictable move. Now. Lightly kick your popgun over the floor toward me . . . that's right . . . and kneel down. You don't want to make me jumpy. Not at this range. A Zuvre blast from here will scramble your face so badly your own parents wouldn't recognize you. But that was hardly their strong point, was it?"

I guess I have ten seconds to live. "It was unwise of you to handle an intruder without backup."

"Your father's file is a sensitive issue."

"So, your bioborg was telling the truth. Osugi and Bosugi don't know you are blackmailing him."

"Why are you worried about my professional ethics when you should be begging for your life?" I glance at my gun, still on the floor halfway between us, letting my eyes linger a moment too long. She may be a professional blackmailer but she is an amateur hit man—she falls for my ploy and lunges at the gun. Her eyes are away from me for only a moment but that is all I need to aim the carrier case in my arms at her and flip open the switchclips without entering the disabling code. The lid-mounted incandescent booby trap explodes in her face. She screams, I roll-dive, her Zuvre fires, glass cracks. I spin, leap, boot her face, wrench her gun from her grip—it fires again. Her fingernails drill into my wrist, I elbow her face, her heel crunches my nose, the Zuvre flies from my hand, but finally I score a full-force blow to her head and follow up with a crushing uppercut. The real Akiko Kato lies motionless on her bioborg twin. I don't think I killed her. Okinawan silverspines thrash on the soaked carpet. Crunching glass, I retrieve the Zuvre—a much more potent gun than my own—and the sealed file on my father, which I stuff into my overalls. I close the door on the stain already spreading over the carpet. I stroll back toward the corridor, whistling "Imagine." That was the easy part. Now I have to get out of PanOpticon, and not by means of a body bag.

Ministry of Law drones fuss around the receptionist still slumped in her rainforest. I summon the elevator, and show appropriately nongenuine concern while I wait. "Sick Building Syndrome, my uncle calls it," I say to nobody in particular. "It affects fish in the same way." I proceed to make myself invisible by boring anyone who may notice my presence. The elevator arrives and an old medic barges out, tossing onlookers aside. "Space," she growls, "I must have space." I slip into the elevator and the doors close on my crime.

"Not so fast!"

A polished boot wedges itself between the closing doors. I consider blasting it away, but outside Akiko Kato's office spyproofing a single shot would alert Security. A guard muscles the doors apart. He has the mass, nostrils, and hair of a minotaur. "Ground Zero, son? Me, too. Okay, elevator, down we go." Our descent begins. "So," says Minotaur. "Are you an industrial spy, or what?"

Adrenaline and confusion swish through my bloodstream in strange ways.

Minotaur keeps a straight face. "You're trying to make a quick getaway. That's why you nearly took off my foot in the door up there."

My laughter goes on too long. "Yep." I rap my toolbox. "Full of top-secret data on PanOpticon's fish. Double agents, you know, the whole tankful." My father's file in my overalls suddenly feels three times bulkier. "To be honest, I was afraid of the fainted receptionist. One glimpse of blood and I'm a goner. I could never do your job."

Minotaur snorts. "Get used to anything." When the elevator doors finally open I say "After you," even though he showed no sign of letting me go first. The elevator is more polite. "Thank you, Guard Murasaki and Mr. Sogabe. I look forward to serving you again." Floorpad arrows return me to the security booth. I am sealed in again. "Have you fully discharged your duties?"

I beam for Ice Maiden. "I get you on the way in and on the way out?"

"Standard procedure."

"You call it standard, I call it the hand of destiny. Yes, the silverspines are fully immunized now. You know, Finny Friends has been in business for eighteen years and we can truthfully say we have never once lost a fish due to negligence. It is a part of our standard procedure to conduct a postmortem on each and every 'friend' in our care, and it is old age each and every time. Or client-sourced alcohol poisoning around the end-of-year party season. I could tell you about it over dinner, perhaps?"

"We have nothing whatever in common."

"We are both carbon-based life-forms. That's a big head start. We wouldn't have to talk about fish. We could talk about anything you like."

The pause chills as it lengthens. "Let's talk about why your toolbox contains a Zuvre .441 Lone Eagle."

How, oh how, could I have been so stupid? "Absolutely impossible."

"A Zuvre .441 registered under the name . . . Akiko Kato."

"Oh!" I laugh, setting down the toolbox, opening it up and taking out the offending item. "Do you mean this Zuvre .441?"

"I do mean that Zuvre .441, yes."

"I can explain. This is for—"

I am not playing for time. She is. The glass flowers with the first shot. Alarms scream. The glass mazes with the second shot. Gas hisses above me. The glass cracks with the third shot. I sledgehammer my body through. The lobby beyond is full of shouting and running and jaggedness and a thousand flashing arrows. Men and women crouch, terrified. Guards' boots pound. I glimpse Minotaur, a dozen Minotaurs, a dozen dozen Minotaurs. "The man in the overalls," I hear Ice Maiden say, "the fish man!" I engage the double safety catch, set the Zuvre on continuous plasma fire, and lob it at the onrushing squadron of guards. Three seconds doesn't give me enough time to make the entrance, and the explosion lifts me up and hurls me into the revolving doors with the force of a typhoon and literally spins me down the steps outside. Chaos, smoke, and sprinkler water belch from the PanOpticon lobby. Around me are dominoing traffic collisions and what any fugitive from injustice needs most—panicking crowds. "A madman!" I rave. "Madman with grenades! Call the cops! Call the helicopters! We need helicopters! Everywhere!" I hobble away down Omekaido Avenue, past Jupiter Cafe—this will give Dowager and Donkey something to gossip about, just look at them gawping. She is still at the sink. Her neck is still an oasis of soft calm in this sandblasted world. I hurry into a Fukuya department store and head for Menswear.

Thirty minutes later I emerge in a sharp gray suit and a pair of John Lennon sunglasses. I hail a taxi and ask the bioborg driver to take me to Kita Senju. I remove my father's file from my brand-new briefcase, and mentally record the moment for posterity. Upon this day, August 24, at 14:50, in the back of an autotaxi rounding Yoyogi Park, under a sky murky as a teenage boy's underfuton, I, Eiji Miyake, less than twenty-four hours after my arrival in the metropolis of Tokyo, officially bring to an end 7,290 days of ignorance and discover my father's true identity. I imagine Anju on the seat next to me, swinging her legs. "See?" I wave the file at her. "I promised I would. Now we'll know his name, his face, his house, who he is, what he is." The taxi swerves to avoid a fleet of ambulances and fire engines. "Open it then," says Anju, "c'mon, bro, open it." I slit open the seal with my thumbnail.

Far things feel near.

Page 1.

The air-reactive ink is already vanishing from ghost-gray to absolute white.

◆

Lao Tzu growls at his vidboy. "Damn, damn, *damn* bioborgs! Every damn time!" I drink my dregs, put on my baseball cap, and stare at PanOpti-con. Time to locate my maker. I limber up. "Say, Captain," Lao Tzu croaks, "no chance of a spare cig in that box, is there?" I show him the empty carton. He looks doleful. Well, I need some more anyway. I have a stressful business meeting ahead. "Is there a machine in here?" "Over there." He nods at a cluster of potted plants. "You'll find one hidden in the greenery. I smoke Carlton, as a rule." I hunt for the right change, but I have to break yet another thousand-yen note. Walk a hundred meters in Tokyo, check your wallet, and you discover another thousand yen has mysteriously spent itself. I mean it. I decide to order one last coffee before facing the real Akiko Kato. The adrenaline forcefield gen-erated by my last coffee is already dying away. I deploy my incredible powers of telepathy. Hey! Waitress! You with the celestial neck! Take off your rubber gloves and come serve me a coffee! My telepathy lets me down today—I get Dowager instead. This close up I notice her nostrils are hairdryer-plug-compatible—two pinched slits. She nods when I thank her for the drink, as if she is the customer, not me. How to Be a Tokyoite, Lesson 1: nonobligatory thank-yous are weird. I walk back to my window seat, trying not to spill my coffee, sit down, open my Carltons, and fail to coax a flame from my cheapo lighter. Lao Tzu slides me a box of courtesy matches from a bar called Mitty's. I light my cigarette—then his—as he is concentrating on a new game. His fingers are crocodile-tough. He takes a deep drag, and sighs with a gratitude only us smokers can understand. "Thanks a million, Captain. My son nags at me to give up, but I tell him, 'Hey, I'm dying anyway—who am I to interfere with nature?'" I make a vague sympathy noise. Nothing prospers in Tokyo but pigeons, crows, rats, roaches, and lawyers. I sugarize my coffee, rest my teaspoon on the meniscus, and slooooooowly dribble the cream onto the bowl of the spoon. Pangaea rotates, floating unruptured before splitting into subcontinents. Playing with coffee is the only pleasure I can afford in Tokyo. The first three months' rent on my capsule wiped out all the money I saved working for Uncle Orange and Uncle Pachinko, leaving me with a chicken-and-egg problem: if I don't work, I can't stay in Tokyo and look for my father; but if I work, when do I look for my father? *Work.* A slag-heap word that blots out the sun. My two saleable talents are picking oranges and playing my guitar. I must be five hundred kilometers from the nearest orange tree, and I have never, ever played my guitar for anyone. Now I understand what fuels dronehood. This: you work or you drown in debt and the underclass. Tokyo turns you into a bank balance with a carcass in tow. The size of this single number dictates where the carcass may live, what it drives, how it dresses, who it sucks up to, who it may date and marry, whether it cleans itself in a gutter or a Jacuzzi. If my landlord, the honorable Buntaro Ogiso, stiffs me, I have no safety net. He doesn't seem to be a con man, but successful con men never do. When I meet my father—at most a couple of weeks away—I want to prove I am standing on my own two feet, and that I am not looking for handouts. Dowager heaves out a drama-queen sigh. "You mean to tell me this is the very last box of coffee filters?"

The waitress with the perfect neck nods.

Donkey joins in. "The very last?"

"The very, very last," my waitress confirms.

Dowager shakes her head. "How can this possibly have happened?"

Donkey maneuvers. "Well, I sent the purchase order off on Thursday!"

My waitress shrugs. "Deliveries take three days."

Dowager clouds over. "I hope you aren't trying to blame this crisis on Eriko."

"And I hope you aren't trying to blame me because I was the one to notice we are going to run out of coffee filters by five o'clock. I just thought I should say something." Stalemate. "Look. Why don't I take some petty cash and buy some more?"

"I am the shift supervisor. I make these decisions."

"I can't go," Eriko the Donkey whines. "I had my hair permed this morning. Any minute now it's going to rain buckets."

Dowager turns back to my waitress. "Go and buy a box of filters. There's a supplier right next to the subway entrance, behind the clock." She pings the register open and removes a five-thousand-yen note. "Keep the receipt, and bring back the exact change, or you'll ruin my bookkeeping." My waitress removes her rubber gloves and apron, takes an umbrella, puts the note in her purse—actually, she has a boy's wallet—and leaves without another word. Dowager squints after her, as if taking aim down a telescopic lens. "That young miss has an attitude problem."

Donkey tuts. "Those rubber gloves! She thinks she's a hand-cream model."

"Students today are too coddled. What is it she studies, anyway?"

"Snobology."

I watch her wait at the light to cross Omekaido Avenue. This Tokyo weather is extraplanetary. Outside is still oven-hot, but a dark roof of cloud is ready to buckle under the weight of rain at any moment. The pedestrians waiting on the island in the middle of Kita Street sense it. The two young women taking in the sandwich board outside Nero's Pizza Emporium sense it. The battalions of the elderly sense it. Hemlock, nightingales, E minor—thunnnnnnnnnnnder! Belly-flopping thunnnnnnnnnnnder, twanging a loose bass. Anju loved thunder, our birthday, treetops, the sea, and me. Her goblin grin flashed when it thundered. Raindrops are heard—shhhhhhhhh—before raindrops are seen—shhhhhhhh—quivering ghost leaves—dappling the pavements, smacking car roofs, drumming tarpaulins. My waitress opens up a big blue, red, and yellow umbrella. The light turns green and the pedestrians dash for cover, sheltering under ineffective tents of jackets or newspapers. "Our poor hand-cream model will get drenched," says Donkey, with a concern that wouldn't fool anyone. The downpour erases the far side of Omekaido Avenue. "Drenched or undrenched, we need coffee filters," replies Dowager. My waitress disappears. I hope she finds somewhere dry. Jupiter Cafe fills with holiday refugees being nice to one another. Lightning zickers, and the lights dip in counterpoint. The refugees all go "Wooooooooo!" I help myself to a match and light another Carlton. It would be stupid to confront Akiko Kato until after this storm passes. Dripping in her office I would be about as formidable as a drowning gerbil. Lao Tzu chuckles, chokes, and gasps for air. "My, my, I ain't seen rain like this since 1971. Must be the end of the world."

□

One hour later and the Kita Street–Omekaido Avenue intersection is a churning confluence of rivers. The rain is incredible. Even on Yakushima, I cannot remember rain quite this heavy. The holiday atmosphere has died, and the customers are doom-laden. The floor of the Jupiter Cafe is, in fact, underwater; we are all sitting on stools, counters, and tables. Outside, traffic stalls and begins to disappear under the foaming water. A family of six huddles on a taxi roof. A baby wails and will not shut up. Group dynamics organize the customers, and there is talk of moving to a higher floor, staying put, navy helicopters, El Niño, tree-climbing, North Korean submarines abducting refugees. I smoke another Carlton and say nothing: too many captains pilot the ship up the mountain. The taxi family is down to three. Junk swirls by. Somebody has a radio, but can tune it to nothing beyond torrential static. The flood level creeps up the window—now it is over halfway up. Submerged mailboxes, motorbikes, traffic signals. A crocodile cruises up to the window and snoutbutts the glass. I wish somebody would scream. Something is twitching in the corner of its mouth—a plump hand with an engagement ring. The beast's eye settles on me. I know that eye. The animal sidles away with a twitch of its tail. "Tokyo, Tokyo," cackles Lao

Tzu. "If it ain't fire, it's earthquake. If it ain't earthquake, it's bombs. If it ain't bombs, it's floods." Dowager crows from her perch, "The time has come to evacuate. Young mothers and babies second, senior ladies first, so get out of my way." "Evacuate to where?" asks a man in a dirty raincoat. "One step outside, the current'll sweep you clean past Guam!" Donkey calls from the safest place of all, the coffee-filter shelf. "Stay inside and we'll drown!" The pregnant woman touches her bump, and whispers, "Oh, no, not now, not now." A priest remembers his drinking problem and swigs from his hip flask. Lao Tzu hums a sea shanty. The wailing baby will not shut up. I see an umbrella shoot down the fiercest artery of the flood, a red, blue, and yellow umbrella, followed by my waitress, rising, falling, flailing, and gasping! She needs me! I don't think. I jump up on the window counter and unfasten the top window, which is still above the water level. "Don't do it," chorus the refugees, "it's certain death!" I frisbee my baseball cap to Lao Tzu. "I'll be back for this." I kick off my sneakers, lever myself through the window, and—

—the torrent is a mythical force submerging and buoying me at a cruel velocity. Lit by lightning, I recognize Tokyo Tower, in floodwater up to its navel. Lesser buildings sink as I am swept by. The death toll must be in the millions. Only PanOpticon appears safe, rising into the heart of the tornado. The sea slants and peaks, the wind howls a symphony of the insane. Sometimes the waitress is close at hand, sometimes far away. Just when I don't think I can stay afloat any longer, I see her paddling toward me on her umbrella coracle. "Some rescuer you turned out to be, Miyake," she says, gripping my wrist. She glances behind me, and unspeakable horror is reflected in her face. I turn around and see the gullet of the crocodile closing in. I whip my hand out of hers and shove the umbrella away as hard as I can, turn around, and face my death. "No! Eiji! No!" my waitress screams. I am strong and silent before my nemesis. The crocodile rears and dives, its fat body feeding into the water until its tail vanishes. Was it only trying to scare me?

"Quick," calls my waitress, but barbed teeth mesh my right foot and yank me under. I pound the crocodile but I may as well be punching a mighty cedar. Down, down, down, I kick and struggle in slow motion, but I only succeed in thickening the high-speed clouds of blood spewing from my punctured calf. We reach the floor of the Pacific. It is heavily urbanized—then I realize the crocodile has chosen to drown me outside Jupiter Cafe, proving that reptiles have a sense of irony. The customers and refugees look on as if the crocodile and I are a circus act. The storm must have passed, because everywhere is swimming-pool blue and tap-dancing light and I swear I can hear "Lucy in the Sky with Diamonds" playing. The crocodile watches me with Akiko Kato eyes, suggesting that I see the funny side of having my bloated corpse stowed in a lair and being snacked on over several weeks. I lighten as I weaken. I watch Lao Tzu help himself to my final Carlton and doff my cap. Then he mimes stabbing himself in the eye and points to the crocodile. A thought unsilts itself—yesterday my landlord gave me my keys—the one for the storefront shutter is three inches long and might serve as a minidagger. Twisting into striking range is no easy feat, but the crocodile is taking a nap, so it fails to notice me fit the key between its eyelids and ram the sharp point home. Squeeze, squelch, squirt. Crocodiles scream, even underwater. The jaws unclamp and the scaly terror of the salty deep thrashes off in spirals. Lao Tzu mimes applause, but I have already gone three minutes without air and the surface is impossibly distant. I kick feebly upward. Nitrogen fizzes in my brain. Sluggishly I fly, and the ocean sings in ten thousand soprano chorus lines. Face submerged, searching for me from the stone whale, is my waitress, loyal to the last, hair streaming in the shallows. I and the girl with kaleidoscope eyes gaze longingly at each other, until, overcome by the beauty of my own death, I sink in slow, sad circles.

As a cord of scarlet sun picks the lock of dawn, the priests of Yasukuni Shrine light my sandalwood funeral pyre. My funeral is the most majestic within living memory. The whole nation is united in mourning. Traffic is diverted around Kudanshita to allow the tens of thousands to come and pay their respects. The flames lick my body. Ambassadors, my uncles, heads of state, Yoko Ono, all in black. My body blackens and blazes. His Imperial Majesty wished to thank my parents, so here they are reunited for the first time in nearly twenty years. The journalists ask them how they feel, but they are both too choked with emotion to reply. I never wanted such an ostentatious ceremony, but, well, heroism is heroism. My soul rises with my ashes and hovers among the television helicopters and pigeons. I rest on the giant torii gate, wide enough to drive a battleship under, enjoying my new perspective of human hearts.

"I should never have abandoned those two," thinks my mother.

"I should never have abandoned those three," thinks my father.

"I wonder if I can keep his deposit," thinks Buntaro Ogiso.

"I never even asked him his name," thinks my waitress.

"I wish John were here today," thinks Yoko Ono. "He would write a requiem."

"Brat," thinks Akiko Kato. "A lifelong earner comes to a premature end."

◆

It would be stupid to confront Akiko Kato until this storm passes. Dripping in her office I would be about as formidable as a drowning gerbil. Lao Tzu chuckles, chokes, and gasps for air. "My, my, I ain't seen rain like this since 1971. Must be the end of the world." But no sooner has he spoken than the storm turns itself off at the main. The pregnant women laugh. I think about their babies. During those nine aquamarsupial months, what do babies think about? Gills, swamps, ocean trenches? When does thought begin? Do sperm scheme against other sperm, the way commuters elbow ahead in the Tokyo rush hour? Do the unborn know they are? At what age did Anju and I learn that the world is actually two: one outside, and one inside, which we call "imagination"? A stupendous discovery, you would have thought, but I have no memory of the day. For babies in wombs, imaginings must be reality. On Omekaido Avenue, pedestrians peer upward from under umbrellas, awnings, and doorways, checking the lack of rain with the backs of their hands. Umbrellas close. Clouds scroll offscreen. Jupiter Cafe's doors slide open and my waitress comes back, swinging a bag. "Took your time," Dowager thanks her. My waitress hands her the filters. "Next time I'll do my very best to pick a supermarket with shorter lines." "Did you hear the thunder?" asks Donkey, and I suspect she is not such a bitch really, just a weak person under the influence of Dowager, who does not like camaraderie among her crew. "Of course she heard it! Everybody in Tokyo heard it! My Aunt Otane heard it, and she's been dead nine years." My money says Dowager tampered with the life insurance and shoved Aunt Otane down a very long flight of highly polished stairs. "The receipt? The change?" My waitress stows her umbrella away and gives Dowager the receipt and coins. She has an invisible irony field cloaking her, which intercepts and destroys incoming attacks. The clock says 14:31. I bisect an almond flake with my thumbnail and draw pentagrams in the ashtray with a toothpick. Here is an unpleasant thought: How do I know Akiko Kato is actually working in PanOpticon today? Suppose I barge past her secretary, flaming with righteousness, only to arrive at her desk to find a "Back Thursday" Post-it note stuck to her computer monitor? I would look like a complete idiot. The entire office would remember me and laugh at me. In my wallet I carry Ms. Kato's card, which I borrowed from my grandmother's fireproof box when I was eleven. I had intended to study voodoo and use it as a totem. AKIKO KATO, ATTORNEY, OSUGI & BOSUGI. I make a deal with myself. I will order an iced coffee, smoke one final Carlton: and then I call. There. If Akiko Kato answers the phone I will go straight over. So I wait until my waitress is at the counter, and go up to place my order with her. She is about to meet my eyes, when Dowager growls "Dishes!" and my girl goes back to the sink. "Refills aren't free," Dowager tells me. I cannot change my mind now, even if I am in danger of needing a caffeine detox program. "Uh . . . I know. An iced coffee, please." I am served brusquely, and wait until the bioborgs kill Lao Tzu. I swap a Carlton for a match, and devise a telephone strategy brilliant enough to reduce hardened Tokyo PAs to putty.

"Good afternoon, Osugi and Bosugi, how may I help you?"

I inject my voice with its maximum authority. "Ye-es"—My voice squeaks as though my balls are still in puberty free fall. I blush—I am nearly twenty!—fake a cough, and restart three octaves below. "I would like to ask if Ms. Akiko Kato is in the office."

"Do you want to speak with her?"

"No, I would like to, I mean, yes, please, thank you, I would like to."

"To what, sir?"

"Uh . . . to speak with her."

"May I ask who's calling?"

"I am a, uh, business associate. A professional one."

"I see, and do you conduct your business anonymously or do you have a name people can call you by?"

I am sweating. "I have a name."

"I can't put you through to Ms. Kato without a name."

"Taro Tanaka." The duddest of all dud names.

"Taro Tanaka. And your call would be concerning . . . ?"

"Uh . . ."

"Hello? Is anyone there?"

"Yes. Sorry?"

"Mr. Tanaka, I asked you why you want to speak with Ms. Kato."

"Oh, I see. Sorry. Uh, it's a confidential matter."

"Of course, but what do you wish to discuss with Ms. Kato?"

"Uh . . . legal matters."

"Naturally, Mr. Tanaka. Well. Ms. Kato is with the senior partners at the moment, and can't come to the phone. If I could take down your number, company, and a rough outline of your business, I can ask Ms. Kato to return your call later today, or maybe tomorrow. Or possibly the day after."

"Naturally, uh, yes."

"So?"

"Uh . . ."

"Mr. Tanaka?"

I fall, drown, whatever, and hang up.

A C or a D, but not quite an automatic fail. I found out that Akiko Kato is in her PanOpticon lair. As I sit here jingling the icebergs in my coffee glass they fuse, clink. I pour in the twin juglets of syrup and cream, and watch them swirl and bleed. If I were Zax Omega I could antigrav up to your office window in a few seconds. That would get your attention quickly enough. Do you daydream about meeting me? How do I appear in your daydreams? The pregnant women are talking about the agony of childbirth. I learn that male doctors never administer anesthetic

because they believe the pain strengthens the mother-baby bond. I learn
that their friend was told by her husband to drive herself to the hospital
when her labor pains began, because he had to play golf with his boss.
My waitress is doing a tour of the tables, emptying ashtrays into a
bucket. Come this way, I order her telepathically, empty mine. Mine is
the only ashtray in the entire cafe she forgets. Dowager is on the telephone, simpering sweetly. Donkey appears to have shrunk to a micro-
scopic height when I was looking away. A guy crossing Kita Street
catches my attention: I swear I saw him cross from the same point
before I made the phone call. I focus on him, tracking his progress
among all the puddle hoppers. He waits for the green man. He crosses
Omekaido Avenue and waits for the green man. He recrosses Kita Street
and waits for the green man. He recrosses Omekaido Avenue and waits
for the green man. I follow him for one, two, three more circuits. What
is his story? Is he a private detective, a bioborg, a lunatic brought out by
the humidity? My bladder tells me it will no longer be ignored. I walk to
the toilet door and push, but the door pushes back. I go back to my seat,
embarrassed, and avert my eyes when the door opens, so the occupant
will not suspect me. This is how I lose my place to a submissive-looking
high school girl, who reemerges fifteen minutes later as a boob-tubed
Neo-Tokyo wet dream. I race to the door but lose—again—to a mother
with a leg-crossing infant. "Emergency!" she giggles at me, and slams the
door in my face. My bladder shrieks at me that I am violating the terms
of its contract. I stay by the door this time and try to think of sand dunes.
Toiletless Tokyo plays this trick on you—to use a toilet you have to go
into a cafe, where you have to buy a bladder-filling drink, and so the
endless cycle goes on. On Yakushima I just found a bush to piss behind.
The mother and kid finally come out and I hold my breath, fumble with
the lock on the other side, and dispose of my three coffees. I run out of
breath, and have to breathe in. Urine, margarine, chemical pine. Not so
smelly, but I think better of wiping the rim. After washing my hands I
squeeze a blackhead, and my initial success persuades me to gamble on
less profitable sites until I resemble the victim of a flying-crab swarm. I
try out my reflection from various angles. I, Eiji Miyake, Experienced
Tokyoite. Is my rugged Kyushu tan already pasting over? My reflection
plays the staring game: we tie, both looking away at the same time. An

impatient knocking starts up on the door. "Sorry, just coming!" I call. I ruffle back my gelled hair—extra-hard formula—and worry at the lock until it opens.

◻

The knocker is Lao Tzu. "Thought you'd passed out in there, Captain." I mumble an apology for making him wait, and resolve to attack Pan-Opticon without delay. Then one of those megaweird coincidences takes place. Cutting across the foreground strides Akiko Kato *herself,* in the flesh, right here, right now, only five millimeters of glass and two meters of air, max, separating us. In slo-mo she turns her head, looks straight at me, our eyes meet, she looks away and carries on walking. First I am slugged by disbelief—my imagination must be running away with me, right? Then I am slugged by belief. It was her. In my fantasy earlier she had not aged: in reality she has, but even so, I know it was her, I know it. Lidded cunning, aquiline nose, wintry beauty. Go, Miyake! Chase after her! Jupiter Cafe's doors take an age to open, then I am running in pursuit—

Baseball cap, idiot!

I dart back to Jupiter Cafe, bang into a cyclist as we flounder in the mirroring veer-right-veer-left-veer-right trap, retrieve my cap, and race to the crossing, where the green man is flashing already. After two hours or more in the air-conned cafe my skin tingles, crackles, and pops in the dire afternoon heat. Akiko Kato—wearing a lethally smart navy blue business suit—has made the far side, and I must either risk the traffic turning and sprint across or else risk losing her before she enters PanOpticon. I sprint. The donorcycles rev, the taxis nudge forward, the angry red man stands with his hands on his hips, but I make the far bank without bouncing off a hood. i dodge upstream through the crowd, clipping insults and dropping "Excuse me!"s. I am within hailing distance when she reaches the revolving door of PanOpticon, but she ignores the entrance and continues walking toward Shinjuku Station. Now I have the chance to catch her up and detain her, but I feel now that doing so would make her less sympathetic to my cause. What woman would help a man who has been blatantly stalking her? Worse still, what if she misunderstands before I can begin explaining? What if she screams, "Rapist! Pervert! Help!" and a pack of Tokyoites turns on me? However, I cannot just let her melt into the crowds either, not since this woman is the key to finding my father. So I compromise for the time being, and just trail her, reminding myself that she does not know the adult Eiji Miyake's face. Yes, I should wait until she enters a shop or cafe or train compartment, then I can position myself for an accidental encounter. I feel power, anxiety, and weakness. She never turns around, not once. Why should she? We pass under a row of scraggly trees, dripping dry. The afternoon is growing old: freed schoolgirls mill around cosmetics shops, with sophisticated Tokyo bodies. I cannot believe I spent so long cooped up in that stuffy coffee shop. Still, my stakeout finally paid off. I stay a steady ten meters behind Ms. Kato, focusing on her navy blue–pinstriped shoulders. She gives off an aura. A jet in the blue. A damp underpass takes us under rail tracks as a train passes. We emerge into dense sunshine on busy Yasukuni Avenue, lined with plush bistros and cell-phone shops blaring intricate guitar riffs. I clang my shin on a bicycle—following people in real life is not easy. The sun steam-irons the pavement and gutter, rinsed air magnifies the heat, and sweat gums my T-shirt to my skin. Between a shop that sells ninety-nine flavors of ice cream and a Belgian waffle shop, Akiko Kato turns and disappears down a narrow side street. I hack through a jungle of housewives waiting outside a Milanese boutique, and find myself in an alley that could be from a gangster movie: no sun, trash cans on wheels, sooty canyon walls. My quarry stops outside what appears to be a cinema—not a respectable one, not down here—and turns around to see if anyone is following her. She has already seen me, so there is no point trying to hide. I glance at my watch and quicken my stride, worriedly, lowering my baseball cap as I rush past her. I smell her perfume: rose-musk and high treason. Rounding the next corner, I stop and peer back—she has already entered the building. The Ganymede Cinema. I double back. Today's film is not porn—it is a feature movie called, oddly, *PanOpticon*. The poster shows only a row of screaming Russian dolls and tells me nothing of what the story might be about. I hesitate. I want a cigarette, but I left my pack at Jupiter Cafe, so I make do with a champagne candy. I have to decide now.

The deserted lobby swarms with psychedelic carpet. Where are all the customers? If this place showed Disney or movies people have heard of, it would be packed. I fail to notice the step, trip, and nearly twist my ankle. The walls are decorated in mildewed glitz and the air is heavy with neglect. A sorry chandelier glows brownly. The woman in the ticket office puts her needlepoint embroidery down with obvious annoyance. "Yes?"

"This is, the, uh, Ganymede Cinema?"

"No, this is the battleship *Yamato*. What do you want?"

"I'm a customer."

"Well, how nice for you."

"The, uh, movie. What is it about?"

She feeds a scarlet thread through a needle's eye. "Can you see a sign on my desk that says 'Plot Synopses Sold Here'?"

"I only—"

"Can you see a sign on my desk that says 'Plot Synopses Sold Here'?"

"No."

"Think really hard. Why is there no such sign?"

Normally, I would just leave, but I know Akiko Kato is in the auditorium. Meeting her here is perfect: "Excuse me, but you wouldn't by any chance be . . ." So I say, meekly enough considering, "One ticket, please."

"Thousand yen."

"Is that the cheapest ticket?"

She does not even deign to answer. I get a note out of my wallet and say goodbye to my budget for the day. She hands me a square of perforated silver paper the size of a chewing gum wrapper, which is exactly what it is. I follow a sign reading: SCREEN THIS WAY. MANAGEMENT IS NOT RESPONSIBLE FOR ACCIDENTS IN THE STAIRWELL. The steep stairs descend in short flights at right angles to the stairs ahead and the stairs behind. Posters of previous presentations line the sweaty walls, but I cannot recognize a single one: *Dark as the Grave Wherein My Friend Is Laid*. I expect each stairway to be the last, but it never is. Is it getting warmer? *Fahrenheit 451*. In the event of fire, customers are kindly requested to crispen without undue panic. *The Life and Times of John*

Shade. I smell bitter almonds. Suddenly there are no more stairs, but a woman with the bruised shaven skull of a chemotherapy patient. When I meet her eyes, I experience a jolt: her sockets are void. I clear my throat. "Hand it over," she says, barely moving her lips, as if she is learning ventriloquism.

"I beg your, uh, pardon?"

"Your ticket. My accursed sister sold you a ticket."

"Oh . . . here. I'll put it in your left—"

So much for consideration for the blind. Her right hand darts out and she rips the ticket in two. "Popcorn."

"I'll, uh, give the popcorn a miss, thank you."

"What is wrong with my popcorn?"

"Nothing . . . I just don't feel like any popcorn."

"So you are refusing to admit that you dislike popcorn?"

"I had a big lunch."

"I hate it when you lie to me."

"You must be mistaking me for somebody else."

She shakes her head. "Mistakes never make it this far down."

"Okay, if it makes you happier, I'll buy some popcorn."

"There isn't any."

I'm missing something. "Why did you offer to sell me some?"

"Your imagination has gotten the better of you."

This is getting irritating. Then I have a thought. "Did the last lady buy any popcorn? She would have arrived here less than a minute ago."

"If you have eyes to see, see, and stop wasting my time." She stands aside and holds open the curtain. The steep cinema auditorium has a population of exactly three. In the front row I recognize Akiko Kato's head and shoulders. A tall man sits beside her. In the center aisle an elderly form sits twisted in a wheelchair, apparently dead. His head is unhinged backwards, his jaw gapes, and he is motionless. I follow his gaze upward to the night sky painted on the ceiling, but its constellations are none that Anju and I ever learned in our astronomy class. I creep down the far aisle, hoping to stay unobserved by Akiko Kato and her companion. I have an urge to eavesdrop before I introduce myself. Plus, if I approach her from the front I cannot pretend to accidentally recognize her. A loud bang goes off from the projectionist's room—either a shotgun or an inexpertly opened bag of potato chips—and I drop down below a row of seats. After some seconds, I reemerge. Neither of them turned around, I think. The lights fall fast as an equatorial sunset—not that I would know—and the curtain squeaks up on a rectangle of flickering light. An ad for a driving school starts without warning, complete with the YMCA song. The ad is much older than me, or the school accepts only drivers who are of the 1970s persuasion. Next comes an ad for a plastic surgeon called Apollo Shigenobu. He grafts permanent grins onto women whose husbands, the surgeon promises, won't recognize them—or your money back! His nurses and customers join hands and sing about facial correction. I enjoyed the "Coming Soon" trailers at the cinema in Kagoshima because it saved the expense of watching the film, but in the Ganymede Cinema there are none. A titanium voice announces the movie: *PanOpticon,* by an unpronounceable director, winner of a film festival in a city I could not locate. No titles, no music. Straight in.

In a monochrome wintry city an omnibus nudges its way through nervous crowds. A middle-aged passenger watches the snow, wartime newspaper vendors, policemen beating a black marketeer to bruised mush. Beyond a burnt skeletal bridge, the omnibus shudders to a halt and the man asks the driver for directions. By way of reply he receives a nod at the enormous sky-obscuring wall. The man walks over the frozen slush and follows the base of this wall, past craters, gutted machines, and wild dogs. A hairy lunatic talks to a fire in circular ruins. Finally the man comes to a low wooden door, where he must stoop to knock. He waits. He knocks again. Nothing. Then he notices a tin can hanging from a length of string—the string vanishes into the masonry of the giant wall. "Is anybody there?" The language is hisses and crackles but the subtitles are Japanese. "I am Doctor Polonski. Warden Bentham is expecting me. Is anybody there?" The doctor puts the can to his ear and hears drowning submariners. The wooden door opens, apparently by itself, and the doctor enters, nearly tripping over the very short man on the other side. "Toadling at your service, Doctor." The croaky dwarf unbows, and jangles the keys on his belt. "This way, if you will." Snow underfoot is gravelly. Incantations whirl, fade, and rise again. The two walk through a maze of uninhabited cages. "This is where we keep the invisible men," says Toadling, with a straight face. Guards are playing cards. "Your destination, Doctor," says Toadling, rapping on a door and pushing it open. "The warden will see you without delay."

Doctor Polonski finds himself in a scruffy office. Distaste shows through his professional demeanor for a moment: Warden Bentham is decrepit and drunk. "Doctor." The warden rubs his eyes. "How good of you to come. Take a seat. Do."

"Thank you." Doctor Polonski treads gingerly from floorboard to floorboard, half of which have been removed, to the only free chair in the room, one designed for a nine-year-old. Warden Bentham indicates a peanut in a tall glass of liquid. "I am penning a treatise on the behavior of various bar snacks in brandy soda."

"Indeed?"

The warden clicks a stopwatch and indicates a cluster of bottles on a shelf. "What's your poison, Doc?"

"Not while I'm on duty. Thank you."

The warden shrugs and empties the last drop of brandy into an eggcup. He drops the bottle between the floorboards and cups his hands to his ears. Several seconds later come a distant tinkle and scream. "Down the hatch, Doc." Warden Bentham then drains his eggcup. "Dear Doc, permit me to cut to the quack. The quick, I mean, the quick. The heart of the matter. Our own Doctor Koenig was blown up by a land mine on Christmas Eve. His post has remained vacant ever since. I am so frustrated by our War Cabinet—Oh, we had such high hopes for our reform institute. Our plan, you know, was to watch our inmates as lovingly as the fathers most of them never had, and set them free from the cages in their heads by empowering their imaginations. Such vision, we had! All we get sent are looters and politicals. Why, I myself—"

"Warden," interrupts Doctor Polonski. "The heart of the matter?"

Warden Bentham nods, leans forward, and whispers: "The Voorman Issue."

Polonski shifts on his tiny chair, carefully. He is afraid of joining the brandy bottle in the abyss below. "Voorman? He is a prisoner here?"

"Indeed, Doctor, indeed."

"And why is Voorman an issue?"

"He believes he is God."

The doctor looks interested for the first time. "God."

"Each to his own, I know, but he has persuaded the prison population his delusion is the truth. We isolated him, but to no avail. The chanting you may have heard earlier? The psalm of Voorman, for the morning mass. I fear disturbances, Doctor Polonski. Revolts. Riots. I want you to examine the man. Ascertain whether his madness is an act, or whether his tapirs truly run amok. If a psychiatrist of your stature decides he is clinically insane, I can parcel him off to a military asylum and we can all go home for tea and cupcakes."

Doctor Polonski considers. "Of what crime was Voorman convicted?"

The warden shrugs. "No idea."

"No idea?"

"We burned all the files last winter for fuel."

"You burned the files?"

"During the cold snap, yes."

"But . . . how do you know when to release the prisoners?"

"Release?" The warden scans the labels on his remaining bottles. "The prisoners? Doctor, if you weren't already a shrink I'd ask you, 'Are you out of your mind?'! How could I feed my children if I let our prisoners go?"

Akiko Kato glances behind her—I duck down. At the end of the row a rat stands on its hind legs in the silvery screenlight. It twitches its nose at me before climbing into the upholstery of an unsprung seat. "Well, Ms. Kato," begins her companion in an imperious voice, "I only hope you have summoned me from my committee for an emergency as urgent as you claimed."

"An apparition appeared in Tokyo yesterday, Minister."

"A ghost story. Please tell me there is more."

"The ghost was your son, Minister. Eiji Miyake is here."

My father says nothing for the longest time.

And I . . . uh, I . . .

"Eiji is alive?"

"Very much alive, Minister. He is a vengeful spirit. He is looking for you."

"What does he want? Money?"

No! I nearly cry out. No, I will wait while Akiko Kato unwinds more rope I can use to hang her later on. Soon.

"Not money, Minister. Blood. There is no easy way to tell you all this . . ." She makes it sound very easy indeed. "Your son is a crack addict. Salivating psychosis on two legs. He has spent his teens in and out of juvenile detention centers. I have here an e-mail swearing he will kill you for his stolen childhood."

My father reads the paper Kato unfolds. His voice is weak. "Surely—"

"And not only you, Minister. Here. He says he wants to make you watch the destruction of your family. To make up for what happened to his sister."

Voorman sits cross-legged on a wire bed-frame. He is straitjacketed. The cell is a palace of filth. "So, Mr. Voorman . . ." A column of flies hovers above an iron bucket. Doctor Polonski paces over chunks of fallen ceiling. "How long have you believed yourself to be God?"

Voorman has a magnetic voice. "Let me ask you the same question."

"I do not believe I am God." The doctor steps on something crunchy.

"But you believe you are a psychiatrist."

"Correct." The doctor scrapes a still-twitching cockroach onto a half-brick. "I have been a psychiatrist since I graduated from medical college, obtained my license, and began practicing my profession."

"I have been God since I began practicing *my* profession."

The doctor leans against a desk to take notes. "Tell me a little about what your profession involves. On a day-to-day basis."

"Postcreation maintenance, mostly, Doctor."

"Of?"

"Of the universe you inhabit. It is only nine days old, so you can imagine the wrinkles that still need ironing out."

The lead of Polonski's pencil breaks. "A considerable body of evidence suggests that the universe is older than nine days."

"I know. I created the evidence myself."

The doctor fishes in his pocket for a new pencil stub. "I am forty-five years of age, Mr. Voorman. How do you account for my memories of my childhood?"

"I created your memories when I created you."

"So everything around us was born in your imagination?"

"Precisely. You, this prison, gooseberries, the Horsehead Nebula. And the fossils. The creationists are right, I'm afraid, although they are wildly liberal in their estimates."

"That must add up to a considerable workload."

"A workload greater than your pitiful hippocampus—no offense—could conceive. The worst part is, if I stop imagining every last atom it will all go *poof! Solipsist,* Doctor, only has one *l.*" Polonski frowns and changes the angle of his notebook. Voorman sighs. "I know you are skeptical, Doctor. I made you that way. Perhaps I can propose an experiment to verify my claims?"

"What do you have in mind?"

"Pure objective realism. Belgium."

"Belgium?"

"I doubt anyone will miss it. Do you?"

My father is motionless. He has a full head of hair—I will never need to worry about baldness. So, my father is a politician. This explains a lot. I hug myself in the darkness. Now I am over the initial shock, today is turning delicious. Soon I will announce my presence, and Akiko Kato will be exposed as a lying viper. Her cell phone trills—she gets it from her handbag, snaps "Not now!" at the caller, and folds it away. "Look, Minister. The general election is three weeks from tomorrow. Your face is going to be on every candidate board in the city, and on television two or three times a day. This is not the time for you to keep a low profile. If your son discovers your identity, your life will be in peril."

"If I could only meet Eiji, just once, and reason with—"

"He has a criminal record as long as your wife's fur rack. And suppose he is deterred from attacking you physically—just imagine the damage he could wreak if the media got wind of this. 'Abandoned Ministerial Love-Child Swears, *"I want to kill my father!"'* No, Minister, we must practice damage limitation now."

My father sighs in the flickering dark. "What do you suggest?"

"Liquidation, of course."

My father quarter-turns. My nose! "Surely . . . not violence?"

Akiko Kato chooses her words with the utmost care. "I foresaw this day. Plans are in place. Accidents happen easily in Tokyo, and I know people who know other people who specialize in fortuitously timed accidents. Of course, their services do not come cheaply, but precision and discretion never do."

I wait for my father's reply.

The Polonskis live in a third-floor apartment in an old townhouse. Their dining room overlooks the bleak courtyard. Mrs. Polonski has not slept properly since the bombings began. A convoy of tanks rumbles past. Mrs. Polonski slices iron bread with a blunt knife. "Are you still fretting about that Boorman prisoner?"

"Voorman. Yes."

"That warden should be ashamed of himself. Piling more work on you, at a time like this. All the paperwork will land on your desk, too, of course."

The doctor tilts the bowl of his spoon and watches a shred of cabbage. "Oh, I'm not worried about the work. He is one of the most intriguing cases I have ever had, to be honest. I have never met such extreme megalomania in such a passive-aggressive. He is so soft-spoken."

"Is he mad, do you suppose?"

"Well, he promised to make Belgium disappear by this evening."

"That does not sound so passive." Mrs. Polonski tips the rest of the broth into her bowl. "Belgium is another prisoner, I take it?"

Polonski chews his bread absently. "Belgium."

Mrs. Polonski sips her broth. "Is Belgium a type of cheese?"

"Belgium the country. Between France and Holland. Belgium."

Mrs. Polonski is puzzled. "An island?"

The doctor smiles to cover his annoyance. "Bel-gi-um."

"Is this a joke, dear?"

"You know I never joke about my patients."

"Belgium." Mrs. Polonski dislikes the word's taste. "A shire of Luxembourg?"

Her husband sighs. "I cannot believe I married a woman who . . . look, bring me my atlas." The doctor turns to the general map of Europe and his face freezes. Between France and Holland is a polygon of blue called the Walloon Lagoon. Polonski's lips move but no sound comes out. "This cannot be. This cannot be. This cannot be."

"I refuse to believe," insists my father, "that any son I fathered could commit murder, however unfortunate his upbringing may have been. When your agent met Eiji, my son must have been provoked into saying the things you claim he did. Or you are imagining the worst—"

"I am a lawyer," says Akiko Kato. "I am not paid to imagine."

"I cannot rubber-stamp the death of my own son!"

"Then you are rubber-stamping the death of your legitimate family. He will not go away, Minister. He has a sack of hatred instead of a heart."

My father squeezes his temples to help him think, the same way I do. "May I ask you a direct question, Ms. Kato?"

"You are the boss," she replies in the tone of the boss.

"Is our privacy retention agreement a factor in your calculations?"

Akiko Kato's reply is swift and sharp. "That is a dangerous insinuation."

"You must admit—"

"I resent your insinuation so much that the price of my silence is doubled."

My father nearly shouts: "Remember who you are talking to!"

"I am talking to a man with a kingdom to lose, Minister."

Suddenly, I know the time has come to intervene. I stand up, two rows behind my father and this woman of poison and lies. "Excuse me. I might be able to shed some light here." They jump up. Akiko Kato is already hissing: "What do you want and who are you?" I swallow my nerves and announce in a voice loud enough to smother the movie: "We are all busy people, so let's cut the small talk. You already know my name, Ms. Kato, or at least you knew it, once upon a time. Eiji Miyake. Yes, Ms. Kato, *that* Eiji Miyake. Why am I here in Tokyo? Think about it." I turn to my father. He is already analyzing the scene—a true, fearless diplomat. "Sir. It is an honor to meet you, at last. I have waited all my life for this moment. Please do not worry. Your lawyer has spun an evil deception . . ."

Icicles fang the window of Voorman's cell. Bombers drone by. Voorman's eyelids rise with imperceptible slowness. "Good morning, Doctor. You have been watching me for some time. Will Belgium figure in your session notes today?" Polonski nods at the guard with the cattle prod. "Leave us, please." The doctor's eyes are dark and baggy. With much wriggling in his straitjacket, Voorman sits up on his bed. "You slept poorly last night, Doctor. Well, you will grow accustomed to this."

The doctor opens his medical bag with professional calm.

"Wicked thoughts!" Voorman smacks his lips. "So I am not a lunatic or a malingerer, but a demon? A demon from hell? What next? Am I to be exorcised?"

Polonski scrutinizes the prisoner. "Do you believe you should be?"

"Any demon is just a human who possesses a sufficiently demonic imagination."

Polonski sits down, opens his notebook, and produces his pencil. "Let us suppose . . . just suppose . . . that you possess certain 'powers.'"

Voorman laughs until his bed squeaks. "I rendered an entire country nonexistent, Doctor! What more evidence do you need?"

"Then what is God doing straitjacketed in the PanOpticon?"

Voorman yawns in a well-fed way. "Honolulu gets boring, Doctor. Golf is tedious when you can guarantee holes-in-one. Existence starts to drag. I put myself into prison for the novelty value. I see prisons as open-cast irony mines. Inmates are so much more appreciative than congregations. I get to meet people like you, good doctor. Your brief is to prove me either a faker or a lunatic, yet you inadvertently demonstrate my divinity."

"I am not a religious man, Mr. Voorman."

"I know, Doctor, I know. That is why I chose you. Fear not, I bear glad tidings. We are going to change places. Your turn has come to juggle time, gravity, waves, and particles. Your turn has come to sift through the dreck of human endeavor for rare specks of originality. Your turn has come to count the falling sparrows and the pillaged continents. I am going to meet your wife. She prays to me every night, you know, after you have gone to bed. Most beseechingly. I intend to make her smile in a most involuntary way. First I shall proceed to Warden Bentham's office, partake of his brandy, and pronounce you a madman of the first degree."

"You are a sick man, Mr. Voorman. The Belgian trick I cannot yet—"

Doctor Polonski appears to freeze in time.

Voorman whistles a national anthem.

The frame jumps.

The prisoner chokes, "What have you done?"

The doctor flexes his new muscles and tries out his new hands. *"What have you done to me?"*

"If you won't calm down and discuss things like a rational adult—"

"Put me back, you monster! You devil! Guards! Guards!"

The doctor clips his bag shut. "Keep an eye on the Taiwan Straits for me. Oh, and the Balkans. Hot spots." The door scrapes open, the guard enters, and the doctor shakes his head sadly. *"I'm the real Doctor Polonski!"* shrieks the prisoner. *"That abomination has stolen my body! He's going to molest my wife!"* The cattle prod buzzes as the charge builds up. The doctor closes the door behind him.

♦

I try out my reflection from various angles. I, Eiji Miyake, Experienced Tokyoite. Is my rugged Kyushu tan already pasting over? My reflection plays the staring game: we tie, both looking away at the same time. An impatient knocking starts up on the door. "Sorry, just coming!" I call. I ruffle back my gelled hair—extra-hard formula—and worry at the lock until it opens. It is Lao Tzu. "Took your time in there, Captain." I apologize, and decide that the time to assault the real PanOpticon has come. I will stop procrastinating. Straight after one last Carlton. I watch workmen on scaffolding erect a giant TV screen against the flank of PanOpticon's chromium neighbor. The waitress with the perfect neck has finished her shift—the clock says 14:58—and has changed out of her uniform. In her real life she wears a purple sweater and whitish jeans. How drop-dead cool can a girl be and not burn a hole in this dimension? Dowager is giving her a talking-to about something over by the cigarette machine when Donkey rings the help-me bell. My waitress glances at the clock anxiously, feels her cell phone and turns toward me to speak into it, cupping the mouth end. Her face lights up and I feel a cold blade of jealousy slip between my ribs. Before I know it, I am choosing another brand of cigarettes. Of course eavesdropping is wrong and I would never do it, but if I innocently overhear, who can blame me? "Yeah, yeah, yeah," she is saying, "let me speak to Nao, will you?" Naoki a boy or Naoko a girl? "I think I might be a little late, so start without me." Start what? "The rain was unbelievable, wasn't it?" She practices piano movements with her free hand. "Yes, I remember how to get there. No problem." Get where? Naoki's house? "Room 162. I know we only have two weeks left, yes, but I could play it blindfolded." She looks at me looking at her and I remember I am supposed to be choosing cigarettes. On an advertisement a legal-looking woman smokes Salem. "See you in twenty minutes or so. Bye-bye." She puts the phone in her shirt pocket and deliberately clears her throat. "So, did you catch all of that, or would you like me to go over any bits you may have missed?" To my horror I realize that she is talking to me. My blush is so hot I smell burning bacon. I look up at her—I am still crouching, to extract my Salems from the machine. I search for words to defuse her contempt while keeping my dignity intact. I say "Uh . . ." Her stare is a merciless death ray. I stand up, but fail because my hand is trapped in the jaws of the cigarette machine's dispensing slot. I finally get my hand back and touch the leaves of the rubber plant. "Uh . . . I was wondering if these plants were real, or, uh . . . artificial. Are. I mean." Together, my waitress and I watch my lie writhe in its final pathetic throes. There. Dead. "Some things are real," says my waitress, "and some things are fake.

Some things are full of shit." Dowager returns to resume her talk, I cock-roach back to my seat. I will shortly leave and run under a heavy truck, but I need a Salem to steady my nerves before I do this. Lao Tzu returns, posturing his behind. "Eat big, shit big, dream small. Say, Captain, no chance of a spare cig, is there? Just one?" I light a pair of Salems with one match. The girl with the flawless neck has finally escaped Jupiter Cafe. She gazelles over the puddles of Omekaido Avenue. I should have been honest just now, I should have said, "Yes, I was eavesdropping. It was wrong, but you seem so fine and wholesome and true that I had to find out more about you. Please excuse me. I will strive to be a good dog in the future." That would have made her smile, even. Too late now. One small lie and your credit is blown at the credibility bank. Forget her. She is way out of your class, Miyake. She is a musician at a top Tokyo university with a conductor boyfriend called Naoki. I am unemployed, and I managed to graduate from high school only because of the usual sympathy vote from teachers. She is from a good family and sleeps in a bedroom with real paintings and CD-ROM encyclopedias. Her film-producer father allows Naoki to sleep over at their Kamakura residence. Her father and Naoki get on well. Naoki has money, talent, and immac-ulate teeth. You, Miyake, are not actually from a family as such. You sleep in a capsule in Kita Senju with your guitar, and your teeth are not exactly prize specimens of the art of the dentist. "What a beautiful young creature," sighs Lao Tzu, watching her disappear on the far side of the intersection. "If only I were your age, Captain, if only . . ."

Perhaps my humiliation with the musician-waitress explains why I do not lose my nerve and head straight back to Shinjuku Station. Either I feel I must rally my forces to save the day, or I feel two slaps in the face from life is no worse than one. I nearly get hit by an ambulance crossing Kita Street. The handful of traffic lights on Yakushima are there only for effect. Here they separate living pedestrians from accident victims. Yes-terday, when I got off the coach at the bus station, I noticed that Tokyo smells of the insides of pockets. Today I have not noticed that smell, so I must smell of the insides of pockets too. I walk up the steps of PanOpticon. It is the tent pole of the Tokyo sky. Over the last eight years I have imagined this moment so many times . . . how strange to be living in this moment. The revolving door creeps around. Inside, the refrigerated air makes the hairs on my forearms rise—when it gets this cold outside in winter they put on the heating. The marble floor is the white of bleached bone. Palm trees sit in bronze urns. A one-legged man crutches across the lobby. Rubber squeaks, tubular metal clinks. Trombone flowers sway in the air-con breeze, looking for babies to feed on. My left sneaker makes a stupid eeky-eeky sound. Nine interviewees in a row wait in nine identical armchairs. They are my age and may very well be clones. Droneclones. I know what they are thinking: What is that country boy stinking of pickles doing in PanOpticon? I ignore them, reach the building guide by the elevators, and look up and down for Osugi & Bosugi, Legal. The prize is within my grasp. I should be ringing my father's doorbell by dinnertime. "Hey! Where do you think you're going, exactly?"

I turn around. The guard at reception is waving his baton this way. Eighteen droneclone eyes swivel from it to me. "Didn't learn how to read, is that it? Look!" He points at a large sign hanging over the reception desk. VISITORS *MUST* REPORT TO RECEPTION. I backtrack and give him a deep, apologetic bow. He folds his arms, unimpressed. "So?"

"I have, uh, business with Osugi and Bosugi."

"Well, how swanky. Your appointment is with *whom* exactly?"

"Appointment?"

"Yes, appointment. As in, 'appointment.'"

"I was hoping to see Ms. Kato."

"And is Ms. Kato aware of this imminent honor?"

"Not exactly, because, well, let me—"

"So you have no appointment."

"Well, if you would just let me—"

"Yes or no?" The bastard is enjoying this.

"No, but look—"

"No, you look. You are standing in a private building. This is not a village marketplace. You cannot just breeze in. Nobody passes by this desk unless they are employees of PanOpticon, or somebody with an appointment—which I verify—with somebody who works here. Not on my watch. I am speaking simply enough, for you, I hope?"

Eighteen droneclone ears tune in to my Kyushu accent. "Can I make an appointment through you, then?"

Way wrong. The guard has stopped enjoying himself. "Do I look like a secretary? I am employed to keep time wasters, salesmen, and assorted scum out. Not usher them in." My attempts at damage control are blown up on the runway. "I don't care how you do things in the rice-field ditch you crawled from, but in Tokyo this is how we do things: first, you scuttle away before I get really irritated. Then, you arrange your own appointment with Ms. Kato. You come back on the right day, five minutes before you are expected, preferably not on my shift so I don't have to see you again. You report to Security. Here. Your appointment with Osugi and Bosugi is confirmed. Then, and only then, you are permitted to step into one of those elevators. Now. I have important business to attend to." He snaps open a sports paper.

Postdownpour sweat and grime regrunge Tokyo. The puddles steam dry. A street musician sings so off-key that passersby have a civic duty to smash his guitar on his head and relieve him of his coins. I head back toward the Shinjuku subway because I have nowhere else to go in this mortgaged city except my capsule. The crowds are beaten senseless by the heat and march out of step. I am beaten senseless by boiling annoyance and tired guilt. I feel I have broken a promise. I cannot understand this. My father's doorbell is lost at an unknown grid reference in the city street guide. Could be around this corner, could be halfway to Yokohama. A tiny nugget of earwax beyond the reach of my little fingernail is driving me crazy. John tries to cheer me up by singing "Nobody Told Me," but I feel too sorry for myself to hum along. I pass a kendo hall. Bone-splintering bamboo-sword screams escape through the window grille. On the pavement is an unexplained pair of shoes. Maybe their owner suddenly turned to vapor and wafted away. Buses and trucks clog arteries, pedestrians squeeze through gaps. During Anju's and my dinosaur period, we found a theory claiming the great extinction occurred because the dinosaurs gagged to death on their own dung. We laughed for an hour, nonstop. Trying to get anywhere in Tokyo, the theory no longer seems so laughable. I feel I am gagging to death here. I hate its sidewalk-to-rooftop advertising, its capsules, tunnels, tap water, air, its MEMBERS ONLYs and its PRIVATE—KEEP OUTs. If I could, I would turn into a nuclear warhead and blast this concrete dung pile from the surface of the world. I mean it.

two

❖

Lost Property

Sawing the head off a thunder god with a rusty hacksaw is not easy when you are eleven years old. The hacksaw keeps jamming. I jiggle it loose, and nearly slip from the thunder god's shoulders. If I fall backward from this height I snap my spine. Outside the shrine a blackbird sings in dark purples. I wrap my legs around the god's muscled torso, like when Uncle Tarmac gives me a piggyback. I drag the blade across his throat. Again, again, again. The wood is stone-hard, but the nick deepens to a slit, the slit becomes a groove. My eyes sting with sweat. The quicker, the better. This must be done, but there is no point getting caught. They put you in prison for this, surely. The blade slips and cuts my thumb. I wipe my eyes on my T-shirt and wait. Here comes the pain, in pulses. The flap of skin pinkens, reddens, and blood wells up. I lick it and taste ten-yen coins. Fair payment. Just as I am paying the thunder god back for what he has done to Anju. I carry on sawing. I cannot see his face from where I am, but when I cut through his windpipe both our bodies shudder.

◆

Saturday, September 2, is already one hour old. One week since my Jupiter Cafe stakeout. On the main thoroughfare through Kita Senju the traffic is at low tide. I can see the Tokyo moon down a crack between the apartment buildings across the street. Zinc, industrial, skidmarked. My capsule is as stifling as inside a boxing glove. The fan stirs the heat. I am not going to contact her. I mean it. No way. Who does she think she is, after all this time? Across the road is a photo developer's with two FUJI-FILM clocks—the left clock shows the actual time, the right shows when the photos will be ready, forty-five minutes into the future. Girders creak, cables hum, the sodium streetlamp outside buzzes. I wonder if this building gives me insomnia. Sick Building Syndrome, Uncle Yen calls it. Below me, Shooting Star is shuttered up and waiting for the night to pass. In the last week I have learned the routine: ten to midnight, Buntaro drags in the sandwich board and takes out the trash; five to midnight, the TV goes off, and he washes up his mug and plate; around now a customer may come sprinting down the street to return a video; at midnight on the nail, Buntaro pings open the register and cashes out. Three minutes later the shutters roll down, he kicks his scooter to life, and off he goes. A cockroach tries to tic free of the glue trap. My muscles ache from my new job. I should chuck out Cat's bowl, I suppose. Keeping it is morbid, now that I know the truth. And the extra milk, and the two cans of quality cat food. Is it edible, if I mix it into a soup or something? Did Cat die instantly, or did she lie on the roadside thinking about it? Did a passerby knock her on the head with a shovel to put her out of her misery? Cats seem too transdimensional to get hit by traffic, but it happens all the time. All the time. Thinking I could keep her was crazy in the first place. My grandmother hates cats. Yakushima islanders keep chained-up dogs as guards. Cats take their own chances. I know nothing about litter trays, when you bring cats in, when you take them out, what injections they need. And look what happened to it when it moved in with me: the Miyake curse strikes again. Anju climbed trees like a cat. A summer puma.

"You are so, so slow!"

I shout back up through the early mist and floppy leaves. "I'm snagged!"

"You're scared!"

"I am not!"

Anju laughs her wild zither when she knows she is right. The forest floor is a long way down. I worry about rotted-through branches snapping. Anju never worries because I always do it for her. She skip-reads her way up trees. She finds fingerholds in coarse bark and toeholds in smooth bark. Last week was our eleventh birthday, and already Anju can climb the gym ropes faster than any of the boys in our class, and, when she is in the mood, multiply fractions, read seventh-grade texts, and recite most Zax Omega adventures word for word. Wheatie says this is because she grabbed most of the brain cells when we were growing inside our mother. I finally unsnag my T-shirt and climb after my sister, as gracefully as a three-toed sloth with vertigo. Minutes later I find her on the top branch, copper-skinned, willow-limbed, moss-stained, thorn-scored, her ponytail knotted back. Waves of spring sea wind break on the woods. "Welcome to my tree," she says. "Not bad," I admit, but it is better than "not bad." I have never climbed so high before. We already trekked up the razor escarpment to get here, so the view is awesome. The fortress-gray mountain faces, the green river snaking out of the gorge, the hanging bridge, mishmash of roofs and power lines, port, timber yards, school soccer ground, gravel pit, Uncle Orange's tea fields, our secret beach, its foot rock, waves breaking on the shoals around the whalestone, the long island of Tanegashima where they launch satellites, glockenspiel clouds, the envelope where the sea seals the sky. Having bombed as tree-climber-in-chief I appoint myself head cartographer. "Kagoshima is over there . . ." I am afraid to let go and point, so I nod. Anju is squinting inland. "I think I can see Wheatie airing the futons." I can't see our grandmother but I know Anju wants me to ask "Where?" so I don't. The mountains rise toward the interior. Miyanoura Peak props up the sky. Hill tribes live in the rainshadow—they decapitate the lost tourists and make the skulls into drinking bowls. And there is a pool where a real kappa lives—it catches swimmers, rams its fist up through their assholes, and pulls out their hearts to eat. Yakushima islanders never go up into the mountains, except for the tourist guides. I feel a lump in my pocket and remember. "Want a champagne bomb?"

"Sure."

Anju suddenly monkey shrieks, swings, and dangles down in front of me, giggling at my panic. Scared birds beat away nearby. Her legs grip the branch above.

"Don't!" is all I can blurt.

Anju bares her front teeth and chickenwings her arms. "Anju the bat."

"Anju! Don't!"

She swings to and fro. "I vant to suckkk your bluddd!" Her hair clasp falls away and her ponytail streams earthward. "Aw! That was my last one."

"Don't dangle like that! Stop it!"

"Eiji's a jellyfish, Eiji's a jellyfish!"

I imagine her falling, ricocheting from branch to branch. "STOP IT!"

"You're even uglier upside down. Hold the candies steady, then."

"Swing back up first!"

"No, I was born first so you have to do what I say. Hold it steady!" She extracts a candy, unpeels the wrapper and watches it flutter away into the sea greens. Watching me, she puts the candy in her mouth and lazily swings herself back upright. "You really are such a wuss!"

"If you fell Wheatie would murder me."

"Wuss." Anju swings herself back upright.

My heartbeat gradually calms down.

"What happens to you when you die?" So Anju.

I don't care as long as she stays upright. "How should I know?"

"Nobody says the same thing. Wheatie says you go to the pure land and walk in gardens with your ancestors. Boooring. Mr. Endo at school says you turn into soil. Kakimoto-sensei says it depends what you were like in this life—I'd get changed into an angel or a unicorn, but you'd come back as a maggot or toadstool."

"So what do you think?"

"When you die they burn you, right?"

"Right."

"So you turn into smoke, right?"

"I guess."

"So you go there." Anju lets go of the tree and shoots the sun with both hands. "Up, up, and away. I want to fly."

A careworn buzzard rises on a thermal.

"In an airplane?"

"Who wants to fly in a smelly airplane?"

I suck my champagne bomb. "How do you know airplanes smell?"

Anju crunches her champagne bomb. "Airplanes must smell. All those people breathing the same air. Like the boys' changing room in the rainy season, but a hundred times worse. No, I mean proper flying."

"Like with a jetpack?"

"No such things as jetpacks."

"Zax Omega has a jetpack."

Anju airs her recently acquired sigh. "No such thing as Zax Omega."

"Zax Omega opened the new building at the port!"

"And did he arrive by jetpack?"

"No," I admit, "by taxi. But you're too heavy to fly."

"Sky Castle Laputa flies and that's made of rock."

"If I can't have Zax Omega no way are you having Sky Castle Laputa."

"Condors, then. Condors weigh more than me. They fly."

"Condors have wings. I don't see any wings on you."

"Ghosts fly without wings."

"Ghosts are dead."

Anju picks champagne bomb shrapnel from her teeth. I have no idea what she is thinking. Leaf shadows hide my twin sister. Parts of Anju are too bright, parts of Anju are so dark she isn't even here.

◆

Jerking off usually sends me to sleep. Am I normal? I've never heard of a nineteen-year-old insomniac. I am no war criminal, no poet or scientist, I'm not even lovelorn. Lustlorn, yes. Here I am, in a city of five million women, cruising into my sexual prime, single as a leper. Let me see. Who is riding the caravan of love tonight? Zizzi Hikaru, wet-suited as per the beer ad; the glam-rock mother of Yuki Chiyo; the waitress from Jupiter Cafe; Insectoid Woman from *Zax Omega and Red Plague Moon*. Back to good old Zizzi, I guess. I hunt through my pockets for some tissues before the festivities commence.

I ferret around for matches to light my postcoital Mild Seven, but end up having to use my gas stove. Well, that was a failure. I am wider awake than ever. Zizzi was disappointing tonight. No sense of timing. Is she getting too young for me? FUJIFILM says 01:49. I clean myself up. What now? Practice my guitar? Write an answer to one of the two epoch-shifting letters I received this week? Which one? Let's stick with the simpler: Akiko Kato's reply to the letter I wrote after failing to see her. The single sheet of paper is still in the plastic bag in the freezer with the Other. I put it on the shelf next to Anju but it kept laughing at me. It came—when was it? Tuesday. Buntaro read the envelope as he handed it to me. "Osugi and Bosugi, Legal. Chasing lawyer ladies? Be careful, kid, you could end up with injunctions slapped on where it hurts. Want to hear my lawyer joke? What's the difference between a catfish and a lawyer? Guess—go on. No? One is a scaly, bottom-dwelling scum sucker, and the other is a catfish." I tell him I'd already heard it and dash up the video-box-stacked stairs to my capsule. I tell myself I am expecting a negative answer, but I wasn't expecting that Akiko Kato's "No" would pack such a slap. I already know the letter by memory. Its greatest hits include: *Disclosure of a client's personal data constitutes a betrayal of trust that no responsible attorney could consider.* Pretty final. *Furthermore, I feel obliged to refuse your request that I forward mail that my client has stated categorically he does not wish to receive.* Not much room for doubt there. Not much room for a reply, either. *Finally, in the event that legal proceedings are initiated to force data regarding your patrimony to be released, assisting you at this early stage represents a clear conflict of interest. I urge you not to pursue this matter, and trust that this letter clarifies our position.* Perfectly. Plan A is dead on arrival.

Mr. Aoyama, substationmaster of Ueno, is bald as a rivet head and has a perfect Adolf Hitler mustache. This is Tuesday, on my first working day at Ueno Station lost-property office. "I am far busier than you can imagine"—he speaks without taking his eyes off his paperwork—"but I make a point of addressing new recruits on an individual basis." Wide silences yawn between his sentences. "You know who I am." His pen scratches. "You are"—he checks a sheet—"Eiji Miyake." He looks at me, waiting for a nod. I nod. "Miyake." He pronounces my name as if it were a toxin found in his food. "Previously employed on an orange farm"—he shuffles sheets, and I recognize my writing—"on an island of no importance south of Kyushu. Most bucolic." Above Aoyama are portraits of his distinguished forebears. I imagine them bickering over who will come alive every morning to pilot the office through another tiresome day. His office smells of sun-faded card files. A computer buzzes. Golf clubs shine. "Who hired you? The Sasaki woman?" I nod. A knock on the door, and his secretary appears with a tray of tea. "I am addressing a trainee, Mrs. Marui!" Aoyama speaks in an appalled hiss. "My ten thirty-five tea becomes my ten forty-five tea, does it not?" Careworn Mrs. Marui bobs an apology and withdraws. "Go over to that window, Miyake, look out, and tell me what you see."

I do as he says. "A window cleaner, sir."

The man is immune to irony. *"Below* the window cleaner."

Trains pulling in and pulling out in the shadow of the Terminus Hotel. Mid-morning passengers. Luggage haulers. The milling, the lost, the late, the meeters, the met, the platform-cleaning machines. "Ueno Station, sir."

"Tell me this, Miyake. What . . . *is* . . . Ueno Station?"

I am at a complete loss.

"Ueno Station," Aoyama replays his grave spiel, "is an extra*ordinary* machine. One of the finest-tuned timepieces in the land. In the world. And this fireproof, thiefproof office is one of the nerve centers. From this console I can access . . . nearly everything. Ueno Station is our lives, Miyake. You serve it, it serves you. It affords a timetabled career. You have the privilege to be a minute cog in this machine. Even I began in a position as lowly as yours; but with punctuality, hard work, integrity—" The phone rings and I stop existing. Aoyama's face switches to a higher-watt glow. His voice beams. *"Sir!* What a pleasure—yes . . . indeed . . . indeed . . . A superb proposal. And may I venture to add— Yes, sir. Absolutely . . . at the membership brokerage? Priceless . . . superb . . . and may I propose—indeed, sir. Rescheduled for Friday? How true . . . we're all very much looking forward to hearing how we performed, sir. Thank you, sir . . . indeed . . . And may I—" Aoyama replaces the handset and gazes at it.

After some seconds I cough politely.

Aoyama looks up. "Where was I?"

"Minute cogs and integrity, sir."

"Integrity." But his mind is no longer here. He closes his eyes and pinches the bridge of his nose. "Your probationary period is six months. You will have the chance to take the Japan Railways examinations in March. So, the Sasaki woman hired you. I make no secret of the fact that she is not an ideal role model. She is one of these men-women. Never quit work, even after marriage. Her husband died—sad, of course—but people die all the time and she expects a man's job by way of compensation. So, Miyake. Rectify your accent problem. Listen to NHK radio announcers. Dump the junk that modern magazines stuff your head with. If I ever see you with a stud in your ear, I shall fire you on the spot. In my day high schools trained young tigers. Now they turn out peacocks. You are dismissed."

I give him a bow as I close the door, but he is watching empty space. The office outside is empty. The tray is on the side. To my own surpise, I lift the teapot lid and spit into it. This must be work-related stress.

The lost-property office is an okay place to work. I have to wear uncool Japan Railways overalls, but I finish at six sharp and Ueno Station is only a few stops down the line from Kita Senju, near Shooting Star. During my three-month probation period I get paid weekly, which suits me fine. I am lucky. Buntaro got me the job. When I got back from PanOpticon last Friday, he said he heard from a contact that there might be a job going there, and would I be interested? You bet, I said. Before I knew it I had an interview with Mrs. Sasaki. She is a stern old bird, a Tokyo version of my grandmother, but after talking for about twenty minutes she offered me the job. I spend the mornings cataloging—writing date/time/train labels on the items collected by conductors and cleaners when the trains terminate, and housing them on the right metal rack. Mrs. Sasaki runs the lost-property office and deals with the high-value items in the side office—wallets, bank cards, jewelry—which have to be registered with the police. Suga trains me to do the low-value ones, stored in the back office. "Not much natural light in here, right?" says Suga. "But you can tell the month from what gets handed in. November to Feb.: skis and snowboards. March: diplomas. June is all wedding gifts. Swimsuits pile up in July. A decent rain will bring hundreds of umbrellas. Not the most inspiring job, but it beats leaping around a garage forecourt or delivering pizzas, imho." Afternoons I spend on the counter, waiting for claimants or answering the phone. Rush hours are busiest, of course, but during mid-afternoon my job is almost relaxing. My memory is the most regular visitor.

The leaves are so green they are blue. Anju and I play our staring game: we stare at each other and the first one to make the other smile and look away wins. I make stupid faces but they bounce off her. Her Cleopatra eyes spark bronze. She wins—she always does—by bringing her eyes close to mine and opening wide. Anju returns to her higher branch and looks at the sun through a leaf. Then she hides the sun with her hand. The webby bit between her thumb and forefinger glows ruby. She looks out to sea. "The tide is coming in."

"Going out."

"Coming in. Your whalestone is diving."

My mind is on miraculous soccer exploits.

"I really used to believe what you told me about the whalestone," she says.

Bicycle kicks and diving headers.

"You spouted such rubbish."

"Uh?"

"About it being magic."

"What being magic?"

"The whalestone, hearing aid!"

"I never said it was magic."

"You did. You said it was a real whale that the thunder god had turned into stone, and that one day when we were older we would swim out to it, and once we set foot on it the spell would be broken, and it would be so grateful that it would take us anywhere we wanted to go. Even to Mom and our father, if we told it to. I used to imagine it happening so hard that I could see it sometimes, like down a telescope. Mother putting on her pearls, and Father washing his car."

"I never said all of that."

"Did too. One of these days I'll swim out to it."

"No way could you *ever* swim that far. Girls can't swim as well as boys."

Anju aims a lazy kick at my head. "I could swim there, *easy*!"

"In your dreams. Way too far."

"In *your* dreams." Waves break at the foot of the gray humpback.

"Maybe it really is a whalestone," I suggest. "A fossil one."

Anju snorts. "It's just a stupid rock. It doesn't even look like a whale. And next time we go to the secret beach I'm going to show you and swim out there, me, and stand on it and laugh at you."

The Kagoshima ferry crawls along the horizon.

"This time tomorrow—" I begin.

"Yeah, yeah, this time tomorrow you'll be in Kagoshima. You'll get up really early to catch the ferry, arrive at Kagoshima Junior High School at ten o'clock. The eighth graders, the seventh graders, then your match. Then you go to the restaurant of a hotel with nine floors and eat while you listen to Mr. Ikeda tell you why you lost. Then you come back on Sunday morning. You already told me a zillion times, Eiji."

"I can't help it if you're jealous."

"Jealous? Twenty-two smelly boys kicking a bag of air on a square of muck?"

"You used to like soccer."

"You used to wet our futon."

Ouch. "You're jealous because I'm going to Kagoshima and you're not."

Anju stays aloof.

The tree creaks. I didn't expect Anju to lose interest in our argument so soon. "Watch," she says. She stands up, feet apart, steadies herself, takes her hands away—

"Stop it," I say,

and my sister jumps into empty air

my lungs wallop out a scream

Anju flashes by me

and lands laughing on a branch below, swinging down to a lower branch. I hear her laughter long after she has vanished in the leaves.

◆

FUJIFILM says two o'clock has come and gone. A single night is stuffed with minutes, but they come undone and get blown away, one by one. My capsule is stuffed with Stuff. A shabby colony in the empire of stuff. An old TV, a rice-husk futon, a camping table, a tray of cast-off kitchen utensils courtesy of Buntaro's wife, Machiko-san, cups containing fungal experiments, a roaring fridge with chrome trimmings. The fan. A pile of *Screen* magazines, off-loaded by Buntaro. All I brought from Yakushima was a backpack of clothes, my Discman, my Lennon CDs, and my guitar. Buntaro looked at my guitar doubtfully the day I arrived. "You don't intend to plug that thing in anywhere, do you?" "No," I answer. "Stay acoustic," he warns. "Go electric on me, and you're out. It's in your lease." I am not going to contact her. No way. She will try to talk me out of looking for my father. I wonder how long it will take for Cockroach to die. The glue trap is called a "cockroach motel," and has windows, doors, and flowers printed on the side. Traitor cockroaches wave six arms—"Come in, come in!" It has an onion-flavored bait packet—curry, shrimp salad, and beef jerky are also available at all good Tokyo supermarkets. Cockroach greeted me when I moved in. It didn't even bother pretending to be scared. Cockroach grinned. Who has the last laugh now? I have! No. It has. I can't sleep. In Yakushima night means sleep. Not much else to do. Night does not mean sleep in Tokyo. Punks slalom down shopping malls. Hostesses stifle yawns and glance at their patrons' Rolexes. Yakuza gangsters fight on deserted construction sites. High schoolers younger than me engage in gymnastic love-hotel sex bouts. In an apartment high above a fellow insomniac flushes a toilet. A pipe behind my head gargles.

Last Wednesday, my second day as a drone at Ueno Station. I am taking a dump during my lunch break, smoking a Salem in the cubicle. I hear the door open, a zipper scratch, and urine firing against porcelain urinal. Then the voice begins—it is Suga, the computer nerd whose part-time job I am taking over at the end of the week, when he goes back to college. Obviously he thinks he is alone in here, because he says this: "Excuse me, are you Suga? Are you responsible for this? Yes, you are Suga, aren't you?" His voice isn't his real voice—it is a cartoon voice, and it must scrape the lining off his vocal cords to produce it. "I don't *wanna* remember, I don't *wanna* remember, I don't *wanna* remember. Don't make me. Can't make me. Won't make me. *Forget* it! *Forget* it! *Forget* it!" His voice reverts to its bland, nasal calm. "It wasn't my fault. Right. Could have happened to anyone. Right. To anyone. Right. Don't listen to them."

I am in a fix. If I leave now the embarrassment reading will be off the scale. I effectively heard him mutter his intimate secrets in his sleep, and I hardly know the guy. But if I stay here, what might he reveal next? How he chopped up the corpse in his bath and put it out with the garbage bit by bit? If he finds me listening, it will look as if I was eavesdropping. What a mess. I cough, flush the toilet, and take a long time to pull my trousers up. When I emerge from my cubicle Suga has disappeared. I wash my hands and walk the roundabout way back to the office, via the magazine stands. Mrs. Sasaki is dealing with a customer. Suga is in the back eating his lunch, and I offer him a Salem. He says no, he doesn't smoke. I forgot, he told me that yesterday. I go to the mirror and pretend to have something in my eye. If I show him too much kindness he may work out that it was me who heard him being memory-whipped. Nerds may be nerds but you need some brains to be one.

Later, back at the claims counter, Suga perches on his stool reading a magazine called *MasterHacker*. Suga has a weird physique—he is overweight around his belly, but he has no butt. Long dangly E.T. arms. He suffers from eczema. His face has been medicated into submission, but the backs of his hands flake, and even in this heat he wears long-sleeved shirts to hide his forearms. A trolley of lost items from the afternoon trains is in the back office waiting for me. Suga smirks. "So you already had the Assistant Stationmaster Aoyama experience?" I nod. Suga puts down his magazine. "Don't let him intimidate you. He isn't as big-time as he makes out. The man is losing it, imho. A big shake-up is being announced, Mrs. Sasaki was saying last week. Not that I care. Next week I'm doing my IBM internship. Week after, back to college. I'm getting my own postgrad research room. You can come and see me when

I'm not supervising. Imperial University, ninth floor. Near Ochano-mizu. I'll draw you a map. You can get the front desk to call up for me. My Ph.D. is in computer systems, but between you, me, and the lost property—all that academic crap is a cover for this—" He waves *MasterHacker*. "I'm one of the five best hackers currently working in Japan. We all know each other, right. We break into systems and leave our tags. Like graffiti artists. There is *nowhere*, right, in Japan I can't hack into. There's a secret website in the Pentagon—you know what the Pentagon is, right, the American defense nerve center—called Holy Grail. This site is protected by their top computer brains, right. If you hack into Holy Grail it proves that you are better than they are, and men in black appear to offer you a job. That is what I'm going to do. Imperial University has the fastest modems this side of the twenty-fifth century. Once I get access to those babies, I am in. Then, whoosh, I am out of this shit hole commonly known as Tokyo. Deep joy. You suckers won't see me for dust."

Suga reads *MasterHacker* while I work. His eyebrows twitch up every time he reaches the bottom of a column of text. I wonder what Suga wouldn't call a shit hole. Weird, but when I remember that I'll only be here until I find my father, I almost like Tokyo. I feel I'm on holiday on another planet, passing myself off as a native alien. I might even stay on. I like flashing my JR travel pass to the train man at the barrier. I like the way nobody pokes their nose into your business. I like the way the ads change every week—on Yakushima they change every ten years. I like riding the train every day from Kita Senju to Ueno: I like the incline where it dives below the ground and becomes a submarine. I like the way submarines pass by at different speeds, so you can fool yourself you are going backward. I like the glimpses of commuters in parallel windows—two stories being remembered at the same time. Kita Senju to Ueno is crammed beyond belief in the morning. We drones all swing and lurch in droozy unison as the train changes speed. Normally only lovers and twins get this close to other people. I like the way nothing needs to be decided on submarines. You just stand there. I like the muffled clunking. Tokyo is one massive machine made of smaller components.

The drones only know what their own minute component is for. I wonder what the total of Tokyo does. I already know the names of the stations between here and Ueno. I know where to stand so I can get off nearest the exit. Do not ride in the first compartment, says Uncle Tarmac—if the train collides, this is the crumple zone—and be extra alert on the platform as the train pulls in, in case a hand in the small of your back shoves you over the edge. I like the brew of sweat, perfume, crushed food, grime, cosmetics. I like how you can study reflected faces, so deeply you can almost leaf through their memories. Submarines carry drones, skulls carry memories, and one man's shit hole may be another man's paradise.

"Eiji!" Anju, of course. Moonlight bright as a UFO abduction, air heady with the mosquito incense that my grandmother uses to fumigate the lived-in rooms. Anju whispers so as not to wake her. "Eiji!" She perches on the high windowsill, hugging her knees. Bamboo shadows sway on the tatami and faded fusuma. "Eiji! Are you awake?"

"No."

"I was watching you. You are a boy-me. But you snore."

She wants to wake me up by getting me angry. "I do not."

"You snore like a piggy puking. Guess where I've been."

Let me sleep. "Down the toilet."

"Out on the roof! You can climb up the balcony pole. I found the way. So warm out there. If you stare at the moon long enough you can see it move. I couldn't sleep. A pesky mosquito woke me up."

"A pesky sister woke me up. My soccer match is tomorrow. I need sleep."

"So you need a midnight snack to build you up. Look."

On the side is a tray. Omochi, soy sauce, daikon pickles, peanut cookies, tea. I see trouble ahead. "When Wheatie finds out she'll—"

Anju scrunches up her face and voice for a Wheatie impression. "Your mother may have made your bones, young missy, but inside that head of yours is going to be all *my* handiwork!"

I have to laugh. "You went down to the kitchen on your own?"

"I told the ghosts I was one of them and they believed me." Anju jumps and lands at my feet without a sound. I know resistance is pointless so I sit up and bite into a squeaky pickle. Anju slides under my futon and dunks an omochi into a saucer of soy sauce. "I had my flying dream again. Only I had to keep flapping *really* hard to stay above the ground. I could see lots of people moving about, and there was this big stripy circus tent where Mom lived. I was about to swoop down on it when the mosquito woke me up."

"Be careful about falling."

Anju chews. "What?"

"If you dream about falling and hit the ground you really die in your bed."

Anju chews some more. "Who says so?"

"Scientists say so."

"Crap."

"It is not crap too! Scientists proved it!"

"If you dreamed of falling, hit the ground, and died, how could anyone know that you were dreaming of falling in the first place?" I think this through. Anju enjoys her victory in silence. Frogs start up and die down. In the distance the sea is sleeping. We chomp one omochi after another. Suddenly Anju speaks in a voice I don't remember her using. "I never see her face anymore, Eiji."

"Whose face?"

"Mom's. Can you?"

"She's ill. She's in a special hospital."

Anju's voice wavers. "What if that isn't true?"

Huh? "Sure it's true!" Seeing Anju near tears makes me feel as if I've swallowed a knife. "She looks like how she looks in the photographs."

"The photographs are old." Why now? Anju wipes her eyes on her nightshirt and looks away. I hear her jaw and throat sort of clench up and her voice comes out wrong. "Wheatie sent me to buy a box of detergent at Mrs. Tanaka's while you were at soccer practice this afternoon. Mrs. Oki and her sister from Kagoshima were there. They were at the back of the store and they didn't notice me at first, so I heard everything."

The knife reaches my gut. "Heard what?"

"Mrs. Oki said, 'Of course the Miyake girl hasn't shown her face here.' Mrs. Tanaka said, 'Of course, she has no right to.' Mrs. Oki said, 'She wouldn't dare. Dumping her two kids on their grandmother and uncles while she lives it up in Tokyo with her fancy men and fancy apartments and fancy cars.' Then she saw me." The knife turns itself. Anju gasps between tight chains of sobs.

"What happened?"

"She dropped her eggs, and hurried out."

A moth drowns in the moonlight.

I wipe Anju's tears. They are so warm. Then she brushes me away and hunches up in a stubborn crouch. "Look," I say, wondering what to say. "Mrs. Oki and her sister from Kagoshima and Mrs. Tanaka are all witches who drink their own piss." Anju shakes her head at the daikon pickle I offer her. She just mumbles. "Broken eggs. Everywhere."

♦

FUJIFILM says 02:34. Sleep. Sleep. You are feeling sleepy. Your eyelids are veeeeeerrry heavy. I don't think so. Let me sleep. Please. I have to work tomorrow. Today. I close my eyes but see a body falling through space. Cartwheeling. Cockroach is still fighting the glue. Cockroaches have sensors that start the legs running even before the brain registers danger. How do scientists find these things out? Cockroaches even eat books if nothing juicier comes along. Cat would have kicked Cockroach's butt. Cat. Cat knows the secret of life and death. Wednesday evening, I get home from work. "Good day at the office, dear?" asks Buntaro, drinking iced coffee from a can. "Not bad," I say. Buntaro drains the last drops. "What are your coworkers like?" "I haven't met many. Suga, the guy I'm replacing, believes he is a sort of archcybercriminal. Mrs. Sasaki, my boss, doesn't seem to like me much but I sort of like her anyway. Mr. Aoyama, her boss, is so uptight I'm surprised he can walk without squeaking." Buntaro lobs his can into the trash, and a customer comes with a stack of videos to return. I climb up to my capsule, slump on my futon, and read Akiko Kato's letter for the hundredth time. I practice my guitar as the room fills with suburban dusk. I can't afford any light fittings yet, so all I have is a decrepit lamp that the previous tenant stowed in the back of the closet. I suddenly decide to admit to myself that the vague hope I have entertained all my life, that by coming to Tokyo I would bump into my father sooner or later, is laughable. Instead of setting me free, the truth makes me too depressed to play the guitar, so I fold my futon into a chair and switch on the TV, salvaged from the trash last week. This TV is a pile of crap. Its greens are mauves and its blues pink. I can find five channels, plus one in a blizzard. All the programs are crap, too. I watch the governor of Tokyo announce that in the event of an earthquake all the blacks, Hispanics, and Koreans will run amok, loot, rape, and pillage. I change the channel. A farmer explains how a pig gets fat by eating its own shit. I change the channel. Tokyo Giants trounce Hiroshima Carp. I get the box of discount sushi from the fridge. I change the channel. A memory game comes on in which contestants are posed questions about tiny details in a section of film they have just watched. I imagine a shadow crouching in the corner of my eye. It launches itself at me and I half-drop my dinner.

"Gaaah!"

A black cat lands at my feet. It yawns a mouth of hooks. Its tail is dunked in white. It has a tartan collar. "Cat," I blurt pointlessly, as my pulse tries to calm itself. It must have jumped onto my balcony from a ledge and entered through the gash in the mosquito netting. "Get lost!" Cat is the coolest customer. I do the sudden stomp people do to intimidate animals, but Cat has seen it all before. Cat looks at my sushi and licks its lips. "Look," I say to it, "go and find a housewife with a freezer full of leftovers." Cat is too cool to reply. "One saucer of milk," I tell it, "then you go away." Cat downs it as I pour. More. "This is your last saucer, okay?" As Cat laps more genteelly, I wonder when I started talking to animals. It watches me blow the fluff off the last of my sushi. So I end up eating a box of crackers while Cat chews on fresh yellowtail, octopus, and cod roe.

Leave Ueno Station through the park entrance, go past the concert hall and museums, skirt around the fountain, and you come to a sort of tree garden. Homeless people live here, in tents made of sky-blue plastic sheeting and wooden poles. The best tents even have doors. I guess

Picture Lady lives there. She appeared at the claims counter just before my lunch break on Thursday. It was the hottest day this week. Tarmac as soft as cooking chocolate. She wore a headscarf tied tight, and a long skirt of no clear color or pattern, and battered sneakers. Forty, fifty, sixty years old, hard to tell beneath the ingrained grime. Suga saw her coming, did his smirk, announced it was his lunch break and slipped away. The homeless woman reminds me of the farming wives on Yakushima, but she's more spaced out. Her eyes don't focus properly. Her voice is cracked and hissed. "I lost 'em."

"What have you lost?"

She mumbles to her feet. "Has anyone given 'em to you yet?"

My hands reach for the claim pad. "What is it you lost?"

She shoots a glance at me. "My pictures."

"You lost some pictures?"

She takes an onion out of her pocket and unpeels the crispy brown skin. Her fingers are scabby and dark.

I try again. "Did you lose the pictures on a train or in the station?"

She keeps flinching. "I got the old ones back . . ."

"It would help me if you could tell me a little more about—"

She licks the onion. "But I ain't got the new ones back."

"Were the pictures valuable?"

She bites. It crunches.

Mrs. Sasaki appears from the side office, and nods at Picture Lady. "Roasting weather we're having, isn't it?"

Picture Lady talks through onion cud. "I need 'em to cover up the clocks."

"We don't have your pictures today, I'm afraid. Maybe tomorrow you'll come across them. Have you looked around Shinobazu Pond?"

Picture Lady scowls. "What would my pictures be doing there?"

Mrs. Sasaki shrugs. "Who knows? It's a cool spot on a hot day."

She nods. "Who knows . . ."

I watch her wander away. "Is she a regular customer?"

Mrs. Sasaki straightens up the desk. "We're a part of her schedule. It costs nothing to be civil to her. Did you work out what her 'pictures' are?"

"Some sort of family albums, I figured?"

"I took her literally at first, too." Mrs. Sasaki speaks carefully, the way she does. "But I think she's talking about her memories." We watch her disappear in the shimmer. Cicadas wind up and wind down.

The moon has moved. Anju sips her tea, calm again. I am between sleeping and waking. I am doing my best to remember our mother's face. I think I remember a perfume she wore, but I cannot be sure. Remembering her voice is easier. I feel Anju settle inside my sleeping curl. She is still thinking. "The last time we saw her was at Uncle Yen's in Kagoshima. The last time we left Yakushima."

"The secret beach birthday. Two years ago?"

"Three. Two years ago was the rubber dinghy birthday."

"She left suddenly. She was staying all week, then she just wasn't there."

"Want to know a secret?"

I am awake again. "A real one?"

"'Course it's a real one. I'm not a little kid."

"Go on, then."

"Wheatie told me never to tell anyone, not even you."

"What about?"

"When she left that day. Mom, I mean."

"You kept a secret for three years? I thought she left because she was ill."

Anju yawns, indifferent to what I think or thought.

"Tell me."

"I was sick that day. You were at soccer practice. I was doing homework on the downstairs table. Mom started making tempura." Anju's voice has gone sort of limp. I prefer it when she blubbers. "She dipped weird stuff into the batter."

"What weird stuff?"

"Stuff you can't eat. Her watch, a candle, a tea bag, a lightbulb. The lightbulb popped when she put it in the oil and she laughed funny. Her ring. Then she arranged everything on a dish with shiso leaves and put it in front of me."

"What did you say?"

"Nothing."

"What did she say?"

"She said she was playing. I said, 'You've been drinking.' She said, 'It's all Yakushima's fault.' I asked her why she couldn't play without drinking. She asked me why I didn't like her cooking. She said to eat my dinner up like a good girl. I said, 'I can't eat those things.' So she got angry. You remember how she got on her visits sometimes?"

"What happened then?"

"Auntie Money came and led her to the bedroom. I heard her"— Anju swallows—"she was *crying*."

"Mom was crying?"

"Auntie Money came back and told me that if I told anyone what had happened, even you, a doctor might take Mom away, because the doctor might not understand." Anju frowns. "So I kind of made myself forget it. But not really."

An owl hoots.

I must go to sleep.

Anju rocks herself, slowly, slowly.

A dog in the distance barks at something, real or remembered.

"Don't go to Kagoshima tomorrow, Eiji."

"I have to go. I'm in defense."

"Don't go."

I don't understand. "Why not?"

"Go, then. I don't care."

"It's only two days. I'll be back tomorrow."

Anju snaps at me. "You're not the only one who can do grown-up things!"

Why is she angry now? "What do you mean by that?"

"Me to know and you to guess!"

"What are you going to do?"

"You'll find out when you get back from your soccer game!"

"Tell me!"

"I can't hear you! You're in Kagoshima!"

"Tell me!" I'm worried.

Her voice turns spiteful. "You'll see."

"Who cares what you do anyway?"

"I saw the pearly snake this morning!"

Now I know my sister is lying. The pearly snake is a stupid tale our grandmother tells to scare us. She says it has lived out in the Miyake storehouse since before she was born, and that it only ever appears to warn of a coming death. Anju and I stopped believing her ages ago, only our grandmother never noticed. I am offended that Anju thinks she can awe me into submission with the pearly snake. I listen to the March midnight bird trying to remember the words to its song. It always loses track, and starts in again. Every year I reremember this bird, but by the rainy season I forget it again. Much later, I try to make friends with my sister, but she is asleep, or pretending to be.

◆

FUJIFILM smuggled three o'clock over the border without my noticing. Two more hours to dawn. I am going to be exhausted all day at work. Mrs. Sasaki warned me Saturday is busier, not quieter, than weekdays, because commuters are more careful with their baggage than weekend shoppers and Friday nighters, and because a lot of people wait until Saturday before coming in to claim lost items. I guess the media people will be snooping around for follow-up stories about Mr. Aoyama. Poor guy. Sudden and rude as a bullet through a drumskin, the telephone riiiiiiiiings. That noise drills me with guilt and dread. The telephone riiiiiiiiings. Weird. I only got my number last week. Nobody knows it. The telephone riiiiiiiiings. Suppose a pervert is out there, trawling for kicks at random? I answer, and before I know it I have a psycho in my shower. No way am I answering. The telephone riiiiiiiiings. Buntaro? Some kind of emergency? What kind of emergency? The telephone riiiiiiiiiings. Wait. Someone at Osugi & Bosugi knows my number—suppose a co-worker of Akiko Kato read my letter before she shredded it, and felt an unaccountable empathy with my plight. She contacts my father, who has to wait until his wife is asleep before daring to contact me. He is whispering coarsely, fiercely, in a closed-off part of his house. "Answer!" The telephone riiiiiiiiings. I have to decide now. No. Let it die. Answer it! I dive off my futon, trap my foot in a folding peg-frame, stub my toe on my guitar case, and lunge for the receiver. "Hello?"

"Never fear-o, 'tis a Nero!" A singing man.

". . . hello?"

"Never fear-o, 'tis a Nero." A mildly irritated man.

"Yes, I thought you said that."

"I never wrote that stupid jingle!" A buttered voice.

"Me neither."

"Look here, young man—you delivered some flyers to our office, which promise that the first two hundred people to phone up off-peak and sing 'Never fear-o, 'tis a Nero!' are entitled to one free medium-size pizza of their choice. That is what I just did. I'll have my regular Kamikaze: mozzarella crust, banana, quail eggs, scallops, triple chilis, octopus ink. Don't chop the chilis. I like to suck them. Helps me concentrate. So—am I one of the first two hundred or am I not?"

"Is this a joke?"

"It had better not be. All-night overtime makes me ravenous."

"I think you misdialed."

"Impossible. This is Nero's pizzeria, right?"

"Wrong."

"Are you quite sure?"

"Yep."

"So I called a private residence after three in the morning?"

"Uh-huh."

"I am so, so dreadfully sorry. I don't know what to say."

"Not to worry. I have insomnia tonight, anyway."

"But I was so patronizing! I thought you were a numbskull pizza boy."

"No problem, really. But you have one weird taste in pizzas."

He chuckles with devious pride. He is older than I thought. "I invented it. At Nero's they nickname it the Kamikaze—I heard the telephone girl tell the chef. The secret is the banana. It glues all the other tastes together. Anyway, I mustn't take up any more of your time. Once more—my sincerest apologies. What I did to you was inexcusable. I didn't mean to do it, but it just happened. Goodbye." He hangs up.

❖

I wake up alone at the end of night. Anju's futon is a discarded pile. Could she be out on the roof? I slide the mosquito net across. "Anju? Anju!" The wind sifts the bamboo, and the frogs start up. Fine. She wants to sulk, let her. Fifteen minutes later, I am dressed, breakfasted, and walking down the track to Anbo harbor with my sports bag and my new baseball cap Anju bought me with her pocket money from Uncle Tarmac. I catch sight of the Kagoshima ferry lit up like a starship on its launchpad and feel a *vhirrr* of excitement. This day is finally here. I am leaving for Kagoshima, on my own, and I refuse to let my stupid jealous sister make me feel guilty about leaving her for one night. I refuse. How can I even be sure what she said last night about our mother was true? She's been acting weird lately. And then a fantastic idea comes to me. It is the greatest idea of my life. I am going to train, train, and train, and become such a brilliant soccer player that I will play for Japan on my twentieth birthday against Brazil in the World Cup final. Japan will be down 8–0 in the sixtieth minute, then I will be called on as a substitute and score three hat tricks by the end of injury time. I will be in newspapers and on TV all over the world. Our mother will be so proud that she gives up drinking, but better still our father sees me, recognizes me, and drives to the airport to meet the team jet. Of course Anju is waiting there too, and our mother, and we are reunited with the world watching. How perfect. How obvious. I am burning with genius and hope. A light is on in Anbo, and crossing the hanging bridge I see a flash. A salmon leaps.

Where the river widens into an estuary, the valley is steep and narrow. Wheatie and the Anbo old people call it the Neck. It is the most haunted place, but I'm not afraid. I half-fear and half-hope Anju will ambush me. The faces between the pine trees are not really there. Where the water floods the track in the rainy season, a torii gate marks the beginning of the path that winds up the hill to the shrine of the thunder god. Wheatie warns us not to play there. She says that apart from the jomon cedars themselves, the thunder god is the oldest on Yakushima. Show disrespect to the thunder god, and the next time you cross water a tsunami will come and drown you. Anju wanted to ask if that was what happened to our grandfather, our mother's father, but I made her promise not to. Mrs. Oki told a kid in our class that he drowned facedown in a ditch, drunk. Anyway, the villagers never bother the thunder god with small-fry favors like exams, money, or weddings—they go to Kakimoto-sensei's new temple next to the bank for that. But for babies, and blessings for fishing boats, solace for dead relatives, they climb the steps to the shrine of the thunder god. Always alone.

I check my Zax Omega watch. Plenty of time. The road to the World Cup starts today in Kagoshima, and I will need all the help I can get. Finding our father is big fry. No fry is bigger for Anju and me. Without another thought I sling my sports bag behind a mossy rock and, fueled by energy from my stupendous brain wave, start running up the muddy steps.

◆

I replace the phone. Weird guy, the way he kept apologizing. Maybe the telephone call will break the insomnia spell. Maybe my body will realize how tired it is, and finally shut down. I lie on my back and stare upward, doing chess knight moves on the ceiling tiles until I forget which ones I've already landed on. Then I begin again. On the third attempt I am overwhelmed by the pointlessness of the exercise. If I can't sleep I may as well think about the letter. The Other Letter. The Big Letter. It came—when?—Thursday. Yesterday. Well, the day before yesterday. I get back to Shooting Star utterly exhausted. Thirty-six bowling balls were left on platform 9, the farthest platform from the lost-property office. Suga had performed his disappearing act so I had to lug them over one by one. They were claimed later by a team that was waiting for them at Tokyo Station. I am learning that laws of probability work differently in the field of lost property. Mrs. Sasaki once had a human skeleton wind up on her trolley, stuffed inside a backpack. A medical student left it on the train after a professor's going-away party. Anyway, I get back to Shooting Star, dripping sweat, and Buntaro is perched on his stool behind the counter spooning down green-tea ice cream, studying a sheet of paper with a magnifying glass. "Hey, kid," he says. "Want to see my son?" This is weird because Buntaro had told me that he doesn't have any kids. Then he shows me a page of inky fuzz. I frown at my proud landlord. "The miracles of ultrasound scans!" he says. "Inside the womb!" I look at Buntaro's belly, and he does a "very funny" face. "We decided on his name. Actually, my wife decided. But I agree. Want to know what name we decided?"

"Sure," I say.

"Kodai. *Ko* as in 'voyage,' *dai* as in 'great.' Great Voyage."

"That is a really cool name," I tell him, meaning it.

Buntaro admires Kodai from various angles. "See his nose? This is his foot. Cute, huh?"

"The cutest. What's this shrimpy thing?"

"How do you think we know he's a he, genius?"

"Oh. Sorry."

"Another letter arrived for you. I would rig up a special mailbox for you, but then I'd miss out on the fun of steaming open my tenants' private letters. Here you go." He hands me a plain white envelope, originally postmarked in Miyazaki, and forwarded by Uncle Yen in Kagoshima. I slit it open and unfold three sheets of crumpled paper. On the video screen helicopters collide and buildings explode. Bruce Willis takes off his sunglasses and squints at the inferno. I read the first line and realize who the letter is from. I shove it into my jacket pocket and climb the stairs—I don't want Buntaro to see the shock on my face.

On the steps to the thunder god shrine, spiderwebs tug, tear, and stick to my face. Boiled-candy spiders. I trip and muddy up my knees. I try to forget the ghost stories I heard about how dead children live on these steps, but once you try to forget something you already remember it. Colossal ferns tower over me. Freshwater crabs skitter into rooty cracks. A deer thuds and disappears into a thicket. I focus on the ultimate reunion with our father once my ultimate plan bears fruit, and run, and run, and suddenly I am standing in the shrine clearing right at the top. I can see for miles. Inland mountains heave and lurch toward the breaking sky. Light smooths the sea over. I can see the windows on the Kagoshima ferry. I approach the bell nervously and look around for an adult to ask permission. I've never woken a god up before. Wheatie takes Anju and me to the harbor shrine every New Year's Day to change our zodiac amulets, but that is a jolly affair of relatives, neighbors, and having our heads patted. This is the real thing. This is sober magic. Only me and the thunder god in his mildewed drowse. I grip the rope that swings the bell hammer—

The first gong is to slosh through the forest, scaring pheasants.

The second gong is to make swing-wing fighters wobble in turbulence.

The third gong is to slam shut forever the iron doors.

I wonder if Anju heard the bell in her sulking place. When I get back tomorrow I will tell her it was me. She will never admit to it, but she will be mightily impressed by my daring. This is like something she normally dreams up. I approach the shrine itself. The thunder god scowls. His face is hatred, typhoon, and nightmare all knotted up. I can't back out now. He's awake. My coin clatters into the donation box, I clap three times and close my eyes. "Good morning, uh, thunder god. My name is Eiji Miyake. I live with Anju and Wheatie in the last house up the valley track, past the big Yokata farmhouse. But you probably know that. I woke you up to ask for your help. I want to become the greatest soccer player in Japan. This is a big, big thing, so please don't give me piles like you did the taxi driver."

"And in return?" asks the silence.

"When I'm a famous soccer player I'll, uh, come back and rebuild your shrine and stuff. Until then, anything that I can give you, you can have. Take it. You don't have to ask me, just take it."

The silence sighs. "Anything?"

"Anything."

"Anything? Are you sure?"

"I said anything, and I mean it."

The silence lasts nine days and nine nights. "Done."

I open my eyes. The fin of an airliner trails rose and gold. Doves spin predictions. Down in Anbo harbor the Kagoshima ferry sounds a solitary horn, and I can see cars arriving. The million and one clocks of the forest flutter, dart, shriek, and howl into life. I rush off, flying down the muddy steps where the ghosts of the dead children are dissolving in the first sunlight.

◆

Miyazaki Mountain Clinic
August 25

Hello Eiji,

How do I begin this? I already wrote a bad-tempered letter, then a moaning one, then a witty one that began, "Hello, I am your mother, nice to meet you." Then one that began with "Sorry." They are crumpled up, near the trash can on the other side of my room. I am a lousy shot.

Hot summer, isn't it? I knew it would be when the rainy season didn't happen. (I suppose it is still raining in Yakushima, though. When doesn't it?) So, you're nearly twenty now. Twenty. Where do all the years go? Want to know how old I'll be next month? Too old to tell anyone. I'm at this place receiving treatment for nerves/drinking. I never wanted to come back to Kyushu, but at least the mountain air here is cool. My therapist has advised that I write to you. I didn't want to at first, but she is even more persistent than me. That looks wrong—I want to write to you, but after all this time, it's so, so much easier not to. But I have this story (more a serial memory). My therapist says I can stop it hurting me only by telling you about it. So if you like, I'm writing out of selfishness. But here goes.

Once upon a time I was a young mother living in Tokyo with infant you and infant Anju. The apartment was paid for by your father, but this story isn't about him, or even Anju. This is about you and me. In those days, it looked like I was onto a good thing—a ninth-floor split-level apartment in a fashionable quarter of the big city, flower boxes on the balcony, a very rich lover with his own wife to wash his shirts. You and Anju, I have to admit, were not part of the plan when I left Yakushima, but it seemed that the life I led twenty years ago was better than the life of orange farming and island gossip that my mother (your grandmother) had arranged (behind my back, as usual) with Shintaro Baba's people to marry me into. Believe me, he was every bit as much a slob a quarter of a century ago as I'm quite sure he is now.

This isn't easy to write.

I was miserable. I was twenty-three, and everyone told me I was beautiful. The only company young mothers have is other young mothers. Young mothers are the most vicious tribe in the world if you don't fit in. When they found out I was a "second wife" they decided I was an immoral influence and petitioned the building manager to have me removed. Your father was powerful enough to block that, but none of them ever spoke to me afterward. As you know, nobody on Yakushima knew about you (yet), and the thought of living with all the knowing glances was too much.

Around that time your father began seeing a newer-model mistress. A baby is not a sexy accessory on a woman. Twins are twice as unsexy. It was an ugly ending, you don't want the details, believe me. (Maybe you do, but I don't want to remember them.) When I was pregnant, he swore he'd take care of everything. Naive young petal that I was, I didn't realize he was only talking about money. Like all weak men, he thought that if he acted confused enough, everyone would forgive him. His lawyers took over and I never saw him again. (Never wanted to.) I was allowed to live in the apartment, but not to sell it—it was during the bubble economy, and the value of the place was doubling every six months. This was shortly after your first birthday.

I was not a well woman. (I've never been a very well woman, but at least now I know it.) Some women take to motherhood like they were mothers even before they were mothers—I was never cut out to be a mother, even when I was one. I still hate little children. All the money your father's lawyer sent for your maintenance I spent on an illegal Filipina nanny so I could escape the apartment. I used to sit in coffee shops watching people walk by. Young women my age, working in banks, doing flower arranging, shopping. All the little ordinary things I had looked down on before I became pregnant.

Two years passed. I got a job in another hostess bar, but I was jaded. I'd already caught my rich patron, and every time I went home you and Anju reminded me where rich patrons leave you. (Diapers and bawling and sleepless nights.) One morning you and I were alone in the house—you'd had a fever, so the nanny took Anju to kindergarten. Not the local one—the young-mother mafia had threatened to boycott it if it admitted you, so we had to get a kindergarten in another neighborhood to take you. You were bawling. Maybe because of the fever, maybe because there was no Anju. I'd been working all night so I washed down some pills with vodka and left you to it. Next thing I knew you were rattling my door—you were walking by this time, of course. My migraine wouldn't let me sleep. I lost it. I screamed at you to go away. So of course you bawled some more. I screamed. Then silence. Then I heard you say the word. You must have gotten it from kindergarten.

"Daddy."

Something broke in me.

Quite calmly, I decided to throw you off the balcony.

New ink, new pen. Pretty dramatic point for my pen to die. So. Quite calmly. *I decided to throw you off the balcony.* Those eight words explain our lives since. I'm not saying they justify what I did, not at all. I don't mean I wanted to throw you over the balcony. I mean I was going to. Really. It is so hard to write this.

This is what happened. I flung open my bedroom door—it opened outward—and slid you clean across the polished wooden landing, over the lip of the stairs and out of sight. I froze, but I couldn't have stopped your fall, not even if I was superhuman. You didn't cry as you fell. I heard you. Imagine a sack of books falling downstairs. You sounded like that. I waited for you to start screaming, and waited, and waited. Suddenly time moved three times as fast, to catch up with itself. You were lying at the bottom, with blood squirting out of your ear. I can still see you. (I still do, every time I go down any stairs any-where.) I was hysterical. The ambulance people had to shout at me to stop me jabbering. Then, when I put down the phone, guess what I saw? You were sitting up, licking the blood on your fingers.

The ambulance man said that children go limp sometimes, like rag dolls. That saved you from major damage. The doctor said you were a lucky boy, but he meant I was a lucky woman. The vodka on my breath pretty much shot down my story about you climbing over the stair guard. Actually, we were all of us lucky. I know I was going to kill you, and could have spent the rest of my life in prison. I can't believe I'm finally writing this. Three days later I paid the nanny a month's money and told her I was taking you to see your grandmother. I was mentally unfit to raise you and Anju. The rest, you know.

I'm not writing this for your sympathy or forgiveness. This story is beyond all that. But the memories even now keep me awake, and showing you them is the only way I know to ease them. I want to get well. I mean—

—you can tell from the creases, can't you, I just crumpled this up and threw it at the trash can. I knew I could never get it in, so I didn't even bother aiming. And guess what? It fell straight in, without even touching the sides. Who knows? Maybe this is one of those times when superstition pays. I'll go and slip this under Dr. Suzuki's door, before I change my mind again. If you want to call me, phone the number on the letterhead. Up to you. I wish—

FUJIFILM is pushing four o'clock. What is the proper way to react to the news that your mother wanted to kill you? After three years of noncommunication. I'm used to my mother being out there, somewhere; but not too near. Things are painless that way. If I move anything, I'm afraid it will all start all over again. The only plan I can think of is Do Nothing. Truth is, I do not care. It is my father's "nowhere" that I can't handle, not my mother's "somewhere." I know what I mean even if I can't put it into words. Cockroach is still struggling. I want to see it. I crawl over to the fridge—so humid tonight. The motel starts vibrating as I pick it up. Cockroach panics. A part of me wants to free it, a part of me wishes it instant death. I force myself to peer in. Bicycling feelers and furious wings! So revolting I drop the motel—it lands on its roof. Now Cockroach is dying upside down, poor shiny bastard, but I don't want to touch the motel. I look for something to flip it over. I fish in the trash—gingerly, in case Elder Brother of Cockroach is in there—and find the squashed box Cat's biscuits came in. On Thursday, after I read the letter I put it down and did nothing for I don't know how long. I'm about to reread it when Cat appears. She jumps on my lap and shows me her shoulder. Clotted blood and soft skin show where a gobbet of fur has been gouged off. "You've been fighting?" I forget about the letter for a moment. I don't know anything about first aid, especially cat first aid, but I think I should disinfect the wound. Of course I don't have anything as practical as antiseptic fluid so I go downstairs and ask Buntaro.

Buntaro pauses the video at the moment the *Titanic* upends and people fall down the mile-long deck. He takes a cigarette from his box of Caster and lights it without offering me one. "Don't tell me. Upon receiving another letter from his mysterious lawyer lady, telling our hero it is all over, he becomes so depressed that he decides to disembowel himself, but all he has is a pair of nail scissors, so—"

"I have a wounded cat on my hands."

Buntaro clouds over. "A what, kid?"

"A wounded cat."

"You're keeping pets in my apartment?"

"No. It just wanders in when it's hungry."

"Or when it wants medical attention?"

"It's just a scratch. I want to dab some disinfectant on it."

"Eiji Miyake, animal doctor."

"Please, Buntaro."

He grumbles and sifts under the register for a while. He pulls out a dusty red box and causes a landslide of junk around his feet, and hands it to me. "It better not be bleeding on my tatami."

"You tight-assed, whining parasite, you've fleeced every outgoing tenant for replacement tatami, but you haven't actually changed it since 1969, have you?" is not what I tell my landlord and job benefactor. Instead I just shake my head meekly. "She isn't bleeding now. She just has this sort of wound that needs seeing to."

"What's this cat look like? My wife might know the owner."

"Black, white paws and tail, and a tartan collar with a silver bell."

"No owner, no name?"

I shake my head. "Thanks for this." I tap the box and begin my get-away.

"Don't get too attached," Buntaro calls up the stairs after me. "Remember the 'Thou shalt not have pets except cactuses' clause in your lease."

I turn around and peer down at him. "What lease?"

Buntaro taps his forehead. He loves reminding me I am at his mercy.

I seal up my capsule and attend to Cat. The witch hazel must sting her—it always stung me and Anju when Wheatie doused our cuts with it—but Cat doesn't even flinch. "Girls shouldn't get into fights," I tell her. I chuck the cotton wool away and return the first-aid box to Buntaro. Cat makes herself comfortable in my yukata. Weird. Cat trusts me to look after her, me of all people.

A head appears on the claims counter. Its owner is a spindly girl of maybe eleven, in a Mickey and Donald jogging suit and with red ribbons in her hair. Her eyes are enormous. "Good afternoon," she says. "I followed the signs. Is this the lost-property office?"

"Yes," I answer. "Have you lost anything?"

"Mommy," she says. "She always wanders off without my permission."

I tut. "I can relate to that." What do I do? Suga skipped the "lost child" chapter, and now he is collecting the trolley from Ueno annex. Mrs. Sasaki is on her lunch hour. Somewhere her mom is running around in hysterics, imagining train wheels and organ-harvesting child kidnappers. I flap. "Why don't you sit on the counter," I tell the girl. She clambers up. Right. What do I do? "Aren't you going to ask me my name?" asks the girl.

"Of course I am. What's your name?"

"Yuki Chiyo. Aren't you going to call Mommy on the big speaker?"

"Of course I am."

I go into the side office. Mrs. Sasaki mentioned the PA system on my first day, but Suga never showed me how to use it. Turn this key, flick this switch. I hope. A green light flashes under SPEAK. I clear my throat and lean into the microphone. The sound of me clearing my throat fills Ueno. When Yuki Chiyo hears her name she hugs herself.

I, however, am broiling with embarrassment. Yuki Chiyo studies me. "So, Yuki. How old are you?"

"Ten. But Mommy tells me not to speak to strangers."

"You already spoke to me."

"Only because I needed you to call Mommy."

"You ungrateful tadpole."

I hear Aoyama marching this way before I see him. His shoes, his keys. "You! Miyake!"

Obviously I am in deep shit. "Good afternoon—"

"Do *not* 'Good afternoon' me! Since when have you had the authority to make a general override announcement?"

My throat is dry. "I didn't realize that—"

"Suppose a train were hurtling into Ueno with a snapped brake cable!" His eyes froth. "Suppose I were making an evacuation announcement!" Veins bulge. "Suppose we receive a bomb warning!" Is he going to fire me? "And you, *you* blanket out my warning with a request for a lost girl's mother to proceed to the lost-property office on the second floor!" He pauses to reoxygenize. "You, *you* pollute the order of this institution with your youthful—liberal—modern—"

"Tra-la-la-la-la!" A leopard-skin woman pads up to the counter.

"Mommy!" Yuki Chiyo waves.

"Dearest, you know it upsets Mommy when you go off like this! Have you been making trouble for this handsome young stripling?" She nudges Aoyama aside and deposits her designer bags on the counter. A perky, vixen smile—I guess I am the stripling. "I am so frightfully sorry. What can I say? Yuki plays this little game whenever we go shopping, don't you, dearest? My husband says it's just a stage she's going through. Do I have to sign anywhere?"

"No, madam."

Aoyama smolders.

"Let me give you a little something for your trouble."

"Really, madam, no need."

"You are a darling." She turns to Aoyama. "Oh, good! A porter!"

I kill my snicker a fraction too late. Aoyama radiates nuclear fury. "No, madam, I am the assistant stationmaster."

"Oh. Well, you look like a porter in that getup. Come on, Yuki."

Yuki turns to me as her mother leads her away and sticks her tongue out. Oh, don't mention it. Aoyama breathes deeply until his fury has cooled into malice. "You, Miyake, *you,* I am *not* going to forget this! I am going to file a report about this *outrage* to the disciplinary committee this very afternoon!" Off he storms. I would have preferred the fury. I wonder if I still have a job. Suga steps out from the back office. "Quite a talent you have there for annoying people, Miyake."

"You were there all along?"

"You seemed in control of the situation."

I want to kill Suga so I say nothing.

I am on the ferry! So many times Anju and I watched it disappear to the world over the horizon, now I am actually on it! The deck sways, and the wind is strong enough to lean back into. Yakushima, the enormous island I live on, is slowly but surely growing smaller. Mr. Ikeda is scanning the shoreline with his army binoculars. Seabirds follow the boat, just hanging there. The seventh graders are arguing about what will happen when the ferry sinks and we have to fight for the lifeboats. Others are watching the TV, or being thown out of places you are not supposed to be in. One kid is vomiting in the toilets and some classmates are discussing the contents. The engine pounds away. I smell engine fumes. I watch the hull slice through the spray-chopped waves. If I hadn't already decided on being a soccer star I would become a sailor. I look for the shrine of the thunder god, but it is already hidden in the morning haze. I wish Anju were here. I wonder what she'll do today. I try to remember the last day we weren't together. I go back as far as I can, but no such day ever was. Yakushima is now the size of a barn. I watch new islands rise ahead and fall behind. I can fit Yakushima inside the O of my thumb and first finger. A tooth is wobbling loose. Mr. Ikeda is on the deck too. "Sakurajima," he shouts at me above the wind and the engine, pointing ahead. I watch the volcano grow and take up a third of the sky.

The torn crater belches graceful, solid clouds of smoke over another third. "You can taste the ash," shouts Mr. Ikeda, "on your tongue! And over there, that's Kagoshima!" Already? The voyage is supposed to take three hours. I consult my Zax Omega watch and find that, yes, nearly three hours have passed. Here comes Kagoshima. Huge! You could fit the whole of Anbo, our village, between two jetties in the harbor. Enormous buildings, vast cranes, huge freighters marked with place-names I mostly haven't heard of. I guess when I was here last my memory was switched off. Or maybe it was night? This is where the world starts. Wait until I tell Anju. She'll be amazed. Amazed.

◆

According to FUJIFILM, four o'clock slipped by fifteen minutes ago. The best I can hope for now is a couple of hours of sleep, so I can be a zombie at work instead of a decaying corpse. Yesterday was the last day of Suga, so I'll be on my own all afternoon. I can still see the body falling. Cockroach is quiet. Has he escaped? Is he plotting revenge? Is he asleep, dreaming of stewing garbage? They say that for every single cockroach you see, there are ninety relatives out of sight. Under the floor, in cavities, behind cupboards. Under futons. "Poor Mom," she is hoping I'll think. "Okay, she dumped us at our uncle's when we were three, but let bygones be bygones. I'll phone her this very morning." No *way*! Forget it! I imagine I can hear Tokyo stir. My neck itches. I scratch. My back itches. I scratch. My crotch itches. I scratch. Once Tokyo itself wakes, all hope of sleep is doomed. The fan stirs the heat. How dare she write me a letter like that? How dare she? I was tired when I went to bed. What happened?

"My final Friday," says Suga. "Deep joy. Tomorrow, freedom. Imho, you should go back to college, Miyake. It beats earning a living for a living." I am not really listening—this is the morning after I discovered that when I was three years old my mother decided to throw me off a ninth-floor balcony—but when he says that word again I give in. "Why do you keep using that word?"

Suga acts puzzled. "What word?"

"*Imho.*"

"Oh, sorry," Suga says, not sounding at all sorry, "I forgot."

"Forgot what?"

"Most of my friends are e-friends. Other hackers. We use our own language, you know. *Imho* stands for the English 'in my humble opinion.' Like, '*I* think that . . .' Cool word, or what?"

The telephone rings. Suga looks—I answer.

"Pleased with yourself, Miyake?" A voice I know, simmering with malice.

"Mr. Aoyama?"

"You work for them, don't you?"

". . . For Ueno Station, you mean, sir?"

"Drop the act! I mean what I mean! I know you work for the consultants!"

". . . Which consultants, sir?"

"I told you to drop it! I see right through you! You were in my office to snoop. To filch. To assess. I know your little game. Then there was your provocation the day before yesterday. That was to get me out of my office, while my files were copied. It all adds up now. Oh yes. Deny it! I dare you to deny it!"

"I swear, Mr. Aoyama, there has been some mistake here . . ."

"A mistake?" Aoyama shouts. "How right you are! The biggest mistake of your treacherous little life! I have served Ueno since before you were born! I have friends at the transport ministry! I went to an influential university!" I cannot believe his voice could get any louder, but it does. "If your masters believe *I* can be 'restructured' to an end-of-the-line deep freeze in Akita with two platforms and a company dormitory made of paper, they are grievously mistaken! My lackey years are long behind me!" He breaks, pants, and launches his final assault. "Ueno has standards! Ueno has systems! Your scumbag parasite know-nothing masters want war, I will give them war, and you, you, *you,* you worm, you cockroach, you *flea,* you will get blasted by crossfire and I will spit on your grave!"

He hangs up.

Suga sort of sneers. "What was that about?"

Why me? Why is it always me?

❖

"How can I say this tactfully?" Mr. Ikeda paces to and fro during our
halftime pep talk. "Boys. You are utterly, utterly crap. Shambolic. Sub-
human. In fact, submammalian. A disgrace. A sickening waste of ship-
ping fuel. A nonteam of myopic, crippled sloths. We have a *miracle* to
thank that the enemy is not nine goals up, and the name of this miracle
is Mitsui." Mitsui chews gum, enjoying the taste of despotic favor. He is
a gifted and aggressive goalkeeper—it is lucky he lacks the imagination
to diversify into playground bullying. Mitsui's father—a taxi driver—is
Yakushima's most notorious alcoholic, so our goalkeeper has been calcu-
lating the flight paths of projectiles from an early age. Ikeda goes on. "In
a more civilized century, I could have insisted that the rest of you commit seppuku. You will, however, shave your heads in shame if we lose.
Defenders. Despite Mr. Mitsui's valiant work, how many times has the
enemy hit the crossbar? Nakamori?"

"Three times, sir."

"And the post?"

I suck my warm orange, readjust my shin pads, watch the enemy
team having their pep talk—their coach is laughing. The stale smell of
boys and soccer uniforms. The afternoon has clouded over. The volcano
puffs. "Miyake? The post?"

"Uh, twice, sir," I guess.

"'Uh, twice, sir.' Uh, yes. Uh, Nakayama, *midfield* means 'middle of
the field,' not 'middle of the penalty area.' *Attack* means we attack the
enemy goal. How many times has their goalkeeper had to touch the ball?
Nakamura?"

"Not very often, sir."

Ikeda massages his temples. "Not once, *actually*, sir! Not once! He
has made three—separate—dates with three—separate—cheerleaders!
Listen to me! I am videoing this match, and, boys, it is my birthday
tomorrow. If you do not give me a goalless draw, I warn you, you will
remember my displeasure until your deaths. In the second half the wind
is on our side. Your orders are to dig in and hold out. One more thing. Do
not give away a penalty. I got the enemy coach drunk last night, and he
boasted that their penalty taker has never missed. Ever. And remember,

if you feel your poor little limbs flagging: my camcorder is watching and will exact retribution on a man-by-man basis."

The referee blows his whistle for the second half. We lose possession of the ball three seconds later. Briefly I remember my deal with the thunder god. Fat lot of good he turned out to be. I do my best to look good for Ikeda's camcorder—running around, shouting "pass," groaning, and generally avoiding the ball as cleverly as I can. "Possess and push!" screams Ikeda. Our 4-3-3 formation buckles into 10-0-0, and our penalty area becomes a pinball zone of kicks, screams, and curses. I fake a spectacular injury but nobody is watching. Time after time Mitsui pulls off a brilliant save, a daring pounce, a midair punch. "Positions!" screams Ikeda. If only I could be as good as Mitsui. I would make the national sports papers tomorrow. Time after time the enemy launches an attack, but the mass of defenders reinforces our luck. The breeze rises to a wind. I make a daring aerial challenge—and win—but the ball hits the top of my head, squashing it, and carries on deeper into our half. I have to do a throw-in at one point, but the referee blows his whistle for a foul throw—I don't know why, but Ikeda will make me pay anyway. Nakamori and Nakamura, our star strikers, are both given yellow cards for punching each other. I turn around and the ball bounces off my face. A corner. "Cretins!" screams Ikeda. Elbow fights with a mutant boy twice my height with a killer's eyes. A tooth that is coming loose suddenly becomes very loose. Mitsui pulls off a diving save. An enemy supporter throws a rice ball at Nakata, our winger, who runs into the crowd and drop-kicks the offender when the ref is looking away. Nakayama takes a free kick, boots the ball up the field—the wind picks it up—and we all banzai charge after it. "Positions!" screams Ikeda. My tooth is hanging on by a strand of gum. The enemy appears to be falling back. We surge. I hear military bands. A wall of enemy strikers is surging this way—they have the ball—a trap? A trap! "Sphincters!" screams Ikeda. I have no breath left but I run back, hoping to salvage an iota of mercy from the postgoal trial. Mitsui is sprinting out to narrow the angle, roaring like a Zero. The enemy striker toe-pokes the ball under his nemesis a moment before impact—I hear the bones crunch—unable to brake in time I springboard over the bodies—the heel of my sneaker hits a nose—momentum rockets me forward, and without thinking I dive, skimming over the empty goalmouth of grit, and grapple the ball to a halt just this side of the goal line.

Rushing silence.

The referee's whistle drills through my head. Red card for Mitsui, yellow one for me, a stretcher and a drive to the hospital for the striker, a verbal sewer from Ikeda, a penalty to the enemy, and yet another problem for our team. We now have no goalkeeper. Ikeda arrives in a whirlwind of abuse and snarls down from his chariot of ire. "You looked pretty useful with your hands just then, Miyake. *You* go in goal." My teammates adopt the proposal at bushfire speed. Sacrificial lambs cannot answer back. I traipse to the goalmouth. The skin is sandpapered off my knees and thighs. The enemy walls in the penalty area. Fathoms yawn either side of me. The ace enemy penalty kicker gloats, curling his rattail lock of hair around his little finger. Moments drum. The drumming slows. The whistle blows. The world sets. Here he comes. Thunder god. Remember me? We had a deal.

◆

Suga empties the contents of his locker into his shoulder bag. I hear police sirens. This is when? Only yesterday. The long corridor that passes the lost-property office links two sides of Ueno, so it is always quite busy—but we hear a special commotion approach and lean out over the counter to see. A TV crew streams past—a presenter, an NHK cameraman bristling with lenses, a boom operator, and a young man heaving a trolley thing. They are not the usual local station film-the-fuzzy-duck crew. Their sense of mission clears a way through the oncoming commuters. "Looks worthy of further investigation," says Suga. "Hold the fort, Miyake. I can sniff scandal." He bolts off and the telephone rings—"Lost property? I'm calling about a friend's wig." I groan. We have hundreds of wigs.

Luckily it is a glam-rock wig with sequined spangles, so I can identify it in the five minutes it takes Suga to return. "Aoyama's flipped!" Suga is feverish with gossip. "Deep-fried his circuitry! On my last day, too!"

"Aoyama?" I remember the telephone call.

"A report was published today. The top Tokyo JR people decided to kick him sideways. All the big Tokyo stations are being shaken up by the new governor, and Aoyama is a symbol of the old school of untouchables. The consultant—this guy who spent ten years teaching at Harvard Business School—gave him the news in front of a gang of junior managers. It was like a 'How to Demote Somebody' seminar."

"Grim."

"Not as grim as what happens next. Aoyama gets out a crossbow, right—"

"A crossbow?"

"A crossbow! And aims it at the consultant's chest, right. He must have seen the news coming. He tells all but one of the juniors to leave if they don't want to witness a bolt puncturing a human heart. Deep madness. Aoyama then throws a reel of mountaineering rope to the remaining junior, and orders him to tie the consultant to the chair. Then he tells the junior to leave. Before Security can get there, Aoyama locks the door from the inside."

"What does he want?"

"Nobody knows yet! The police were called, so the TV people came too. The director was up there, trying to fight the press hacks away, but we're going to be on the evening news whatever happens! Deep thrill. The SWAT teams will be here soon, and negotiators in bulletproof jackets. Nothing this exciting *ever* happens in Ueno. National news!"

I dive left and I know the ball is veering right. The ground whacks the breath from my body, my skeleton crunches, and the enemy roars. I spit out my tooth. It lies there, no longer a part of me. White, a speck of blood. Why bother getting up? Ever? I have lost the match, my friends, my soccer, my fame, my hopes to meet my father—everything except Anju. I should never have left Yakushima. The islanders will remember my shame for all time. How can I go back now? I lie in the goalmouth dirt—if I begin to sob here, how can I—

"Get up, Miyake!" It's Nakamori, the team captain.

I look up. The rattail kid is holding his head in his hands. The enemy is stalking away. The referee is pointing to the twelve-yard box. I look in our goal. Empty. Where is the ball? I realize what happened. *The ball went wide.* The thunder god musses my hair. Thank you. Oh, thank you. I place the ball for the goal kick. Can the thunder god save my luck for another twenty-five minutes? Please. "Nice save," sneers an enemy supporter. "Positions!" screams Ikeda. "Go go go!" I look for a friendly face on our team, but nobody will make eye contact in case I kick the ball to them. What do I do? The wind increases. "Look," I vow to the thunder god, "let me be as great a goalkeeper as Mitsui, just for this game, and my future is yours. I know you saved me just now. Don't turn your back on me now. Please. Please." I run back a few paces, turn, take three deep breaths, sprint at the ball, and—it is a perfect, clean, power-ful, rocket-fueled, divine kick. The thunder god intercepts the ball at house height and volleys it over the field. The ball soars over the enemy strikers. Their defenders are still jogging back into their half, unaware the goal kick has been taken. Some spectators gawk. Some players look around, wondering where the ball has gone. The enemy goalkeeper is having his photo taken with a girl, and the ball falls to earth before he realizes his services are needed. He dashes out in panic. The ball bounces over the goalkeeper, the thunder god nods it back down into the back of the net, and the miracle is complete.

◆

The walk back from Kita Senju Station to Shooting Star usually clears my head, but it is impossible not to think of Aoyama holed up in his office with a crossbow bolt aimed at the head of an executive with red suspenders and pinstripes. Suga stayed around after work, but I wanted to get away from the police and gaping crowds. I didn't even say goodbye to Suga. At Shooting Star, Buntaro is glued to the TV, spooning green-tea ice cream. "My, my, Miyake. You are a harbinger of doom." "What do you mean?" "Look at the TV! Nothing like this happened at Ueno until you started working there." I fan myself with my baseball cap and watch the screen. The camera shows an outside zoomed-in view of Aoyama's office, taken, I guess, from the Terminus Hotel. The blinds are drawn. *Ueno Station Under Siege.* "There is absolutely no question," a policeman assures a cluster of interviewers, "of a forced-entry operation at this present moment in time." "Lull him into a false sense of security," says Buntaro. "What do you make of this Aoyama character? Does he seem like a man on the edge of grand lunacy? Or does he seem like a publicity stunter?"

"Dunno . . . just unhappy." And I spat into his teapot. I retreat upstairs.

"Aren't you going to watch?"

"No."

"Oh, by the way. About your cat. The cat."

I peer down. "You found her owner?"

Buntaro keeps one eye on the TV. "No, kid, but she found her maker. Unless she has a secret twin she never told you about. Real coincidence. I was cycling here this morning and what did I see by the drainage channel down the side of Lawson's? One dead cat, flies buzzing. Black, white paws and tail, a tartan collar with a silver bell, just like you described. I did my civic bit and called the council when I got here, but someone had already reported it. They can't let things like that lie around in this heat."

This is the worst day on record.

"Sorry to be the bearer of ill tidings and all."

The second worst, I mean.

"Only a cat," I mumble. I enter my capsule, sit down, and appear to lack the will to do anything except smoke the rest of my Dunhills. I don't want to watch TV. I bought a noodle cup and a pint of mushy strawberries walking back from Kita Senju, but my appetite has vanished. I listen to the street fill up with evening.

Yakushima never returns to its full size when the ferry takes us back the following morning. The day is glossy with sunshine, but that heightens the illusion that this boundless island is a scale model. I look out for

Anju on the seawall—and when I can't find her I have to admit my ela-
tion is dented. Anju is a gifted sulker, but a thirty-six-hour sulk is a long
haul, even for my sister. I zip open my sports bag—the man-of-the-
match trophy glints back. I look for the thunder god's shrine on its
cliff—and this time I find it. The passengers pour down the gangplank,
my teammates disappearing into waiting cars. I wave goodbye. Mr.
Ikeda claps me on the shoulder and actually smiles. "Want a lift?"

"No, thanks, sir, my sister'll be walking down to meet me."

"Okay. Practice first thing tomorrow. And well done again, Miyake.
You turned the game around. Three–nil! Three–nil!" Ikeda is still fat
with revenge. "That wiped the snotty, shitty sneer off the fat face of their
moron coach! I caught his despair on camera! I'll get that shot made into
New Year's cards, eh? Show his shame to the world!"

I kick the same stone from the harbor up the main street, over the
old bridge, and all the way up to the Neck. The stone obeys my every
wish. Sun mirrors off the rice fields. I see the first dragonflies. This is
the beginning of a long road. At the end is the World Cup. The abandoned house stares with empty sockets. I pass the torii gate, and think
about running up to thank the thunder god right now—but I want to see
Anju first. The hanging bridge trembles under my footsteps. Tiny fish
cloud the leeward sides. Anju will be at home, helping our grandmother
make lunch. Nothing to worry about. I slide open the front door—"I'm
back!"

Anju's foot thumps—

No, it was only the old house. I can tell from the shoes that my
grandmother is out too. They must have gone to see Uncle Tarmac, but
somehow missed me around the new harbor building while Mr. Ikeda
was talking to me. I pour myself a glass of milk, and dive onto the sofa.
On the insides of my eyelids I watch the exact parabola of the soccer
ball curving over a volcano and under a distant crossbar.

♦

"Miyake!" Buntaro, of course. I lift my head too quickly and yank my
neck cords. A hammering on my capsule door. "Come quick! Quick!
Now!" I clatter downstairs, where customers cluster around Buntaro's
TV. The outside of Aoyama's office, high above the tracks. *Live from*

Ueno Station Hostage Crisis Center. The picture is being taken with a night camera—light is orange and dark is brown. I don't need to ask what is happening because the commentator is telling us. "The blind is up! The window is being opened and—a figure, Mr. Aoyama has—yes, that is him, I can confirm that, the figure climbing out of the window is Mr. Aoyama—he is on the ledge—the light is going on behind . . . please wait while—I'm receiving . . ." Background radio scratchings. "The hostage is unharmed! The police have taken the office! Whether they broke down the door or—now, Aoyama appears to have honored his promise not to—but the question now is— Oh, oh, he surely isn't thinking of jumping . . . The face at the window, I can confirm that is a police officer, attempting to talk Aoyama out—he is dealing with a very disturbed man at this moment in time—he will be saying that—"

Aoyama jumps from the ledge.

Aoyama is no longer alive but not yet dead.

His body cartwheels, and falls for a long, long time.

Footsteps in the hallway wake me up. I open my eyes—my trophy shines on the table, proof that I didn't dream the whole glorious afternoon. Evening lights the worn wooden room where my uncles and mother spent their childhoods. And here are my grandmother and Mr. Kirin, one of Yakushima's four police officers. "I'm back," I say, worried. "We won."

My grandmother doesn't care. "Did Anju say she was going anywhere?"

"No. Where is she?"

"If you're lying I'll, I'll, I'll—"

Mr. Kirin gently sits my grandmother down and turns to me. "Eiji . . ."

I want to be sick. "What happened to Anju?"

"Anju seems to have run away . . ."

He knows more.

"She wouldn't, not without telling me. Never."

My grandmother's voice is broken. "So what did she tell you? She told me she was going to Uncle Tarmac's yesterday evening. He called me this lunchtime to find out why she had changed her mind. If this is a game you two cooked up, you are in a sackload of trouble!" Mr. Kirin sits down on the other end of the sofa. "I want you to think, Eiji. Is there a secret place where she might have gone?"

First I think of trees. Then, with sickening certainty, I think of the whalestone. To get even with me. Her swimsuit . . . I run upstairs. I open our drawer. I was right—it's gone. I think of the thunder god. *Anything that I can give you, you can have. Take it.* Mr. Kirin fills the bedroom doorframe. "What is it, Eiji-kun?" I get the words out before everything crashes down. "Look in the sea."

◆

Nearly five o'clock, says FUJIFILM. I get up and piss. In my toilet-cube mirror a drone looks back at me in mild surprise. I need a cigarette. The packet of Dunhills is empty, but I find one rolled under the ironing board. I light it on the gas stove, and go onto the balcony to smoke it. Dawn sketches outlines and colors them in. Tokyo roars, far off and near. So that is the end of Mr. Aoyama. He ran out of minutes, so he jumped. I wash the fungus out of a mug and make myself a cup of instant coffee. I take Anju's photograph out to the balcony, and drink my coffee in her company. I think about the letter from my mother, and a deal presents itself. Should I? I must wash my dishes today. I look in the cockroach motel—I look again. Cockroach escaped. A leg and a smear of cockroach shit remain. I take in my laundry and fold it into a neat pile. I tune my guitar and run through some bossa nova chords, but all those sunlit breezes are not how I feel. Very well, Mother. You are my Plan B. I'll give you what you want, if you tell me how to find our father. Nearly six o'clock. Early, but people at clinics get up early. That's the point. Before I change my mind I dial.

"Good morning, Miyazaki Mountain Clinic."

"Morning. Could you put me through to Mariko Miyake's room, please."

"Not possible, I'm afraid."

"Is it too early?"

"Too late. Mrs. Miyake checked herself out yesterday evening."

Oh, no. "Are you sure?"

"Quite sure. She even took our towels as a souvenir."

"Look, this is her son. I need to contact her. It's urgent."

"I'm sure it is, but once our guests decide to leave us they never hang around."

"Did she leave a forwarding address?"

She doesn't bother to pretend to check. "No."

"How was she?"

"You'd need to talk to her counselor—"

"What time does he start work?"

"She. But Dr. Suzuki would never discuss a patient with anyone. Even the patient's son."

If only I had called yesterday, if only, if only. "Did you meet her?"

"Mrs. Miyake? Of course. I'm a senior nurse."

"Can you tell me if she was—okay?"

"It depends what you mean by okay."

"Well, you've been really helpful. Thanks so much."

She uppercuts my irony. "It was my pleasure, sir."

Click, buzz, click, purrrrrrrrr.........

Plan B down the drain. The submarines are running, and I feel wide awake, but it is still too early to leave for work. What a night. I feel I lived through it, rather than just remembered it. Buntaro called me down for a smoke later, in the quiet hour between eleven and midnight. We talked for a little while. I nearly forget that he is not a decent human being but my bloodsucking landlord. I put *Plastic Ono Band* into my Discman and lie down on my futon, just for a moment. Deep bells and beatboxes.

Plastic Ono Band is long over when a pattering sound pads into my dreams. At first I think it is a pipe dripping splashes, but then I feel her settling inside the curl of my body. I open my eyes. "Hey." My voice is a croak. "I thought you were supposed to be dead." She yawns, indifferent to what I think or thought. She regards me with her bronze-spark Cleopatra eyes.

❖

The fibers in the neck of the thunder god tear, snap, and scream. I am still gripping it—I never expected it to come loose so soon—it comes away, the saw goes clattering down, I reshift my weight too far, lose my balance, and slide down between the thunder god's back and the shrine wall. I seem to be falling for the longest time. The floor whacks the breath out of my body. I don't break my back, but within an hour I will have turned into the incredible walking bruise. My enemy's head rolls away, wood on wood, and comes to a rest on its side, looking right this way. Hatred, revenge, jealousy, rage—all twisted into the same contortions, and pulled tight. A smear of my blood over one nostril. The woods are too quiet. No adult, no police car, no grandmother. The blackbird has gone. Only the cannon boom of the ocean against the rocks a long way down. The gods are all related, and from this day on they are going to be in a conspiracy against me. I will live a life without luck. So be it. I get to my feet. I pick up the head, cradling it like an infant, and take it outside to the edge of the rock face. The sea breaks over the whale-stone's humpback, and the spray flies. One, two, three—I watch the severed head of the thunder god, all the way down. It vanishes in a white crown.

three

♋

Video Games

catch a glimpse of my father being bundled into an unmarked van across the baseball field. I would recognize him anywhere. He hammers on the back window, but the van is already through the gates and disappearing into the smoking rubble of Tokyo. I leap onto our patrol stratobike, take off my baseball cap, and rest it on the console. Zizzi flashes me a peppermint smile and off we zoom. Lavender clouds slide by. I train my gun on a chili-pepper schoolboy, but for once things are exactly as they appear. The sunroof of a midnight Cadillac flips open, and out pops a lobster-mobster*Bang!* Shell and claws everywhere. I drill the rear window and the vehicle explodes in paintbox flames. The van swerves down the road to the airport. In the underpass an ambulance cuts us up—a scalpel-slashing medic leaps onto the front of our stratobike, eyeballs afroth with plague*Bang!* In the nuts! *Bang!* The mutant staggers, but refuses to die*Bang!* Blasted through a billboard. *Reload.* "You're my top gun," croons Zizzi. We get to the airport just in time to see my father dragged into a vanilla Cessna aircraft. I dare not risk a shot at his kidnappers at this range. A mighty chokmakopter eclipses the sun, and zombie spawn abseil to earth. I pulp dozens in midair, but the semolina army of death sludges up too quickly. "Zax, honey!" says Zizzi. "Megaweapon in McDonald's!" I fire at the golden arches and collect the twenty-third-century rapid-fire bazooka. It purrs as I scythe—soon the runway is a spill of twitching limbs. I pepper the chokmakopter until it nose-dives into the fuel trucks. Octane fuchsia explosions light the world. "Way to go, Zax! Stage Two—Pursue your father's abductors to their laboratory!" We soar in pursuit of the Cessna—I click my trigger to skip the preamble. We enter the underworld. The sewers are quiet. Too quiet. A gigahydra erupts, nine heads dripping lime slime from nine lassooing necks*Bang!* Cleft like a cabbage. *Reload.* But from the stump two new heads are born. "Deep-fry the freak!" screams Zizzi—I aim at the beast's trunk and activate my flamethrower. *Whoooooorrrsh!* It shrivels in my swath of strawberry fire. A lily-white Lilith, one*Bang!* and she's history. A swarm of cyberwasps—*bangabangabanga. Reload.* My hand is killing me. The tunnel narrows to a dead end. An unseen iron door creaks open—a scientist in silhouette. "My son! You found me! At long last!" I relax and flex my gun hand. "You are just in time"—he rips off his false beard, his briefcase morphs into a grenade launcher—"to die!" The gritty gloom swarms with intelligent missiles, homing in on my body heat. *Bangabangabanga!* I miss most of them, and can't even take aim at the impostor. Scarlet pixels of lifeblood splatter the screen. "Zax," begs my sister, "don't leave me here—insert a coin to continue. Honey, don't quit now."

◆

"Honey," mimics a voice over my shoulder, "don't quit now!" I replace my gun and turn around to face my spectator and his sarcastic applause. My first thought is that he is far too cool to be hanging out in video arcades. Older than me, a sleek ponytail, an earring. Pop-star good looks. "First time in the underworld, right?" His real voice is tailored Tokyoite.

I nod. The real world fades in.

"It was the same for me, my first time in the underworld."

Laser zaps, vampire howls, coin rattles, cyclical video-game music. "Oh."

"You see your father, so you let your guard down. A dirty trick! Next time, shoot the egghead on sight. It takes about nine shots to kill him."

"Well. Sorry I died and spoiled your fun."

The most casual of shrugs. "You're doomed from the first coin. You pay to postpone the ending, but the video game always wins in the long run."

My last half-Marlboro has died in the ashtray. "Very deep."

"Actually, I was waiting for my date in the pool hall upstairs. Looks like she's playing the be-late-keep-him-on-tenterhooks game. So I came down to make sure she hadn't fucked up and was waiting outside. I saw you, wrapped up in *Zax Omega and Red Plague Moon,* and had to stay to watch. Did you know your tongue pokes out when you concentrate?"

"No."

"It's a two-player game, really. It even took me two weeks to master it."

"That must have cost you a fortune."

"No. My father owns a man who owns a distributor."

No reply presents itself. "Well, hope your date shows up soon."

"The bitch had better. Or I'll flay her alive."

Saturday night in Shibuya bubbles and sweats. One week since my sleepless night, I decided to come exploring. It never ends! Uncle Yen took me out last year to his bar in Kagoshima, but that is nothing compared to this. Neither are the prices. Drones drink in squadrons, ties loose, collars undone. She-drones have their office uniforms stuffed into shoulder bags. I damn drones too much, considering I am one now. But I only pretend to be one. Maybe we all start out that way. Same as Mr. Aoyama. Couples on dates. Americans and beautiful women in moonglasses. I bet the waitress with the perfect neck has a whole phone book of boyfriends like my spectator in the video arcade. A giant DRINK COCA-COLA cascade of magma maroons and holy whites. I suck a champagne bomb and walk on. Hostesses wave geriatric company presidents into taxis. In an amber-lit restaurant everyone knows one another. A giant Mongol warrior scooters past, flanked by bunny girls handing out leaflets advertising a new shopping complex somewhere. Girls in cellophane waistcoats, panties, and tights sit in glass booths outside clubs, offering chitchat and 10-percent-off coupons. I imagine scything through the crowds with the twenty-third-century megaweapon. The clouds are candy colored from the lights and lasers. Outside Aphrodite's Soapworld a bouncer runs through the girls pinned up on the board. "Number one is Russian—classy, accommodating. Two, Filipina—attentive, well-trained. The French girl—well, need I say more? The

Brazilian—dark chocolate, plenty of bite. Number five, English—white chocolate. Six is German—home of the weiner. Not an ounce of flab on the Koreans. Number eight are our exotic black twins, and number nine—ah, number nine is beyond the grasp of ordinary mortals—" He catches me gawking and cackles. "Come back in a decade or so, sonny, with your summer bonus." I wander past an electronics shop, and on TV notice someone oddly familiar walking past an electronics shop. He stops, examines the TV, amazed and semi-appalled at how he must appear to other people. I buy a new pack of Marlboros. As I pass by the red lanterns of a noodle shop and smell the kitchen vapors pumped out, I suddenly remember how hungry I am. I peer through the window—it looks greasy enough to be affordable, even for me. I slide open the door and enter through the strings of beads. A steamy hole with a roaring kitchen. I order fried tofu noodles with green onions, help myself to a glass of iced water, and sit by the window, watching the crowds wash by and crunching ice cubes. Happy twentieth birthday, Eiji Miyake. Now I can begin to talk about My Teenage Years. Buntaro handed me a fine crop of cards this evening—one from each of my four aunts. The fifth letter was another one from the ministry of unwelcome missives, which, evidently, is still operating its Get Miyake campaign. I light up a Marlboro and take out the letter again to reread, trying to figure out whether it is a step forward, backward, or sideward.

Tokyo
September 8

Eiji Miyake,

I am your father's wife. His <u>first</u> wife, his <u>real</u> wife, his <u>only</u> wife. Well, well. My informant at Osugi & Bosugi tells me you have been trying to contact my husband. How dare you? Was your upbringing so primitive you were never taught <u>shame</u>? Yet somehow I always suspected this day would come. So, you have learned of your father's influential status and are seeking quick cash. <u>Blackmail</u> is an ugly word, done by ugly people. But blackmail demands panache and pliable victims. You possess <u>neither</u>. Presumably, you believe you are clever, but in Tokyo you are a greedy boy from the countryside with a mind mired in <u>manure</u>. I <u>will</u> protect my daughters and my husband. We have paid enough, <u>more</u> than enough, for what your mother did. Perhaps this is <u>her</u> idea? She is a <u>leech</u>. You are a <u>boil</u>. My message to you is simple. If you <u>dare</u> to attempt to intimidate my husband, to show your face to any of our family, or to request a <u>single</u> yen: then, as a boil, you will be <u>lanced</u>.

I drain the soup from the bottom of the bowl. A dragon chases its tail around the world. So. For my coming-of-age birthday I also received a paranoid stepmother who underlines too much, and two or more stepsisters. Unfortunately the letter itself won't help me find my father—it was unsigned, unaddressed, and posted in a northern ward of Tokyo, which narrows down the search to about three million people, assuming it was even written there. My stepmother is no fool. Her negative attitude is yet another hurdle. On the other hand, to be pushed away, I have to be touched. Also, my father didn't write the letter himself—so at worst, this means he still isn't sure about meeting me. At best, it means he hasn't actually been told I am trying to contact him. It is at this moment that I realize I don't have my baseball cap. This is the worst unbirthday present I could receive. I call myself a name that earns a dubious glance from my neighbor. That cap was the last present I had from Anju. I think back—I had it in the video arcade. I leave, and backtrack through the currents of pleasure seekers.

Zax Omega and Red Plague Moon is still plying for trade, but my baseball cap has gone. I search the rows of students pummeling the offspring of *Street Fighter*; a crowd of kids gathered around *2084*; the booths of girls digitizing their faces with those of the famous; the alleys of salarymen playing mah-jongg with video stripstresses. All these people like my mother paying counselors and clinics to reattach them to reality: all of us people here paying Sony and Sega to reattach us to unreality. I identify the jowly supervisor by the way he jangles his keys. I have to yell into his ear. I smell the wax. "Anyone handed in a cap?"

"Wha'?"

"I left a baseball cap here, thirty minutes ago?"

"Why?"

"I forgot it!"

"You forgot why you left it?"

"Never mind."

I remember my spectator. In the upstairs pool hall, he said. I find the back stairs and go up. The sudden quietness and gloom are sub-aquatic. Three rows by six of ocean blue tables. I see him on the far side, playing alone, and on his head is my baseball cap. His ponytail is fed through the strap gap. He pockets a ball, looks up, and gestures me over. "I figured you'd be back. That's why I didn't chase after you. Want to win it off my head?"

"I'd rather you just took it off your head."

"Where's the fun in that?"

"There isn't any. But it is my cap."

He sizes me up. "True." He presents my cap with a courtier flourish. "No offense meant. I'm not really myself tonight."

"I should thank you for rescuing it."

He smiles an honest smile. "You're welcome."

My move. "So, uh, how late is she now?"

"When does 'late' become 'stood up'?"

"I dunno. Ninety minutes?"

"Then the bitch has well and truly stood me up. And I had to pay for this table until ten." He gestures with his cue. "Play a few frames, if you're not busy?"

"I'm unbusy. But I'm too broke to bet."

"Can you afford one cigarette per game?"

I am sort of flattered that he takes me seriously enough to offer me a game of pool. All I have had in the way of company since I got to Tokyo has been Cat, Cockroach, Suga, and Buntaro's sarcasm. "Okay."

Yuzu Daimon is a final-year law student, a native of Tokyo, and the most gifted pool player I have ever met. He is brilliant. I mean it. He lets me win a couple of frames out of politeness, but by ten o'clock he mops up seven more in U-turn-spinning, jump-shotting, unerring style. He sinks shots the way a master hit man assassinates. We hand in the cues and sit down to smoke our winnings. My plastic lighter is shot: a flame flicks from Daimon's thumb. It is a beautiful object. "Platinum," says Daimon.

"Must be worth a fortune."

"It was my twentieth-birthday present. You should practice more." Daimon nods at the table. "You have a good eye."

"You sound like my sports teacher in high school."

"Oh, please. Say, Miyake, I've decided Saturday owes me compensation for being stood up. What say we go to a bar and find a pair of girls."

"Uh, thanks. I'd better pass."

"Your girlfriend will never find out. Tokyo's too big."

"No, it's nothing like that—"

"So you don't have a woman waiting anywhere?"

"Not a nonimaginary one, no, but—"

"You're trying to tell me you're gay?"

"Not as far as I know, no, but—"

"Then you took a vow of celibacy? You're a member of a cult?"

I show him the contents of my wallet.

"So? I'm offering to foot the bill."

"I can't mooch off you. You already paid for the table."

"You won't be 'mooching' off me. I told you, I'm going to be a lawyer. Lawyers never spend their own money. My father has a hospitality account of a quarter of a million yen to get through, or his department will face a budgetary reassessment. So you see, by refusing you put our family in a difficult position."

That's quite a lot of money. "Every year?"

Daimon sees I am serious, and laughs. "Every *month*!"

"Mooching off your father is even worse than mooching off you."

"Look, Miyake, I'm only talking about a couple of beers. Five at most. I'm not trying to buy your soul and definitely not your body, no offense. C'mon. When's your birthday?"

"Next month," I lie.

"Then consider it a premature birthday present."

Santa Claus works behind the bar, Rudolf the Red-Nosed Reindeer emerges from the toilets holding a mop, and elves in floppy hats wait on the tables. I watch snowflakes dance on the ceiling, smoking a Marlboro lit by the Virgin Mary. Yuzu Daimon drums along to psychedelic Christmas carols. "It's called the Merry Christmas Bar."

"But it's September ninth."

"It's December twenty-fifth every night in here. It is what we call a chick magnet."

"I might be being naive, but might your girlfriend have just been held up?"

"You are being beyond naive, Miyake. What decade was this Yakushima place shipwrecked in? The bitch stood me up. I know it. We had an arrangement. A special arrangement, not the sort you just forget about. If she wanted to be there, she would have been, and I am now as single as a newborn babe, and she is jet trash to me. Jet trash. And don't turn around right now, but I believe our feminine solace has just arrived. Over in the nook between the fireplace and the tree. The one in the coffee leather, the other in the cherry velvet."

"They must be models. They wouldn't look at me twice. Once."

"I said I'll pay for your drinks, not massage your ego."

"I mean it."

"Bullshit."

"Look at how I'm dressed."

"We'll say you work as a roadie."

"I'm not even well-dressed enough to be a roadie."

"Then we'll say you work as a roadie for Metallica."

"But we've never met them."

Daimon buries his face in his hands and chuckles. "Ah, Miyake, Miyake. What do you think bars are for? Do you think all these people enjoy paying exorbitant prices for pissy cocktails? Finish your beer. Whiskey is the drink you take on missions to penetrate the enemy interior. No more buts! Look at Cherry. Imagine yourself untying the cords of that bodice thing she's wearing with your front teeth. A simple yes or no will do: do you want her?"

"Who wouldn't? But—"

"Santa! Santa! Two double Kilmagoons! On the rocks!"

·   ·   ·

"So, after the rape," Daimon says in a loud voice as we take the adjacent table, "their world is bulldozed. Razed. She stops eating. She rips out the telephone. The only thing she shows any interest in are her dead son's video games. When her husband—my oldest friend, as I told you— leaves home for work in the mornings she is already there, hunched over the pistol, wasting men on the sixteen-inch Sony. When he gets back, she hasn't moved a muscle. Breakfast dishes still on the table, she doesn't care. *Bangabangabang! Reload.* Back in the real world, the police drop the case—sexual assault during a night on the bare mountain? Forget it. Most men just can't begin to understand what an experience like that . . . I despair of our sex, sometimes, Miyake. So. Nine months pass this way. She doesn't leave the house once. Not a single time. He is going frantic with worry. Finally he asks a psychiatrist for advice. Some- how, the shrink concludes, she has to be reintegrated into society or risk sinking into self-willed autism. Now, they originally met in their univer- sity orchestra—she was a xylophonist, he was a trombonist. So he buys two tickets for *Pictures at an Exhibition,* and day by day, erodes away at her resistance until she agrees to come. Cigarette?"

"Excuse me?" Daimon leans over to Coffee. "May I?"

I could swear there was an ashtray when we sat down.

"Sure."

"Thanks so much. The night of the concert, she takes sedatives, they get dressed up, have a candlelit dinner somewhere high up, and they take their seats in the front row. The trumpet starts—you know"— Daimon hums the opening bars—"and she freezes. Her eyes are *ice.* Her fingernails sink into his thigh until they draw blood. She starts trem- bling. Forget the embarrassment, he has to get her out of there before she gets hysterical. Out in the foyer she tells him. The cymbal clasher— in the orchestra—she swears on her ancestor's tomb that he was the man who raped her."

I notice Coffee and Velvet are tuned in.

"I know what you're thinking. Why not go to the cops? Nine cases out of ten, the judge tells the woman she was asking for it by wearing her skirt too high, and the rapist gets away with signing an apology form. She tells him that unless he avenges her honor, she'll throw herself from the top of the Tokyo Hilton. Now. You met him. He's no mug. He does his homework, and gets an unregistered gun with a silencer, surgical gloves. One evening, while the orchestra is performing Beethoven's Fifth, he breaks into the cymbalist's apartment—he lives alone with his pet crystals. What he finds backs up his wife's story. Internet porn printouts, S and M gear, manacles hanging from the ceiling, a seriously worn and torn inflatable Marilyn Monroe. He hides under the bed. After midnight the cymbalist gets back, listens to his answering machine, has a shower, and gets into bed. My friend has a sense of the dramatic, and growls: 'Even a monster should check under his mattress.' *Bangabangabanga!*"

"Quite a story."

"Not over yet. My damn lighter isn't working—" Daimon leans over to Coffee, who is already opening her designer handbag. "I'm terribly sorry to trouble you—thanks so much." She even lights it for him, and then one for me. I nod shyly. "Revenge is medicinal. You probably remember the local rags—'Who Banged the Cymbal?'—but a successful murder is only a question of planning, and the police have no clues. His wife recovers in a matter of *days*. She starts teaching at her school for the blind again. Chucks out the video games. And come spring, when the Saito Kinen Orchestra goes to Yokohama, this time *she* insists that they buy front-row tickets. Like before, but happier. He can live with his conscience—he only dispensed natural justice. The state would have done the same if it had sharper cops. They get dressed up, have the candlelit dinner, and they take their seats in the front row. The string section starts in—and she freezes. Her eyes are *ice*. Her breathing changes. He thinks she's having some sort of attack, and manages to get her out into the lobby. 'What?' he asks. 'The second cellist! It's him! The man who raped me!' '*What?* How about the cymbal clasher I killed last year?' She shakes her head like he's crazy. 'What are you talking about? The second cellist is the rapist, I swear on my ancestors' grave, and if you don't avenge my honor I'll electrocute myself.'"

"Unbelievable!" gasps Coffee. "Like, what did he do next?"

Daimon rotates, Coffee crosses her legs, and we become a foursome. "Went to the cops. Confessed to the cymbal player's murder. By the time he was brought to trial, his wife had accused nine different men of raping her, including the minister for golf."

Cherry is aghast. "Did all that really happen?"

"I swear"—Daimon blows a wobbly smoke ring—"every word is true."

When I get back to the table after placing my order with Santa, Daimon's arm is around Coffee's chair. "Like, aha"—Coffee pokes out her tongue between her white lips—"Santa's little helper." Her face is marshmallowed with cosmetics. Velvet swivels toward me. Her tights whisper and Godzilla wakes up. "Yuzu-kun tells me you're in the music biz." I smell her perfume, moistened and salted with sweat. "I'm modeling at the moment, doing a series of shoots for Tokyo's biggest chain of body-correction clinics." She leans toward me, her Lark Slim awaiting a flame, and in my nether regions Godzilla rears his fearsome head. Daimon spins his lighter across the table. Velvet's face glows. A whole evening without thinking of Anju, until now.

♋

Velvet wraps her arms around my chest as we lean into the first corner, less than a second behind Daimon's Suzuki 950. My Yamaha 1000 bucks and growls down a gear. The sun-buckled stadium, the golden trumpets, the giant BRIDGESTONE airship: the touch of Velvet's hands makes it hard to concentrate. Daimon clips a row of dancing police cones, and above the din I hear Coffee puppy-squeal. "C'mon!" Velvet whispers in my ear, just for me, and her whisper is a love ghost potholing naked in the curves of my inner ear. I feel as hard and full as the Yamaha fuel tank. Coffee whoops. "Better than the real thing! Giddyup!" Daimon leans into the chicane. "Realer than the real thing," he mutters. I follow his drive line, and down the long straight I nearly pass him, but Coffee watches my screen and tells Daimon when to block me— "Gotcha!" she laughs—I skid through a patch of oil, at 180 k.p.h.— Velvet's fingers dig into me, the rear wheel overtakes the front, but I keep my bike on the road. We scissor through the zoo, I glimpse zebras streaming, manes flowing. Coffee retrieves her cell phone—it beeps

"The Star-Spangled Banner"—and proceeds to have a conversation about where she is and how totally unbelievable her night is. Recklessly I lean my Yamaha into the long, banking curve—I cut inside Daimon and we are neck and neck. "Say, Miyake, this is as valid or as stupid a test of masculinity as anything else, don't you agree?" I risk a side glance—"I guess." He flashes a dangerous grin. "Like, a twenty-first-century duel," comments Coffee, putting her phone back in her bag. "For sure!" replies Velvet. "Miyake is going to make you eat grit, right, Miyake?" I say nothing but her little finger mines my navel and threatens to worm farther down until I say "Okay." "Settled, then," replies Daimon, and veers into me. Velvet screams as I lose control and slam into an oncoming Jomo fuel tanker. BAAANNNNNNGGGGGGGGG! When the fun-size nuclear explosion dies down, Daimon and Coffee are disappearing into the distance, small as a period. "Nasty accident," tuts Daimon. My Yamaha stutters into second gear. "Like, ruthless!" laughs Coffee. "No way he'll catch up now." Daimon glances over at me. "Poor Miyake. Remember, it's only a video game." An absurd idea comes to me, which owes more to two whiskeys on two beers than original thinking. I skid the Yamaha through a U-turn, and discover that, yes, I can drive counterclockwise. The "seconds elapsed" tick down. The zebras in the zoo stream backward. A programmer as nutty as Suga must have written the software. Velvet's hands tweak my nipples to show approval. We pass the start line—"Laps Completed" reads "–1." I tear up the swing bridge—the bike flips up as we leap through space, and shudders as we land on the far ramp. Here comes Daimon on his Suzuki. "Like, what?" Daimon begins a sentence with "You—" I mirror his evasive swerve, and skid straight into his headlamp, round as the moon on a bright day. No explosion. Our bikes freeze in midtilt, the music stops, and the screens die.

◆

"I am not used to not winning." Daimon gives me a look that would worry me if it were from a stranger. "Deep down, you are one sneaky son of a bitch, Miyake."

"Poor Daimon. Remember, it's only a video game."

Daimon does not smile. "Never punch above your weight class."

Coffee makes a *ge?* confused noise. "Like, where'd the veloco-drome go?"

"I think"—Velvet dismounts—"Miyake busted the video machine, big time."

Daimon swings off his Suzuki. "Let's go."

"Like, where?" Coffee slips off.

"A quiet little place where they know me."

"Did you know," asks Coffee, "if you pluck your nasal hair instead of trimming it you can burst a blood vessel and die?" Daimon leads us through the pleasure quarter as if he created it. I am lost, and hope I won't need to find my own way back to the Shinjuku subway. The crowds have thinned a little from before, the pleasure seekers all harder core now. A sports car nudges by, throbbing with bass. "Lotus Elise 111S," says Daimon. Coffee's cell phone beeps "Auld Lang Syne," but she can't hear the caller despite shouting "hello?" a dozen times. Jazz brays through an open door. A line of the hippest people wait outside. I enjoy the envious stares Daimon and I earn. I would die to hold Velvet's hand. I would die if she slapped my hand away. I would die if she wanted me to take it and I never realized. Daimon tells us a long story about misunderstandings with drag queens in Los Angeles that makes the girls shriek with laughter. "But, like, L.A. is really dangerous," says Coffee, "everyone has guns. Singapore's the only really safe place abroad." "Ever been to L.A.?" asks Daimon. "No," says Coffee. "Ever been to Singapore?" asks Daimon. "No," says Coffee. "So somewhere you have never been is less dangerous than somewhere else you have never been?" Coffee rolls her eyes. "Like, who says you need to go to a place to know about it? What do you think TV is for?" Daimon defers. "Hear that, Miyake? This must be feminine logic." Coffee waves her arms in the air. "Like, long live girl power!" We walk down a passage-way, lit with signs for stand bars, where an elevator is waiting. Coffee hiccups. "Which floor?" The elevator doors close. I shudder with cold. Daimon adjusts his reflection, and decides to switch on his good humor. "Ninth. Queen of Spades. I have a great idea. Let's get married." Coffee giggles and presses 9. "I accept! Queen of Spades. Like, freaky name for a bar." If the floor numbers were not changing I would not have known the elevator was rising. Coffee picks some fluff off Daimon's collar. "Nice jacket." "Armani. I'm very choosy about what comes into contact with my skin. That's why I chose you, my divinity." Coffee rolls her eyes and looks at me. "Is he always like this, Miyake?" "You can't ask him," smiles Daimon, "Miyake's too good a friend to be honest with you." I look at the four reflections of our four reflections. Hyperspace hums. "Stay in here too long," I say, "and you'd forget which one was you." A gong bronzes, the elevator doors open, and Daimon leaps into an abyss of night. Velvet, Coffee, and I sway unsteadily. We are on the roof of a building so high Tokyo has disappeared. Higher than clouds, higher than the wind. The stars are near enough to prod. A meteor arcs around. I see a curtain in the night behind Orion and the illusion is obvious—we are in a miniature planetarium, less than ten meters across. A gong bronzes, and a grapefruit dawn blushes up the sides of the dome from the floor. "Like," gasps Coffee, "totally unbelievable." Velvet looks quietly impressed. Daimon claps. "Miriam! As you can see, I couldn't keep myself away."

A woman in an opal kimono and full geisha makeup slips through the curtain. She bows exquisitely. Everything about her is exquisite, from her lacquer hair clip to her sunset slippers. "Good evening, Mr. Daimon." A pillow-hushed voice. Her cosmetics conceal whatever is beneath, but from the way she moves I put her in her mid-twenties. "This is an unexpected pleasure."

"I know it is, Miriam, I know it is. I heard you were due to be going on an exotic vacation tonight—but here you are, still. Well, well. Meet my new bride." He kisses Coffee, who giggles but squirms closer. "Do tell me Dirty Daddy isn't on the premises."

"Would you be referring to . . . whom, Mr. Daimon?"

"Such diplomacy!" He stage-whispers at me: "Miriam is a bona fide pro."

The woman glances at me.

"Mr. Daimon senior isn't here tonight, Mr. Daimon."

Daimon sighs. "That father of mine. Off rutting Chizumi *again*? At his age? Has anyone else around here noticed how fat he's grown? Talk about excess baggage. Does Chizumi dish you the dirt on Mr. Daimon senior, Miriam? Is the trysting wig-on or wig-off? . . . Ah, I can see you're not going to answer. Well, if he isn't here, I can worship at the altar of my passion"—he encircles Coffee's waist—"in the Daimon clan's private room. Naturally, the evening's festivities go on Father Rat-fuck's bill."

"Naturally, Mr. Daimon, Mama-san will invoice Mr. Daimon senior."

"Why so formal, Miriam? What happened to 'Yuzu-chan'?"

"I'll have to ask you to sign for your friends in the guest book, Mr. Daimon."

Daimon waves his hand. "Whatever."

I ignore an inner voice warning me to get in the elevator and leave right now, because I lack excuse or explanation. I am still buzzing with alcohol, but I see something dangerous in the way Daimon . . . I dunno, in the way he is. The moment passes. Daimon sweeps us on, in Daimon we trust. The enchanted land awaits.

Miriam the hostess leads us through a series of curtained anterooms—I forget which way we faced when we came in. Each curtain is embroidered with a kanji too ancient to read. Finally we enter a quilted chamber, unchanged since the 1930s. Tapestries of ancient cities hang on the windowless walls. Stiff leather chairs, an unattended mahogany-brass bar, a pendulum swinging too slowly, a dying chandelier. A rusty cage with an open door. The parrot inside opens its wings as we pass. Coffee squeals like a rubber sole on varnish. A number of older men sit around in clusters, discussing secrets in low voices and slow gestures. Smoke at dusk. Girls and women fill glasses and occupy the arms of the chairs. They are here to serve, not to entertain. Alchemy has distilled all color into the girls' kimonos. Persimmon golds, cathode-ray indigos, ladybug scarlets, tundra olives. A ceiling fan paddles the thick heat. In the shadow of a monstrous aspidistra a piano plays a nocturne to itself, at half-speed.

"Wow," says Velvet.

"Freaky," says Coffee.

A powerful odor similar to my hairspray makes me sneeze. "Mr. Daimon!" A thickly rouged woman appears behind the bar. "And companions! My!" She wears a headdress of peacock feathers, and flutters a faded actress's wave. She wears sequined evening gloves. "How green and growing you all look! That's young blood for you."

"Good evening, Mama-san. Quiet, for a Saturday?"

"Saturday already? The days don't find their way up this far."

Daimon cocks a smile. Coffee and Velvet are welcome wherever there are men's imaginations to strip them, but in my jeans, T-shirt, baseball cap, and sneakers, I feel as out of place as a shit shoveler at an imperial wedding. Daimon clasps my shoulder. "I want to take my brother-in-arms here—and our imperial consorts—to my father's room."

"Sayu-chan can show you—"

Daimon cuts in. His smile is nearly vicious. "But Miriam is free."

Messages pass between Daimon and Mama-san. Miriam looks away miserably. Mama-san nods, and sort of hikes up her face. "Miriam?" Miriam turns back and smiles. "What joy that would bring me, Mr. Daimon."

"I mostly drive my Prussian blue Porsche Carrera 4 Cabriolet. I have a weakness for Porsches. Their curves, if you look closely, are *exactly* those of a kneeling woman, bent over in submission." Daimon watches Miriam pour the champagne. Velvet kneels up. "What about you, Eiji?" We are on "Eiji" terms. "I'm, uh, more of a two-wheel sort of person." Velvet bubbles: "Oh, *don't* tell me you drive a Harley?" Daimon barks a laugh. "How did you guess? Miyake's Harley is his, how can I put it, his pelvic thrust of freedom between gigs, right? You get so much shit in a rock star's entourage, you wouldn't believe it. Groupies, smackheads, drummers, Miyake's been through it all. Splendid, Miriam, you didn't spill a drop. I suppose you get a lot of practice. Tell me, how long has it been you've been holed up here as a waitressImeana hostess?" Miriam is ghostly but dignified in the lamplight. The room is intimate and too warm. I smell the girls' perfume and cosmetics and recently laid tatami. "Come now, Mr. Daimon. Ladies never discuss years."

Daimon undoes his ponytail. "Years, is it? My, my. You must be very happy here. Well, everyone, now the champagne has been poured, I wish to propose two toasts."

"What are we, like, drinking to?" asks Coffee.

"One: as Miyake here knows, I recently broke free from a female vampire who peels promises the way a whore—and this is an appropriate description—peels condoms on and off."

"I know exactly the sort of woman you mean," nods Coffee.

"We understand each other so deeply," sighs Daimon. "Shall we get married in Waikiki, Lisbon, or Pusan?"

Coffee toys with Daimon's earring. "Pusan? The toilet of Korea?"

"Poisonous little country," agrees Daimon. "You can have that earring."

"Like, great. Here's to freedom." We chime our flutes.

"What's your second toast?" asks Velvet, stroking a chrysanthemum drooping from a vase.

Daimon gestures at Coffee and Velvet. "Why—a toast to the flower of true Japanese womanhood. Miriam, you're a woman, you know about these things. What qualities should I look for in a wife?"

Miriam considers. "In your case, Mr. Daimon, blindness."

Daimon places his hands over his heart to stop the bleeding. "Oh, Miriam! Where is your compassion tonight? Miriam is the duck-feeding type, Miyake. She treats her waterfowl with more compassion than her lovers, I hear."

Miriam replies, "Waterfowl are more dependable, I hear."

"Dependable? Or dependent? No matter. Don't you agree that Miyake and I are the two luckiest men in Tokyo?"

I cannot meet her stare. I wonder what her real name might be. "Only you know how lucky you are," she says. "Will that be all, Mr. Daimon?"

"No, Miriam, that will not be all. I want some grass. Instant karma mix. And you know how peckish drugs make me, so bring something peckable in half an hour or so."

The room has a fusuma screen that opens onto a balcony. Tokyo rises from the floor of the night. Four weeks ago I was helping my cousin repair Uncle Orange's tea-plantation cultivator. Now look. A six-story can of KIRIN LAGER BEER pours dandelion neon, over and over. Across a light-year of streets, buildings, and neon murk I can see aircraft warning lights pulse on PanOpticon's crown. Altair and Vega fade in and out on either side of the Milky Way. Traffic noises ebb up. Velvet leans out. "Miles and miles," she says to herself. Her hair shifts in the hot breeze. "I do declare," says Daimon, the friend who is giving me all this on a plate, "I have rolled the perfect joint this side of the whorehouses of Bogotá."

"And just how would you know?" Coffee bends down to light it.

"I own a dozen." He wriggles out of his jacket and slings it away.

Velvet leans out farther. "Are those islands or ships? That loop of lights, so far away from here?"

Daimon peers through the railings. "Reclaimed land. New airport."

Coffee looks. "Let's go out there and see how fast your Porsche runs."

"Let's not." Daimon puckers the joint into life, holds the smoke down, and exhales a happy aaaaaaaaa . . . Coffee kneels, and Daimon holds it to her lips. Uncle Money gave me a stern lecture about drugs and Tokyo that Velvet will make me ignore, gladly. Coffee purses her lips as dragon smoke uncurls from her nostrils. "Did I tell you"—Daimon gazes into the flame of his lighter—"that this lighter is a piece of history? It used to belong to General MacArthur during the Occupation." "Like, sure it did, if you say so," scoffs Coffee. "I say so, but never mind. Get me a zabuton, my coffeecreamyhoneyhole, let your lungs soak up this beauty, we'll drive to Tierra del Fuego and repopulate Patagonia . . ." While Coffee is fetching a cushion from the tatami room the cell phone in her bag beeps the Moonlight Sonata. Daimon heaves a mighty sigh— "Irritating!"—and he passes the joint to me. I give it to Velvet. Daimon answers the phone in a fair imitation of the royal crown prince. "I bid you a splendid evening." Coffee dives, giggling. "Mine!" Daimon scissors her to the floor between his legs. She writhes, giggling, mantrapped. "No, I'm terribly sorry, but you can't speak with her. Her boyfriend? Really? That's what she told you? How awful. I'm fucking her later tonight, you see, so go and rent a naughty video, you sad fuck. But first, listen very carefully to this—this is how your death sounds." And he tosses the phone over the balcony.

Coffee's giggle has its plug pulled.

Daimon smiles wild as a stoned toad.

"You just threw my phone over the railing!"

Daimon dribbles giggles. "I know I just threw your phone over the railing."

"It might have hit somebody on the head."

"Well, scientists warn us that cell phones harm the brain."

"My phone!"

"Oh, I'll buy you another one. I'll buy you another ten."

Coffee weighs up various factors. "The most up-to-date model?"

Daimon grabs the zabuton, lies back, and does a gangster impression. "I'll buy ya da factory, shweetie." Coffee does a little-girl pout and holds the champagne glass to her ear. "I can hear bubbles." Velvet takes my earlobes in a thumb pinch, pulls my head toward hers, seals my mouth with hers, and marijuana smoke rushes in. Stolen chocolate, smeared and soft. "Ohohohohohohohoho," observes Daimon, "do that inside, you two. It looks like I—and my newlywed—have been overtaken by the young upstart once again." I open my eyes, and gasp, and cough. Velvet prods me in the chest, so I go inside.

"You sit there," she says, pointing to the far side of the low table. A monk in heat, a dog in a cassock. Her forearms glisten with sweat. She blows out the candle. We take solemn turns with the joint and say nothing. Our fingertips might brush. Hers contain an electric current. Bioborg. I make out her outline in the glow of the night city, even filtered through the paper. She doesn't actually touch me, and her demeanor warns me against touching her until she tells me to. The bright tip of the joint travels through the turfy air. Sometimes I am me, sometimes I am not quite. Pearls, moonstone, teeth enamel. A time/space irregularity explores my limbs. Onto the dark, I airbrush her breasts, her hair, her face. If I sneezed right now Godzilla would probably explode in my boxer shorts. "You smoke this all the time?" Her words are twists in the smoke. "Ever since my twentieth birthday." A scroll, doll, droll troll, a bowing chrysanthemum in a vase. "So how old are you, roadie?" I even hear her lush hair hush. "Twenty-three. You?" Bitter snowflakes flurry. Lying is so easy. "I am one million today." One spanky whoop from Velvet and a grrrrrrrrr from Daimon, and Velvet and I are laughing hard enough to fracture ribs, even though no sound comes out. Then I forget why I was laughing, and

I sit up again. "Keep your hands on the table," she warns me severely, "I hate boys whose hands get everywhere." After a couple of attempts our mouths meet and we kiss for nine days and nine nights.

The fusuma to the balcony slides open. Velvet and I jump apart. Daimon stands in the moonlight, his torso stripped, with a sort of vampire Miffy the Bunny painted across his chest in lipstick. His nipples are Miffy's greedy eyes. "Miyake! Stoned or boned? Want to swap yet?" The shoji to the outer corridor slides open. Miriam stands in the entrance, holding a tray of sticky pearls and cubes of watermelon and lychees. I glimpse shock, anger, and hatred before professional indifference regains control. "Miriam! Bearing nibblies! Caviar, no less? One of her chief assets, Miyake, is her sense of timing." She removes her slippers, steps up, and sets the tray on the table. "Pardon me." She withdraws. "Oh, Miriam, you don't need me to pardon you, not with your powerful and influential patrons to take care of you." Pigletty Coffee appears, doing herself up, supporting the fusuma frame to stop it from collapsing. She sees Miriam. She is used to ordering domestics. "Show us to the powder room."

Daimon speaks to Eiji, but Eiji finds it hard to concentrate because his head keeps rolling into the corner so he has to get up and screw it back on. Coffee and Velvet have been in the ladies' room since time began. "I use a quiet East Shinjuku love hotel near the park, attached to a four-star place so you can order up decent food from the kitchen." Eiji is somehow uneasy. Daimon peers in. "Not still worried about money?" Eiji tries to shake his head but nods it by accident. "Money is only this stuff my father has too much of." The girls, thinks Eiji, is it all right, just to— Daimon hears his friend's thoughts, buttons up his shirt, and wags a finger. "These two are strictly a double act, Miyake. Either both get laid, or they both go home to their lavender-scented lacy bedrooms. You back out on me now and I'll be left with the most expensive wank on my hands since Michael Jackson last played at the Budokan. And yours has at least evolved problem-solving intelligence. Mine has a fashion sense where her brain should be." Eiji is about to say something but forgets what he was going to say the moment before he begins. "Girls are like video games, Miyake. You pay, you play, you leave." Eiji is all gratitude. He tries to express this, but his words are flowing out like endless rain into a paper cup, they slither wildly as they make their way across the universe, so he gives up. Another hostess brings the coffee. "Who, the *fuck*, are you?" Daimon demands. The hostess bows. "Aya-chan, Mr. Daimon. Miriam-san has become unwell." Daimon snarls: "Trot back to Mama-san and remind Mama-san who my father is, and what a miserable fuck I can be if I . . ." But his sentence trails off. He pinches the head off the chrysanthemum, and pulls off the petals. "Forget I said that, Aya-chan. Give this to the ghost of Miriam, with my profoundest respects." He hands her the flower stump, which Eiji thinks is sort of cute. Eiji sits in the front of the taxi. Daimon sits in the back with his two concubines. The streets clear, they go over a wide bridge. Atlas holds up his globe in the foyer, Daimon gazes up at the screen showing rooms lit and unlit and prices and presses panels and gets keys. Another elevator ride. Daimon kisses Eiji on the lips and jump-shots him into the room behind. A ten-second shower and uncurious porn on pay TV. Nine different types of condom. A pink H flashes on and off outside. Heads on stalks, sunflower heads. Coffee comes in, a lemon towel around her lozenge honey skin, sort of numb somehow now, rather factually the legendary swimming pool of sex laps, she draws the curtain, close your eyes, she says, and slips into bed, her skin slides out, berries swell, yeah okay you can but you are *not* to touch me there, snagged on a twig, yeah okay, does he normally swap over like this? Your friend? Yuzu Daimon? What a name, *Yuzu*, like the fruit? I guess. Shush. Waxy chocolate, cheap and teeth biting midriff, mossy nooks, nervous push, no I said you are *not* to touch me there, Godzilla retreats, nervous of this promised land, sweat tricklets down our back, hoisting, lowering, raising, all technical stuff, *that's it there*, Godzilla changes his mind again, roots dig in harder, boughs thrash back and forth, her fingers grasp, her toes find leverage, swimming in the blue, the sheets of blue, billowing and grunty and lethargic, she gasps for air, she dives, winces, and *yes* is this all there is *no* and surface and *yes* and under and *no* and surface and *yes* and under and surface and under *coming* and *coming* if *coming* you—don't—wake—up—before—you—hit—the—ground—you

I wake up in a round bed, alone as a toy tossed away, down stairs. This love-hotel room is a temple of pink. Not flower pink—offal pink. The curtains are soiled with morning. I hear jackhammers, traffic crossings, and crows. Husky sunflowers bend in their vase. My head is cork-screwed from temple to temple. My tongue has been salted and sun-dried and shit on. My throat has been attacked by geologists' hammers. My elbows and knees have been friction-burned raw. My groin smells of prawn. The bedsheets are twisted, and the undersheet is dashed with crusty blood. So, two virgins defrocked each other. *That* groin sneeze was sex? That was no Golden Gate Bridge to a promised land. It was a wobbly plank across a soggy bog. Nobody even gives you a badge to sew on. This room is a public tissue—love hotels must have the highest sex-per-cubic-meter ratios this side of . . . where? Paris. I grope for a ciga-rette—empty. Still. All things considered, I got off lightly. The telephone riiiiiiiiings. Daimon calling from the room next door, I bet.

"Good morning, sir, this is Reception." A man, brisk and breezy.

"Uh, g'morning."

"This is just to remind you that your suite is booked until seven . . ."

My watch is on the bedside. 6:45. "Okay."

"After seven hourly charges reapply."

"Okay, I'll be right out."

"Will you be paying cash or credit, sir?"

"*What?*"

"When your lady friends left just now they didn't know if you are paying cash or credit? Two rooms for all night comes to fifty-five thou-sand yen, provided nothing is taken from the minibar, and that you vacate the room in the next fifteen minutes."

Cold shock squeezes down my colon.

Still brisk, less breezy. "So I'm calling up to ensure there has been no kind of unpleasant misunderstanding. Has there?"

Would vomiting help?

"I said, there is no kind of problem, is there, sir?" Not-so-veiled menace.

"No, none at all. Uh, I'll pay cash, I think. I'll be right down."

"We'll be waiting for you in the entrance lobby, sir."

I get dressed in my gummy clothes and dart into Daimon's room. Nobody. Identical to mine, only on the mirror, scrawled in some sort of jelly, are the characters ONLY A VIDEO GAME. Daimon, you prime-time bastard. Miyake, you idiot. I turn out my jeans pockets and find 630 yen, in small change. This isn't happening. I try to wake up. I fail. This is definitely happening. I am 54,370 yen short. I need a fantastic plan in the next nine minutes. I sit on the toilet and shit as I run through my alternatives. One: "You see, the guy I was with, he promised he would pay for everything on his, uh, father's expense account." The yakuza king places his fingertips together. "Eiji Miyake, employed in a lost-property office? A position of trust. How fascinated your employers would be to learn how you spend your weekends. I feel it is my civic duty to report this matter unless you are willing to compensate us with certain *duties,* not all of which, I must warn you, could be described as *pleasant.*" Two: "Buntaro! Help! I need you to bring me fifty-five thousand yen to a love hotel right now or you'll have to find another tenant." Not a choice that would pose him much difficulty. Three: the yakuza king licks his razor blade. "So, *this* is the thief who attempted to escape from my hotel without paying for services consumed." I raise my bloodied head and swollen eyelids. My tongue lies in his shaving bowl.

If only crises could be flushed away down toilet bowls too.

In movies people escape along rooftops. I try to open the window, but it isn't designed to open, and anyway, I can't crawl down the sides of buildings. I see people in the littered streets and envy every single one of them. Could I start a fire? Trigger alarms and sprinklers? I follow the fire alarms to the end of the corridor, just so I feel I'm doing something. "In the event of fire, smoke alarms will automatically unlock this door." Uncle Tarmac says love hotels are designed to stop people doing runners—the elevator always takes you straight to Reception. What else do people do in movies? "Out the back way," they hiss. Where is this "back way"? I try the other end of the corridor. "Emergency stairs. No exit."

Back ways are through kitchens. I dimly remember Daimon, may his bollocks fester, telling me there was a kitchen. Hotel kitchens are in the basement. I slip through the door and start down the stairs. Stupidly, I look over the handrail. The floor far below is the size of a stamp. The Aoyama escape route. I go as fast and quietly as I can. What will I say if they catch me here? That I get claustrophobic in elevators? Shut up. I get down to the ground floor. A large glass door opens into Reception. A huge male receptionist is standing there. An ex–sumo wrestler, waiting for me. The stairs continue down one more floor. I can beg for mercy, or up the stakes and continue down. The receptionist narrows his eyes, running his finger down a ledger. I slip by the glass door—a statue of Atlas and the globe blocks his line of sight—and creep down the stairs to a door marked STAFF ONLY. Please let it be open. It doesn't open. I barge it. It judders open. Thank you. Beyond is a stuffy corridor of pipes and fuse boxes. At the end mops are stacked against another door. I turn the handle and push. Nothing doing. I try to shoulder it open. The door is locked. Worse still, I hear the glass door opening one floor above—and I didn't close the STAFF ONLY door behind me. "Hey? Anyone there?" Mr. Sumo. Doom pisses hot dread on my head. What can I do? Desperate, I knock on the locked door. I hear Mr. Sumo's shoes on the steps. "Anyone there?" I knock again. And suddenly a bolt slides, the door is yanked open, and a chef is glaring at me—behind him a fluorescent-lit kitchen chops and bubbles. *"You,"* he snarls, "had *better,*" his eyes as friendly as the bed-bound demon's in *The Exorcist,* "be the new mousseboy."

Huh?

"Tell me you're the new mousseboy!"

Mr. Sumo is fifteen seconds from my jugular vein.

"Yes, I am definitely the new mousseboy."

"Well, get in here then!" He pulls me through, slams the door behind me, and, giving me my first lucky break of the morning, bolts it shut. *Head Chef Bonki* is sewn into his hat. "What, the *hell,* are you doing turning up for your first morning *forty-five minutes late,* looking like a vagabond? *Take off that baseball cap in my kitchen!*" Behind him, junior chefs and kitchen hands watch the human sacrifice. I take off my cap and bow. "I'm very sorry." Cream, steam, mutton, and gas. I see no windows and no doors. How do I get out of here? Head Chef Bonki snarls. "Master is *disappointed*. And when Master is disappointed, *we* are disappointed. We run a *very* . . . tight . . . ship!" He suddenly yells at the top of his voice and blasts what are left of my nerves away. "And what do we do to members of the crew who let the ship down?" The kitchen staff chants back in an air-punching chorus. "To the sharks! To the sharks! To the sharks!" I seriously consider giving myself up to Mr. Sumo, after all. "Follow me, mousseboy. Master will conduct his inspection." I am hustled between shining counters and racks of pans, past a rack of time cards. A door. Please let there be a door. "This is where you check in, if Master forgives your disgraceful start." Mr. Sumo must be at the bolted door by now. All these knives worry me. A boy with a sunken nose scrubs floor tiles with a toothbrush—the chef deals him a powerful kick for no apparent reason. We come to a poky office full of the chug, grind, and kiss of a knife-sharpening lathe. On the far side is an open door—steps lead up to a yard of trash bags. The chef raps on the door-frame, and shouts. "The new mousseboy has reported for active duty, Master." The lathe dies.

"Final*mente*." Master does not turn around. "Show the scoundrel in." His voice is far too high for his bulk. The head chef stands aside and prods me forward. Master turns around. He is wearing a blowtorcher's mask that reveals a petite mouth. He holds a cleaver sharp enough to castrate a bull. "Leave us, Head Chef Bonki. Hang the sign on the door." The office door clicks shut. Master tests the blade on his tongue. "Why prolong your little deception?"

"Sir?"

"Come now. You are not the mousseboy who served me so *amply* at Jeremiah the Bullfrog's."

Lie, quick! "Uh, true. I'm his brother. He got sick. But he didn't want to let down the crew, so he sent me instead." Not bad.

"How su*preme*ly sacrificial." Master advances. Not good.

The door touches my back. "My pleasure," I say. Do I hear banging?

"*My* pleasure. *Mine,* I tell you. Touch it. Mousse is springy."

I see my face in the black glass of his mask wondering what, exactly, the new mousseboy is supposed to do. And what happened to the old one. "You are the best in the business, Master." Sudden commotion is loose in the kitchen. There is no guaranteed way around my captor to the yard door. Master pants. I smell liver pâté on his breath. "Tweak it. Mousse is delicate. Slice it. Oh yes. Mousse is soft. So soft. Sniff it. Mousse will yield. Oh yes. Mousse *will* yield." Four fat fingers swim toward my face.

A shout. *"Hey!"*

"Irksome. Irksome." Master lifts up a tiny curtain next to my head that covers a peephole. His mouth stiffens. He picks up his cleaver, knocks me aside, flings the door open, and barges through. "Whore-house vermin!" he screams. "You have been warned!" I glimpse Mr. Sumo throwing assistant chefs over counters. "You have been warned!" shouts Master. "You have been warned what happens to pimps from the dark side who bring herpes and syphilis onto my spotless ship!" He hurls his cleaver and I hear a piercing shriek. No point hanging around to examine the damage—I am out through the door, running up the steps, leaping over the plastic garbage bags, scattering through the crows, sprinting across the backyard, down a side street, and I don't stop zigzag-ging and checking behind me until seven-thirty.

At seven-forty I suddenly know where I am: Omekaido Avenue. That zir-conium skyscraper is PanOpticon. I walk a little farther toward Shinjuku and get to the intersection with Kita Street. Jupiter Cafe. The morning is already shallow-frying. I check my money. If I walk back to Ueno, I can afford my submarine back to Kita Senju and buy a light breakfast.

Jupiter Cafe is air-conned soggy cool. I buy coffee and a pineapple muffin, sit at my window seat, and examine my ghostly reflection in the window: a twenty-year-old Eiji Miyake, hair matted with sweat, smelling of pot and, apparently, sex, and sporting—I see to my horror—a love bite the size of Africa over my Adam's apple. My complexion has completed its metamorphosis from Kyushu tan to drone paste. The waitress with the most perfect neck is not working this morning—if she saw me in my present condition, I would give a howl, age nine centuries, and desic-cate into a mound of dandruff and fingernails. The only other customer is a woman with a toolbox of makeup studying a fashion magazine. I vow mentally never to stroke another woman again, ever. I savor my muffin and watch the media screen on the NHK building. Missile launchers recoil, cities catch fire. A new Nokia cell phone. Foreign affairs minister announces putative WW2 Nanking excesses are left-wing plots to destroy patriotism. Zizzi Hikaru washes her hair in Pearl River shampoo. Fly-draped skeletons stalk an African city. Nintendo proudly presents *Universal Soldiers*. The kid who hijacked a coach and slit three throats says he did it to stand out. I watch the passing traffic, until I hear a hacking cough. I never noticed Lao Tzu appear. He takes out a pack of Parliament cigarettes, but has lost his lighter. "Hello again, Captain." I lend him my lighter. "Morning." He notices my love bite, but says nothing. In front of him is a flip-up video game screen, book-size but designed in the twenty-third century. "Brand-new vidboy3—ten thou by ten thou res, four gigabytes, wraparound sonics, Socrates artificial intelligence chip. Software was launched only last week: *Virtua Sapiens*. A present from my daughter-in-law"—Lao Tzu shifts on his stool—"on doctor's orders, to stave off senility." I slide the ashtray between us. "That's nice of her." Lao Tzu flicks ash. "You call getting my cretin son to sell off my rice fields to a supermarket owner *nice*? So much for filial duty! I let the brat have the land to stop the tax wolves attacking when I die, and *this*"—he prods the machine—"is how I get repaid. I got to go shake the hose— you get leaky at my age. Care for a test drive while I'm gone?" He slides his vidboy3 over the counter toward me and wanders off to the rest room. I take off my baseball cap, plug myself in, and press RUN. The screen clears.

♋

Welcome to Virtua Sapiens
[all rights reserved]

```
I see you are a new user. What is your online title?
>eiji miyake
Congrats for registering with Virtua Sapiens, Eiji
Miyake. You will never be lonely again. Please select
a relationship category. Friend, Enemy, Stranger,
Lover, Relative.
>relative
```

Okay, Eiji. Which relative would you like to meet
today?
>my father, of course
Well, excuse me. Please hold still for three seconds
while I digitize your face. An eye icon blinks and a microlens
built into the screen frame blinks red. Okay--now hold extra still
while I register your retina. One wall, a floor, and a ceiling
appear. A whirlpool carpet bitmaps the floor. Pinstripes unroll up the
walls. A window appears, with a view of plum blossoms tossing in a
spring storm. Curtains of rain blur the glass. I even hear the rain. The
room is gloomy. A lamp appears on the left and glows cozy yellow. A see-
through sofa appears under the window. The sofa is inked in with zig-
zags. And in the center of the sofa appears my father, right foot folded
on left knee, which looks cool but cannot be comfortable. The program
has given him my nose and mouth, but made him jowlier and thinned
his hair. His eyes are those of a mad scientist on the eve of world domi-
nation. His wrinkles are symmetrical. He is wearing a black dressing
gown—he sort of glows, as if he got out of the bath five minutes ago.
My father leans over to screen right, where a wine bucket appears—he
slides the bottle out and reads the label. "Chablis, 1993." A crisp, clear,
even voice, perfect for weather forecasting. He pours himself a glass,
makes a great show of savoring the bouquet, and sort of snorts it through
his lips. He winks. An enamel smile flashes. "Welcome home, son.
Refresh my memory, will you—how long has it been?"
>never, actually
His eyebrows shoot up. "Such a long time? Time flies like an arrow!
What a lot of news we have to catch up on. But you and I will get on like
a house on fire. So tell me about school, son."
>i left. i am 20
He sips his wine, sloshing it around his tongue, and runs a hand back
through his hair. "Is that so, son?" He leans forward toward the screen
between us—the resolution is amazing—I flinch backward. "So you
must be at university, right? Is that a cafeteria I see in the background?"
>i didn't bother applying for university. no parents
to pay and no money

My father leans back and lounges a lazy arm over the back of the sofa. "Is that so, son? That strikes me as a pity. Education is a wonderful thing. So how do you spend your time, exactly?"

>i am a rock star

His eyebrows shoot up. "Is that a fact, son? Tell me. Are you a successful rock star, with fame and fortune, or are you one of the unwashed millions still waiting for your lucky break to come along?"

>very successful. all over the world

He winks and flashes an enamel smile. "I know meeting your old man after all this time is tough, son, but honesty is always the best policy. If you are such a big noise in the entertainment world, how come I've never heard of you in *Time* magazine?"

>i perform under an alias to protect my privacy

He knocks back the rest of his wine. "It isn't that I don't believe you, son, but could you tell me your alias? I want to boast about my rock star son to my buddies—and bank manager!"

>john lennon

My father slaps his knee. "The real John Lennon was assassinated by Mark David Chapman in 1980, therefore I know you are pulling my leg!"

>mind if I change the subject?

He comes across all serious, and puts down his glass. "Time for a father-and-son heart-to-heart, is it? We don't have to be afraid of our feelings anymore. Tell me what's on your mind."

> who are you exactly?

"Your father, son!"

>but as a human, who are you?

My father refills his glass. Lightning fuses the sky, the plum blossom scratches the windowpane, and the purple on gray is transformed to black on titanium white. I guess the program needs more time to respond to unlikely or general questions. My father chuckles and places his feet together. "Well, son, that is one big question. Where would you like me to begin?"

>what sort of man are you?

My father rests his left foot on his right knee. "Let me see. I'm Japanese, fifty next birthday. By profession I am an actor. My hobbies are snorkeling and wine appreciation. But fear not—all these details will come to light as our relationship unfolds—and I trust you'll be visiting again soon! I would like to introduce you to a special person. What do you say?"

>ok

The screen pans to the right, past the wine bucket. A woman—in her late thirties?—sits on the floor, smoking, humming snatches of "Norwegian Wood" between drags. She is wrapped in a man's shirt, and black leggings hug her shapely legs. Long hair flows down to her waist. She has my eyes. "Hi, Eiji." Her voice is tender and pleased to see me. "Can you guess who I might be?"

>snow white?

She smiles sideways at my father and puts out her cigarette. "I see you have your father's sense of humor. I'm your mother."

>but mommy dear, you haven't seen daddy for 17 years

The program processes this unexpected input while the storm headbutts the window. My mom lights another cigarette. "Well, we had a few fences to mend, I admit. But now we get on like a house on fire."

>so you finally ran out of suckers to give you money?

"That hurts, Eiji." My virtual mother turns away and sobs alarmingly like my real one, a sort of dry, hidden quaking. I am typing in an apology, but my father responds first. He speaks in a slow and threatening thespian lilt. "This is a home, young man, not a hotel! If you can't keep a civil tongue in your head, you know where the door is!" What a pair of virtual parents the program generated for me! They are thinking, "What a virtual son reality generated for us." The plum blossoms suffer wear and tear in the unseasonal weather.

◆

"Hello? Wakey! Anybody home?" A man in Jupiter Cafe shouts so loud he drowns out the sound of the virtual rainstorm. "Wrong change, little lady! If you never learned to add up they shouldn't let you on a register!" I unplug myself and turn around to see what the fuss is about. A grizzly drone in a stained shirt snarls at the girl with the most perfect neck in creation—when did she get here? She stares back, surprised but unfazed. Donkey is washing dishes, staying out of trouble, while my girl struggles to be polite with this human hog. "You only gave me a five-thousand-yen note, sir."

"Listen to me, girlie! I gave you a ten-thousand-yen note! Not five! Ten!"

"Sir, I am quite sure—"

He rears up on his two hind legs. "You saying I'm fibbing, girlie?"

"No sir, but I am saying you are mistaken."

"You a feminist?"

The line of customers ruffles uneasily, but nobody says anything.

"I—"

"I gave you a ten thousand, you abortion bucket! Correct change! *Now!*"

She pings open the register. "Sir, there isn't even a ten-thousand note in here."

Hog slavers and twitches his tusks. "So! You steal from the register as well!"

Maybe I am still semistoned from the hash, or maybe *Virtua Sapiens* reshuffled my sense of reality, but I find myself walking over and tapping the guy on his shoulder. He turns around. His mouth is one bent sneer. Hog is larger than I thought, but it is too late to back out so I attack first and hardest. I douse his face with coffee and headbutt his nose, really *really* hard. Christmas lights flicker in my eyes—Hog backs off, leaking a bubbly "Aaaaaaaaa" noise. Blood trickles from his nose through his fingers. I steady myself and my hand gropes for something to brandish. The pain in my forehead crushes my voice jagged. "Get out *right now* or I'll *smash* your *fricking teeth* into *tiny fricking splinters* with"—I look at what I'm holding—"this ashtray!" I must look deranged enough to mean business—after wheezing about police and assault in a beaky voice, Hog retreats. The customers look on. Lao Tzu pats my shoulder. "Neat work, Captain." Donkey comes over to her coworker, all concern. "Are you okay? I didn't know what was going on . . ." The waitress with the perfect neck slams shut the register, and glares at me. "I could have handled him."

"I know," I reply. The Christmas tree lights fizz dangerously.

"But thank you, anyway." She gives me a cautious semismile, so when the Christmas lights fuse I have something to take my mind off the pain. I sit back down and pain buys up my head.

I wonder if my mother drank at Jupiter Cafe during her time in Tokyo. Maybe after Anju and I were born, maybe in this very seat, waiting for a summons from Akiko Kato. PanOpticon drones work Sundays, too. A steady stream files in and out of the building. Nearly two weeks have passed since my abortive stakeout, and my father is still lost in Tokyo. Could be in a distant suburb, could be that guy reading the sports pages on the next table. Lao Tzu is two stools along, plugged into his nutty game. "Hi." The waitress with the most perfect neck holds a coffee jug. "Refill?"

"No more money, I'm afraid."

"Times must be hard. But this is payment in kind for security services rendered."

"Then I would love a refill. Thank you."

She pours. I watch. She asks, "How is your head?"

I lean on my elbow and cover my throat to hide my love bite. "Fine."

"Anything else?"

"Anything else?"

"Another muffin? I'll pay for it."

"What I would love, if you wouldn't, uh, mind"—my pain makes me braver than I would normally dream of being—"is your name."

That cautious smile never comes quickly. "Ai Imajo."

"Ai Imajo." What a cool name.

"And yours?"

"Eiji Miyake." Not so cool.

"Eiji Miyake," says Ai Imajo, and I feel loads, loads better. She studies the bash on my forehead. "Doesn't it hurt like crazy when you headbutt somebody?"

"Not if you know what you're doing. Apparently."

"So you don't go around headbutting people every day?"

"That was my first headbutt."

"A historic occasion." The intersection lights go green and the traffic buzzes and swarms into the haze. "Where else have I seen you, Eiji Miyake?"

"The day of the storm. Two weeks ago. You thought I was—well, I was, I suppose—listening in to your phone call. At the end of your shift. I was sitting here for a couple of hours. But don't worry. I am completely stable."

"Yeah." Ai Imajo thinks back, nodding. "I remember."

"Damn damn *damn* bioborgs!" Lao Tzu swears at the vidboy3.

"I'm on my break. Mind if I sit here?"

Do I mind? "Sure." And to my joy and mortification—I am so gunked up from a night with a stranger in a love hotel—I find the girl with the most perfect neck in creation sitting beside me, engaging me in conversation. "So. Did you meet up with whoever?"

"Who?"

"Whoever you were waiting for, on the day of the storm."

"No. Not yet."

"Girlfriend?"

I work from the abridged version and leapfrog Akiko Kato. "Relative."

"How long have you been looking?"

"Three weeks . . ."

"Three weeks since you arrived in Tokyo?"

"How do you know?"

Her cheeks dome and her eyes crescent. I love smiles like this. "Your accent. You'll lose it in six months. Where are you from?"

"You won't have heard of where I'm from."

"Try me."

"Yakushima. An island off—"

"—southern Kyushu where the jomon cedars grow, the oldest living things in the eastern hemisphere. Of course I've heard of Yakushima. So how are you finding Tokyo, this difficult town?"

Tokyo, this difficult town. How cool is that? "Full of surprises. Sometimes lonely. Mostly weird. I can't walk in a straight line. I keep bumping into people."

"You have to stop thinking about walking. Like catching peanuts in your mouth—think about it, you miss. How do you know your relative passes by here?"

"I don't, really. I don't even know what he looks like."

"Is he a distant relative?"

"I wouldn't want to bore you."

"Do I sound bored? Why not look in the telephone book?"

"Dunno his name, even."

Ai Imajo frowns. "And does he know your name?"

"Yes."

"Place an ad in the personal columns. 'Relatives of Eiji Miyake—please contact this PO box.' That kind of thing. Most Tokyoites read the same three or four newspapers. Your relative might not read it himself, but somebody else might. You're looking dubious."

I think hard.

Ai Imajo studies me. "What?"

Oh, I love being studied by this girl. "I have no idea."

That smile again, slightly bemused now. "I have no idea what?"

"No idea why I never thought of that. Which newspapers?"

"O Wild Man of Kyushu," says Buntaro back at Shooting Star, "your eyes are a pair of piss holes in the snow." My landlord is eating a blueberry-blooded Popsicle. On the video screen a man in a black suit walks through a desert. A bottleneck guitar swirls with the tumbleweed. The black suit needs a dry cleaning and the man needs a shave and a shower. "Morning. What's the movie?"

"*Paris, Texas,* by Wim Wenders." Buntaro piles in the last of the Popsicle before it collapses down his hand. I watch for a while longer. Not much happens in Paris, Texas. "Sort of slow, isn't it?"

Buntaro licks his hand. "This, kid, is an existentialist classic. Man with no memory meets woman with huge hooters. So. How was your night? No memory or huge hooters? You can't fool me, y'know. I was young myself, once. You are a quick worker, though, I got to grant you that. Two weeks in the big bad city and already harvesting the more fragrant sex."

"I sort of ran into friends."

"Yeah, yeah. Speaking of friends, I saw a monster cockroach earlier."

"Take it up with my landlord."

"Seriously, I thought it was a hairless rat. Then it twitched its antlers. I tried to splat it, but it took off and flew up the stairs. Vanished under your door quicker than you could say 'In the name of all that is holy, what *is* that thing?' Maybe your starving cat ate it. Maybe it ate your starving cat."

"I fed my starving cat before I went out." Good to see Buntaro getting used to the idea of Cat living in my capsule.

"Aha! So your tryst was planned!"

My head throbs. "Leave me alone," I beg. "Please."

"Was I knocking you? Empty what's full, fill what's empty, scratch what itches. But what *is* that unidentified red patch covering your throat?"

Attack is defense. "Your fly is way open."

"Who cares? The dead bird does not leave the nest."

"The bird can't be that dead. Look at your wife."

"The bird is dead. Look at my wife."

"Huh?"

"You'll see what I mean one day, my boy."

I'm about to go upstairs when three high school boys march in. The leader asks me: "You got *Virtua Sapiens*?"

"Never heard of it," says Buntaro. "The sequel of *Homo*?"

"What?"

"It's a video game," I explain. "Out last week."

The second-in-command ignores me. "Got *Broadsword of Zyqorum* then?"

"No software. All videos."

"Told ya!" says the leader, and they troop out.

"You're welcome, guys." Buntaro watches them go. "Y'know, Miyake, I have it on reliable authority—*Baby and You*, no less—that the average Japanese father spends seventeen minutes per day with his kid. The average grammar school boy spends ninety-five minutes per day inside video games. A new generation of electronic daddies. When Kodai is born, he is getting his bedtime stories from his parents, not from sicko druggo psycho freako programmers. I'm already getting ready my big fat 'No' for when Kodai comes running for a video game machine thing."

"What if he comes running in tears because none of the kids in his class will talk to him because his daddy's too mean to buy him a game system?"

"I—" Buntaro frowns. "I never thought of that. What did your dad do?"

"He was in another part of the country."

"What about your mom, then?"

One little lie leads to another. "I had my soccer club. Anyway, I need to, uh, get cleaned up." I climb up to my capsule, shower—by the time I towel myself dry I am sweaty enough for another shower—and unroll my futon. I lie down, but sleep is not coming. Ai Imajo keeps floating up. Her supple neck, her smile. She says my name. I get up and try to do some bottleneck guitar chords, but my fingers are rusty. I check the cockroach motel. Only one guest—a baby. Cockroach has spread the word about motel hospitality. Cat comes back and laps her water dish dry. I fill it up, but she laps it dry again.

Later I go out to buy the *Tokyo Evening Mail*. I take the submarine into Ueno, and find a quiet place in the park to fill out the classified ad box. I make several false starts—it is crucial that I don't write anything that will provoke my stepmother or make it look like I want money. Finally I'm satisfied with Plan C: a short, simple message. I'll post it tomorrow during my lunch break. I suck a champagne bomb. Ueno Park is full of families, kids, couples, old people, rings of foreigners—Brazilians maybe, Chinese, each nationality on its own patch of territory. Museumgoers, photographers, skateboarders. Cicadas in the trees, babies under the trees, an amusement park through the trees. Oily pigeons. Velocidrome motorbikes rip around the far perimeter. The air is cotton candy, incense, zoo, and octopus dumpling–flavored. I walk down to Shinobazu Pond to watch people feed the ducks. I lie down against a tree and put *Mind Games* on my Discman. It is the hottest afternoon in the history of September. I watch clouds. Here comes Picture Lady, arguing with an invisible companion. I wonder if I will ever find the guts to ask Ai Imajo out on a date. I watch a young woman feeding the ducks bread crusts from a paper bag. She has a stack of library books on her bench. I drowse. The woman wheels her bicycle over, as if she wants to talk to me. She studies my face. I press STOP on my Discman and park noises flood back. "No," she finally says, "this is not just one of those coincidences."

"I'm sorry?"

She shakes her head in disgusted disbelief. "Daimon is actually spying on me."

I prop myself up. "Who are you?"

She sets her face hard. "I do not need this."

Uh?

Her finger curses me as she hisses. "Tell him to go fuck himself! Tell him to sell his elopement fantasies to his squeaky schoolgirls! Tell him he is worth nothing! Tell him my country stopped being a Japanese colony at the end of the last war! Tell him if he tries to call I'll change my number! Tell him that if he shows his face at my apartment I'll drive a fork into it! Tell Yuzu Daimon to slime away and die! And all of this applies to you, too."

Ducks honk.

All at once I understand. This woman is Miriam, the hostess at Queen of Spades. The woman who didn't meet Yuzu Daimon at the video arcade yesterday evening. The woman I helped Daimon get even with. This is awful. "I swear," I begin, "I—I had no idea, I wasn't spying on you just now, I—" ducks flap by "—I never realized, I mean, this is all a mistake, I had no idea you would be here—how could I? I mean, I don't even know Daimon, really—"

First, the sycamore tree blips spokes. Second, it sinks in that she kicked me hard and straight and true, in the balls. Third, I writhe on the ground as acorns of agony spatter down around me. Fourth, I hear her voice, cold enough to freeze the pond. "I know *exactly* who you are, Eiji Miyake. You are a leech who tells lies for a living. Exactly like your father." She walks to her bike. I try to ignore the pain and replay her last line. "Wait!" She is already cycling away. I wobble to my feet. *Your father,* she said. "Wait!" She is pedaling away, over the causeway between the duck pond and the boating lake. I try to run but the pain takes my breath away. "Miriam! Wait!" Mothers with pushchairs turn to look, a bunch of motorbike kids watch and laugh. Even the ducks laugh. *"Miriam!"* I crouch down, defeated, and watch her disappear into mirages and spray from the fountains. She knows my father! I want to feel hope but I want to bawl with frustration. I hobble back to my stuff, where I find one thing more, lying in the dust between the roots of the sycamore. A library book that fell when Miriam crippled me. What book is it? I can't read a word—it is in Korean.

In the Shibuya backstreets I am lost in no time. Last night and this afternoon seem weeks, not hours, apart. This grid of narrow streets and bright shadows, and the pink quarter of midnight seem to be different cities. Cats and crows pick through piles of trash. Brewery trucks reverse around corners. Water spatters from overflow pipes. Shibuya's night zone is drowsing, like a hackneyed comedian between acts. My eyes begin to get lost in the signboards—WILD ORCHID, YAMATO NADE-SHIKO, MAC'S, DICKENS, YUMI-CHAN'S. Even if I happened to find Queen of Spades, search fatigue would probably stop me seeing. I left Shooting Star without my watch, and I have no idea how fast the afternoon is passing. My feet are aching and I taste dust. So hot. I fan myself with my baseball cap. It makes no difference. An old mama-san waters mari-golds in her third-story window box. When I look back at her she is still watching me, absently.

The phone booth is a safari of porn and smells of never-washed trousers. You don't need to buy sex mangas in Tokyo—just find the nearest pay phone. I and my cousins would have saved a fortune. All the shapes and sizes I ever imagined, and lots of others, too. Threesomes, foursomes, S&M, high school revue, special silver service for octogenarians. "Infor-mation," answers a woman. "What city, please?"

"Tokyo."

"What area, please?"

"Shibuya."

"And the name, please?"

Miss Manila Sunrise pouts over two beach balls—no, surely—

"Name, please?"

—they *can't* actually be her actual, bodily—

"Name, please!"

"Uh, sorry. I'm trying to track down a bar. Queen of Spades."

"Queen of Spades . . . one moment, please." Keyboard taps.

Miss Whippy Cream licks the froth off her stilettos.

Keyboard taps. "Queens of England . . . Queer Sauna . . . sorry. Nothing."

"Are you sure? It was there last night. Could it be a new number?"

Mrs. Mopp rides a broom, speech ballooning: "In! Out! Shake it all about!"

"New numbers are added to the computer as they are registered."

"So if Queen of Spades isn't on your computer . . ."

"Then it must be unlisted."

Weird. "What kind of bar wants to hide its telephone number?"

"A very exclusive one, I imagine. Sorry, but I can't help you."

"Oh well. Thanks for trying."

I hang up. One big card is handwritten in childish letters. It has no telephone number. "If you want sex with me, I'm standing outside." I look around. She looks right at me through the glass. Sixteen? Fifteen? Fourteen? Her eyes have a damaged look. She presses her lips softly against the glass. I scuttle away, faster than Cockroach.

The police-box door is stiff. I have to grind it open. Ancient Aum Shinrikyo wanted posters, Dial 110 posters, Join-the-Police-and-Serve-Japan posters. One offer I'll pass, thanks. Filing cabinets. The same black-and-white clock with the gliding second hand you get in all government buildings. A Citibank calendar, rustling in the breeze from the paddling fan. The cop is tilted back with his hands behind his head, deep in meditation. One eyelid rises. "Son?"

"Excuse me. I'm looking for a bar."

"You're looking for a bar." His words leak from the side of his mouth.

"Yes."

"Will any bar do? Or does it have to be one bar in particular?"

"I'm looking for one bar in particular."

"You're looking for one bar in particular."

"Yes."

A sigh as long as the end of the world. The other eyelid rises. Two bloodshot eyeballs. A long silence. He leans forward, his chair screeches, and he slowly unfolds a map on the desk. Upside down. "Name?"

"Eiji Miyake."

A long stare. "Not your name, genius. The name of the bar."

"Uh, sorry. Queen of Spades."

The cop focuses and darkens. "You are a member of this bar?"

I swallow. "Not exactly. I went there last night."

He frowns as if I am being evasive. "Somebody took you?"

I nod. "Yeah."

He peers at me from another angle. "And you want to go back? Why?"

"I need to speak to a sort of—friend—who works there."

"You need to speak to a sort of friend who works there. How old exactly did you say you are?"

"I, uh, didn't."

"I know you didn't, genius. That is why I asked. How old are you?"

What is this about? "I'm twenty."

"ID."

Nervously, I open my wallet and hand over my driver's license. The cop scrutinizes it. "Eiji Miyake, resident of Kagoshima Prefecture. In Tokyo to work?" I nod. He reads. "Date of birth, September ninth. You were twenty yesterday, correct?"

"Correct."

"So upon visiting said bar you were under the minimum legal drinking age. Correct?"

"I went to Queen of Spades yesterday. On my birthday."

"You went to said bar yesterday. On your birthday."

"All I want is the address of this place, Officer."

He searches my face for clues for a long time. Eventually he hands back my license. "Then all I can suggest is you obtain said address by calling said sort of friend. Queen of Spades is not listed on any map of mine." The end. I bow and leave, struggling to slide the door shut as he memorizes my face.

I admit defeat. My legs are about to unscrew and fall off. I explored every street and alley in Shibuya, twice at least, but Queen of Spades is no longer here. I buy a can of Calpis and a packet of Seven Stars and sit down on a step. Could I find Daimon back at the pool hall? No. He will avoid the place for a long time, to avoid me. If only Miriam had said she knew my father last night. How did she know my name? Because Daimon mentioned it several times. "Miyake" is pretty common, though. Daimon signed me in, and she must have seen the weird kanji for "Eiji." My father must have talked about me. I swig from my can and light a Seven Star. My father moves in these exclusive club circles—about the only thing I know about him is his wealth. I imagine smoke swirling in my lungs, dust in sunny mine shafts. Bumping into Miriam at Shinobazu Pond—not so outlandish, really. She feeds ducks, how many places can you feed ducks in Tokyo? I balance my cigarette on the lip of the can and flick through Miriam's dropped library book. Wow. Being kicked in the balls by the same woman who hostesses my father. No. Something is wrong. All these coincidences are too weird. Still. Finding where they join into an explanation is a sort of Plan D. I wonder if my father is a womanizer, like Daimon's father seems to be? I always imagined him as a sort of faithful adulterer. Still, I am here to meet him, not judge him. The cigarette rolls off the can, which, all on its own, has begun to vibrate, wobble, and . . .

. . . fall over, the ground groans, windows sing, buildings shake, shit *I* shake, adrenaline seeps, a million sentences drop dead, elevators die, millions more Tokyoites dive under tables and into doorways—I curl into a sort of ball, already flinching under the mass of falling masonry— and the whole city and I hurl up shining prayers to anyone—*anyone*— God, gods, kami, ancestors—who might be listening: stop this stop this stop this *now*, please, please, please don't let this be the big one, not the big one, not today, not now, not another Kobe, not another 1917, not today, not here. Calpis runs in a delta over the thirsty sidewalk. Buntaro told me you get vertically oscillating earthquakes and horizontally oscillating ones. Horizontal ones are okay. Vertical ones floor cities. But how do you tell one from the other? Who cares, just STOP!

The earthquake stops.

I uncrouch, newborn and dumb, not believing it quite yet. Silence. Breathe. Relief tests its feeble muscles. People switch on their radios to find out if it was just a local snore or if Yokohama or Nagoya has been rubbled off the map of Japan. I right my can and light another cigarette. Then I see something else I can't trust myself to believe, quite yet. Across the road from my step is the entrance to a passageway. The passageway runs into the building and ends at an elevator. Next to the elevator is a signboard. On the signboard, next to number 9, two trapezoid eyes stare straight back at me. I know those eyes. The eyes of the queen of spades.

The elevator doors open with a bronze gong. A bucket of soapy water stands beside the projector. A woman in dungarees is cleaning tiny holes in the planetarium with a toothpick. She glances at me from her stepladder, obviously not worried by the possibility of aftershocks. "We open at nine, I'm afraid, sir." Then she sees how scuzzy my clothes are. "Not another trendy young sales geek, *please*." So I skip the pleasantries too. "I was hoping I could have a quick word with Miriam."

I am scanned. "Who are you exactly?"

"My name is Miyake. I was here last night with Yuzu Daimon. Miriam was our hostess. I just need to ask her one question. Then I'll go."

The woman shakes her head. "I think you'll go right now, actually."

"Please. I'm not a psycho or anything. Please."

"Miriam isn't working tonight, anyway."

"Can I just have her telephone number?"

She toothpicks a hole. "What is this question of yours?"

"A personal one."

I have never been so looked at until today. She jerks her thumb toward the curtain door. "You'd better speak to Shiyori." I thank her and make my way through to the smoking chamber. The tapestries are rolled up and sunlight leans against the windows in solid bars. Women in T-shirts and jeans sit around slurping somen noodles. A mechanical parrot is being operated upon by a fragile lady. When I enter, all conversation stops. "Yeah?" asks one of the girls.

"The girl in the entrance told me to ask for Shiyori."

"That's me." She pours herself some oolong tea. "What do you want?"

"I need to speak with Miriam."

"She isn't working today."

Another girl rearranges her chopsticks. "You were here last night. One of Yuzu Daimon's guests."

"Yes."

The vibes turn from indifference to hostility. Shiyori washes out her mouth with tea. "So he sent you over to see how his little prank went down, did he?" "I don't understand," says another, "how he gets a kick out of the way he treats her." Another girl chews a chopstick blunt. "The way I see it, if you think Miriam is going to want to be in the same room as you, you are crazy."

"I had no idea there was anything between them."

"Then you are a blind moron."

"Fine. I am a blind moron. But I have to speak to Miriam about something."

"What is so urgent exactly?"

"I can't talk about it. Something she said."

The women fall quiet as the parrot woman puts down a tiny screwdriver. "If you wish to speak with Miriam, you need to become a member of this club." I realize she is the mama-san from last night. "Prospective members must collect nine nominations from existing members, excluding Yuzu Daimon, who is now barred. The application fee is three million yen—nonreturnable. If the selection committee approves your application, the first annual payment is nine million yen. Upon receipt of this, you are free to ask Miriam anything you wish. In the meantime, tell Yuzu Daimon he would be wise to leave the city for a long time. Mr. Morino is most displeased."

"Could I just leave a note for—"

"No. You can just leave."

I open my mouth—

"I said, you can just leave."

Now what?

"Masanobu Suga?" The receptionist at Imperial University looks blank. "A student? But it's four in the afternoon on Sunday! He'll probably be having breakfast."

"He's a postgraduate. Computers."

"In that case he won't have gotten out of bed yet."

Her colleague leans over and mouths, "Flake-face."

"Oh! Him. Suga, yeah. Go on up. Nine-eighteen."

Another elevator. The doors open at the third floor, and some students get in. I feel as though I am an enemy intruder. They carry on their conversation. I had imagined students only ever talk about philosophy, engineering, and whether love is something sacred or merely sexual programming: they are discussing the best way of getting past the hydra in *Zax Omega and Red Plague Moon*. So this is where the top students in my high school were bound. I summon the courage to tell the students to attack the hydra with the flamethrower, but the doors open for the ninth floor. I always thought universities were wide and flat. In Tokyo they are tall and thin. The corridor is deserted. I walk up and down a few times, trying to figure out how the room numbers work. Perhaps this is a part of the entrance examination. Finally I see "Masanobu Suga. Abandon hope, all Microsofters who enter here." I knock. "Enter!" I push the door open. The air stinks of armpit, and the Doraemon bedspread over the window keeps the room as dank and dark as one. Bongo drums, manuals, magazines, computer equipment, a Zizzi Hikaru poster, a pot containing a stump, a complete set of manga entitled *Vulvavaders from Cloud Nine,* a pile of dead cup-ramen packs, and a mountain range of paper files. At Ueno lost property, Suga was forever harping on about paperless offices. The man himself is in the corner, hunched over his keyboard. Tappetty-tap-tap-tap-tappetty-beepetty-beep-beep-beep. "Shit!" He swivels around and peers at his visitor. He works to access my face and name, though only nine days have passed since Suga quit Ueno. "Miyake!"

"You said I could come and see you sometime."

Suga frowns. "But I never thought you actually would . . . How is the lost-property business? Mrs. Sasaki still freezing the ground beneath her feet? And did you see Aoyama's final dive on TV? It was all over the news until that high school kid went and busjacked the holiday coach. See that? Cut the passengers' throats. Goes to show, if you're going to perform a dramatic suicide like Aoyama, schedule it clear of any major news stories."

"Suga, I came to—"

"You're lucky I'm in. Pull up a chair. You might find one under— never mind, sit on that box. I got back from my week at IBM yesterday. You should see their labs! They put me on the phone-line help desk to wipe asses. Deep grief. I wanted to be in R and D to check out the new stuff, right. It took me a few minutes to hatch my escape plan. My first call comes in, this bumpkin from Akita with an accent even thicker than yours, no offense. 'I'm having some trouble with my computer. Screen's all blank.' 'Oh dear, sir. Can you see the cursor?' 'The what?' 'The little arrow, sir, that tells you where you are.' 'Don't see no arrow. Don't see nothin'. Screen's all blank, I tell ya.' 'I see, sir. Is there a power indicator on your monitor?' 'On my what?' 'On your monitor, sir. The TV. Does it have a little *on* light?' 'No light, no nothin'.' 'Sir, is the TV plugged into the wall?' 'No idea, can't see nothin', I tell ya.' 'Not even if you crane your head around, sir?' 'How could I? It's as black as night in here, I'm tellin' ya.' 'Maybe it would help if you turned the lights on, sir?' 'I tried, but they won't come on—the electric company is testing all the wiring, and there won't be no power until three o'clock.' 'I see, sir. Well, I have good news.' 'You do?' 'Yes, sir. Do you still have the boxes the computer came in?' 'I never throw nothin' away.' 'Splendid, sir. I want you to pack your computer up and take it back to the store you bought it from.' 'Is the problem that serious, then?' 'I'm afraid it is, sir.' 'What do I tell 'em at the shop, then?' 'Are you listening carefully, sir?' 'I am.' *'Tell them you're too much of a shit-for-brains to own a computer!'* And then I hang up."

"That was your escape plan?"

"I know my calls are monitored by the moron in charge of me, right. Plus, I know they know I'm too valuable to chop. So the supervisor agreed my talents might be more profitably employed in another department. I suggested R and D, and off I went. Miyake, what is that thing you're carrying?"

"A pineapple."

"I thought so. Why are you carrying a pineapple?"

"This is a present."

"I thought they came in cans. Who are you giving a live pineapple to?"

"You."

"Me?" Suga is mystified. "What do you do with them?"

"People slice them into chunks with a knife, and, uh . . . eat them."

Suga suddenly beams. "Hey, thanks. I forgot lunch. Guess where I am?" He nods at his computer, and pulls a beer free from its six-pack—I shake my head. "French Nuclear Energy. Their antihacking tech is iron age."

"I thought your Holy Grail is in the Pentagon."

"Oh, shit." Suga hiss-pisses beer everywhere. "It is. The French are zombies."

"Zombies? I know their Pacific nuclear tests suck, but—"

Suga shakes his head. "Zombies. No hacker worth his silicon ever hacks directly. We hack into a zombie computer, and go fishing from there. Often, we zombify another zombie via the first. The hotter the target, the longer the zombie conga."

Time to get to the point. "I have a favor to ask. A delicate one."

"What do you want me to hack into?"

He looks at me as he swigs his beer. I realize there is a whole lot more to Suga than I judged. I judge people too fast. I get out the library book that Miriam dropped in the park. "This might be difficult, Suga, but could you get into a Tokyo library computer and look up the address of the person who has borrowed this book?"

Suga wipes away the beer froth. "You must be joking."

"Can you do it?"

"Can I piss straight when I whiz?"

Miriam's Korean name is Kang Hyo Yeoun. She is twenty-five, and has three books on loan from the library service. I take an overground train to her apartment in Funabashi. It is a run-down neighborhood, but sort of friendly. Everything needs a new coat of paint. I ask a woman who works in a cake shop next to the station where I can find Miriam's address, and she draws me a map and says goodbye with a crafty wink. I walk past a long row of bicycle stalls, turn a corner, and there is the sea, for the first time in a month. Tokyo Bay sea air has a gasoline tang. Cargo ships lie berthed, loaded and unloaded by cranes with four legs and llama necks. Fiery weeds sprout from wrinkled tarmac. A *yakiniku* restaurant smokes the evening with meat and charcoal. A garage band rehearses a song called "Sonic Genocide." A taxi driver stands in a corner of the quay, rehearsing his golf swing, watching imaginary holes-in-one land in the calm evening. A window-grilled pawnshop, a bright curry shop, a laundromat, a liquor store, a gateball ground, and Miriam's apartment. It is an old three-story affair. I smoke a Seven Star in a record few drags. The first floor has already been abandoned. The metal stairs jangle as I climb up. One decent typhoon and the whole structure would be blown clean across Hokkaido. Here it is. 303.

Her face appears in the gloom above the door chain.

She slams the door.

I hammer, embarrassed. I crouch down to speak through the mail slot. "I brought your library book. You dropped it in the park. This is nothing to do with Daimon. Miriam, I don't even know him! Please." No reply. A dog with its head in a lampshade walks past. Its overweight owner is several paces behind, panting. He scowls, daring me to laugh. "Bob had his bollocks lopped off. The restraint is to stop him licking where he shouldn't." He unlocks the apartment next to Miriam's and disappears. Miriam's door opens. She is smoking. I am still crouched down. The door chain is still on. "Here is your book."

She takes it. Then she silently judges me.

"You gave Daimon my message?"

"I tried to tell you, I don't know Daimon."

She shakes her head in frustration. "Why do you keep saying that? If Daimon didn't send you, how did you know where to come?"

"I, uh, got your address from the library."

She accepts this without me needing to explain the illegal part. "And so you returned my book from the kindness of your heart?"

"Not only that, no."

"So what do you want?"

She shifts, and reflected amber light catches the side of her face. I understand why Daimon fell in love with her. I understand nothing else. "Do you really know who my father is?"

"What?"

"In Ueno Park, you talked about my father as if you know him."

"He's a regular at the club! Of course I know him!"

I swallow. "What is his name?"

"What are you talking about? Your father is Yuzu Daimon's father."

Plan C buckles past its crumple zone. "He told you that?" Oh, it all falls into place now. "Plan C" was a fat name for a skinny little lie.

"He signed you in to Queen of Spades as his stepbrother. His—your—father keeps a couple of mistresses at any one time, so you aren't the first one."

I look away, hardly able to believe this. No, this is all too easy to believe.

"You are not his brother?" Miriam probes. "That was all Daimon bullshit?" My father rejoins the unknown millions. I don't answer her. She sort of yowls. "That selfish, stupid jerk. Just to get back at me . . . Listen, Eiji Miyake, whoever you are. Look at me!" She stubs out her cigarette. "Queen of Spades is not . . . an ordinary place. If you ever go back there, bad things could happen to you. Oh, hell. This could be very bad. By admitting you, Daimon—well, he broke a major rule. Normally, male guests are blood relatives only. Listen to me. Do not go back there, ever. Steer clear of Shibuya, in fact. And do not come back here, ever. Understand?"

No, I do not really understand, but what can I do but nod? She closes the door. It is the last moment of the day. The sunset would be beautiful, if I were in the mood. A dying SF-movie sun sits on a WARNER CINEMA multiplex. I wonder what subway line takes you to that sort of sunset, and what station you need to get off at. I amble back the way I came and find a video arcade. Inside are a whole row of full-sized

2084 machines, doing brisk business with schoolkids. *Zax Omega and Red Plague Moon* has moved on. Today has been a bad day. I change a thousand-yen note into hundred-yen coins.

♋

Photon fire bursts around me, and my final comrade falls. I get the prison guard in my sights and fricassee him. Eerie silence. Is the shooting finally over? Eight stages since the red door. The metal walkway clanks as I walk over the pile of guards and fallen rebels. It is down to me. Here is the prison door. "Prisoner: Ned Ludd. Crime: Cyber-Terrorism. Sentence: Life Incarceration. Security Access: Orange." Inside is my father, the man who will free humanity from the tyranny of OuterNet. The revolution to reverse reality starts now. I fire the OPEN pad, and the door slides sideways. I enter the cell. Darkness. The door slides shut and the lights come on. OuterNet intelligence officers! With old-fashioned revolvers? I open fire, but my photon gun is dead. The whole cell is a dampening field. Somewhere I took the wrong turn. Somewhere I failed to read the sign. Before my eyes, my ENERGY bar shrinks to .01. I cannot move. I cannot even stand. A man—I recognize him, he is the farmer from the soy farm during my waking hours—walks over, loosening his tie. "My name is Agent K00996363E. The revelation is this, Player I8192727I. Ned Ludd is a project created by OuterNet to detect antigame tendencies among players, and assess their potential danger to OuterNet. Your susceptibility to indoctrination is evidence of defective wet-programming. The very idea that ideology can ever defeat the image is proof of insanity. OuterNet will reprocess your wetware, in accordance with Propagation of Game Law 972HIJ. This grieves me, I81, but it is for your own good." He brings his face up close. It is not hateful. It is tender and forgiving. "Game over."

four

Reclaimed Land

So this is how I die, minutes after midnight on reclaimed land somewhere south of Tokyo Bay. I sneeze, and the swelling in my right eye nearly ruptures. Sunday, September 17. I cannot call this unexpected. Not after the last twelve hours. Since Anju showed me what death was, I have glimpsed it waiting in trains, in elevators, on pharmacy shelves. Growing up I saw it booming off the ocean rocks on Yakushima. Always at some distance. Now it has thrown off its disguise, as it does in nightmares. I am here, this is real. A waking nightmare from which I will never wake. Splayed on my back, far from anyone who knows me, my LIFE bar at zero. My body is racked and I am running a temperature as high as this bridge. The sky is spilling with stars, night flights, and satellites. What a murky, gritty, pointless, unlikely, premature, snot-sprayed way to die this is. One gamble that was rigged from the beginning. Very nearly my last thought is that if this whole aimless story is to go on, God the vivisectionist is going to need a new monkey for his experiments. So many stars. What are they for? How did I get here?

◆

Wednesday afternoon, I go to the bank near Ueno Station to pay for my ads in the personal columns. The bank is a ten-minute walk down Asakusa Avenue, so I borrow an orphaned bike—the company car of the lost-property office. It is too rickety for anybody ever to want to steal, but saves my lunch break nearly a quarter of an hour's walk down a busy road hot with fumes and the dying summer. No shade in Tokyo, and all the concrete stores the heat. I park the bike outside and go in—the bank is busy with lunchtime, and burbling with bank noises. Drones, telephones, computer printers, paper, automatic doors, murmurs, a bored baby. Using an ATM to pay for Plan D—the newspaper personal ad—is the cheapest way, as long as I don't make a single mistake typing in the long string of digits, otherwise my money will go flying into the wrong account. I am taking my time. A virtual bank teller on the screen bows, hands clasped over her skirt. Please wait. Transaction being processed. I wait, and read the stuff about lost cards and cheap credit. When I next look at the virtual bank teller she is saying something new. I gag on disbelief. Father will see you shortly, Eiji Miyake. I triple-check—the message is still there. I look around. This must be a practical joke, and someone must be on-site to enjoy it. A bank teller stands at the head of the row of machines to help people in difficulty, and she sees the look on my face and hurries over. She has the same uniform and expression as her virtual coworker. I just point dumbly at the screen. She traces her finger across the screen. "Yes, sir. The transaction is now processed. This is your card, and don't forget to keep your receipt safe and sound."

"But look at the message!"

She has a Minnie Mouse voice. "'Transaction completed. Please take your card and receipt.' No problem here, sir." I look at the screen. She is right. "There was another message," I insist. I look around for a practical joker. "A message with my name on it."

Her smile tightens. "That would be most irregular, sir."

People in the line are tuning in. I flap. "I know how irregular it is! Why else do you think I . . ." A uniform in a yellow armband arrives on the scene. He is only a couple of years older than me but he is already Captain Smug, Samurai of Corporate Finance. "Thank you, Mrs. Wakayama," he dismisses his underling. "I am the duty manager, sir. What is the trouble?"

"I just transferred some money—but—"

"Did the machine malfunction in any way?"

"A message flashed up on the screen. A personal message. For me."

"What leads you to conclude the message was for you, sir?"

"It had my name."

Captain Smug puts on a sympathetic frown from a training seminar. "What did this 'message' say exactly, *sir*?"

"It told me my father wanted to see me."

I feel housewives in the line bristle with curiosity and turn to one another. Captain Smug does a passable imitation of a doctor humoring a lunatic. "I think it might be quite possible that our machine uses characters that may be somewhat tricky for you to read."

"I may not have a job in a bank but I can read, thank you."

"But of course." Captain Smug eyes my work overalls. He scratches the back of his neck to show he is embarrassed. He glances at his watch to show I am embarrassing. "All I am saying is that either some misunderstanding has occurred here, or you just witnessed a phenomenon that has never before occurred in the history of Tokyo Bank, nor, so far as I am aware, in the history of Japanese banking. Does this sort of thing happen to you often?"

I put my card back into my wallet and cycle back to Ueno Station. I am so on edge all afternoon that Mrs. Sasaki asks what the matter is. I lie about feeling feverish, so she gives me some medicine and I have to drink it and lie again about feeling better. During my tea break I use the ATM in the station, which gives balance statements but does not make payments. Nothing unusual happens. I search the faces of lost-property customers for knowing glints. Nothing. I wonder if Suga did it. But Suga doesn't know about my father. Nobody in Tokyo knows about my father. Except my father.

Riding the submarine back to Kita Senju, I look around. Paranoia, but. No drone catches my eye, only a little girl. Who in Tokyo knows about my father? My stepmother, and Akiko Kato. Neither of them would need to communicate with me in such a weird way. Walking back from the station, I catch myself looking in the road mirrors for stalkers. In the supermarket I buy a 50-percent-off okonomiyaki and some milk for Cat. "Buntaro," I think while I wait in line. I got my capsule because a relative of my guitar teacher in Kagoshima knows a friend of Buntaro's wife—could he have found out about my father? But what sort of video store owner is powerful enough to use ATM screens as a personal telegraph system? Some sort of unholy alliance between Suga and Buntaro? I get back to Shooting Star to find my chief suspect on the phone with his wife, running his hand through his thinning hair. They are talking about kindergartens for Kodai. He nods at me and makes a nagging goose with his hand. I watch a scene or two from a movie called *Jacob's Ladder,* about a man who cannot distinguish between nightmares and reality. "I know what you're thinking, kid," Buntaro says, putting down the receiver. "Kodai isn't even born yet. But these places have waiting lists longer than Grateful Dead guitar solos. Get into the right kindergarten, and the conveyor belt goes all the way up to the right university." He shakes his head, sighing. "Listen to me. Education Papa. How was your day? You look like you had your bone marrow sucked out." Buntaro offers me a cigarette and strikes himself off my list of suspects. Unlikely as it seems, the sole remaining candidate is now the likeliest: my father. What are we up to now? Plan E.

On Thursday lunchtime I go back to the same branch of the same bank to try out the ATM again. The same woman is on duty—she avoids eye contact the moment she recognizes me. I insert my card, type in my PIN, and the virtual bank teller bows. What dark room has no exits but only entrances into darker rooms? Father is watching. I search for meaning—is this a warning? I look around for Minnie Mouse, but Captain Smug has been lying in wait for me. "Another inexplicable message, sir?"

"If this isn't an inexplicable message," you Lord of Irony—I rap the screen with my knuckles—"then give me another name for it."

"Oh dear, sir, not exactly Bill Gates, are you? Perhaps the message was telling you that you lack the funds necessary to complete your transaction?" Of course the screen has returned to normal: my pitiful bank balance. I look around—is somebody watching? Erasing the message when a witness comes up? How? "I know this sounds weird," I begin, not sure where to continue. Captain Smug just raises his eyebrows. "But somebody is using your ATM to mess your customers around." Captain

Smug does mock fascination. "Shouldn't that worry you?" Captain Smug folds his arms and tilts his head at an I-went-to-a-top-Tokyo-university angle. I storm off without another word. I cycle back to the lost-property office, as suspicious of parked cars and half-open windows as yesterday. My father was influential enough to have his name left off my and Anju's birth certificates, but surely this is another league. Only the elite of the elite could swing this. I spend the rest of the afternoon attaching labels to forgotten umbrellas, and weeding out for destruction the ones we have held for twenty-eight days. Might my stepmother be somehow trying to intimidate me? If it is my father, why is he playing these pranks instead of just calling me? Nothing makes sense.

Friday is payday for us probationary stop gap employees recruited in the middle of the year. The bank is packed—I have to wait several minutes to get to a machine. No sign of Minnie, but Captain Smug hovers in the wings. I pull my baseball cap down low. A woman with ostrich feathers in her hat keeps sneezing over me, and groaning. I insert my card and ask for fourteen thousand yen. The virtual bank teller smiles, bows, and asks me to wait. So far so normal. `Your breathing space is all used up. Father is warning you.` I am expecting this: from under the visor of my cap I study the line of impatient people. Who? No clue, no idea. The machine shuttles my money. The virtual bank teller bows again. `Father is coming for you today.` Come on, then! What else do you think I am in the city for? I drum the virtual teller with the bases of my fists. "You aren't from Tokyo, are you, sir?" Captain Smug is at my shoulder. "I can tell because our Tokyo customers usually have the manners to refrain from assaulting our machines." "Look at this! Look!" I show him the screen and curse. What did I expect? `Please take your money and remove your card.` It beeps. I know if I say anything to Captain Smug, or even look at the guy, I will be seized by an urgent desire to make him hurt, and I don't think my cranium could take another headbutt less than seven days since the last. I ignore his unconcealed why-do-all-the-weirdos-come-on-my-shift? expression, take my money, card, and receipt, and walk around the bank lobby for a while, trying to meet stares. Queues, marble floors, number chimes. Nobody looks at anyone in banks. Then I notice Captain Smug talking to a security man. They are glancing in my direction. I slink off.

Between the bank and Ueno is the seediest noodle shop in all of Tokyo. As Tokyo has the seediest noodle shops in Japan, this is probably the seediest noodle shop in the world. It is too seedy even to have a name or even a definite color. Suga told me about it. It is as cheap as it should be—unusual for Tokyo—and you can drink as much ice water as you want. Plus, they have comic book collections going back twenty years, including some Zax Omegas that even I have never seen. I park my bike in the alley around the side, smell burnt tar through the fan outlet, and walk in through the strings of beads. Inside is murky and flyblown. Four construction workers sit around four greasy bowls in silence. The cook, an old man who died several days ago, has been allowed to rot on his stool. The single round light is dappled with the bodies of dead insects, and the walls are decorated with spatters and dribbles of grease. A TV runs an old black-and-white yakuza movie, but nobody watches it. A gangster is chucked into a concrete mixer. Fans revolve their heads, this way and that. With a shudder, the cook reanimates his corpse and sits up. "Yeah? What can I do for you?" I order a tempura-egg-onion soba, and sit at the counter. Today, the message said. So this time tomorrow I will know everything: whether this Plan E is the true lead, or if it is yet another dud. I must keep a lid firmly on my hopes. I feel excited and my hopes boil over. Who else could it be but my father? My noodles come. I sprinkle on some chili pepper and watch it spread on the jellyfish of grease. Tasted better, tasted worse.

Outside in the glare, the bike is missing. A black Cadillac, the sort that the FBI uses for presidential missions, takes up the side alley. The passenger door inches open and a lizard pokes his head out—short, spiky white hair, eyes too far apart. "Looking for anything?" I turn my baseball cap around to shade my eyes. Lizard leans on the Cadillac roof. He is about my age. A dragon tail disappears up one arm of his short-sleeved snakeskin shirt, and a dragon head twists out of the other.

"My bike."

Lizard says something to somebody in the Cadillac. The driver's door opens, and a man in sunglasses and with a Frankenstein scar down the side of his face gets out, walks around the back of the Cadillac, and picks up a mangle of metal. He brings it around and hands it to me. "This it?" His forearms are densely muscled and his knuckles are chunky with gold. He blocks out the sun. In shock, I hold the metal for a moment before dropping it.

"It was, yeah."

Lizard tuts. "People are such mindless vandals, ain't they? Break-down of the family unit, it is." Frankenstein shunts my ex-bike aside with his foot. "Get in"—he jerks his thumb at the Cadillac—"Father sent us to pick you up."

"*You* came from my father?"

Frankenstein and Lizard find my surprise funny. "Who else?"

"And did my father tell you to trash my bike?"

Lizard clears his throat and spits. "Get in the car, ya lippy cock-wart, or I'll break both yer fucking arms right here, right now." Traffic drags its heat and din to the next red light. What choice do I have?

The Cadillac purrs over the Sumida River bridge on air cushions. The tinted windows retune the bright afternoon, and the air-con chills the inside to fridge-beer temperature. I get goose bumps. Frankenstein drives, Lizard is in the back with me, sprawled pop-star fashion. I could almost enjoy the ride if I was not being abducted by yakuza and if I wasn't going to lose my job. Maybe I could find a phone and call Mrs. Sasaki to say—what? The last thing I want to do is lie to her. Mrs. Sasaki is okay. I tell myself these things are trifles—my father has sent for me. This is it. Why am I unable to get excited? Northside Tokyo slides by, block after block after block. Better to be a car than a human, out here. Highways, overpasses, off-ramps. A petrochemical plant runs pipes for kilometers, lined by those corkscrewing conifers. A massive car plant. Acre upon acre of white body shells. So my father is some kind of yakuza man. Makes sense, sort of. Money, power, and influence. The white lines and billowing trees and industrial chimneys are dreamlike. The dashboard clock reads 13:23. Mrs. Sasaki will be wondering why I am late. "Any chance I could make a phone call?" Lizard gives me the finger. I push my luck: "All I—" But Frankenstein turns around and says, "Shut the fuck up, Miyake! I cannot *stand* whining children." My father gives me no status. I should stop guessing, sit back, and wait. We pass through a tollgate. Frankenstein moves into top gear and the Cadillac eats up the expressway. 13:43. The buildings get more residential, and densely pyloned mountains shuffle this way. On the right the sea pencils in the horizon. Lizard yawns and lights a cigarette. He smokes Hope. "Traveling in style, or what?" says Frankenstein, not to me. "Know how much one of these babies costs?" Lizard toys with a death's-head ring: "Fuck of a lot." Frankenstein wets his lips: "Quarter of a million dollars." Lizard: "What's that in real money?" Frankenstein thinks: "Twenty-two million yen. Give or take." Lizard looks at me: "Hear that, Miyake? If ya pass yer entrance exams, slave in an office all yer life, save yer bonuses, get reincarnated nine times, ya'll be able to zip around in a Cadillac too." I stare ahead. "Miyake! I'm talking to ya!" "Sorry. I thought I had to shut the fuck up." Lizard whistles and a switchblade knife hisses open. "Watch yer lippyliplip"—the knife flashes at my wrist, the blade slices through the casing of my wristwatch and scrapes through its innards— "fuckhead." The knife is spinning back in his fingers. Lizard's eyes flare, daring me to open my mouth. He wins his dare and laughs a scratchy, staccato laugh.

Xanadu, way out beyond Tokyo Bay, is having its grand opening today. Bunting flutters over the expressway exit, a giant BRIDGESTONE airship floats above the enormous dome. The glands in my throat start to throb. Valhalla opens in the new year, and Nirvana and its new airport monorail terminus are still under construction. The traffic slugs to a crawl. Coaches, family wagons, jeeps, sports cars, coaches line up bumper to bumper through the tollgate. Flags of the world hang limp. An enormous banner reads "Xanadu Open Today! Family Paradise Here on Earth! Nine-Screen Multiplex! Olympic Pool! Krypton Dance Emporium! Karaoke Beehive! Cuisine Cosmos! California Lido! Neptune Sea Park! Pluto Pachinko! Parking space for 10,000—yes, 10,000!—automobiles."

A motorbike cop waves us into an access road. "Cadillacs get you in anywhere." Lizard stubs out another Hope. "That guy is one of ours," says Frankenstein as the window slides down, "the good old days are back. Before your time every fucking cop in the fucking city recognized our family." The Cadillac veers up a slope straight into the sun, tinted by the windshield into a dark star. Over the top we enter a construction site, hidden from Xanadu by a great wall of metal sheeting. Gravel piles, slab stacks, concrete mixers, unplanted trees with roots in sack diapers. "Where are all the happy workers?" asks Lizard. "Holiday for the Grand Opening," says Frankenstein. Rounding a block of portable toilets comes Valhalla. This is a dazzling black glass pyramid built of triangles rising from building rubble. The Cadillac drives down a ramp into shadow, surfing to a halt in front of a barrier arm. A porter slides open the window of his box. He is about ninety and either is drunk or has Parkinson's disease. Frankenstein's window lowers and Frankenstein glowers. The porter repeatedly salutes and bows. "Open," growls Frankenstein, "fucking Sesame." The arm rises and the porter bows out of sight. The Cadillac cruises into the black, reverses, and halts. I feel a lurching thrill, despite my charming companions. Am I really in the same building as my father?

"Out," says Lizard.

We are in a basement car park smelling of oil and cinder blocks. Two Cadillacs are parked alongside ours. My eyes need more time to adjust—it is too dark to see the walls. Frankenstein pokes me in the small of my back. "March, cub scout." I follow him—a ball of dim light flickers on and off. A round window in a swing door. Beyond is a gloomy service corridor smelling of fresh paint and echoing with our footsteps. "Hasn't even been built yet and the lighting's already fucked," notes Lizard. Other corridors run off from this. It occurs to me to be afraid. Nobody knows I am here. Wrong: my father knows. I try to fix landmarks in my memory—right at this fire hose, straight on past this noticeboard. Frankenstein halts by a men's toilet. Lizard unlocks it. "In you go."

"I don't need the toilet."

"It wasn't a fucking question."

"When do I meet my father?"

Lizard smirks. "We'll tell him how eager ya are." Frankenstein foots the door open, Lizard clamps my nose and shoves me in—the door is locked before I regain my balance. I am in a white bathroom. The floor tiles, wall tiles, ceiling, fittings, sinks, urinals, cubicle doors—everything is snow-blindingly white. No windows, no other exits. The door is metal and unkickdownable. I bang on it a couple of times. "Hey! How long are you going to leave me in here?"

Behind me a toilet flushes.

"Who's there?"

A cubicle door unbolts and swings open. "Thought I recognized that voice," says Yuzu Daimon, doing up his belt. "What timing, Miyake. So what are you doing in a bad dream like this?" Daimon washes his hands, watching me in the mirror. "Are you going to answer my question or am I going to get the silent treatment until our prison guards come back to take me away?"

"You really have a nerve."

He shakes his hands under the dryer but nothing happens, so he dries them on his T-shirt. Its picture shows a cartoon schoolgirl lowering a smoking gun; her speech bubble reads "So that's what it feels like to kill . . . I like it." "Still sulking about the love hotel, Miyake?"

"I can see you as a lawyer."

"Oh, wow, thanks for the compliment." He turns around. "Look, are you going to keep up this period of mourning or are you going to tell me why you are here?"

"My father brought me."

"And your father is who?"

"I dunno yet."

Daimon decides not to laugh. "That seems rather careless of you."

"Why are you here?"

"To have the shit kicked out of me. You may get to watch."

"Why? Did you abandon them in a love hotel?"

"Sharp, Miyake, sharp. Ever thought of law?"

"No. I have this fatal flaw. I trust people, occasionally."

Daimon pretends to wince.

"But I still want to know why you're here."

"Long story."

I look at the door.

"Okay." Daimon perches on the washbasin. "Sit on any chair you like."

There are no chairs. "I'll stand."

The toilet cistern stops filling and the silence sighs loudly.

"This is an old-fashioned war-of-succession tale. Once upon a time there was an ancient despot called Konosuke Tsuru. His empire had its roots way back in the Occupation days, in outdoor markets and siphoned-off cigarettes. You don't happen to . . . ?" I shake my head. "Half a century later Konosuke Tsuru had progressed to breakfast meetings with cabinet members. His interests span the Tokyo underworld and the Tokyo overlords, from drugs to construction—a handy portfolio in a country whose leaders' sole remedy for economic slumps is to pour concrete down mountainsides and build suspension bridges to uninhabited islands. But I digress. Tsuru's right-hand man was Jun Nagasaki. His left-hand man was Ryutaro Morino. Emperor Tsuru, Admiral Nagasaki, and General Morino. With me so far?"

I give the patronizing slime a slight nod.

"On his ninety-somethingth birthday Tsuru receives a massive heart attack and an ambulance ride to Shiba Park Hospital. This is February of this year. A delicate time—the hatred Morino and Nagasaki have for each other was used by Tsuru as a check on his underlings. Tradition would demand that Tsuru name a successor, but he is a tough old dog and vows to pull through. Nagasaki decides to usher in his manifest destiny seven days later by staging his Pearl Harbor—not against Morino's forces, which are on red alert, but on Tsuru's, which believe themselves to be sacred. Over a hundred key Tsuru men were wiped out in a single night, all within ten minutes. No negotiation, no quarter, no mercy." Daimon shoots me with his fingers. "Tsuru managed to get himself lugged out of the hospital—one rumor says he was battered to death with his own golf clubs, another rumor says he got as far as Singapore, where a relapse caught up with him. He is, as they say, history. By dawn the throne was Nagasaki's. Any questions from the floor at this point?"

"How do you know all this?"

"My father is a corrupt chief of police."

A blunt answer from a slippery liar. "He must be phenomenally corrupt to be able to afford Queen of Spades."

"He is in the pay of Nagasaki. It is not toy money. Next question."

Next. "You were explaining why you are here."

"If this was a yakuza movie, the Tsuru faction survivors would team up with Morino and stage a war of honor. Nagasaki broke the code and must be punished, right? Reality is less exciting. Morino dithers, losing valuable time. The Tsuru survivors work out which way the wind is blowing and surrender to Nagasaki's offer of amnesty. They are promptly killed, but never mind. By May, Nagasaki not only has Tsuru's Tokyo operations under his thumb, but the Korean and Triad gangs too. Nobody ever managed that. Ever. By June he is helping to choose the godfather of the Tokyo governor's grandchild. When Morino sends an ambassador to Nagasaki proposing they divide the kingdom, Nagasaki sends the ambassador back minus his arms and legs. By July Nagasaki has the lot, and Morino has sunk to scaring brothel owners for insurance money. Nagasaki is content to watch Morino go extinct, rather than dirty the sole of his boot by stamping on him."

"Why does none of this make the newspapers?"

"You straight citizens of Japan are living in a movie set, Miyake. You are unpaid extras. The politicos are the actors. But the true directors, the Nagasakis and the Tsurus—you never see. The show is run from the wings, not under the spotlights."

"Are you going to get around to telling me why you ended up here?"

"Okay. I fell in love with the girl Morino fell in love with."

At last I see. "Miriam."

Daimon's mask slips and shows a real face. The door bangs open and Lizard appears. "Comfortable, ladies?" He flicks open his knife, spins it, catches it, and points it at Daimon. "You first." Daimon slides off the washbasin counter, still looking at me, puzzled. Lizard smacks his lips. "Time has come to kiss yer oh-so-charming face goodbye, Daimon." Daimon smiles in return. "Is your dress sense a charity fundraiser or do you actually believe you look cool in that pantomime mobster getup?" Lizard smiles back. "Cute." He whacks Daimon in the windpipe, grabs the back of his head, and slams his face into the metal door. "I get such a hard-on from casual violence," says Lizard. "Say something cute again." Daimon picks himself up, bloody-nosed, and stumbles into the corridor. The door is relocked.

Either I am losing my mind or the bathroom walls are bending inward. Time bends too. My watch is dead so I have no idea how long I have been in here. A cockroach navigates the floor. I cup my hands and drink some water. To distract myself from the swarm of unguessable questions I play a favorite game: searching for Anju in my reflection. I often catch sight of her around my eyes. I try a variation on this game: concentrate on my mother's face; subtract that face from my own; the remainder should be my father. Could my father actually be this Ryutaro Morino or Jun Nagasaki? Daimon implied Morino brought us here. But he also implied Morino is washed up. Too washed up to own a fleet of Cadillacs. I suck a champagne bomb. My throat is sore. By now Mrs. Sasaki will have decided that Aoyama's suspicions about me were accurate—I am an unreliable dropout. The cockroach reappears. I suck my last champagne bomb. Lizard watches me from the mirror—I jump. "Here comes the moment ya've been waiting for, Miyake. Father will see you now."

Valhalla is one enormous leisure hotel. When it is completed it will be the plushest in Tokyo. Sugar chandeliers, milky carpets, cream walls, silver fittings. Air-cons are not yet installed, so the passageways are at the mercy of the sun, and under all this glass I am drenched with sweat in thirty seconds. Thick smells of carpet underlay and fresh paint. On the far side of the construction-site perimeter fence I see the vast dome of Xanadu, courtyards, and even a fake river with fake caverns. The windows tint the outside world sepia, the same tones you get in wartime newsreels. The air is dry as a desert. Lizard knocks on room 333. "Father, I got Miyake with me."

My stupendous mistake dawns on me.

Father does not mean my father: *father* means "yakuza father." I would laugh if the afternoon were not now so dangerous. A voice rasps out a moment later. "Enter!" The door is unlocked from inside. Eight people sit around a conference table in a spotless meeting room. At the head sits a man in his fifties. "Sit the infant down." His voice is as thirsty as sandpaper. Cavernous eye sockets, plump lips, mottled and flaky skin—the sort used on young actors playing old roles—and a wart on the corner of his eye bigger than an amorous nipple. My way-too-late fear was quite correct. If this troll is my father, I am Miffy the Bunny. I take the defendant's chair. I do not even know what the charge is. "So," says the prosecutor and judge. "You are Eiji Miyake."

No point denying anything. "Yes. Who are you?"

Death gives me a choice of sorts. A point-blank bullet through the brain or a thirty-meter fall. Frankenstein and the stage manager of this black farce are placing bets on which one I will choose right now. Beyond hope is beyond panic. Here comes the Mongolian, strolling up the unfinished bridge. My right eye is so swollen the night swims. Yes, of course I am afraid, and frustrated that my stupid life is ending so soon. But mostly I feel the weight of the nightmare, stopping me waking. I am cattle in a cage, waiting for the bolt through my skull. Why gibber? Why beg? Why try to run when the only escape is a drop through blackness? If my head survived the fall, the rest of my body would not. The Mongolian spits, and folds a fresh strip of gum into his mouth. He pulls out his gun. After Anju I dreamed of drowning several times a week, right up until I got my guitar. In those dreams I handled fear by ceasing to struggle, and I do the same now. I have less than forty seconds. I unfold the photo of my father one last time. Dad is still uncreased. Yes, we do look alike. My daydream was right in that respect, at least. He is fatter than I thought, but hey. I touch his cheekbone and hope, somewhere, he knows. Down below on the reclaimed land Lizard whoops—"A twitcher!" *Bang!* Picking off the wounded is more interesting to him than how I die. "Ya got the shivers too, huh?" *Bang!* "Guns! The ultimate fucking video game!" *Bang!* I jump each time he fires. One of the Cadillacs wheel-screeches into life. My father sits in the driving seat of the car in the photograph, smiling at whatever Akiko Kato is telling him as she gets in. A black-and-white day gone by. This is the closest I got to meeting him. Stars.

◆

"Who am I?" The yakuza head repeats my question, although his lips barely move and his voice is tone-dead. "My accountant calls me Mr. Morino. My men call me Father. My subscribers call me God. My wife calls me 'Him' to her friends, 'You' to my face. My lovers call me Incredible." A ripple of amusement. "My enemies call me the stuff of nightmares. You call me Sir." He retrieves a cigar from an ashtray and relights it. "Sit down. Your trial is behind schedule." I do as I am told and look around at my jury. Frankenstein, chomping a Big Mac. A weathered, leathered man, who appears to be meditating, rocking very slightly to and fro, to and fro. A woman who is using a laptop computer, pianist-fast. She reminds me of Queen of Spades's mama-san until I realize she *is* Queen of Spades's mama-san. For her part, she plainly has no interest in renewing our acquaintance. On the left are three police sketches from the catalog of yakuza henchmen. A horn section on pause. Through an opening, in the corner of my eye, a girl dressed in a loose *yukata* sucks a Popsicle. When I try to meet her eye she retreats out of sight. Lizard takes the chair next to me. Ryutaro Morino watches me, over the pile of junk food boxes. The sound of breathing, the creaking of Leatherjacket's chair, the tapetty-tap-tap of the computer keyboard. What are we waiting for? Morino clears his throat. "Eiji Miyake, how do you plead?"

"What is it you think I have done?"

Lizard's knife scores a deep cut along the table edge. It stops an inch from my thumb. "What is it you think I have done, *sir*?"

I swallow. "What is it you think I have done, *sir*."

"If you are guilty you know the charge."

"So I must be innocent, *sir*."

I hear the Popsicle girl in the next room titter.

"He pleads Not Guilty." Morino nods his head gravely. "Then explain why you were at Queen of Spades on Saturday, September ninth."

"Is Yuzu Daimon here?"

Morino gives one nod, my face whacks the tabletop, my arm is yanked above my head one degree away from snapping off. Lizard grunts in my ear. "What d'ya suppose ya just did wrong? Just then? Guess!"

"Didn't—answer—the—question." My arm is released.

"Bright boy." Morino blinks. "So. Explain why you were at Queen of Spades."

"Yuzu Daimon took me there."

"Sir."

"*Sir.*"

"Yet you told Mama-san here last Saturday that you didn't know Daimon."

Mama-san glances at me for the first time. "I warned you—I cannot tolerate whining juveniles. Can anyone tell me what 'fifteen billion' is in Russian?" Leatherjacket replies. Mama-san carries on typing. Morino waits for my answer.

"I didn't know Daimon. I still don't. I left my baseball cap in a video arcade, went back, he had it, gave it back to me, we started talking—"

"—and a beautiful friendship was born. But Queen of Spades is a choosy club. Yuzu Daimon signed you in as his stepbrother. Are you saying this is a lie?"

I wonder what the consequences will be.

"Did you hear my question, Eiji Miyake?"

"Yes, it was a lie. Sir."

"I say that Jun Nagasaki sent you to spy."

So this is why I am here. I see a very faint glimmer of hope. At least I only have to convince them of the truth. "Not true."

"So you know the name Jun Nagasaki?"

"Since an hour ago, yes. Only the name."

"You went to Queen of Spades with Yuzu Daimon to harass a hostess—you know her as Miriam."

I shake my head. "No, sir, I did not."

"You went to Queen of Spades with Yuzu Daimon to persuade her to defect into Jun Nagasaki's circle of beagle-fucking traitors."

"No, sir."

Violence stains Morino's motionless face. His voice would freeze nitrogen. "You are fucking Miriam. You are fucking my little girl."

This is the crunch. I shake my head. "No, sir. No. No."

Frankenstein rattles french fry splinters in a cup.

Morino leans back, and the pressure eases, minutely. He opens a gray file folder. "So for your next trick, you will explain this photograph." The horn section passes it down to me. A letter-size black-and-white picture of a shabby apartment building. The zoom lens focuses on the third floor, where a kid my age is handing something through a door. A dog with its head in a lampshade pisses in a flower box. I recognize Miriam's apartment, and me. The pressure redoubles. This is really why I am here today. This is bad. No lie is going to get me out of here. But where will the truth get me? Morino clunks his knuckles out of their sockets. "My breath is bated. As they say." Morino clunks his knuckles into their sockets. My mouth is a sandbox. "Now. Why did you show your zit-puss face at the home of my little girl?"

I tell him everything from Shinobazu Pond in Ueno Park to the conversation with Miriam. The only bit I leave out is Suga—I claim to do the library hacking myself—and I hope this lie is small enough to smuggle through. Morino nicks the tip off a new cigar. I finish. Judgment hangs. Lizard swivels on his chair. "Father?" Morino nods. "Don't sound right to me. Computer dorks just don't lug suitcases around stations for a living." Mama-san shuts down her laptop. "Father?" Morino nods. "I know Miriam matters to you very much, but we need to be in other places very urgently to keep the operation on track. This nondescript fruit-farm boy is, I am quite sure, exactly what he appears to be. Nagasaki does not employ spies in diapers; his story fills in the blanks in Daimon's; and he hasn't laid a paw on Miriam."

Morino respects her. "How do you know?"

"One: you had Miriam tailed by the best surveillance agent in Tokyo for the last two weeks. Two: I'm a woman."

Morino narrows his eyes to read me better. I lower my eyes. Frankenstein's cell phone beeps. He goes into the adjoining room to answer. An airship floats into view behind Morino's head. Higher up, a jet glints in high-altitude sunshine. Mama-san takes a disk from her computer and seals it shut in a case. "Soon," barks Frankenstein into his phone. "Keep them there. We'll be there soon." He resumes his seat. Morino finishes reading me. "Eiji Miyake. The court finds you guilty. Guilty of being a dumb fuck who sticks his nose through wrong doors. The mandatory sentence is having your testicles cut off, dipped in soy sauce, and placed in your mouth, which will be duct-taped until said members are chewed and swallowed by the detainee." I glance around at the jurors. Nobody is smiling. "However, the court will suspend this sentence on condition that you observe an exclusion order. You will never go near Queen of

Spades. You will never go near my little girl. Even if you see her in your dreams, I will discover your lapse, and the sentence will be executed. I make myself clear?"

I dare not taste the freedom I can smell. "Completely, sir."

"You will return to your nondescript life."

"Yes, sir."

Mama-san stands, but Morino does not yet dismiss me. "When I was a boy half your age, Miyake, my friends and I would capture dune lizards on the Shimane coast. Dune lizards are cunning. You grab one: they detach their tails and skitter away. How do I know you are not leaving us with a tail?"

"Because you scare me."

"Your father is also afraid of me, but that man has left me with a zooful of tails in his time."

The horn players nod. I hear Popsicle giggle.

"Did you just say my father?"

Morino breathes smoke. "Ye-es. You know I did."

"My real father?"

"Ye-es."

"As in . . ."

"As in the flesh-and-blood man who banged up your mother, Mariko Miyake, twenty years ago. Who else would I mean?"

"You *know* him?"

"We meet professionally, on occasion. You seem surprised." Morino watches me flounder. "So, my operative hit the nail on the head. My, what an astute hunch. You really don't know who your father is, do you? To think, these things happen in real life. A semiorphan comes to Tokyo in search of the father he has never met. So you thought the ATM messages my banking people sent you were from your *real* father?" His lips bulge slightly in lieu of a laugh. Lizard snickers. Morino taps the file folder—"Everything about your father is in here." He fans himself with it. "You were buried deep, but my agent can dig up anything. I had you investigated—and your father cropped up. Surprised? Amazed. Still. You can fuck off now." He tosses the file folder into a metal trash can. Lizard stands and kicks my chair.

"Mr. Morino?"

"Are you still here?"

"Please give me that file folder."

Morino narrows his eyes at Lizard and nods at the door.

"Sir—but if you don't need that information anymore—"

"I don't need it, no, but I enjoy causing you needless suffering. Son will escort you to the lobby. Your friend and mentor Yuzu Daimon is waiting for you. He is feeling drained. Now walk away from this room, or you will be beaten senseless and dumped down a hole." I follow Lizard, and glance back one final time at the trash can before door 333 closes on my father.

I resolved to walk past Yuzu Daimon, to show my contempt by just ignoring him. That was before I see his body slumped on the sofa. I have known a few people who died, but I have never actually seen one—so pale, so utterly still—what do you do? My heart is a manic punchbag. The sofa creaks as his limbs shift. His eyes flicker open. His eyeballs wander, then find me. "So—what did they—do to you?"

A sort of weird crunching of gears.

"What did they do to you, Miyake?"

I can finally speak. "They let me go."

"Two miracles in the same day. Untouched?"

"Scared shitless, but untouched. And not as scared shitless as I was a moment ago. I thought you were dead! What did they do to you?"

Daimon ignores this. "Why—you went to . . . Miriam's—why?"

"She dropped a library book when she kicked me in Ueno Park the day after. I took it back. That was all."

A laugh tries to twitch his mouth.

Despite myself I am concerned for him. "What did they do to you?"

"One liter of blood."

I must have misheard. "They took one liter of your blood? Isn't that . . ."

"More . . . than a blood donation, yes. Much more. But it was only my first offense, so they let me off lightly."

"But what are they going to do with your blood?"

"Test it—sell it, I imagine."

"Who to?"

"Miyake . . . please. I have no . . . energy . . . for an . . . exposé of illegal markets . . ."

"Can you move? I think you should get to a hospital."

Speaking is costing Daimon a lot. "Correct, Doctor, yes. I had a sixth of my blood removed as a payment in a yakuza vendetta. Awful, isn't it? Yes, I know I'm lucky to be alive. But please don't contact the police, because my dear old dad is on the take too."

"Okay, but hanging around in this building is a very bad idea."

"One minute . . . two minutes . . . let me . . . get some breath."

I explore the lobby. The exit will let us leave, but not reenter. The passageway back to the interview room is blocked by a grille locked by Lizard. The glass walls of the lobby are covered by taped plastic sheeting. I peel back a corner—a construction site, the perimeter fence, and Neptune Sea Park, only a soccer-ball kick away. Sunbathers roast on the boardwalks. The Pacific is as glossy as a monster-movie sea. I sneeze. Not a cold, not now, please. I am afraid Daimon will slip into a coma if I don't haul him away. "Try to stand up."

"Leave me alone."

"I want to call your parents."

Daimon half-sits. "No, no, definitely, no. Believe me this once. Calling my parents is the very, very worst thing . . ."

"Why?"

Daimon shakes his head as if avoiding a fly. "Politics. Politics."

So now what? "How much money have you got?"

"Every yen is yours if you leave me alone."

"Don't tempt me. Near the entrance to Xanadu I saw a taxi stand. You and I are going to walk over there. You can either give in now, or make me shout at you for ten minutes and then give in. Up to you."

Daimon sighs again. "So masterful when you get roused."

We get weird looks as we wade through the crowds, but everyone assumes Daimon is slouched on my shoulder because he is dead drunk, and the crush parts for us. Atomic September sunshine drenches the day. My Japan Railways overalls are gluey with sweat, stale and fresh.

People flow into Xanadu and out again. The air is crammed with silvery helium balloons and tinsel music. Swarms of conversation pieces, smoke from a corn-on-the-cob stand. I see our reflection in a pair of mile-wide sunglasses. We look terrible. A giant black rabbit produces a midget magician from a top hat, and the world claps. Somewhere a piano and strings perform something beautiful. I feel Daimon heaving. "Do you want to be sick?" I ask him. "No. I was laughing at the funny side of today." I wonder where the funny side is. "Do you have any idea how embarrassing it is for me having my hide saved by you, Miyake?" Zax Omega leaps across our path, selling models of himself. "Yeah," I say. "I imagine it must be pretty humiliating, considering." Daimon says nothing more until we get to the taxi stand. His feet drag heavier, and his breathing is rawer. The taxi door swings open all by itself—down south you still have to open them by hand. "Do you know Kita Senju?" I ask the driver. He nods. "Do you know the Tenmaya store five minutes from the station with the, uh, fake Holland clock thing?" The driver nods. "This video store is right on the same street." I scribble Shooting Star's address. "Please take my friend there." The taxi driver looks dubious, balancing a very good fare against Daimon's grogginess. "Only a bit of sunstroke. In ten minutes he'll be himself again." The fare wins, and the taxi drives Daimon away. I turn back and face the way I came. I have an appointment back in Valhalla with a discarded file folder in a metal trash can.

The Mongolian is climbing nearer. A man-shaped hole in the dim dark. I can see his almost-smile. The impact of his cowboy boots against the concrete counts off my remaining moments. Lizard and the Cadillac headlights strobing the battleground may as well be events from another lifetime. Are Morino and Frankenstein still watching? If I take my eyes off the Mongolian, I am afraid my killer will halve the distance when I look back. I have a nightmare where that happens. If this is not a nightmare, what is? My adrenaline is fighting my fever, but I have no way to use this loaned energy. No amount of adrenaline will keep me alive when I hit the ground after that drop. No amount of adrenaline will let me disarm a real, live mercenary with a real, live gun. Fuck, no. I am dead. Who will miss me? Buntaro will find a new tenant by next Saturday. Mom will enter her cycle of guilt, blame, and vodka. Again. Who knows what my father will feel? Blame, regret, grief? I would hope so. My stepmother will probably buy a new hat to celebrate. Akiko Kato will have a little paperwork to process. Cat will find a new pad. She was only ever in it for the milk. My uncles, their wives, and my cousins back in Yakushima will be shocked and distraught by the news, of course, but they will all agree that Tokyo is trouble and Japan is not the fortress of safety it used to be. My grandmother will receive the news with a blank face and a long silence that will last half a day. Then she will say, "His sister called him, so he went." My list ends there. And this is assuming that my body turns up. Burying me in a pit under a future runway with the others down there would surely make a whole load more sense. Buntaro will report me in a week as a missing person, and everyone will shrug, say he trod in his mother's footsteps, assume I am working in a spare-parts factory in a disposable town, and forget me. Here comes my killer, checking his gun. What was it all for? Anju was overwhelmed by the ocean. I am just underwhelmed. I sneeze again. Sneezing, now! I want to ask my nose, Why bother? The breeze is cool off the drained sea.

◆

I decide to kill an hour before I reenter Valhalla. First, I find a telephone. I call Mrs. Sasaki at Ueno, but the moment I hear her voice I hang up in panic, or shame. Either I must tell her an outright lie—or I tell her the outright truth. I cannot do either. So I call Buntaro, who is much easier to handle—he jumps down the telephone line. "Guess what, kid! Kodai's eyes are actually open! Inside my wife! Open! Imagine that! And get this—he is sucking his thumb! Already! The doctor said this is unusual, so early on. Early developer, the doctor actually said that."

"Buntaro, I—"

"I was watching a baby video earlier. Maternity is . . . beyond belief. Ever wondered if embryos get thirsty? They do! So they drink up the amniotic fluid, and then pee it out again! The same as being hooked up to a never-ending supply of Budweiser. Except amniotic fluid tastes better. Waiting to be born must be nine months of bliss, same as a bar where you never have to pay the bill. Pity is, we never remember a thing."

"Buntaro, a friend is—"

"Have you any idea how much pregnancy rearranges a woman's internals? By the third trimester, the uterus is touching the breastbone. Placental mammals really have it tough. That's why—" A woman in the background at Shooting Star screams her lungs out. "Hang on, I'll turn down the volume. Watching *Rosemary's Baby*. Get a few pointers if Kodai turns out to be the son of the Prince of Darkness. A midwife at the hospital was saying—"

"Buntaro!"

"Is anything the matter?"

"Really sorry, but I'm calling from a box and my card is about to die. A friend is coming to Shooting Star by taxi. He donated some blood, but they took too much and he needs to lie down—please, when he gets there, would you show him up to my room? I'll explain later. Please."

"And will his trousers be needing pressing? Or how about a massage, or—"

My card dies. Perfect. I hang up.

A platoon of boyfriends and girlfriends—not to mention the battalion of bothered young families five years will transform the couples into—swills me down a shopping mall to a podium. Musicians perform something twiddly and ribboned. Mozart, maybe. By accident I find myself in the front row. A fat cellist, two thin violinists, a dumpy viola player, and a girl playing a Yamaha grand piano. She has one of those perfect necks—curves, smoothness, toughness, hollows, bumps, all just so. She is in a cream silk dress—sweat dapples mark her spine—and she plays barefoot. Her hair hangs down over her face. The music finishes and everyone claps. The string section basks in the applause—the pianist just turns around and gives a modest bow. Ai Imajo. It really is Ai Imajo. I look for a hiding place but I am walled in by handbags, strollers, and melting ice creams. Ai Imajo looks right my way and a blush grenade goes off in my face. Then I realize she is looking but not seeing. She is still dazzled by the brightness of the music. Of course, just because I recognize her does not mean that she recognizes me. Then Ai Imajo smiles at me—I check behind me to make sure Beethoven has not appeared—and then she mimes a headbutt. I manage a feeble nod before getting pushed back by penguins carrying bushes of flowers. Wish I had some. A hippopotamus woman looped in beads makes the microphone scream with feedback. I wander off to find a quiet and shady corner of Xanadu, if there is such a thing, and just sit in peace. I do not even think about embarrassing Ai in front of her music-student friends.

Valhalla blots out the sun. When my hour is up, I slip through a gap in the perimeter fence and into its unfinished shadow. I can see three security guards smoking in the mouth of the main entrance, but sneaking up between rows of blocks, piping, coils of cable, and drainage channels is easy. If I am being watched from Valhalla itself I am in trouble: I hope seeing Ai Imajo has used up today's coincidence quota. I nearly trip over a coil of cable. It sidewinds into life and enters Valhalla through a ventilation duct. No place for a snake, Snake. Avoiding the guards' field of vision I get to the foot of the pyramid, and begin looking for a way in. The building is vast—it takes about five minutes per side to skirt. I pass the hotel lobby entrance, and curse myself for not leaving it wedged open with something—I could probably have forced the inner shutter somehow. Twenty minutes later I am back to the main entrance and its three guards. I consider trying to pass myself off as a boilermaker or something—I am still in my work overalls—but when I creep close enough to overhear them discussing the best way to cripple a man (go for the kneecaps or go for the tendons) I change my mind. I backtrack to the basement ramp that Frankenstein drove down earlier in the afternoon. I spy on the guard lodge from behind a backhoe. Its window faces acrossways, not up the ramp. I think if I stay against the wall I can reach it without being seen. Then, maybe, I can crawl past. The main danger is from any vehicles ascending the ramp as I am making my way down. Still, there were only three Cadillacs in the entire car park. I think.

It works. I reach the lodge without being caught. On the guard's TV I hear "And it's a clash of the Giants and the Dragons in front of sixty thousand on this sweltering afternoon in the Dome as homeboy Enoki limbers up, and I can well imagine what must be going through the mind of that young battler!" I smell pork *katsu* and hear a microwave ping. I get down on my knees and scramble past—my foot slips in fine gravel, surely he must have heard? I carry on anyway, past his door, under the barrier arm and away, bracing myself for a shout and alarms. I dash behind a column, my heart percussion-capping. Nothing. He must be stone deaf. I am now an unauthorized intruder. Calm down. I am walking into a building to pick up a piece of unwanted trash. The three Cadillacs are still parked in a row, which is not a good sign, but as long as my father is safe in the metal trash can I can find a hiding place some-where in the hotel and retrieve it when the yakuza have gone. Staying in the darkest wedges of shadow I make my way to the portal door and slip through. I sort of remember the way. Snake is wandering this maze of swinging doors too. Grown to canoe length. I pass the toilet where Dai-mon and I were put on ice—abrupt laughter rings out. My nerves snap, I dart ahead and clear the next corner just as the laughter spills into the corridor. It follows me for the next three turnings. Then it dies down. Then it changes direction and heads toward me—does it? I double back in panic—I thought I doubled back—and end up down a dead end with a drinks machine in the alcove. I listen. The voices of two men are get-ting nearer. Maybe I can squeeze down the side of the machine—I can, but as I try to twist around behind it my foot gets caught in a loop of cable. At that moment the voices appear in front of the machine. I freeze. If I move they will hear me. If they look down the side of the machine they will see my leg. I feel a sneeze getting nearer. No. Dread snuffs it. A transformer juts into the small of my back. It hornet-hums and is hot as an iron.

"My, my, my, what do we have here."

"Imported Stella Artois. Nectar of the gods."

"Time for a quick can?"

"Why not? And guess what? Kakizaki is AB rhesus negative."

"My, my. I hope you bled him dry. AB-neg is liquid ruby for the right billionaire."

"Drier than dry, poor fuck. I see it as an act of mercy. You heard about the neck trusses on the lip of the pits? Fuck, this machine won't take five thousands. Got anything smaller?"

I am going to sneeze right now.

Coins are fed in. "Neck trusses? I thought Morino said to use tape?"

"We did, but Nabe wriggled too much. Morino ordered no sedatives. So there was nothing for it but neck trusses and nine-inch nails. Kakizaki's the lucky one. Whiter than cod, he is, he'll hardly feel a thing."

Beers clunk through the machine's guts. The men open their beers and walk away, still discussing carpentry. I sneeze and hit my head on the side of the machine. The voices do not return.

I find room 333 by accident while I am still looking for a hiding place. I press my ear against it. Apart from my pulse pounding my eardrums I hear nothing. I think. I test the handle: very, very carefully. It is tightly sprung, but feels unlocked. Holding my breath, I open the door a sliver and peer in. I can see the metal trash can with the file folder. The window is slightly open, and a breeze combs the blinds. Remembering the adjoining room, I creep in. Nobody here. Relief washes through me, then triumph hoses me down. This insane risk has paid off. I open the file folder—and groan. A single photograph falls to the floor and lands blank side up. A message is ballpointed on it: *An Arabic proverb: "Take whatever you want," says God, "and pay for it." Pluto Pachinko, Xanadu, now.* I turn the picture over. Two certainties. One: the woman is Akiko Kato. Two: from the angle of his jaw to the slope of his eyebrows, the man in the driver's seat is my father. I am looking at the face of my father. I know it.

Pluto Pachinko is so thick with sweat, smoke, and sheer din you could swim up to the mirrorballs on the disco ceiling. I would swap a whole lung for a cigarette right now instead of waiting fifty years—but I am afraid if I delay for one moment I will miss Morino and Plan F, the most promising so far, will drive off with him. Never mind, just by breathing in here I can absorb enough nicotine to calm a rhino. Customers cram the aisles, waiting for a free seat. My eldest uncle—owner of the only pachinko parlor on Yakushima—told me that new places rig several of the machines to pay out more generously, so they can muscle in on the marketplace. The clatter and glitter of cascading silver balls hypnotize the ranks of drones and she-drones. I wonder how many babies are slowly cooking to death in the bowels of Xanadu's car park. I start a second lap, searching for a staff-only door. I find a girl in a Pluto uniform. "Hey! Where's Dad's office!"

She is cowed. "Whose office, sir?"

I scowl. "The manager!"

"Oh—Mr. Ozaki?"

I roll my eyeballs. "Who else?"

She takes me behind the help desk, punches in a code on a combination door and holds it open. "Up these stairs, sir. I'd show you up myself, but I'm not supposed to leave the floor."

"I should hope not." I close the door, impressed with my performance. A complex lock springs closed. Steep stairs leading to one door. Underwater quiet. I climb the stairs, and then nearly lose my footing when I notice Leatherjacket calmly watching me from the top step. "Uh, hello," I say. Leatherjacket looks at me and chews gum. He is cradling a gun. The first real gun I have ever seen. I point at the door. "Can I go in?" Leatherjacket chews, and tilts his head a fraction. I knock twice and open the door.

Inside, a man flies through the air, and through a mirror on the far side of the room. The mirror breaks into applause—the man drops out of view, to the drone-packed parlor below. The scene lurches. I gape— did I do that? Pachinko din from downstairs fills the office, unfiltered. Morino watches me from behind the desk with a finger on his amused lip and one ear cupped. I just have time to register the three horn players—they did the hurling—and Mama-san knitting, before the chain reaction from below breaks out. Chaos, screaming, shouting. Morino rests his elbows on the desk. His smile is deep contentment. A jag of mirror falls from the frame. From outside Leatherjacket closes the door behind me. The cyclone subsides as the stampede clears the pachinko parlor below. Lizard and Frankenstein peer through the frame to inspect the damage. Morino sort of smiles with his eyelids. "Fine timing, Miyake. You witnessed my declaration of war."

I am trembling. "The man . . ."

"Take a seat. What man?"

"The man they—threw out—through the window."

Morino inspects a wooden box. "Ozaki? What about him?"

"Won't he need—" I swallow "—an ambulance?"

Morino unclips the box. Cigars. "I expect so."

"Aren't you going to call one?"

Morino looks inside. "Excellent! A Montecristo. Call an ambulance? If Ozaki wanted an ambulance called, he should have thought through the consequences of pissing on my shoes."

"But—the police—aren't you . . ."

Morino slides the cigar under his nose.

"Police?" Frankenstein watches the chaos flood out of Pluto Pachinko. "Police work in your world. We police ours." He nods at Lizard and he and Frankenstein leave. I feel as if my stomach has been gouged out. Mama-san's knitting needles click. The horn players are on pause.

Morino unwraps the cigar. "What do you know about cigars? Nothing. So listen. Learn. The Montecristo is the king of cigars. Pure perfection. Pure Cuban—filler, wrapper, binder. For a rat's penis like Ozaki to even look at a Montecristo is blasphemy. I told you to sit down." I obey, numb. "You are here because you want information. Am I right?"

"Yes."

"This information cost me good money. How do you intend to pay?"

I try my best to ignore the fact that this man just had someone thrown through a window, and pull myself into focus. "I would be grateful if . . ." My sentence dies.

Morino dabs the cigar with his tongue. "I am sure your gratitude is five-star gratitude. But I have metropolitan overheads. Your gratitude is worth flea shit. Try harder."

"How much?"

Morino takes a tool from the desk and circumcises the cigar. "Why is it always money, money, money with kids nowadays? Little wonder Japan is becoming this moral and spiritual graveyard. No, Miyake. I do not want your money. We both know you have none. No. I propose you pay with loyalty."

"My loyalty?"

"There a fucking echo in here?"

"What would giving you my loyalty mean?"

"So like your father. Living in small print. Your loyalty? Let me see. I thought we could spend the rest of the day together. Go bowling. An outing to a dog show. A bite to eat, and afterward a get-together with some old friends. Midnight comes around, we give you a ride home."

"And in return—"

"You receive—" He clicks his fingers and a horn player hands him the file folder. Morino leafs through it. "Your father. Name, address, occupation, résumé, personal history, pix—color, black and white— itemized telephone bills, bank accounts, preferred shaving gel." Morino fastens it shut. "You give me and my family a few hours of your precious time, and your historic search ends in glory. What do you say?" From the deserted pachinko floor below I hear glass crunching and electric shut- ters lowering. It occurs to me that saying "No" may have consequences far worse than being denied a file folder, bearing in mind what I have witnessed.

"Yes."

A wet dab, and a needle plunges into my left arm, just above the elbow. I yelp. Another horn player grips me tight. He shoves his face up to mine, and opens his mouth wide, as if he wants to bite off my nose. I have a close-up view of his mouth before I can turn away, then I turn back. His tongue is a clipped stump. A formless giggle. The horn players are all mutes. The syringe fills with my blood. I stare at Morino as a syringe in his arm fills up with blood. He seems surprised at my shock. "We need ink."

"Ink?"

"For the contract. I am a man of the written word." The syringes are removed and my arm is released. Morino squirts both syringes into a teacup, and mixes our blood with a teaspoon. My puncture is dabbed with disinfectant. A horn player spreads a sheet of calligraphy paper in front of Morino, and hands him a writing brush. Morino dips the brush, breathes deeply, and in graceful strokes, draws the characters for *loyalty*, *duty*, and *obedience. Mori-No.* He rotates the paper on the desk. "Quickly," Morino orders, "before the blood clots." I pick up the brush, dip it, and write *Mi* and *Yake*. Red already stiffens to dung brown. Morino watches with a critical eye. "Penmanship is a dying art."

"At my high school we practiced with ordinary ink."

Morino blows the paper dry, and rolls it into a scroll case. Everything seems prepared. Mama-san puts the scroll case into her handbag. "Perhaps now, Father," she says, "we can finally attend to business?"

"Yes." Morino puts down the cup of blood and wipes his mouth. "Bowling."

A basement shopping mall will connect Xanadu with Valhalla and Nirvana. It is still a gloomy underpass, lit by roadworker lamps and strewn with tarpaulins, tiles, wood planking, sheet glass, and a prematurely delivered army of boutique dummies huddled naked in misty polyethylene. Morino is ahead, a megaphone in one hand. Mama-san walks behind me, and the horn players bring up the rear. Somewhere above my head in the real world, Ai Imajo is playing Mozart. Words from Morino could be the voice of darkness itself. "Our ancestors built temples for their gods. We build department stores and theme parks. In my youth I went to Italy with my father, on business. I still dream about the buildings I saw. What we lack in Japan is the necessary megalomania." Down here is chilly and damp. I sneeze. My throat feels tight. Finally we climb to the surface on a dead escalator. "Welcome to Valhalla," says Thor, a thunderbolt in one hand and a bowling ball in the other. Through a temporary door in a plywood wall we enter a far greater darkness. At first I cannot see a thing—not even the floor. I can only feel the emptiness. I follow the vapor trail and ember light of Morino's cigar. In the distance is a suffused glow. This is a bowling alley. We walk past lane upon lane. I lose count. Minutes seem to pass. "Ever go bowling much on Yakushima, Miyake?" Sometimes Morino's voice seems far, sometimes near. "No," I answer. "Bowling keeps youngsters out of trouble. Safer than falling out of trees or drowning in undertows. Once, I went bowling with your father. A clever bowler, your dad. An even better golf player, though." I don't believe him, but I probe anyway. "What golf course did you play at?" Morino waves his cigar at me—its tip is a firefly in the gloom. "Not a crumb until midnight. That is the deal. Then you stuff yourself with all the details you can stomach." Suddenly we are here. Leatherjacket, Frankenstein, Lizard, Popsicle. Mama-san sits down and gets out her knitting. Morino smacks his lips. "Our guests are accommodated?" Frankenstein jerks a thumb down the lit alley. Instead of tenpins are three wax human heads. The center head moves. The left head tics. I should not be here. This is a nightmarish mistake. No. This is a sort of interrogation. Morino is not sick enough to hurl bowling balls at real people. He is at root a businessman. "Father," says Mama-san. "I have to say. This is an unspeakable act."

"War is war."

"I mean, Father, we will be wasting their retinas."

"Oh. I beg your pardon. Yes, I understand your concern, Mother, I really do. But my conscience won't let me stop a dead man seeing his destiny coming."

"*Morino!*" shouts Centerhead, hoarsely. "I know you're there!"

Morino raises his megaphone to his lips. His amplified voice is a dust storm. "Congratulations on a fine opening day, Mr. Nabe." Echoes slap away and back. "There seemed to be a minor ruckus in the pachinko parlor, but I'm sure everything is sorted out now."

"Release us! This instant! Jun Nagasaki owns this city!"

"Wrong, Nabe. Jun Nagasaki thinks he owns it. But I know I own it."

"You are stark fucking *insane*!"

"And you," Lizard shouts back, "you are stark fucking *dead*!"

The megaphone crackles. "You, Nabe, were always a walking lobotomy. Your death suits you perfectly. But you, Gunzo—I thought you had the sense to grab your turd money and run for the tropics."

Lefthead speaks. "We're more useful to you alive, Morino."

"Maybe. But you are more pleasing to me dead."

"I can show you how to strangle Nagasaki's supply lines."

Morino hands the megaphone to Leatherjacket, who deposits his chewing gum in a tissue. "Good afternoon, Gunzo."

"*You?*"

"I favor customers who pay on time." He has a dusky foreign accent.

"I don't fucking *believe* it!"

"Your inability to believe is the cause of your present dilemma."

Centerhead shouts, "You're dead, you slimy Mongolian traitor!"

The slimy Mongolian traitor hands the megaphone back to Morino, smiles, and puts in a new stick of gum.

Lefthead cries, "I can be your messenger to Nagasaki, Morino!"

"Ya ain't our messenger," shouts back Lizard, "yer our fucking message!"

"Most succinct, son," comments Morino approvingly. "Most concise. You can throw first." Lizard bows graciously and selects the heaviest bowling ball. I tell myself this is just a bluff. I should not be here. Lizard steps onto the concourse, and lines up a shot. "Shoot us, Morino!" shouts Centerhead. "Let us die honorably!" Frankenstein shouts back, "What do you know about honor, Nabe? You sold your hole to Nagasaki before he could say 'Bend over'!" Lizard steps one, two, and—wham! A fast, uncurving line, my gut knots, I try to wake myself up, or just look away, but when Centerhead screams I look, idiot that I am—and see the worst sight of my life, bar none. Righthead—Kakizaki, I guess— is no longer recognizable. I want to vomit but nothing comes. Kakizaki is a staved-in cavity of bone and blood. The horn players burst into wild applause. Lefthead is shut down with shock. Centerhead gasps, drowning, spattered with red specks. Lizard bows again and comes back to the console seat. "Superb technique," praises Frankenstein. "Watch it on the replay, shall we?" I turn around and keel, putting my head between my knees. I jump up when the megaphone combusts "Miyaaaaaakeeeeeeeee!" down in my ear. Lizard gestures at the bowling alley. "Yer on."

"No."

The horn players mime confusion and surprise.

Morino stage-whispers: "Yes! We signed a contract."

"You said nothing about being an accessory to murder."

"Your vow says you will do what the Father tells you to," says Frankenstein.

"But—"

"And Father is telling you to bowl."

"I—"

"A moral conundrum for a responsible young man," considers Morino. "To throw or not to throw. Throw, and you risk doing that double-dealing abomination down there some damage. Not throw, and you cause a fire in Shooting Star and inflict a miscarriage upon your landlord's wife. Which would weigh heavier on your conscience? Think about it." He wants to lock me into this violence, to ensure I will never talk. The locks click shut. "Thought about it?" I get up, hoping for an unseen plot twist to get me out of here. I pick up a ball, the lightest. It weighs a lot. No. I cannot do this. This act is not in me. I hear laughter, and look back. Lizard lies on his back with his legs apart, his jacket partly wrapped around a balloon. Nipples, a navel, and a triangle of pubic hair are scribbled on the balloon with a black marker. Franken-stein kneels over him, lowering a long knife. "No," Lizard cries in falsetto, "please don't hurt me, mister, I got a baby in my growbag." "Sorry, Mrs. Buntaro," sighs Frankenstein, "but this is what you get for letting rooms to tenants who break vows with powerful men . . ." Lizard screams at the top of his lungs, "Please! My baby, my baby! *Mercy!*" The knife tip presses down on Mrs. Buntaro's rubbery belly, Frankenstein bunches his other fist into a sledgehammer, and *Bang!* Popsicle lolls and rolls a tickled laugh. Mama-san knits, Morino claps. A huddle of faces hanging in blackness, glowing from the monitor and console lights. In a single motion they turn and stare at me. I cannot tell which floating face gives the final order. "Bowl." I must miss, but not obviously. I should not be here. I want to apologize to the heads, but how can I? I march onto the concourse, and try to breathe—one, I aim for the gutter, a meter down from Rightdeadhead. Two, my gut coils up and—the ball flies away too early, my fingers made the holes sweaty. I crouch there, too sick to watch, too sick not to. The ball veers toward the gutter, and rolls along its edge for the middle third of the alley. But then spin swings the ball back—straight toward Centerhead. His face seems to refract, his howl grows louder as the ball rumbles down the alley, and the horn players behind me cheer in unison. And I close my eyes. Groans of disappoint-ment from behind. "You shaved his stubble," consoles Morino. I'm trem-bling and I can't stop. "Wanna watch the rerun?" leers Lizard. I ignore him, wobble back, and collapse on the end seat. I close my eyes. The gleaming, clotting blood.

"Clear the decks!" Frankenstein halloos. "My specialty, this—the windmill express!" I hear much grunting, his run-up, and the thunder of a rocketing bowl. Three seconds later, rapturous applause. "Eggshelled!" shouts Lizard. "Bravo!" says Morino. Centerhead shrieks over and over, but Lefthead is ominously quiet. On the insides of my eyelids I can see the end of the alley. I scrunch my eyes up even tighter, but I still have this Technicolor view. I probably will until I die. I should not be here in this twisted psychotic afternoon. My body refuses to stop trembling. I retch once, and twice, but nothing comes up. Noxious glued-okonomiyaki fumes. When did I last eat? Weeks ago. If I could, I would walk away. Never mind the document wallet. But I know they won't let me. A hand slides into my crotch. "Got any candy?" Popsicle. *"What?"* Champagne bombs? "Got any candy?" Her breath is rotting yogurt. Lizard grabs her hair and pulls her off. "You cheap little fucking *slut!"* Slap, slap, lash. Morino picks up his megaphone. The survivor is still shrieking. "Cut you a deal, Nabe?" The shrieks are blocked by desperate, breathless sobs. "If you shut your racket up for the next bowl, you are a free man. Not a squeak, mind you!" Nabe breathes in hoarse throat-rips. Morino lowers the megaphone and looks at Mama-san. "Will you?"

"My bowling days are behind me." The knitting needles click.

"Father," says Leatherjacket, "I think I have the basics of this game."

Morino gestures at the balls. "You are one of us, now. Please."

"I'll tidy up Gunzo. Gunzo I always disliked."

A steady roll, a quaver of fear from Nabe, and a blat. Applause.

"Oh dear, Nabe," bellows Frankenstein, "I distinctly heard a squeak."

"No!" comes the broken voice.

Morino gets to his feet. "Try to see the funny side! Humor is the soul of the soul." I should not be here. Morino takes his time choosing a bowling ball. "Yuck. This one has been used already." He wipes his hand on a handkerchief. Nabe is sobbing, softly, as if he lost a teddy bear and nobody cares. Morino paces—one, two—rumble, the ball flies. One short, sawtoothed howl. A chopstick snapping. Two heavy objects thump into the pit.

Three Cadillacs glide down the fast lane. A nowhere land, not city, not country. Access roads, service stations, warehouses. Afternoon drains away the day into a hole of evening. I am still branded with what I saw in the bowling alley, and always will be. I do not know how it is I can think at all. I guess the burn will not hurt until the shock wears off and my nerves come back to life. I think about the places I could be if I never reentered Valhalla. I could be chatting with Ai Imajo in a coffee shop. I could be feeding Cat and smoking with Buntaro. I could be bombing around the coast road on Yakushima on Uncle Tarmac's motorbike. The moon rises over forest slopes. Where is this? The something peninsula. Frankenstein is driving, Leatherjacket is in the passenger seat. Morino and I sit in the middle seat. He blows wreathes of cigar smoke, and makes several phone calls about "operations." He makes a chain of calls mostly no longer than "Where the fuck is Miriam?" Popsicle is giving Lizard a blow job in the backseat. We enter a tunnel. The roof lights bar-code-scan across the windshield. Mighty ventilators hang from the tunnel roof. I should not be in this nightmare. "I wish you would stop saying that," says Morino, apparently to me. "It's getting on my nerves. We all get the nightmare we deserve. No more, no less." I am still trying to understand this when Frankenstein speaks. "My nightmares always wind up in tunnels. I'm having this ordinary dream, nothing spooky or nothing, then I see the mouth of a tunnel and I think, 'Oh yeah, here comes the nightmare.' I drive into the tunnel and it starts. People hang from the ceiling. Some guy I offed ten years ago comes back and my shooter jams. The tunnel presses in closer and tighter 'til you can't breathe no more." Popsicle slurps. Lizard groans slightly and speaks. "Nightmares are yer law-of-the-jungle stuff. All yer modern gizmos stripped away. Yer just left there, alone, dinner for something bigger and badder and eviller. Watch yer teeth!" He slaps Popsicle, who whimpers. Morino taps ash into the tray. "Interesting stuff, boys. My view is, a nightmare is comedy without a release valve. They tickle, but you can't laugh. And the pressure builds up and up. Got anything to add, Miyake?" I look at this torturer, wondering if this is just another day for him. "No." Morino no longer seems to need to move his lips to speak. "Cheer up, Miyake. People die all the time. Millions every day. Those three killed themselves the moment they double-crossed me. You just helped deliver the sentence. You'll have forgotten all about them in a week. Forgetfulness is the greatest healer." Lizard comes with a contented smack of the lips. Popsicle sits up, wiping her mouth. "Candy!" Lizard mutters and unzips something. "Yer arm's a fucking pincushion. Show me yer thigh. I'll shoot you up there. Don't drool any or it'll be soap powder next time. Clean yerself up." Leatherjacket speaks. "In my homeland, it is said nightmares are our wilder ancestors returning to reclaim land. Land tamed and grazed by our softer, fatter, modern, waking selves." Frankenstein produces a steel comb and pulls it across his hair, keeping his other hand on the wheel. "Sent by who, then?" Leatherjacket folds in a new stick of gum. "Nightmares are messengers, sent by who, or what, we *really* are, underneath. 'Don't forget where you come from,' the nightmare tells us. 'Don't forget your true self.'"

A neon poodle prances across its sign for all eternity. It wears a little doggie bow tie. Our Cadillac joins that of the horn players. Mama-san has taken the third away on business of her own. The men prime their guns and Frankenstein opens my door. "Would you prefer to stay in the nice safe car with a doped-up sex nymphet tart?" Before I work out what to say Lizard swipes at my baseball cap. "Pity. Ya can't." We get out and walk toward the door of the poodle warehouse. An insect electrocutor bristles every few seconds. From inside the warehouse I can hear a roaring, swelling and sinking. Two bouncers appear from the shadows of the entrance and approach the horn players. "Evening, gentlemen. First, I gotta ask for any weapons—house rules, I lock 'em up safe. Second, your cars are not on the list. Who are you with?"

The horn players part and Morino walks through. "Me."

The bouncers blanch.

Morino stares. "I heard a rumor about a dog show tonight."

The more colossal bouncer pulls himself together first. "Mr. Morino—"

"The old Mr. Morino ended the day Mr. Tsuru died. My name is Father now."

"Yes, uh, Father." He flips open his cell phone. "Just you give me a moment and I'll make sure the best, uh, ringside seat is cleared for you and your party—" Morino nods at Frankenstein, who knifes him about where his heart is. Right down to the hilt. A horn player jerks the bouncer's head back and probably breaks his neck. It all happens too fast to register, and too fast for the victim to make a sound. The other two horn players fell the second bouncer. Lizard volleys the gun out of his hand and kisses the tumbled man. No, he doesn't. He bites the bouncer's nose—and spits out specks of dark. At this point I look away. I am fused and burned out by what I have seen today. Thuds, grunts. "Dump the fuckrats behind those crates," orders Morino. The kicked-away cell phone rings. Frankenstein crunches its shell with a single stomp. "Cheap Taiwanese shit. Nothing is made in Japan anymore." Lizard opens the warehouse door. Inside is mulchy and meaty. Row after dim row of pallets stacked with tins of dog food. This place is enormous. Cheers and yells slosh from the distance. The horn players lead the way. I falter, and get a whack from Frankenstein in my coccyx. "No stalling, Miyake, you're one of us until the clock strikes midnight." I obey. I have to. All I can do to calm my survival instinct is to lower my baseball cap. Nobody in the shouting, hundred-plus-strong crowd notices our approach. The horn players plow through the outer walls—yakuza shirts and tattoos to a man. They whirl around angrily, catch sight of Morino, gape, and fall away. We reach the edge of a spotlit pit. A gray mastiff and a black Doberman are straining at their leashes, globs of saliva flying off their fangs. On the far side of the pit a man stands on a crate. He scribbles down the bets the crowd shouts at him. Hairy fat diamonds bulge through his mesh undershirt. I am sandwiched between Frankenstein behind and Morino in front—as safe as it gets—so I have a decent view as Morino pulls a gun from his jacket and shoots the mastiff through the head.

Silence.

A stain eats up the pit floor around the dead dog's head. The Doberman whimpers behind its trainer. The horn players already have their weapons trained on the crowd. They fall back. I should not be here. The mastiff trainer regains his power of speech. "You shot Mr. Nagasaki's best dog!"

Morino acts confused. "Whose best dog?"

"Jun Nagasaki, you, you, you—"

"Oh, him."

The trainer is apoplectic. "Jun Nagasaki! Jun Nagasaki."

"I heard that name too much today. Don't mention it again."

"Jun Nagasaki'll peel your skin off, you, you, you—"

Morino points his gun*Bang!* The trainer buckles over and lands on his mastiff. Their blood pools. Morino turns to Frankenstein. "I warned him. Uncle? I warned him, yes?" Frankenstein nods. "You gave a fair warning, Father. Nobody says you never." The crowd is still anchored in the concrete floor. Morino clears his throat and spits on the trainer. "Guns, and fairy godmothers. Your wildest wish comes true. Right. Every last pig-fucking one of you will leave. Except Yamada here—" He levels the gun at the bookie on the table. "I want a word in your ear, Yamada. Go!" The horn players fire off a round each, and the crowd drains away down the aisles and rows, ushered by the pistol-toting horn players—vampires before dawn don't melt away so fast. The bookie keeps his hands raised. Lizard jumps into the pit and tips the trainer's head over with his foot. Between his eyes is a bloodied joke-shop scab. "Nice shot, Father." From outside I hear cars screech away.

The bookie swallows hard. "If you're going to kill me, Morino—"

"Poor Yamada-kun. You backed the wrong dog again. I am going to kill you, no doubt, but not today. I need you to take a message to your owner. Tell Nagasaki I wish to discuss war reparations he owes me. Tell him I'll be waiting at midnight sharp. The terminal bridge for the new airport. Out beyond Xanadu on the reclaimed land. You think you can remember all that?"

The Mongolian halts ten paces away. His gun is cradled in his hand. The shots and lights from the reclaimed land seem far, far away now. My heart shotguns inside my rib cage. My overalls are scratchy and stinking. My final memories of life are the stupidest things. An unclaimed Haruki Murakami novel I salvaged from lost property, half-finished, in my locker at Ueno—what happened to the man stuck down his dry well with no rope? My mother laughing in Uncle Pachinko's backyard trying to play badminton, drunk, of course, but happy at least. When did that happen? Regret that I never made my pilgrimage to Liverpool. Waking one morning to find a pencil line of snow over my and Anju's futon, where it had blown in through a crack during an early fall. Is this junk the stuff of life? I hear my name, but I know it was only my imagination. I fight to keep control of my breathing, and sneeze. I never looked at Leatherjacket before, not properly. Yours is the last face I will ever see. Not how you imagine the face of death to look. Quite plain, mildly curious, taut. It has an immunity to emotion caused by the acts its master has made it witness. Do it. It would be too tacky for me to beg. So what are my last words? "I really don't want to die." How profound. "I suggest," says Leatherjacket, "that you crouch."

"Crouch?" A crouch-style execution. Why?

"On the ground. A—how do you say?—fetus position."

Why bother? Dead is dead.

"You should crouch for your own safety," my killer insists.

I mangled a stillborn huff that Leatherjacket interprets as a No.

Leatherjacket primes his gun. "Well, I warned you."

So many stars. What are they for?

◆

Tuna, abalone, yellowtail, salmon roe, bonito, egg tofu, human earlobe. The sushi is piled high. The wasabi is mixed in with the soy sauce to kill any impurities in the raw fish. It clots the soy sauce, sticky blood. I must stop thinking about the bowling alley. I must. We drove through the night since the dogs, it seemed, but the clock here says only 22:14. Little over a hundred minutes to go, I tell myself, but I find it hard to believe in anything good. I am in the grip of a cold that will get much worse before it will get any better. I get some water down my throat, it bloats my stomach. Even breathing is hard. We have the restaurant to ourselves. A family was here, but they shuffled out the moment they saw us. The old waitress stays cool, but the chef stays out back, lying low. I would if I could. Frankenstein lobs a sausage at me. "Why the sulky face, cub scout? Anyone would think you lost your parents." Lizard smears wasabi in the soy sauce. "Maybe he realized the mastiff I shot back at Goichi's was his long-lost papa." Morino flicks his cigar tip at me. "Grin and bear it! Remember your heritage! You're a Japanese law-abiding straight! You grin and bear it until your walker buckles and your drinking water is mercury oxide and our whole country is one coast-to-coast parking lot. I'm not knocking Japan. I love it. In most places the muscle is at the beck and call of the masters. In Japan, we, the muscle, *are* the masters. Japan is *our* gig. So grin. Bear it." I may have to bear it, but the only thing I can grin about is that until we leave this restaurant my position cannot get worse. Lizard points to a corner of the room. "Father!" Saliva-shiny sushi cud. "See what I spy with my little eye—they got a karaoke machine!" My position just got worse. "Joy of joys." Morino looks at Frankenstein. "Let loose the wings of song." Frankenstein sings a song in English with a chorus that goes "I can't liiiiiiiiive, if living is without yoo-ooo-ooo, I can't giiiiiiiiive, I can't take any moooooooooore." The horn players bay along with the vowels. The noise is so bad I watch for the sushi to sprout maggots. Leatherjacket sips a glass of milk in the corner. He doesn't seem to belong here either. Morino calls over the elderly waitress who has been nervously serving us. "Sing." Without arguing she performs an enka number called "Cherry Blossoms of the Inland Sea," about a mah-jongg gambler who dies to honor a debt, but only after ninety-nine verses. Lizard sings a song called "Electrode Incest" by a band of the same name. It contains no verses, choruses, or chord changes. The horn players clap wildly as Lizard does a turkey dance on the table and licks the microphone. Finally the song is over and Morino gestures me up.

"No," I say flatly. "I don't sing."

A hail of sushi slaps my face. The horn players boo.

"I don't like music."

"Bullshit," says Morino. "My investigator said you have twenty CDs, loads by that Beatle who got snuffed, a file of sheet music, and a guitar."

"How do you know that?"

"Nightmares do their homework."

I swab rice off my face. "You had my room broken into?"

Morino holds his glass for the waitress to fill. "If I thought you had touched my baby girl, you virtual orphan brat, I would have had *you* broken into. So be grateful."

"I hate karaoke and I'm not going to sing."

Lizard does a snide imitation. *"I hate karaoke and I'm not going to sing."* Then his fist fills my eye and the table becomes the ceiling.

I pick myself up. My eye sort of sings, throbbing up.

"I wanted to do that all day." Lizard examines his knuckles. "Father told you to sing."

I shake my head. There is no blood.

Frankenstein places a chopstick over his index and ring fingers, belches, and snaps the chopstick with his middle finger. "I say Miyake is in danger of a breach of contract, Father."

Morino wags his finger. "You have to make allowances. He was never the same after his sister drowned. They had their own little country. Fuck, they had their own language. What a pity he went off to Kagoshima the day she died, selfish fuck that he is. Hey!" He clicks his fingers at the waitress. "More edamame!" Drugged with cold germs as I am, I cannot guess if Morino has a gift for inspired guesses or a skeleton key to the basements of my mind. Either way, I want to spike his eye with my chopstick. I imagine myself doing it. Squirt. His wart throbs. I swear, the thing is watching me.

According to the Cadillac clock we enter the reclaimed-land perimeter road at 23:04. Thirty minutes later we are still driving. Military band music pumps through the car and a fever pumps through me, or maybe the fever is in the car and the military music in me. Millimeters away from being a killer, I was. I am. Can a chance difference in spin and angle really make me not guilty? I threw. I had to. But I threw. One more hour and the file folder will be mine. Plus a magnificent black eye. I was expecting the pretender to the yakuza throne of Tokyo to be joined by fleets of armored personnel, but no. Just these two Cadillacs. My nose streams uncontrollably, and my neck feels clamped in some sort of truss. Maybe some code of honor binds the two factions to nonviolence. Or, please no, maybe this is a suicide mission. I tell myself if Morino was the kamikaze type he wouldn't have made it to his age, or even his body weight, but I no longer know what to think. Nobody says much. Morino calls Mama-san, at Queen of Spades, I guess. "Is Miriam at work yet? I called her place. Tell her to call my cell phone the moment she gets in." Lizard and Frankenstein smoke their Camels, Morino his cigar. I am too ill to want to smoke. Popsicle whimpers in her narcotic sleep. The sea is calm enough to walk on and the sky is stars, acre after acre. The full moon is a six-watt bulb—I could shatter it with a well-aimed stone. Morino makes another call, but nobody answers. "Suicides tend to check themselves out when the moon is full, a nurse once told me. Suicides, and, for some reason, horses." Finally we slow to a halt, parked at a strategic angle to the horn players' Cadillac, I guess. I get out. My cramped muscles hurt. Yet another construction site. Tokyo suburbs are demolition dumps or construction sites. The giant terminus building is still a giant foundation. Flat as a pool table, the reclaimed land extends all the way to the mountains. A bridge, with the central section missing, rises on either side of where we stand. I can hear the lazy sea a short distance over the embankment. "Say, Miyake." His lighter flame dances. "You can monkey up that bridge." I wonder what the catch is. "Nagasaki is the opposition, and you don't fit the image. I don't want anyone thinking I'm recruiting from kindergarten." Lizard snickers.

"Will you give me the file folder?"

"You are boring me. Not until after fucking midnight. Go."

I have walked several paces when Leatherjacket, standing on a mound of boulders, whistles. I thought it was to me but it wasn't. "Our friends are coming. Nine vehicles."

"Nine." Frankenstein shrugs. "I had hoped for more, but nine is not bad."

I begin running up the slope. The bridge is the nearest thing to a safe haven. On the other hand, it is a perfect cell to keep me in. I get within a few meters of the top. I guess I am thirty meters up—high enough to clamp my lungs and make my balls retract. I peer over the parapet and watch Nagasaki's cars draw up. They park semicircling Morino's two Cadillacs and flick their beams on full. They kill their engines. Four men in each vehicle file out, each with a combat jacket, a helmet, and an automatic rifle, and take up firing positions. Not for the first time today, I feel I have strayed into an action movie. Morino and his men put on sunglasses. No guns, no night vision. Morino holds his megaphone in one hand and keeps the other in his pocket. Thirty-six heavily armed men to seven. A man in a white suit climbs out at leisure, flanked by two bodyguards. I wait for the order to fire. No file folder. It was all for nothing. Morino's voice reverbs over the reclaimed land as if his megaphone is a pinhole for the night to talk through. "Jun Nagasaki. Do you have any final requests?"

"I stand here frankly amazed, Morino. Have you really sunk so low, so quickly? Five tired goons, one ex–arms dealer—I shall kill you myself, Suhbataar, so painfully, so professionally, and so slowly that even you will be impressed—and an unarmed catamite hiding up a bridge." So much for my safe haven. "*This* is your comeback squad? Do you have an aircraft carrier waiting offshore? Are you hoping to kill me by sheer anticlimax?"

"I summoned you here to deliver my verdict."

"Are you a tertiary syphilitic? Are you Ultraman?"

"I'll allow you to apologize with honor. You may kill yourself."

"This is beyond stupid, Morino, this is rude. Let me get this right. You *seriously* fuck up my opening day at Xanadu. Persuading the press that Ozaki fell by accident has been a logistic hernia. You hurl bowling balls at my three managers until their skulls are Lego, and then you damage two innocent bouncers the old-fashioned way and shoot my finest dog. My dog, Morino, is what really hurts. You *amateur*. No operator of style ever, *ever* harms an animal."

"Style? Importing uninspected shitforbeef burgers from the U.S. and killing off Wakayama schoolchildren with O-157, and then getting your Ministry of Agriculture poodles to blame the radish farmers, is this *style*? Blackmailing bank executives over the figures you made them cook by refusing to pay back your bubble economy loans: *style*? You call a 'Pay up, Mr. Food Manufacturer, or pay for a razor blade in your baby products' scam *style*?"

"Your failure to grasp the fact that the world has progressed since 1970 is why I inherited and expanded Tsuru's interests and why you are still drawing your operational revenue by scaring loose change out of Shinjuku bar owners. How, oh *how* do you suppose you will still be alive in five minutes?"

"You are unaware that I have two secret weapons."

"Do you? I am *ablaze* with curiosity."

"The first weapon is your blazing curiosity, Nagasaki. Even in the old days, you spoke before you shot."

"Is your second secret weapon as terrifying as your first?"

"I present to you, ladies"—it is hard for me to catch the next word—"NimQSix."

"'Nim—Q—Six.' A magic robot? A drain unblocker?"

"A plastic explosive developed by the Israeli secret service."

"Never heard of it."

"Of course you never heard of it. The Israelis do not advertise in *Time*. But microcells of NimQSix are embedded in the triggers of the guns your dumb fucking apes are holding. The casings of your swanky Kevlar helmets are peppered with the stuff. My compatriot here, Mr. Suhbataar, oversaw the customization of your equipment when he diverted it from his Russian military supplier."

Some of Nagasaki's men turn to look at their boss.

Nagasaki folds his arms. "In the sad history of sad dumb bluffing fucks with empty hands, Morino, you are the saddest dumbest bluffing fuck of them all. Which weapons do you think I used to wipe out Tsuru? Let me assure you, there is nothing booby-trapped about my hardware."

"First, I needed you to bury the Tsuru faction. For this, I thank you—"

"Thank me when your lying guts are leaking through bullet holes. Now, I have a city to run. Stand away from the motors, you puppy dogs. I ordered those cars myself via our mutual Mongolian and I don't want to damage the paintwork."

Morino stubs his cigar out on the paintwork. "Shut up and learn. NimQSix microcells weigh one twentieth of a gram. A dot on a page. It is a perfectly stable explosive, even under repeat-fire ricochet conditions, *until*—here is the beauty of the piece—it is oscillated by a specific VHF frequency. Then the microcell explodes with a force ample to blow away body parts. The single oscillator east of Syria is built into my cell phone." To me, shivering with cold heat thirty meters up, probably with a sniper aiming at my head, this does not sound overly convincing.

Nagasaki spits. "I am getting bored of this gangster-movie pseudo-science—"

"Humor me for ten more seconds. NimQSix is the future. You really should take the time to educate yourself. I enter the code—I took the precaution of doing this prior to your arrival tonight—and simply press the DIAL button. Like this—"

Blossoms of explosions boom and flame and thunder.

I duck.

Shock waves scalp the air.

The reboom echoes off the mountains.

Finally I peer over the parapet. Nagasaki's men are scattered around where they were standing. The men who are out of the glare of the headlights are shadowy piles, but the ones who fell in the light—red as a slaughterhouse floor. Most of the torsos still have their legs attached, but the gun hands are blown away. And their heads—imploded by their combat helmets—are nowhere. I never learned the vocabulary I need to take this in. Only in war movies, horror movies: nightmares. The Cadillac door opens and Popsicle falls onto her knees. She gives a yelp of disgust, as if surprised by a spider in the bath. "Yaaa!" Lizard bounds around. "Yaaaaaaaa! Fucking *yaaaaaaaaa*haaaaaaaaay!" Nagasaki is still alive—no helmet to remove his skull—and trying to get to his feet. Both arms are shredded stumps after the elbows. Morino struts over and puts the megaphone into his enemy's ear. "Isn't science wonderful?" *Bang!*

The megaphone turns to me. "Seasonal fireworks, Miyake. Now listen. Midnight has passed. So the file folder in the Cadillac is all yours. Yes. Father keeps his word. Unfortunately, you won't be able to appreciate your hard-earned information because you'll be dead as a fucking dodo. I brought you along just in case Nagasaki wheeled your father out of retirement. I credited the cretin with too much cunning, so it seems we have one witness too many to the night's entertainment, instead of a possible bargaining chip. Mr. Suhbataar has asked to put the bullet through your head, and as he is the chief architect of my master plan, how could I say no? If it makes you feel any better, you were a forgettable boy who would have lived the bored, stifled, colorless life of your countrymen. And yeah, your father is a meaningless jerk too. Believe me, you will miss nothing. Sweet dreams."

Why bother? Dead is dead.

"You should crouch for your own safety," my killer insists.

My fear mangles my response to a stillborn huff.

"No?" Leatherjacket primes his gun. "Well, I warned you."

In his hand is not his gun but his cell phone. He enters a number, leans over the parapet, points down at the Cadillacs, and crouches.

The night rips open its guts, I am knocked over by a sheer wall of noise, the bridge shakes, a metallic, stony hail falls, I glimpse a flaming piece of car arcing overhead, and the file folder containing my father is cinders. The night rezips. The echo sonic booms off the mountains. Gravel presses into my cheekbone. I sort of stand—to my surprise, my body still works. Smoke pours upward from the craters where the Cadillacs were parked.

Leatherjacket enters another number into his cell phone. I crouch, wondering what could be left to blow up—is he a walking bomb who explodes his own evidence?—but this time the cell phone is only a cell phone. "Mr. Tsuru? Suhbataar. Your wishes regarding Mr. Nagasaki and Mr. Morino have been realized. Indeed, Mr. Tsuru. Just as they sowed, they reaped." He puts his phone away and looks at me.

Burning and crackling.

My lip is bleeding where I bit it. With the part of me that can still speak, I say something like "Are you going to kill me?"

"I am thinking about it. Are you afraid?"

I nod. Very, very afraid.

"Fear is not necessarily a weakness. I disdain weakness, but I disdain waste. To survive, you must persuade yourself that tonight was another man's nightmare into which you accidentally strayed. Find a place to hide by daybreak, and stay hidden for many days. If you assist the police in any way, you will be killed immediately. Do you understand?"

I nod, and sneeze an enormous sneeze.

By the time I look up, I am alone with the smoke and the night.

five

♌

Study of Tales

THE ALL-CONSUMING

Goatwriter peered out at the starless night. His breath misted up the window. He counted only three noises: the candle spluttering on his writing bureau; Mrs. Comb battling in her sleep, growling "Don't-Care was made to care, Amaryllis Broomhead!"; and Pithecanthropus, snoring in his undercarriage hammock. The whisperings were later than usual tonight. Goatwriter rummaged for his spectacles. He examined a lost volume of poems written by Princess Nukada in the ninth century, and by and by Goatwriter was oblivious to the here and now. This insomnia had been Goatwriter's regular nocturnal guest since midsummer. The Venerable Bus parked itself between midnight and the early hours, Goatwriter woke, and nothing could make him sleep again. He did not mention his insomnia: not even to his best friend, Pithecanthropus, and certainly not to Mrs. Comb, who was sure to prescribe a curative bitterer than the complaint. Nor did he mention the whisperings that often came to him. In the beginning, Goatwriter believed they originated in the Aberdeen waterfalls where the Venerable Bus had rested that week, but this theory was scotched when he heard them again on the Solomon Islands on Maundy Thursday. Goatwriter then wondered if he were going insane, but no, all his mental faculties seemed as muscular as ever. Goatwriter had finally started believing that his whisperings came from his writing brush—the selfsame brush Lady Shonagon used to write her pillow book, thirteen thousand crescent moons ago. What did they want, these suspirations? Goatwriter heard a rush, a rustle, and Princess Nukada was left on the shelf. He pressed his ear against the brush. Yes, syllables were bubbling up again. Goatwriter dipped his brush in ink and began to write the words he heard, slowly at first as words spattered singly, but then quicker, as sentences filled and over-spilled.

"Oh, sir, this is the limit!" Mrs. Comb tore open the morning curtains. "Why will you never wrap up proper when you go about in the wee hours? If your rheumatism plays up again, Muggins here'll be the one who'll have to do your lugging and fetching, you mark my words!"

Goatwriter unglued his eyelids. "Unquiet slumbers, Mrs. Comb."

"Then up and about with you, sir. Your breakfast is done. Zanzibar kippers, grilled to your fancy." The housekeeper looked at the landscape. "A right dreary spot we parked in last night, and no mistake."

Goatwriter found his pince-nez and peered out. The Venerable Bus had rolled to a cold shoulder of moorland. "Inky landscape, paper-pulp sky. We find ourselves in the m-margins, m-my d-dear Mrs. Comb."

"Drabby name for a right drabby place."

"The soil hereabouts is so acidic that all colors wilt. Years ago I heard that a m-marginal d-duke stationed a daffodil plantation, but the yellow bleached away. Even evergreens never greened."

"Aye, well, sir. Your kippers'll be turning cold."

Goatwriter frowned. "Strange to say, Mrs. Comb, but of appetite I am bereft. A splash of tea will suffice. Might I ask you to place the fish on a dish for me to eat by and by? Now, where are the pages that I wrote last night?" Goatwriter looked on his writing bureau. "Where can they be?" Goatwriter looked beneath and behind his bureau. "How vexatious!" Exhausting all the places his ms. could be, he began searching in places it couldn't be. "Curious? No, catastrophic! I wrote invaluable fragments of a truly untold tale!"

Despite decades of service, Mrs. Comb was cross about the spurned kippers. "I daresay you had another writing dream, sir, like the time you dreamed you wrote *Les Misérables*. You very nearly took Victor Hugo to court for flagellism."

The door banged open and the margin wind sprang in, disordering the loose and the fluttery. A fearsome prehistoric creature filled the doorframe. His torso was hairy and mud-spattered. He grunted in the language of clay and bone. Mrs. Comb glared. "Don't you dare clomp your mucky mudluggers on my clean carpet!"

"A good m-morning to you, too, Pithecanthropus." Goatwriter's missing pages were temporarily forgotten. "What have you found there, m-my d-dear fellow?" Pithecanthropus grinned bashfully and opened his cupped palms toward Mrs. Comb. A white, fragile flower drooped from a clod of earth. "A Snowdonian snowdrop!" exclaimed Goatwriter. "Blooming in September! How rare!"

Mrs. Comb was less impressed. "I'll thank you for taking your mucky weeds elsewhere! Such a muckster I never beheld!" She began scrubbing the kipper pan. "Shut the door on your way out! Do you want me and Sir to catch our deaths?"

Pithecanthropus grunted dejectedly and did as bid. Goatwriter felt sorry for his best friend, but he knew better than to come between Mrs. Comb and the perennial object of her scorn.

◆

So I wake up staring at another unfamiliar ceiling. I slip straight into my amnesia game. This is where I am numb and I want to stay numb. I used to play this after Anju went, when my nine-year round of "Eiji is visiting this month" began. Uncles' spare rooms, rice-husk futons, and cousins who held the ultimate warhead in any argument—"Well, if you don't like it here, go back to your grandmother's house!" Anyway, the object of the amnesia game is to remain in cozy ignorance of where I have woken up for as long as possible. I count to ten but I am still clueless. I am getting too good at this game. I examine the evidence. My muscles are strained and sore. I slept on a ballooning sofa in a pale living room. Forget-me-not curtains cover a big bay window. I have a mouth ulcer. *Bang!* goes the memory bomb. Heads in the bowling alley, a cigar-lit Morino, the

Mongolian on a bridge to thin air. My nose and throat are in the corked-up stages of a bad cold: my body takes care of itself despite its idiot brain. How long have I been asleep? Who fed Cat last night? A box of Lark cigarettes is on the table. There are only three left, but I smoke one after the other, lighting them with free matches from a bar called Mitty's. I am too warm. I slept in my clothes, so my various crevices are stewing. I should open the window, but moving would set into motion all the unthinkable consequences. For as long as I lie here, no new crisis can begin, and the distance between me and the deaths of thirty, forty men lengthens. How many people ever witness slaughter, real slaughter, outside of war zones? I groan. I cannot unsee what I saw. It will be national news. International news, most probably. TV will be channel-to-channel Yakuza Wars for the next six months. I groan again. Forensic teams will be crawling over the battlefield with tweezers. The Serious Crime Squad will be interviewing Xanadu shoppers. A girl employed at an already infamous pachinko parlor will have told reporters about a very suspicious character pretending to be the manager's son, moments before poor Mr. Ozaki himself was thrown through the security-floor security window. Police artists will listen, nod, and make charcoal sketches. Oh, shit. What do I do? What will the unseen Mr. Tsuru want done to me? What has become of Mama-san and the Queen of Spades? I have no plan. Worse, I have no cigarettes. I have no tissues to blow my nose. I listen hard, and I hear . . . absolutely nothing.

Sleeping in my clothes was a mistake, but I was afraid to undress in case I was woken up by the sound of the front door behind jimmied and I needed to bolt. I am still afraid. This is worse than waiting for an earthquake. If I feel an earthquake I know what to do—dive under a table and whimper. But what do I do if I hear an intruder searching for me? Hide? Where? I do not even know how many floors this house has. I get up: first stop, toilet. Japanese-squat style, with a bowl of bitter herbs. The kitchen is terra-cotta and spotless—judging from the flour-thumbed recipe books, the owner loves cooking. Each cooking imple-ment hangs from its own hook. There is a cleaning cupboard as tall as me, but it is too obvious a hiding place to be of much use. Through the window I see an empty carport and a strip of front garden. Roses, weeds, and a bird table. A high privet hedge shuts off the house from the outside world. I have no recollection of what lies on the other side. The living room is Japanese—tatami matting, a Buddhist altar with photographs of the recent and long dead, an alcove for flower arrangements and a hanging scroll with kanji that would give me a headache if I tried to read them. There is no TV, no stereo, and no telephone—just a receiverless fax machine on top of an ample bookshelf. The books are old, illustrated collections of tales. *The Moon Princess, Urashima Taro, Gon the Fox.* This house seems too orderly for kids, although it is not a particularly old building. I open the curtains an inch. The back garden is somebody's pride and joy. The pond is bigger than my grandmother's—I can see carp lurking in the green. Late dragonflies skim over the duckweed. A stone lantern sits on an island. Pots of lavender, and a high bamboo grove, thick enough to hide in. Birds nest in an orange mailbox nailed to a silver birch. You could watch this garden for hours. It unfolds itself if you stare long enough. No wonder there is no TV. I go upstairs. The carpet is snowy and lush under my bare feet. A lavish bathroom with sea-horse taps. A master bedroom—the decor suggests a middle-aged couple. The smaller bedroom is used only for guests. Well. No hiding places here. You have to be nine years old to find good hiding places in the average house. Anju won by hiding in the washing machine one time. I assume my tour is complete, but notice a slatted closet door at the end of the landing. Its knob twirls uselessly, but it swings open anyway. Its shelves are not shelves but steep stairs. A knotted rope hangs down to help you haul yourself up. On the third step my head hits the ceiling, which shifts. I push, and a crack of daylight opens as the plywood trapdoor swings up. It seems I have found my hiding place. I emerge into a library-study with the highest book-population density I have seen in my life. Book walls, book towers, book avenues, book sidestreets. Book spillages, book rubble. Paperback books, hardcover books, atlases, manuals, almanacs. Nine lifetimes of books. Enough books to build an igloo to hide in, and then to hide the igloo. The room is sentient with books. Mirrors double and cube the books. A Great Wall of China quantity of books. Enough books to make me wonder if I am a book too. Light comes in through a high triangular window. A sort of wickerwork lightshade hangs down. Apart from the bookcases and sagging shelves, the only item of furniture is an old-fashioned writing bureau with square holes to lose papers and bills in. My grandmother had the same sort. Still does, I guess. On the writing bureau are two piles of paper—one is white and blank as starched shirts, and the other is manuscript laid in a special lacquer tray. I cannot help myself. I sit down and begin reading page one.

♌

Goatwriter worked in the Venerable Bus, trying to reconstruct the fragments of the tale that had whispered before the dawn. Mrs. Comb mangled sheets and time extracted the minutes from hours. Goatwriter finally arose to check the correct spelling of *zwitterion* in his dictionary. He got sidetracked by *gustviter,* and returned with the dictionary to his writing bureau, where he was lured further from his original quest by *durzi* and *theopneust.* Drowsiness laid Goatwriter down, and the winds blew over the margins from the east.

When Goatwriter awoke from his long sleep he was alone. There was no paper on the writing bureau. He looked around. Nothing. For a moment he hoped he was still dreaming. The pages he had worked so hard at reconstructing that very morning had disappeared! Mrs. Comb, he knew, never touched his writing bureau, nor would Pithecanthropus. And since the same fate had befallen the pages Goatwriter had composed during the early hours, only one explanation remained, however shocking: "Thief!" cried Goatwriter. "Thief! Thief!"

Mrs. Comb rushed in, scattering pegs. "Sir! What's the to-do?"

"Burglarized, Mrs. Comb! While I lay sleeping!"

Pithecanthropus burst in clenching a wrench, grunting nastily.

"My reconstructed truly untold tale has been purloined!"

"But how could it be, sir? I saw nothing as I hung out the washing."

Pithecanthropus sniffed, and grunted uneasily. He led Mrs. Comb and Goatwriter to the stern of the Venerable Bus and sniffed the tire-track mud. He pointed at a set of tiny tracks, and grunted conspiratorially. Mrs. Comb gasped. "An unwashed rodent?" verified Goatwriter.

"Bigger than a mouse? Aha! We m-may conclude, thusly, that the thief is a d-dirty little rat! We m-must apprehend this scallywag and teach him a thing or two about copyright law! My d-dear Pithecanthropus—lead the way!"

The early man read the ground with brow furrowed. An anvil cloud lugged itself overhead. The rodent tracks led off the beaten track, down the path not taken, through a sleepy hollow and over a tarn of brackish bilgewater. Mrs. Comb saw him first on the lip of the dike. "Whatever next by 'eck!" A scarecrow, nailed to a T, in a very sorry state. His eyes and ears were pecked away, and wispy hay bled from a wound in his side whenever the wind bothered to blow. Goatwriter had encountered numerous scarecrows in folktales, and knew the protocol. "Ahem. Frightfully sorry to disturb your meditations, Scarecrow . . ."

Scarecrow raised his head so, so slowly.

". . . but have you seen a d-dirty little rat scurry by, carrying pages of a stolen m-manuscript?"

Scarecrow's mouth twitched. "This day . . ."

"Splendid!" replied Goatwriter. "Which way was the vile varmint headed?"

"This day . . . we shall sit . . . with my father . . . in Paradise . . ."

At that exact moment, two hellhounds hurdled the dike, sank their slavering fangs into poor Scarecrow, tore him off his T and savaged him to windblown tatters. Goatwriter was knocked backward by a loose paw. Pithecanthropus swept Mrs. Comb off her feet and into his arms for her own safety. All that remained of Scarecrow were rags nailed to the wood. Goatwriter, lying by the edge of the bilgewater, tried to recall what to do and what not to do with rabid dogs—play dead? Look them in the eye? Outrun an old-world fruit bat out of Hades?

"That'll learn 'im," growled the top dog, "to give the plot away."

"Wot about these three?" sniffed the underdog.

Goatwriter felt the heat of their breath. "Good doggies . . ."

"Talks like a writer," bristled the underdog. "Smells like one. Is one."

"No time, no time," barked the top dog. "Our maker is getting away!"

"Lemme practice on Beardy first," pleaded the underdog.

Pithecanthropus readied himself to defend his friend, but the hell-hounds turned and bounded away over the blank margins until they were but blots on the wizened horizon. "Well!" exclaimed Mrs. Comb. She then recalled that she was nesting in the arms of an extinct biped. "Put me down this very instant, you muckster!"

◆

A door bangs downstairs and the manuscript zooms out of focus. I stop breathing. Somebody is here. Somebody is here for me. Buntaro would have called out by now. So soon? How did they find me? My survival instinct, battered into submission by Morino, asserts itself now. The intruders are searching the living room, the kitchen, the garden, cranny by nook. They will have seen the socks I left on the sofa. My cigarettes. I replaced the plywood trapdoor and pulled up the rope, but did I close the slatted door on the landing? I can hand myself over and hope for mercy. Bad idea. Yakuza do not do mercy. Hide here, under books. But if I cause a bookslide, they will hear it and know I am here. Is there anything up here that could serve as a weapon? I listen for footsteps on the shelves—nothing. Either the intruders are working in silence, or I am only dealing with one. My default strategy is this: hold a three-ton, three-volume set of *A Critical Review of the Japanese "I" Novel* above the trapdoor—when it opens wide enough, lob them through and knock the guy backward. Pray he is a lone operator, jump down, land on him—if he has a gun I am in trouble—bust his ribs, and run for it. I wait. And wait. Concentrate. I wait. Am I sure I heard the bang? I left the back window open an inch—suppose it was just the wind. Concentrate! I wait. Nobody. My arms are aching. I cannot stand this. "Hello?"

The flurry of violence never comes.

Scared by a story I told myself. I am in a bad way.

Later in the afternoon, I go back down. In the spare bedroom closet I find some sheets and towels, and arrange them on the step-shelves behind the slatted door, so hopefully the intruder will think it is a linen closet rather than stairs to sanctuary. I gather up any sign of my residency, and stuff it into a plastic bag under the sink. I must clean up any traces of myself, as I make them. I should be hungry—when did I last eat?—but my stomach seems to be missing. I need a cigarette, but no way am I venturing outside. Coffee would be fine, but I can only find green tea, so I make a pot. I blow my nose—my hearing comes back, but snots up again—open the bay window, and drink my tea on the step. In the pond carp appear and disappear. Whirligigs bend but never puncture the liquid sky. A ruby-throated bird listens for earthworms. I watch ants. Cicadas muzzzmezzzmezzzmezzzmezzzmuzzzzzzzzz. Nowhere in the house is a single clock, or even a calendar. There is a sundial in the garden but the day is too hazy for a clear shadow. It feels three o'clock–ish, but I could be wrong. The breeze shuffles and flicks through the bamboo leaves. A column of midges hovers above the pond. I sip my tea. My tongue cannot taste a thing. Look at me. Five weeks ago I was on the morning ferry to Kagoshima, with a lunchbox from Aunt Orange. I was sure I would find my father before the week was up. Look at who—what—I found instead. What a disaster, what an aftermath! The summer is lost, and other things, too. The fax machine beeps. I jump and spill my tea. A message feeds through from Buntaro, telling me he'll be over around six, if the traffic lets up. When is six o'clock relative to now? Hours need other hours to make any sense at all. Hanging on the wall above the fax machine is a shell-framed photograph of an old man and woman, maybe in their fifties. I guess they own this house. They are sitting at a cafe table in the shade on a bright day. He is about to break into laughter at whatever she has just said. She is reading my reaction to see if I genuinely enjoyed her story, or if I am just being polite. Weird. Her face is familiar. Familiar, and impossible to lie to. "True," she seems to say to me, "but see if you can piece the puzzle together yourself." We watch each other for a while, then I go back to her garden where the dragonflies live out their whole lives.

♌

"And you are quite sure, m-my d-dear fellow," prompted Goatwriter, "that the tracks end in this m-mulch m-mound of Stiltonic stench?" Pithecanthropus grunted a yes, waded into the pyramid of cans, pans, mottled bottles, spud skins, linchpins, and "Vote for Me" leaflets, and picked up some fresh garbage. "Kipper bones!" squawked Mrs. Comb.

"Then one m-must suppose," concluded Goatwriter, "we have hunted our quarry to its hovel."

"*Hovel?*" a voice shot back from the apex of the pyramid. "Gimme my *hovel* an' stuff yer geriatric rust-bucket bus, *any* day o' da month!"

"Aha! The thief sits in residence! Unhand m-my m-manuscript forthwith!"

"Take a hike, ya sewerchewer JoeSchmoe!"

"Soap and water!" gasped Mrs. Comb.

Goatwriter lowered his horns. "Fiend! Ladies are present!"

A tiny hand appeared and flashed the finger. "If dat scrawny bird is a lady I am Frank Sinatra's gallstone, ya hear? Dis is yer last warning! If ya ain't skedaddled by da time I count to five I'll slap harassment suits so fast—"

"Legality! Indeed! A point m-most m-moot! You are the breaker, enterer, thiever of Zanzibar kippers and m-my truly untold tale! We d-demand justice and by Gideon we d-don't intend to leave empty-handed!"

"Magnificent, sir," whispered Mrs. Comb.

"Oooh, a threat!" the thief responded. "Ain't I wetting my didgeri-dungarees!"

Pithecanthropus grunted impatiently, waded deeper into the garbage pyramid, and with a single karate chop removed its top. Inside was a shocked, and then a furious, rat. "Are ya deranged, ya knuckle-dragger? Ya nearly lobotomized me!"

Goatwriter peered through his pince-nez. "Remarkable—the thief would appear to be a *Mus musculus d-domesticus.*"

"Ain't nuffink domestic or mousey about me, punk! I am da ScatRat! Yeah, so I sampled yer moldy kippers—wassa big balooey, Huey? I never lifted no stories or pages! I got *Scientific Whalers' Weekly* to wipe my ●hole! Ya slander my good name once more, I swear, my lawyer'll sue ya all da way to Alcatraz!" Then he spewed a chain of expletives so dire that Mrs. Comb shrieked and covered her ears with her wings. ScatRat hollered all the louder. "Act yer age, not yer egg size! Yer in da margins of da real world here!" With a final one-fingered salute, the rodent vanished into his pile's bowels.

The marginal wind blew a forlorn note.

Pithecanthropus grunted a question.

"I agree, sir," added Mrs. Comb. "Don't-Care should be made to care."

Goatwriter turned away stiffly. "Certainly, friends, this ScatRat is an abominable character, but a lack of m-manners per se is no crime. Such a crude d-degenerate would have no need of stealing m-my truly untold tale. He m-may be too ignorant to read. This m-mystery m-must go unsolved. Let us return to the Venerable Bus. M-my arthritis is telling m-me we shall be leaving these uninviting parts tonight."

Mrs. Comb baked a burdock troll cake to cheer Goatwriter up. Pithecanthropus repaired a hole in the roof. Goatwriter proofread his rewrite, and laid it to rest in his manuscript tray. He was unhappy with it. It lacked the magnificent glow that the earlier two versions had seemed to possess. "Dinnertime, by and by," called Mrs. Comb. "You must be starving, sir. You haven't had a bite all the livelong day."

"Peculiar to pronounce, Mrs. Comb, I could not entertain a m-morsel."

"I wish you'd give over fretting about your story, sir."

"No, no, Mrs. Comb—I just feel exceedingly full."

Pithecanthropus grunted urgently through the hole in the roof.

"Clap that savage trap!" shot back Mrs. Comb. "Sir is out of sorts!"

Goatwriter frowned as his jaws worked. "My d-dear fellow, whatever is distressing you so?"

Mrs. Comb's cookbook thudded. "Sir! What are you eating?"

"Why, only a little paper cud—" Goatwriter's mouth froze as he bit on the hard truth. Mrs. Comb fluttered. "Sir! Nobody stole your pages! You were eating your own pages as you wrote them!"

Goatwriter's words stuck in his throat.

♦

In the parched fog and half-light I wake with a yell. An old woman in black leans over me. I fall off the sofa. "Steady," the old woman says. "Steady, child. You were dreaming. It's me, Mrs. Sasaki, from Ueno Station." Mrs. Sasaki. I unclench, breathe in, breathe out. Mrs. Sasaki? Fog blows away. Eiji Miyake, King of Cool. She smiles and shakes her head.

"Sorry I startled you so. Welcome back to the land of the living. Buntaro neglected to mention I would be visiting this morning, am I correct?"

I get to my feet and sit down straightaway. "Morning . . ."

She puts down a sports bag. "I brought you some items from your apartment. I thought they might make your stay here more comfortable. Though had I known about your black eye, I would have brought a T-bone steak." I am embarrassed that Mrs. Sasaki saw the mess I live in. "I must admit, I thought you would be up by now. Why don't you sleep in the guest room, you foolish youth?"

My mouth is dry as a sandbox. "I feel safer down here, I guess. Mrs. Sasaki—you, Buntaro—how did he know your number at Ueno? How do you know Shooting Star, and Buntaro?"

"I'm his mother." Mrs. Sasaki smiles at my astonishment. "We all have a mother somewhere, you know. Even Buntaro."

Pieces slot into place. "How come neither of you said anything?"

"You never asked."

"It never occurred to me to ask."

"Then why should it occur to us to tell you?"

"My job?"

"Buntaro got you the interview, but you got the job yourself. None of this matters. We shall discuss your position at Ueno over breakfast. One thing at a time. First, you are to clean yourself up. I suggest you shave. You look as if you spent the week camping out with the homeless people in Ueno Park. It is high time you stopped yourself going to seed. While you are in the shower, I will cook your breakfast. I will expect you to eat more than me."

I stay in the shower until my bone marrow is hot and my fingerpads wrinkle. I body shampoo myself three times from scalp to toe. When I come out even my cold is better and I weigh less. I clip my fingernails. Now I shave. I am lucky, I only need to shave once a week. The boys in my class at high school used to boast about how often they shaved, but there are a hundred other things I would rather do with my time than drag steel over my hair follicles. Uncle Yen gave me an electric shaver a couple of years ago, but Uncle Tarmac laughed when he saw it and said real men use blades. I am still on my first packet of Bic disposables. I use the electric one only when I stay with Uncle Yen. I splash on cold water, and rinse my blade under the cold tap—Uncle Tarmac says the cold makes the razor contract and sharpen. I think of him every time I shave. I smear on Ice Blue shaving gel, especially the groove between the upper lip and the nose—why is there no name for that?—and my chin cleft, and the lower jaw hinge where I usually cut myself. Wait until the gel stings. Then start on the flatlands near the ears where it hurts least. I sort of like this pain. Tugged, uprooted. Some pain is best conquered by diving into it. Around the nose. Rinse away, stubbly goo. I chase it down the drain. More cold water. I touch my black eye until it hurts. Clean boxers, T-shirt, shorts. I can smell cooking. I go downstairs and put my shaving stuff back in the sports bag. I catch the eye of the lady in the shell photograph. "There, feeling better now? You worry too much. You are quite safe here. Tell me what happened. Give me your story. Speak. Give it to me."

So. The Mongolian disappeared into thin air. The burning Cadillacs broke into fresh applause. My senses struggled back from wherever, and I knew I had to get away from that place as soon as possible. I started jogging down the bridge. Not running—I knew I had a long night in front of me. I did not look over the parapet again, and I did not look over my shoulder. I was not even tempted. The thick smoke spun with plutonium fumes. It made me cough but it hid the bodies. I willed myself to become a machine whose product was distance. I jogged a hundred paces, and walked a hundred, over and over, along the perimeter road, scanning the moonlit distance for cars. I could hide down the embankment if anything came—the slope was built of those shorefront prefabricated concrete blocks with big hollows—but I had the track to myself. Horror, shock, guilt, relief: all the predictable things, I felt none of them. All I could feel was this urge to put distance between me and everything I had seen. Stars weakened. The fear that I would be caught and nailed to the crimes on the reclaimed land opened emergency reserves of stamina, and I kept my hundred-hundred regime up until the perimeter road curved through the roadblock and onto the main coastal road that led back to Xanadu. The dawn was scorching the horizon and the traffic on the main thoroughfare toward Tokyo was thickening. I was off the reclaimed land now and could pretend to know nothing about what had happened. The aspirin moon was dissolving in the lukewarm morning. Drivers and passengers stared at me—nobody walks out there, there is no sidewalk, just a sort of bulldozed-up ridge of ground. I thought about hitchhiking, but figured this would attract attention to me. I could not cope with small talk. How would I even explain how I came to be there? I heard a fleet of police sirens approach. Luckily I was passing a family restaurant, so I could hide in the entrance and pretend to make a phone call. I was wrong—no police cars, only two ambulances. What should I do? My fever was *taiko*-drumming my brain and my eye throbbed where Lizard had hit me. I had no plan of action beyond calling Buntaro and begging for help, but he wouldn't be at Shooting Star until eleven and I did not have his home number, and I was afraid he would dump my stuff on the sidewalk when he found out what sort of company I kept on my evenings out. Who could blame him? Could Daimon help? I called my own number, but the only response was my own answering machine. I hung up. "Are you okay, dear?" asked a waitress behind the register. "Do you need anything for that eye?" She looked at me so kindly that the only way I could stop myself from blubbering was leaving rudely without answering. I envy her son. The route passed an industrial zone—at least I had a sidewalk to walk on. Every streetlight switched off simultaneously. The factory units went on forever. They all made things for other factory units: stacking shelves, packing products, forklift gearboxes. The drumming was subsiding, but the fever was now steaming the contents of my skull. I had used everything up. I should try to get back to the family restaurant, I thought, and collapse in the lap of the angel of mercy. Collapse? Hospitals, doctors, questions? Twenty-year-olds don't collapse. The restaurant was too far behind me. There was a bench in front of a tiling-sealant factory. I don't know why anyone put a bench there, but I sat down gratefully, in the shade of a giant NIKE sneaker. I hate this world. NIKE. THERE IS NO FINISH LINE. Across a weed-strewn wasteland I could see Xanadu and Valhalla. One great circle. A starter pistol went off somewhere, and the sun sprang

up, running. A bird was singing—a long, human whistling note, then a
starburst of bird code at the end. Over and over. Same bird lives on Yakushima, I swear. I willed myself to get up and make it as far as Xanadu,
where I could find some air-conditioning and a place to sleep until I
could phone Shooting Star. I willed myself, but my body wouldn't move. A
white car slowed down. Beep, beep. Beepy white car. Go away. The door
opened from the inside, and the driver leaned over the passenger seat.
"Look, kid, I'm not Zizzi Hikaru but unless you know of a better offer
coming along, I suggest you climb in." An uncoupled moment as I realized
the driver was Buntaro. A haggard, stressed Buntaro. I was too drained
to even wonder how, who, when, why. I was asleep in thirty seconds.

♌

HUNGER

Mrs. Comb laid her final egg for the week, nestled it in cotton wool,
placed it in her wicker basket, and added the finishing touches to her
shopping list. Polish polish, Parmesan marzipan, toucan candles, and nit
lotion "for the muckster." A knock on her boudoir door preceded a nervous "Ahem . . ."

"Yes, sir?"

The door creaked open and Goatwriter squinted. "I believe m-mar-
ket d-day is with us again, Mrs. Comb?"

"That it is, sir. I'm off shortly to sell my eggs."

"Splendid. I, ahem, sense a dearth of stories hereabouts. I thought
perhaps you m-might take along some recent scribblings to the m-mar-
ket, and see if a storybroker comes along. You never know. Supply,
demand, and all that . . ."

"Right you are, sir." In fact Mrs. Comb doubted very much that
anyone would pay money for Goatwriter's tales in a century of Sundays,
but she slipped the stapled volume into her apron pocket so as not to
hurt his feelings. The door banged open and the wind sprang in. Pithecanthropus stood on the threshold and grunted a question to Mrs.
Comb. "Aye," she replied, "I am going now, and no, you aren't welcome.
You'll scare the customers off." Pithecanthropus grunted a request, and

opened his cupped palms to Mrs. Comb, who nearly dropped her basket in shock. "*Worms!* In my boudoir! Respectable folk live in these parts! Nobody eats worms! How dare you even think about putting those slimy articles in with my fresh eggs! Get out with you, this instant! Be off with you!"

Mrs. Comb pecked her way across the blasted heath. This land had once been lush and green, but now cauliflowers rotted in rows, trees were stripped leafless, and craters pocked the scorched earth. A pipe dribbled sewage into a mire of wire, the stench from which forced Mrs. Comb to smother her mouth with her headscarf.

Without warning, the sky screamed at the top of its lungs.

Mrs. Comb just had time to shelter her basket of eggs and cover her ears before the sonic boom hit, blowing her apron over her head and ballooning her knickerbockers. When, finally, the shock waves subsided and Mrs. Comb got to her feet, she saw a most unusual sight: a hippie and his psychedelic surfboard falling from heaven. Mrs. Comb barely had time to scramble behind a large barrel labeled AGENT ORANGE before impact. Stones and assorted crash noises showered from the crater. Mrs. Comb, too buffeted to say a word even to herself, could only watch the dust settle. She heard a loud groan. "Oh, *man* . . ." The hippie heaved himself over the edge. His dreadlocks were ginger, his sunglasses wraparound, and his halo crooked. Seeing Mrs. Comb, he made the peace sign.

"Two what?" asked Mrs. Comb, finally finding her tongue.

"Two Phantoms on a bombing raid, ma'am, they *totally* blew me away. Never even saw 'em coming. Surprised they can find anything standing to demolish."

"That was a nasty tumble you took. Is anything broken?"

"Only my pride, ma'am. A perk of immortality."

"Beg your pardon?"

The hippie swung his dreadlocks. "Name of God, ma'am."

This was becoming a very unsettling morning for a respectable old hen. Should she curtsy? "Charmed, I'm sure. But if those thundering machines are off dropping bombs, shouldn't you try and stop them?"

God wiped his halo on his shirt. "Would if I could, ma'am, but once the military decides to blast the living bejesus out of a country it takes more than divine intervention to change their minds. Time was, we had a veto on genocide, but now the generals don't even bother letting us know . . ."

"So how do wars ever get stopped?"

"That, ma'am, is one sticky spittoon of guacamole. Tell you the truth, I never wanted to be a god. My daddy insisted, and when he insisted there wasn't no arguing. I flunked the Ivy League colleges, and wound up at a divinity school in Big Sur. Surf was up, sand was golden, and oh, so were the babes, begging your pardon, ma'am. I skipped most of the seminars and just scraped by, mostly thanks to the old man's string-pulling. Only miracle I learned was the water-to-wine scam. This war zone is my first posting. *Heaven,* ma'am, is another word for nepotism, you dig? Cronies of the Almighty get the stable democracies, leaving us nobodies to stick Band-Aids over the never-ending tribal revenge tragedies and the mafia statelets. It sucks, ma'am, well and truly suck-a-roos. Say, you got the time there?"

Mrs. Comb checked her wristwatch. "Five and twenty to twelve."

"*Bonymaronie!* I gotta get my videos back to the store by noon or they'll fine me again!" God clicked his fingers, his surfboard rose from the ashes, and he leapt aboard. "Mighty fine passing the time with you, ma'am. If you run into trouble on my turf, send me a wing and a prayer, you hear?" Crouching in a kung fu position, God surfed away. Mrs. Comb watched the divinity dwindle. "Aye. Well. I won't be holding me breath."

♦

Mrs. Sasaki ladles my miso soup from the pan into a lacquer bowl. Koi-washi fish and small cubes of tofu. Anju loved koiwashi—our grandmother used to serve it this way. The miso paste swirls at the bottom, deep-sea sludge. Yellow daikon pickles, salmon rice balls wrapped in seaweed. Sheer comfort food. I exist on toast and yogurt in my capsule, assuming I get up early enough: real food is too much hassle to make. I know I should be ravenous, but my appetite is still in hiding. I eat to please Mrs. Sasaki. When my grandmother's dog Caesar was dying, he ate just to please his mistress. "Mrs. Sasaki, I have some questions."

"I imagine you do."

"Where am I?"

She passes me the bowl. "You didn't ask Buntaro?"

"Yesterday was weird all day, I wasn't thinking straight. At all."

"Well, you are staying in the house of my sister and brother-in-law."

"Are they the couple in the seashell photo above the fax?"

"Yes. I took that photograph myself. My sister is fond of it."

"Where are they now?"

"In Germany. Her books sell very well there, so her publisher flew her over for a publicity tour. Her husband is a scholar of European languages, so he burrows in university libraries while she tends to her writerly duties."

I slurp my soup. "This is good. Does your sister work in the attic?"

"I was wondering if you would find her study."

"I hope it was okay to go up there. I, uh, even began reading some stories I found on the writing desk."

"I don't think my sister would object. Unread stories aren't stories."

"She must be a special person, your sister."

"I trust you will finish those rice balls. Why do you say that?"

"This house. In Tokyo, but it feels as though it could be in a forest during the Kofun period. No telephones, no TV, no computer."

Mrs. Sasaki purses her lips when she smiles. "I must tell her that. She'll love it. My sister doesn't need a telephone—she was born deaf, you see. And my brother-in-law says the world needs less communication, not more." Mrs. Sasaki slices an orange on the chopping board, and zest stings my nostrils. She sits down. "I do not think it would be wise if you returned to Ueno. We have no proof those people or their associates are looking for you, but nor do we have any proof that they are not. I vote that we shouldn't take any risks. They knew where to find you on Friday. As a precaution, I ensured your Ueno records were misfiled. Poor Assistant Stationmaster Aoyama was the only person who might have noticed. I think you should sit tight here, until the end of the week—if anybody comes asking for you at Shooting Star, Buntaro will tell them you have left Tokyo for good. If not, the coast is clear enough."

This makes sense. "Okay."

"Worry about the future next week." Mrs. Sasaki pours the tea. "In the meantime, rest. You don't so much solve problems, as live through them."

"Please don't think I'm not grateful, Mrs. Sasaki . . ." Green tea with barley grains. "But why are you and Buntaro being so kind to me?"

"'Who' matters more than 'why.' Eat."

"I don't understand."

"No matter, Miyake-kun."

♌

The market town was a razed maze of rubble and scree. The mosque on the hill had taken a direct hit and its windows were empty sockets. The cathedral smoldered without a roof, and the dome of the synagogue had fallen in. Streetcars lay toppled. Abandoned children waited quietly to die by the roadside. White jeeps from aid organizations drove around, one nearly running over Mrs. Comb. She came to an enormous statue that reigned over the kingdom of ruin. OUR BELOVED COMMANDER, read the plaque. In his shadow, a gaunt man sizzled worms over a fire. His family watched, their eyes empty of everything but a dreadful hunger. The commander was as plump as the father was skeletal, only the commander was made of bronze. "Excuse me," asked Mrs. Comb, "but I'm looking for the marketplace."

"You're standing in it."

Mrs. Comb realized he was being serious. "This waste ground?"

"A car bomber struck last week. There is a war on."

"But surely people need to buy and sell food?"

"What food? We are under siege, if you hadn't noticed!"

"A siege?"

"They call them 'sanctions' these days."

"Fancy . . . and who is the war between?"

"No idea."

"But surely you can tell, when the soldiers fight one another?"

"The soldiers? Are you crazy? They might get hurt! They have a gentleman's agreement—never fire at a uniform. The purpose of modern warfare is to slay as many civilians as possible."

"Fancy." Mrs. Comb looked at the rubble-strewn marketplace and said something most unwise. "Looks like I won't be selling any eggs here today, anyway."

"Eggs?"

The word spilled across the gutted landscape. "Eggs!" Orphans crawled from drains. "Eggs!" Old women tapped their canes. "Eggs!" Blind pensioners appeared in doorless doorways, twisting their heads to hear better. "Eggs!" The crowd grew to a mob in a minute, encircling the statue. The gaunt man was shrieking, "They are mine! I found her first!" But nobody paid him any attention. Mrs. Comb was thoroughly disconcerted, and struggled to calm the oncoming frenzy. "Now, by gum, no need to—" The mob surged—a wall of snatching hands collapsed over Mrs. Comb, who squawked in terror as her eggs were pounded underfoot. In panic, she flapped and rose above the crowds, but she was no spring chicken and could only manage a few seconds airborne. As the only roosting site in reach was the handlebar mustache of the Beloved Commander, that was where she rested. The mob, at first, was struck dumb by Mrs. Comb's ascension. A little kid bleated out the truth Mrs. Comb longed not to hear. "She ain't no lady!"

"I most certainly am a lady!" Mrs. Comb called down from her perch. "I'll have you know my father ruled the roost!"

"Ladies don't fly! You're a *hen*!"

A new word devoured the hungry town. Not *eggs*, not even *hen*, but "Chicken! Chicken! Chicken!"

◆

Later the same day. The doorbell chimes and my heart coils up again. I put the manuscript down. Not Buntaro, not Mrs. Sasaki? I am up in the attic study, but I hear a key turned in the front door. An intruder with a skeleton key? I am not imagining it this time—I am learning the silences that fill this house, and I know what is in my head and what is not—there, the door swings open, feet in the entrance hall. "Miyake! Relax! This is Yuzu Daimon! Come out, come out, wherever you are! Your landlord gave me the key." We meet on the stairs. "You look better than when I last saw you," I say. "Not hard," he replies. "But you look even worse.

Sheesh! They did that to your eye?" His T-shirt reads "Whoever dies with the most stuff wins." "I came to bring you my apology. I thought I could chop off my little finger."

"What would I do with your little finger?" I sound sulky.

"Whatever. Pickle it, keep it in an enameled casket: ideal for picking your nose in polite society. What a conversation piece: 'It formerly belonged to the notorious international playboy Yuzu Daimon, you know.'"

"I'd rather use my own finger, thanks. And"—I wave my hand, vaguely—"going back was my decision, not yours."

"Oh well, I bought you ten packs of cigarettes to tide you over," he says. I see he is still unsure whether or not I want to lash out at him. "If I had to cut off a finger every time I needed to apologize, I'd be up to my shoulder blade by now. Marlboros. I remembered you smoked Marlboros in the pool hall on the fateful night. And your landlord thought you might like your guitar to keep you company, so I brought it over. I left it down in the entrance hall. How do you feel?" How do I feel? Weird, but not angry. "Thanks," I say. He shrugs. "Well, considering . . ." I shrug. "The garden is good for smoking."

Once I begin—from the point where I loaded him into the taxi—I cannot stop until the end, the point where Buntaro loaded me into his car. I can't remember talking so long, ever. Daimon never interrupts, except to light our cigarettes and to get a beer from the fridge. To my surprise, I even find myself telling him about my father and why I came to Tokyo in the first place. When I finally finish the sun has gone. "What amazes me," I say, "is that none of what happened has been reported. How can forty people get killed—not quietly, either, but action-movie deaths—and it not be reported?"

"Yakuza wars make the police look useless and the politicos look corrupt. Which, as everybody knows, is true. But if the authorities admit it, the voters of Tokyo may be prompted to wonder why they bother paying taxes at all. So it gets kept off TV."

"But the newspapers?"

"Their pet journalists are fed reports of battles already won and lost higher up the mountainside. Original, story-sniffing journalists get black-listed from news conferences, so newspapers can't keep them. Subtle, isn't it?"

"Then why bother with the news at all?"

"People want their comic strips and bedtime stories. Look . . . a dragonfly. The old poet-monks used to know what week of what month it was, just by the color and sheen of dragonflies'—howd'yacall'em?—fuselages." Daimon plays with his lighter. "Did you tell your landlord the same full, uncut director's version of the other night that you just told me?"

"I toned down the violence. I also left out the death threats to his wife, since the man who made them is . . . dead. I still don't know what is right, and what will give him nightmares and paranoia."

Daimon nods. "Do you dream about it?"

"I don't sleep much." I open a can of beer. "What are your plans?"

"My dad thinks I should disappear for a while, and for once we agree. I'm going back to the States in the morning. With my wife."

I splurt out beer. "You're *married*? Since when?"

Daimon looks at his watch. "Five hours ago."

This is Daimon's sincere smile. I only see it once, and only for a moment.

"Miriam? Kang Hyo Yeoun?"

The smile is put away. "Her real name is Min. A queen with sharp teeth from precolonial Korea, apparently. There is stuff about her I can't tell you, but we figured we owe you her real name. I gather she administered you her famous kick."

"I sewed them back on. Min? Her name never stays the same."

"It will from now on."

We clink cans. "Congratulations. Quick, uh, wedding."

"That is the point of clandestine marriage and elopement."

"I got the impression that you hated each other."

"Hate." Daimon examines his hands. "Love."

"Do your parents know?"

"They've lived separately for ten years—always very respectably, of course. But they kind of forfeited their rights to advise me on . . ." Daimon plays with his lighter. ". . . relationship matters."

"But you think your marriage is . . . wise."

"I think it is one of the most unwise things I have ever done."

I do not understand. "Shouldn't you be with, uh, Min-san?"

"Yes. I need to be leaving to pick up our air tickets. But before I go, will you show me the photograph of your father?" I unfold it from my wallet. He studies it closely, but shakes his head. "Sorry, I never saw the guy. But listen, I'll ask my dad if he can't find out the contact details of the detective Morino was in the habit of using. Yakuza usually use the same one or two trusted people. I can't promise—the police department at City Hall is in pandemonium, nobody knows who's in bed with whom, and Tsuru is apparently back from Singapore, minus chunks of his memories and sanity, but maybe useful as a figurehead. But I can promise to try. After that you'll be on your own, but at least you may have a lead to a Plan B."

"Plan G, or F, maybe. Any lead is better than no lead."

We go to the entrance hall. Daimon puts on his sandals. "Well then."

"Well then. Enjoy your honeymoon."

"That is what I like about you, Miyake."

"What is?"

He climbs into his Porsche, and gives me a quarter-wave.

Back on the balcony step I light another cigarette. The box of Marlboros is way too heavy. I look inside and find Yuzu Daimon's platinum lighter. One side is inscribed: *To General MacArthur on occasion of seventy-first birthday, January 1951, from Aichi Citizens Repatriation Committee— Earnest Beseech to Assist Countrymen Captured USSR.* So the lighter really was the real thing! It must be worth—what?—a lot. Way too much for me to accept. I go back to the entrance hall and peer through the front door, but Daimon is gone. The sound of his sports car is swallowed by the streets. I work out the meaning with an English dictionary from the attic. Giving me this is more of an apology than cutting off a little finger. I wonder how many Aichi citizens ever made it back to their parents.

♌

"Truss the chicken!" cried one section of the mob. "Cut off the drumsticks and roll 'em in herbs!" howled another. "Stuff her with breadcrumbs an' roast her with spuds!" How Mrs. Comb wished Pithecanthropus would rescue her, even if her suspicion that his hair harbored lice and fleas proved correct in the process. A line of starving choirboys sang "Chicken nuggets!" as if their lives depended on their performance. A ladder appeared, and Mrs. Comb realized that soon her refuge would become a trap. How could Goatwriter possibly cope without her? His shirts would be crumpled, and in time he would starve, too. That was when Mrs. Comb remembered the book Goatwriter had given her. "Hold your horses!" she cried, "and you'll sup on something more nourishing than stringy old poultry!"

The mob paused.

Mrs. Comb waved the holy book at them. "Stories!"

"Stories never filled *my* belly," someone called. The ladder moved nearer.

"You never heard the right ones, is why! Listen!" Mrs. Comb turned to page one, wishing Goatwriter's handwriting wasn't so spidery. "'A tightrope artist walked across a high wire. A silent cataract thundered below. Walking on the wire toward him came a girl with eyes as near as Saturn, who asked him: "Do you believe in ghosts?" The tightrope artist frowned, and replied, "I couldn't say, miss. Do you believe in ghosts?" She said, "Of course," and disappeared.'" A cobblestone missed Mrs. Comb by an inch. "I'm still hungry!" howled a wolfman in sackcloth, and the ladder was propped up against the knees of the Beloved Commander. "Wait," gulped Mrs. Comb, "wait! Listen to one more!" She lost her place and turned to page nine. "'Father! Father! Why hast thou forsaken me?'"

The noon sun browned.

A spectral hush fell to Earth.

The mob grew silent—then nervous—and suddenly screamed with hysteria. "Phantoms!" Men, women, and children drained away down cracks and culverts. In half a minute Mrs. Comb was left alone on the Beloved Commander, surveying a marketplace empty but for rubble and the body of a black marketeer whose skull had been staved by a loose cobblestone. "Goodness gracious," Mrs. Comb remarked.

"Great balls of fire!" added God, levitating on his surfboard. "Ma'am."

"God?"

"That is my name, salvation's the game."

"I called you?"

"This here neighborhood ain't what it once was, ma'am. What say I give you a lift somewhere?"

Mrs. Comb realized she was saved. "I'd thank you kindly if you'd take me back to the Venerable Bus. Nothing but a pack of cannibals in these parts, God, nothing but hairless savages."

"They are just hungry, ma'am, very hungry. Jump aboard and hold on tight." Mrs. Comb tightened her headscarf and wondered why human beings despise what is beautiful and good, and seek to destroy the things they need the most. She could not understand it. She could not begin to understand.

◆

Another two or three days of nothing weather. I spend them the same way. I get up late, smoke in the garden, and make some tea and toast. I watch my black eye dapple lighter. I clean up the living room and the kitchen, hide my trash and the more obvious evidence of my presence, and go up to the attic to read. I feel safest up here. I read detective stories by Kogoro Akechi. I read *Kitchen* by Banana Yoshimoto. I read *The Makioka Sisters* by Junichiro Tanizaki. I read a novel by Philip K. Dick about a parallel universe where Japan and Germany won the Second World War, in which an author writes a novel about a parallel universe where America and Britain won. I read *No Longer Human* by Osamu Dazai, which we were supposed to read at school but which I never did. Anju was the reader, never me. Looking back, I was jealous of her books for the hours she gave them. And at high school we had those Japanese classes designed to maim the fun of reading, with all those questions such as *Indicate the word most appropriately describing the emotion we experience when we read the following: "The mournful cries of the seagulls were borne over the waves as my father set sail for the final time." a] nostalgic. b] poignant. c] wistful. d] esoteric. e] heartful.* "We." I hated those classes more than anything else at high school, which is saying a lot.

Who is this "We" jerk-off anyway? I never met him, but the books and teachers made me feel as if there was something wrong with me if I disagreed with "We." This morning I am reading a French novel called *Le Grand Meaulnes*. I am fat on books. For snacks between meals I read the Goatwriter stories by Mrs. Sasaki's sister. There are dozens of them. Mrs. Sasaki says her sister wrote them for her nephew, Buntaro, when he was a little boy—Buntaro had a childhood? Weird. Now she writes them to warm up in the morning. Reading is hungry work. When I feel like lunch I go down to the kitchen and eat some food from the fridge, and an apple or banana. Afterward I trawl the pond for fallen leaves with a big net, and feed the fish. Then I go back up to the attic to read some more until it gets dark. I tape blackout paper to the triangular window, and play my guitar—very quietly, in case somebody hears—until Buntaro or Mrs. Sasaki comes. We eat together and chat—nobody has come looking for me at either Shooting Star or Ueno, so far. After supper, I lock, bolt, and chain the door, do push-ups and sit-ups, and take a shower. I still sleep downstairs on the sofa, where I stand a good chance of hearing intruders before they get to me. I carry on reading until the early hours, and finally fall asleep. My dreams are shallow, floating dreams, zoom lenses, parked cars, people who smile knowingly at me . . .

I can smell again. I never noticed smells so much as now. I remap the house, this time in smells. The living room is polish, tatami, incense. The kitchen is cooking oil, stainless steel, hard currants. The main bedroom is linen, jasmine, varnish. The garden is leaf juice, pond life, and smoke tufts. This house is so quiet. The slightest noise is as impossible to ignore as the shrillest cell-phone conversation on a commuter submarine. I hear things I never normally notice. Fluids through my tubes, my joints as I climb the shelves, the vibrations of cars, crows and doors several streets away, a fly on a windowpane, a futon being beaten.

The fax machine beeps. I put down *Le Grand Meaulnes*, go downstairs, and find the fax lying on the floor. MIYAKE. MORINO'S DETECTIVE WILL RECEIVE MAIL SENT TO ADDRESS BELOW. BE CAUTIOUS. DO NOT GIVE ADDRESS UNTIL SURE OK. WE BOARD FLIGHT 30 MINS. HOPE YOU FIND THE MAN. A post office box in Edogawabashi follows. I write the address down on a cigarette box flap, hide it in my wallet, and set the fax alight in an ashtray with General Douglas MacArthur's lighter. This is an overdramatic act, in a Ken Takakura movie sort of way, but I like flames. I glance up at the photo of Mrs. Sasaki's sister. The wine in her glass is cool and scents the air. "So," she says, "what happens in the next chapter?"

♌

WITCH SHROUDS

Pithecanthropus peered from his undercarriage hammock. The Venerable Bus was on its night journey. White lines sped from the blurry darkness ahead vanished toward the distant past. Pithecanthropus loved the lullaby swing of his hammock and the fingers of the headwind stroking his fur. A piebald rabbit, headlit and hypnotized, hurtled unharmed beneath the wheels, and its nose nearly touched Pithecanthropus's proboscis. "Hot diggity!" thought the rabbit, finding itself alive after all. "The angel of death is one dingo-ugsome critter! Wait until I tell my relatives!" By and by, Pithecanthropus yawned and slid down inside his hammock again, settling in the sediment of wishbones, flat batteries, oily rags, and Stilton rind. His final thought was that it was not the Venerable Bus that moved over the Earth, but the Earth that spun beneath the vehicle's four ancient, spinning, yet stationary wheels.

The bumps of Mrs. Comb's vacuum cleaning in her boudoir, directly above his hammock, awoke Pithecanthropus several hours later. The Venerable Bus's journey had come to an end as the new day dawned. Without stirring, Pithecanthropus could tell they had parked somewhere hot from the aroma of dry-roasted locusts. He crawled out and got to his feet in an ocher desert of pebbles, boulders, and bones. The sun's naked eyeball stared unblinkingly from a pink-dry sky. The desert wind stirred but did not cool the heat. Unswerving as an algebraic constant, the road ran to its vanishing point. Pithecanthropus flexed his mighty biceps, drummed his triple-barreled triceps, and bellowed his morning roar. Mrs. Comb shook the crumbs from the breakfast tablecloth, muttering, as she did every morning, "Must we put up with that ungodly racket *every* morning?" Goatwriter appeared on the steps and climbed down to the baked earth. "Good m-morning." Pithecanthropus bowed shyly to Mrs. Comb and grunted a greeting and a question to Goatwriter. "I believe," the latter replied, "that we have arrived in the Northern Territories, but of Terra Australis or M-mars I cannot be sure. If one consults Sir Joseph Banks's magnum—"

Goatwriter never finished his sentence because a maelstrom of feathers arose from nowhere, engulfed the Venerable Bus, and deprived the writer of the power of speech. Moogurning, phewlitting, macawbering, hallucinogenic birds, many unseen since the days when mythology was common gossip. Mrs. Comb dived for cover under the steps. Pithecanthropus lost his vision in the winged rhythms, and glimpsed his childhood in fossilized forests. Goatwriter was identifying and classifying: "*Archaeopteryx* . . . Thewlicker's goose . . . *Quetzalcoatlus* . . . Greater hopeless auks . . . Nightjars at noon . . ." He closed his eyes and a druggy smile encircled his face. "Fragments . . . I hear fragments . . ." Time spun for a time, until the birds vanished thitherly as suddenly as hitherly. "Extra*ordinary* avifauna!" declared Goatwriter, once he had relocated his tongue. "Come out, Mrs. Comb, the coast is clear! D-do you know, I heard fragments of the truly untold tale? The birds were singing it to me! Excuse m-me, friends, but I m-must repair to m-my writing bureau without further d-delay!"

♦

I sit at the writing bureau with a fresh sheet of paper, and for a moment the page is perfect. The photograph of my father is open on the bureau too. How do you write a letter to a real live private detective? *Dear Sir, you don't know me, but*—rejected. *Dear Sir, I am the late Mr. Morino's personal assistant, and I am writing to ask for a replacement*—rejected. *Dear Sir, my name is Eiji Miyake*—*you spied on me not so long ago for*— rejected. I decide to be uncunning and brief. *Sir: please send a copy of the ID file on Eiji Miyake to Box 333 Tokyo Evening Mail. Thank you.* If it works, it works; if it fails, nothing I could say would have persuaded him anyway. I go back down to the garden and burn the three drafts—if Buntaro or Mrs. Sasaki found out, they would tell me I am insane for seeking out anyone connected with Morino, and of course they would be quite right. But surely, if the detective posed a threat we would know about it by now. He sifted through my capsule for Morino, so he knows where to find me. I put the note into an envelope, address and seal it. That was the easy part. Now I have to go out and post it.

I pull my baseball cap down low, take the key from the hook by the door, and put my shoes on. I raise the latch on the main gate, and enter the real world. No brakes. No mysterious cars. Just a quiet, residential street, built down a sedate slope. All the houses are set back from the road behind high fences with automatic gates. Several have video cameras. Each property probably costs more than a whole village in Yakushima. I wonder if Ai Imajo lives in this sort of street, with that sort of bedroom window, behind that sort of hedge. I hear a girl laughing, and from out of an alley flies a junior high school kid on a bike with his girl standing on the rear wheel spindles. "What a *gross* story!" she repeats, over and over, laughing and flicking back her hair. "*Gross!*"

The slope leads to a busy main road, lined with stores. All motion and noise, every vehicle a mission. I feel as though I am a ghost revisiting a place where I was never particularly happy. I pass a supermarket where mangos and papayas lie exquisitely ribboned. Kids play tag in the aisles. In the supermarket parking lot the men watch TV in their cars. A pregnant girl—my age—walks along, hands on her hump. Builders clamber along girders, a blowtorch hisses magnesium. I pass a kindergarten—children in color-coded hats run along paths of Brownian motion. What is Tokyo for? I haven't decided. I feel uneasy trusting in my anonymity. Nobody stops and points; no traffic crashes; no birds fall out of the sky; no "Hey! Look! There's that kid who witnessed thirty or more men get blown away by gangsters three or four nights ago!" Do soldiers feel this, when they get back from a war? The utter weirdness of utter normality. The post office is full of babies bawling and pensioners staring into inner distance. I wait my turn, looking at the "Have you seen this person?" posters of society's number-one enemies, with the plastic-surgery faces they are fancied to have adopted. "Do not attempt to apprehend these criminals. They may be armed and dangerous." The person behind nudges me. The assistant asks for the third or fourth time. "Yes, sir?"

"Uh, I'd like to mail this, please."

I pay, she gives me my stamps and change, then addresses the customer behind me. It is true. What happened to me last Friday night is locked inside my head, and nothing shows on my face. I lick the stamps, stick them on, and balance the envelope on the lip of the box. Is this wise? I let the letter go, it falls with a papery slap. When did "wise" ever come into it? Onward, Plan G. I look up into the eye of a video camera. Outside, the air is heavier and gustier than it was, and swallows are diving low. Another video camera watches the supermarket parking lot. Yet another is mounted on the bridge to meditate on passing traffic. Who watches for what, and why? I hurry back.

Evening brings rain in slow motion. I am up in the attic. The paper turned white to blue and now is nearly as gray as the ink, but I am content just to sit here and watch the watercourses trickle down the windowpanes. In Yakushima they boast about the rain. Uncle Pachinko says it rains thirty-five days per month. Here in Tokyo, when did it last rain? That summer storm, on the day of my stakeout. I was such a holy fool. What if my father really has no interest in even meeting me? What if he is a yakuza man too? Sometimes the watercourses follow the one before, other times they split off. Then my father owes it to me to tell me himself. His job—his way of life, even—is not the point. In the street outside, the cars of ordinary husbands swish by on their way to ordinary homes. A car cuts its engine outside, and my sense of peace drains away. I peer through the triangular window: Buntaro's beat-up old Honda. Here comes my savior, leaping the flooding drain, covering his bald patch with a newspaper.

♌

Goatwriter sat at his writing bureau, watching the perfect sentences orbit inches above his head, waiting for him to pin them onto paper with his brush. Which was . . . where? Goatwriter looked for his brush. "Most odd," he thought, "I quite clearly remember placing it on my blotter when I heard Pithecanthropus yawning . . ." He searched for it in the places it should be, then might be, and then could not possibly be. Only one conclusion remained. "Thief!" cried Goatwriter. "Thief! Thief!" Mrs. Comb was by his side in a semijiffy. "Let me explain once more, sir. Your snack paper goes in this tray, here, but your writings and what-not go in—" Goatwriter shook his head. "No, Mrs. Comb! It is not my manuscript that has gone missing this time, but my writing brush! Yes, the selfsame brush Lady Shonagon used to write her pillow book, thirteen thousand crescent m-moons ago! The tongue of m-my imagi-nation! The vocal cords of m-my inspiration, without which m-my career is over, m-moreover! I am doomed! The critics will d-de-re-un-in(con)struct me!" Pithecanthropus grunted a question. "The thief surely struck while the d-deployed birds d-decoyed our suspicions!" Mrs. Comb tightened her apron strings. "Never fear, sir, we found us a thief before and we'll find us one again, shan't us, you?" Pithecanthropus was so pleased to be addressed directly by Mrs. Comb that he grunted happily, instead of pointing out that tracking in a muddy margin was one thing, but following tracks across windy sand was an entirely different caul-dron of newts.

"As usual, Mrs. Comb"—Goatwriter forced himself to calm down—"you are right. Yes. Let us apply logic to these d-direst of straits. My writ-ing brush is missing. Where does one find pens, quills, and implements of that kidney? At the ends of sentences. The ends of lines. We m-must focus our energies on locating lines."

"Only one line out here, sir."

"Which line would that be, pray, Mrs. Comb?"

"Why, sir—the line running down the middle of the road."

Goatwriter clapped his hoofs. "Friends. Prepare for war."

Mrs. Comb was tiring and perspiring under her parasol, and worried that her next egg would be laid already hard-boiled. Pithecanthropus panted heavily. The road cooked holes in his soles. Goatwriter saw mirages of intransitive verbs freeze and melt. Pools of lead bubbled in the sand. Time relapsed and collapsed. Goatwriter dabbed his brow with his Paisley kerchief and verified that what he saw was truly true. "Aha! Friends, take heart! The white lines are veering from the road—my writing brush cannot now be far!" Mrs. Comb insisted that they stop for a predesert prickly pear dessert. Somewhat refreshed, they followed the lines into a labyrinth of boulders and crags. Reptiles dry-fried themselves on volcanic rocks. Pithecanthropus grew uneasy—something, he was sure, was watching them. He grunted nothing for fear of upsetting Mrs. Comb. "I say," said Goatwriter, at the head of the expedition. "We seem to be . . . here . . ." The three drew level at the lip of a smooth, white, steep, wide crater with a black hole in its center. "Extra*ordinary*," gasped Goatwriter, "to stumble across radiotelescope technology in this benighted desert . . ."

"You can call it a radiotellythingummyjig if you want to, sir, but I recognize a lavatory bowl when I see one. Must take a month o' Whitmondays to polish, or—"

"Keeeeeeraaaaaaaaawwwk!" For the second time that morning Mrs. Comb was interrupted by a nonexistent bird, but this one was a far nastier piece of work—an evil-eyed saw-toothed pterodactyl with a wingspan that eclipsed the sun. Goatwriter's rear was speared clear down the crater—his hoofs were unable to gain traction on the ceramic surface. Mrs. Comb swooped down on an intercept course, but, unable to pull out of her beak dive, disappeared down the black hole a moment after Goatwriter. Pithecanthropus was not afraid of anything prehistoric, or posthistoric for that matter, but when he thought of his only friend and Mrs. Comb alone in the darkness beneath his feet, his cranium throbbed with anxiety. Without another thought he tobogganed toward the bottomless blackness.

The early man's long fall was broken by tangles and meshes. Far above, a pinhole let in a ray of light. Pithecanthropus grunted. "Yes," replied Goatwriter in wobbly tones, "m-my M-Miltonic d-descent was parried by a potpourri of porous packing. Mrs. Comb? Are you within earshot?" His housekeeper clucked. "It'll take more than a tumble to knock *my* stuffing out, sir. But whatever is this cobwebby muck strung up everywhere? Where can we have landed, I wonder?"

A wall of light opened up and an aristocratic voice rang out. "Welcome to my palatial website, O Goatwriter!" A woman appeared, wearing a Technicolor crown and a power suit. "We have been expecting you." Her hair was sunshine and her lips shiny, but she seemed two-dimensional because she was. The wall was a giant screen that lit a chamber strewn with electrical cables. "My name is Queen Shrouds." Her royal smile was atomic.

"I am unfamiliar"—Goatwriter squinted—"with Your M-Majesty's empire."

"The future is my empire."

"Oh, aye?" clucked Mrs. Comb. "You and whose army?"

Queen Shrouds shone brighter. "My army is the media."

"Right grand, doubtless, but we are looking for a stolen writing brush and we have firm suspicions that it found its way down this hole."

"Indeed." Queen Shrouds deigned to glance at Mrs. Comb. "I had it stolen."

"Grand way for a queen to act," cooed Mrs. Comb. "We call the likes of you 'thief' where I come from!"

"Her Majesty neva stole it Herself, ya scraggy drumstix!" rang a rodent retort. "*I* lifted ya pen from under ya noses when Her Maj digitized da birdstorm!"

Pithecanthropus grunted in amazement. "ScatRat!" gasped Goatwriter. The felon appeared on-screen, leering and harpstringing his whiskers. "But how d-did you arrive—whence?—wherefore?—"

"Being marginalized was a drag! I been trucking along in ya rustbucket ever since da caveman trashed my ScatPad, until dis morning when Her Maj Queen Shrouds made me an offer no honest rat could refuse—I lure ya to her website, an' She uploads me. I am da world number-one CyberRat."

Goatwriter chewed his beard. "Why would you voluntarily renounce your solid state for the virtual?"

"Da whole internet is my rat run now, Beardy! I lightspeed down da cables I used to bust up ma teeth chewin'! Lettuce cut to da quick, Goatee. Queen Shrouds has granted ya dis audience two make ya da same offer."

The queen close-upped. Her kaleidoscopic eyes loomed large. "Indeed, O Goatwriter. On this side of the screen awaits the future! Paper is dead, have you not heard?" Her voice scaled operatic heights. "You shall compose your untold tales in a virtual heaven, and I, as your cyberagent—"

"Aye," pecked Mrs. Comb, "the nub!"

"Silence, hen! Goatwriter, digitize yourself to my loving embrace, and we shall iron out that troublesome speech dddddddddefect! Imagine, you uttering sentences at the speed of charged particles instead of an amputee marathon!"

Goatwriter glared. "Your imagery is tasteless. My stammer discerns my true friends from the false. I refuse!"

Queen Shrouds filed her nails. "Luddites, Luddites ev'rywhere, nor any stop to think. Then I shall digitize you anyway, RAM-raid your virtual brain, synthesize every story you could ever compose, and delete the leftover bytes with those of your tedious companions Mr. Id and Madame Ego. ScatRat! Bring the digitizer online!" The evil queen's face receded to allow space for the awesome cannon contraption ScatRat was lugging on-screen. Goatwriter struggled, but the web of cables held him fast. "Where is the fulfillment in stealing stories from another's pen?" The queen looked genuinely puzzled. "'Fulfillment'? Writing is not about 'fulfillment.' Writing is about adoration! Glamour! Awards! When I was a mere human I learned the language of writers, oh yes. I said 'conceit' instead of 'idea'; I said 'tour de force' instead of 'quite good'; I said 'cult classic!' instead of 'this trash will never sell!' Did it bring me fulfillment? No, it brought me overdrafts and obscurity! But by capturing your imagination in my motherboard, O Goateed One, the literary cosmos will be my cocktail bar! ScatRat! Get ready to fire!"

"Sir," flapped Mrs. Comb, "do something!"

Goatwriter lowered his horns. "You are forgetting one thing."

Queen Shrouds dismissed him. "On the count of three, ScatRat! One, two—"

"I will be heard! Under the riddle clause of the Evil Queen Law," Goatwriter quoted from memory, "'d-disagreements arising between evil queens and captives shall be settled by a riddle posed to the latter party by the former. Unless said riddle is executed it is illegal to store captive in any form by any m-means, electronic, m-mechanical, photocopying, recording, without prior permission of captive and captive's publishers.'"

STOP COUNTDOWN flashed on and off. The wintry iris and laser pupil of Queen Shrouds filled the screen. "O ScatRat. Say it is not so. Do." ScatRat could be heard twanging a whisker. "Just an old formality, Yer Maj! Leave it to ya evva-so-'umble. I'll zip two insolvableriddles@ evilqueens.sup.org an' get da numero uno brainshredda! Relax! Feta cheese is in da bag!" The queen frowned, and uttered, "Make it so!" She closed her eyes in cyberdelectation. "And then his soul," gassy colors popped and fused, "stories," she tossed back her head, "and book deals in ninety-nine languages will be mine! Mine!" Her laughing mouth plunged the website into bucking bronchial blackness. "Miiiiiiiiine!"

◆

I finish my noodles first, so I broach the subject. "Buntaro, I need to talk about money." Buntaro fishes for tempura batter. "What money?" Exactly. "Rent for next month. I dunno how to tell you this, but . . . I don't have it. Not now that the money from Ueno will stop. I know this is a lot to ask, but could you take it out of my deposit?" Buntaro looks worried— about me, or the elusive tempura? I go on. "I am really ashamed, after everything you and Mrs. Sasaki have done for me. But you should know now, so, if, I dunno, if you wanted to give me my marching orders, I mean I would understand, really . . ."

"Got you!" Buntaro holds up the shrimp between his chopsticks and delicately nibbles its head off. "The wife had a better idea, kid. She wants a vacation before she gets too pregnant for the airlines to let her fly. You know, we got to thinking how long it has been since we took a week off together. Guess how long?" I shake my head. "Never! Literally, never. Before I took over Shooting Star we were always too broke, and since then—well, a video store can never sleep. When I work, she rests; when she works, I rest. Nine years have gone by like that. She phoned around a few hotels in Okinawa this morning—off-season, loads of cheap deals. So, our proposal is this: you look after the store next week, and that can take care of rent for October."

"*All* of October?"

"The working hours are brutal, be warned—ten A.M. to midnight, seven days. Added up, it comes to a poor hourly rate. But it would give you a breathing space to land another job."

"You would really leave me in charge of the store?"

"No Al Pacino look-alike has come around asking for you. Hiding here was wise, but you can come out now."

"No, I mean—would you trust me with your, uh, business?"

"My wife does, so I do. And I got a glowing reference from your previous employer." Buntaro starts toothpicking. "Running the store is easy—I can teach you everything in thirty minutes. And my mom will drop by every evening to pick up the cash and do the accounts. What do you say? Do I tell my wife to book our hotel in our subtropical paradise of American heliports and guides whose makeup never runs?"

"Of course. Sure. Thank you."

"No need to, kid. This is business. Let's smoke a Marlboro on the step to seal a mutually beneficial package. But don't tell my wife. I'm supposed to be quitting in time for Kodai's grand opening." We go outside and get through most of a packet, listening to the frogs and the rain in the pond. The rain and smoke keep the mosquitoes away. "By the way," says Buntaro, "does the name Ai Imajo happen to mean anything to you?"

I scratch the back of my head and nod.

"Friend or foe?"

"Friend, I hope. Why?"

"Apparently she appeared at Ueno lost property this morning to report a lost Eiji Miyake. My mother said you had left Tokyo unexpectedly for family reasons. The young lady made a 'nice of him to let me know!' face, thanked my mother, and went away." I stay poker-faced because I know my landlord is watching from the corner of his eye. "Well." Buntaro gets to his feet. "I'll go and tell my wife our good news." I walk through with him to the entrance hall. Buntaro pretends to check for dust. "I must say, you keep this place neat as a palace. Neater than your luxury penthouse, anyway." He slaps his shirt pocket and takes something out. "I am a dolt! I forgot. This pictogram thing came for you today. Well. Sleep tight and pleasant dreams." When Buntaro has gone I take the pictogram into the living room and inspect it by the lamplight. *Nagano, Mountain Paradise.* Something tells me Buntaro's memory lapse was no accident—this is from my mother, forwarded by Aunt Yen. I sit down and balance it on my knee. It hardly weighs a thing, but it weighs so much. Skies gray with snow, mountainsides pink with cherry blossom, snow turquoise with sky, happy hikers, happy skiers. More intimate blame-shifting revelations.

The creator of Goatwriter looks down at me. I cannot see her eyes but I can hear her voice. "I don't think you're being very fair to her." I scowl at her. "You know, we are all of us writers, busy writing our own fictions about how the world is, and how it came to be this way. We concoct plots and ascribe motives that may, or may not, coincide with the truth." I scowl at the envelope, wondering. "Take your mother. You write her part for her. Have you ever wondered how she writes her part? Go on. Open it now. Spare us further agony." Just like Mrs. Sasaki, the author is sympathetic and stern in equal measures. I flick the envelope with my finger, moodily, over and over. "Ah," she sighs, and the drowsy sea in the background sighs too, "the young."

♌

Pithecanthropus, meanwhile, had slipped from the wired jungle and was exploring the edges of the cavernous website. He noticed that all the cables led to a single giant plug. Resting on this plug, hidden in a rack of Phillips screwdrivers, Pithecanthropus, with his keen eyes, made out Goatwriter's beloved writing brush. He stowed it in the waxy hair above his ear, and made his way back to the screen when he heard TV orchestra music announce ScatRat's return. The rodent was dressed in a glittering quizmaster jacket, clutching an envelope marked "Million Dollar Riddle." Queen Shrouds hissed in anticipation. "Let us be quite clear. When you fail to answer, your copyright reverts to me."

Mrs. Comb clucked. "When Sir answers right, we go free—with Sir's pen."

Queen Shrouds ignored her. "ScatRat—let the riddling commence!"

ScatRat slit the envelope with a fang. Drum rolls cued from hidden speakers. "What, pray, is da most mathematical animal in da universe?"

Mrs. Comb tutted. "Well, what kind of a daft question is that?"

ScatRat slurped his side of the screen in a most disgusting manner. "Ya got sixty seconds, Goatee! Go!" A stopwatch appeared in the corner and countdown music began. Goatwriter chewed his beard. "Let me see now . . . the most mathematical animal . . . well, the case for humans is fatally undermined by their television . . . Dolphins excel in the brain weight/body weight means test. . . . However, no cleverer Euclidean geometrician exists than the bolas spider . . . Yet what of the scallop's knowledge of Cartesian oval lenses? Oh . . . crikey . . . what can the answer be?" Only fifteen seconds remained, and Queen Shrouds and ScatRat were already dancing a celebratory rumba. "I can see the rapturous reviews!" The queen clapped gleefully. "Taste the publishers' lunches!" Desperately, Mrs. Comb searched in her handbag for an inspirational snack but all she found was an old chestnut. Pithecanthropus chose that moment to tap Mrs. Comb's wing and show her Goatwriter's writing brush. In the glare of the screen, however, Mrs. Comb's sharp eyes spotted the focus of her loathing jump between the primitive ancestor's eyebrows. "Fleas!" she shrieked. "Fleas!"

Queen Shrouds's rumba halted. "I beg your pardon?"

Goatwriter clopped his hoofs. "By jiminy, yes! Of course, the most mathematical animal is the flea!"

ScatRat's leer disappeared. "Ya gotta say why or it don't count!"

"Ahem." Goatwriter allowed himself a faint smile. "Fleas subtract from happiness, divide attention, add to miseries, and multiply alarmingly."

ScatRat gazed up at his screen idol. "Some ya win, Yer Maj, some ya—" Queen Shrouds muted him with a doubleclick of her fingers. "You corrupted, bugged cybervermin, only one punishment fits this crime!" ScatRat's "noooooooooo" diminished in volume as he was dragged to the recycle bin where all his ones were zeroed. The queen turned her furious gaze to Goatwriter. Gigabytes crackled. "And if you think, O Billy Goat, some legal-eagle babble prevents a real live witch"—Mrs. Comb gasped as the queen tossed away her crown and resumed her hideous cronehood—"yes, Witch Shrouds herself, from seizing the object of her desires, then even for a creator of fiction you are cretinous beyond belief!" She primed the on-screen digitizer. "Five . . . four . . . three . . . two . . ."

Pithecanthropus pulled the plug on the project. The system crashed and the website of the witch vanished as if it had never existed, which in a sense it hadn't, for Goatwriter, Mrs. Comb, and Pithecanthropus found themselves sitting in the sun-blasted desert, too astonished to utter a syllable.

♦

September 20
A ski resort town in the Nagano mountains

Eiji,

If you tried to contact me after I sprung myself from the clinic in Miyazaki, it was sweet of you, but I couldn't stay there any longer. Anywhere on Kyushu is too close to Yakushima for comfort. (If you didn't, I don't blame you. I didn't expect you to.) I may have problems but the patients there were so scary I figured I'd take my chances back in the big bad world. (At least they give you knives and forks out here.) Burn the last letter I wrote. Burn it, please, I won't ask you for a single thing but I'm asking you to do this. The only thing Dr. Suzuki made me realize is that there comes a point in your life, and when you pass this point you can't change. You are what you are, for better or worse, and that is that. I shouldn't have told you about the stairs incident. You must hate me. I would. Sometimes I honestly do. Hate myself, I mean. Be careful of counselors, therapists, head doctors. They poke around, and take things to bits without thinking about how they'll put it all back together. Burn the letter. Letters like that shouldn't exist. (Especially on Yakushima.) Burn it.

So here I am in Nagano. What sunsets they make in these mountains! The hotel is at the foot of Mount Hakuba and the view from my room is swallowed up by the mountain. It needs a different word to describe it every day. You should visit Nagano, someday. In the Edo period all the missionaries from the capital used to "summer" up here. I suppose we have the missionaries to thank for naming these mountains the "Japan Alps." Why do people always have to compare things with abroad? (Like Kagoshima, the Naples of Japan—that always sets my teeth on edge.) Nobody knows what the locals used to call the mountains before anyone knew the Alps, or even Europe, was out there. (Am I the only one who thinks this is depressing?) I'm

staying as a nonpaying guest in a small hotel opened by someone I knew from my days in Tokyo, years and years ago, after I
left you to the tender mercies of your grandmother. He is a big-
shot hotelier now, quite respectable, except for two very expensive divorces, which I'm sure he deserved, just as he deserves
his success now. (He changed before he reached that critical
point where your life is set in concrete.) He wanted me to help
scout for a location for a new hotel he wants to build from
scratch, but he doesn't know how much I drink yet, or he's persuading himself he can "save" me. His favorite two words are
project and *venture*. The snows are due in early November. (Only
six weeks away. Another year on its last legs.) If I have spent the
good-old-days currency I have with my friend by winter, I may
go in search of warmer climes. (Old Chinese [or Yakushima?]
proverb: guests are like fish—after three days they begin to
stink.) I hear Monte Carlo is pleasant for "wintering." I hear
Prince Charles of England may be available.

I had a dream about Anju last night. Anju, a Siberian tiger
running past me in an underpass (I knew it was Siberian because the yellow stripes were white), and a game where you had
to hide a bone egg in a library. Anju won't leave me alone. I paid
a priest a fortune to perform rites for her soul, but now I
think that I should have spent the money on French wine, for all
the good it did. I never dream about you, in fact I never remember any of my dreams, except the Anju ones. Why is that? Dr.
Suzuki seemed to think—ah, who cares. Just burn the letter,
please.

♌

THE STUDY OF TALES

Goatwriter sat at his writing bureau and watched bats stream from the
bracken-matted dusk. Shadows danced in the forest of moss. "I declare,
I could swear . . ." Goatwriter thought. "Not like that sewer-mouthed
ScatRat, I trust, sir," replied Mrs. Comb, who was polishing the stair.

Goatwriter stroked the writing brush of Lady Shonagon, and thought ". . . in the arborescent soul, far and deep, I may glean the truly untold tale. The Venerable Bus penetrated this forest seven days ago and has not moved on. Unprecedented. What might it signify?" The evening was cooling. Mrs. Comb shivered. "Foxtrot pudding for supper, sir. You give your eyes a rest and play a nice round of Blind Man's Scrabble." She hoped they would wake up somewhere else the following morning, but doubted that they would.

The Venerable Bus had traveled nowhere that night. Pithecanthropus was on his morning dig, tunneling through creaking coal seams in search of diamonds for Mrs. Comb's birthday, for he had heard that they were a girl's best friend and might put in a word in his favor. This far down Pithecanthropus could hear the earth furnace boom and clang to its own rhythms. Hours are not found so far below the land, among troll larvae and veins of unknown metals, and Pithecanthropus lost all track of time, so he could not have said when it was that an impossibly distant voice found him at last. He strained to listen. "You hulking great lout! Where are you when I need you?" Mrs. Comb! Needing him! Pithecanthropus swam upward through the loosened earth with a mighty breaststroke, and resurfaced within sixty seconds. Mrs. Comb was flapping in circles as wildly as any headless chicken, waving a note. "Here you are at last! Muckgrubbing around in a crisis!" Pithecanthropus grunted. "Sir has upped and offed! I knew he wasn't himself last night, and this morning I find this note on the stove!" She thrust it at Pithecanthropus, who groaned—all those squiggles skidding over the paper. Mrs. Comb sighed. "Three million years you've had to learn how to read! The letter says Sir has gone into this mucky forest! Alone! He said he didn't want to drag us into anything dangerous! What if he meets a mild cannibal much less a wild animal? What if the Venerable Bus drives off tonight? We'd never see Sir again! And he forgot his asthma inhaler!" Mrs. Comb began sobbing into her apron. The sight wrung Pithecanthropus's giant heart. "First his story, then his pen, and now he's lost himself!" Pithecanthropus grunted imploringly.

"Are—are you sure? You can track Sir in this forest?"

Pithecanthropus grunted reassuringly.

◆

I hear Buntaro let himself in downstairs. "Hang on," I yell, "I'll be right down!" Two o'clock already—today is the last day of my exile. I feel tired again—it rained last night, and fat fingers kept prying me awake. I kept dreaming somebody was trying to force a window somewhere. I tidy the pages of the manuscript on the writing bureau, and pick my way between the books to the trapdoor. I shout down—"Sorry, Buntaro! I lost track of the time." I go down to the living room, where a shadow closes the door behind me. It is not Buntaro. My heart rams itself up my throat. She is a slight, severe, middle-aged woman, unafraid, curious, reading me. She is dressed in forgettable clothes, anonymous as a face in a catalog. You would pass her a hundred times and never notice her. Unless she suddenly appeared in your living room. How owlish and scarred and gray she is. Her stare goes on and on, as if she has every right to be here, and is waiting for the intruder—me—to explain himself. "Who, uh, are you?" I eventually manage.

"You invited me, Eiji Miyake." Her voice you would not forget. Cracked as cane, dry as drought. "So I came."

A passing lunatic? "But I never invited anyone."

"But you did. Two days ago you sent an invitation to my mail drop."

Her? "Morino's detective?"

"Correct. My name is Yamaya." She disarms me with a smile as friendly as a dagger thrust. "Yes, I am a woman, not a man in drag. Invisibility is a major asset in my line of work. However, discussing my modus operandi is not why you asked me to drop by, is it? I hope you will offer me a chair." All too weird. "Sure. Please sit down." Mrs. Yamaya takes the sofa, so I take the floor by the window. She has the eye of a meticulous reader, which makes me the book. She looks behind me. "Nice garden. Nice property. Nice neighborhood."

Over to me, it seems. I offer her a Marlboro from Daimon's final box, but she shakes her head. I light mine. "How did you, uh, trace me?"

"I obtained your address from the *Tokyo Evening Mail.*"

"They gave you my address?"

"No, I said I *obtained* it. I trailed Mr. Ogiso here yesterday evening to note when we could talk undisturbed."

"With respect, Mrs. Yamaya, I asked for a file, not a visit."

"With respect, Mr. Miyake, see it from my point of view. I receive a note from a mysterious nobody asking for the selfsame file I compiled for the late Ryutaro Morino three days before the night of the long knives. How coincidental. I earn a living by unpicking coincidences. Your note was a bleeding lamb tossed into a swimming pool of sharks. I had three theories—you were a potential client testing my professionalism; someone with a potentially lucrative personal interest in Eiji Miyake; or the father of Eiji Miyake himself. All three were worth a follow-up. I do so, and I discover you are the son of the father."

From the garden I hear a crow craw-crawing. I wonder what happened to Mrs. Yamaya to make her so sad but so steel-willed. "You know my father?"

"Only socially."

"Mrs. Yamaya, I would like to ask you more cleverly and indirectly, but, uh, will you please give me the file on my father?"

Mrs. Yamaya forms a cage with her long, strong fingers. "Now we have got to why I am here. Precisely. To consider this very question."

"How much money do you want?"

"Please, Mr. Miyake. You are too poor to bribe a bicycle inspector."

"Then what are we supposed to be considering? Whether or not I deserve it?"

Mrs. Yamaya's murmur could hush a stadium. "*Deserve* is a hazardous verb. It is best to leave it out of the equation."

"So what does enter the equation?"

The garden crow hops over to the balcony and peers in.

Mrs. Yamaya folds her arms. "Consequences."

The doorbell goes and I twitch—hot ash falls on my legs—and a specially rigged light strobes on and off several times, for Mrs. Sasaki's sister's deafness, I guess. I stub out my cigarette. It lies there, stubbed. The doorbell goes again—I hear a slight laugh. Mrs. Yamaya doesn't move. "Aren't you going to answer it?"

"Excuse me," I say, and she nods.

Stupidly, I am too fazed to put the chain on the door, and the two

young men seem so pleased to see me that for a moment I panic—this is
a setup organized with Mrs. Yamaya, and I've walked straight into it. "Hi
there!" they beam. Which one spoke? Immaculate white shirts, conser-
vative ties, sheeny, computer-generated hair—hardly regular yakuza
garb. They irradiate health and positive vibes. "Hello, sir! Is this a bad
time? Because we have *great* news!" They are either going to produce
guns or tell me about a spectacular discount kimono service.

"You, uh, do?" I glance behind me.

"You bet I do! You see, Lord Jesus Christ is waiting outside the door
of your heart at this very moment—he wants to know if you have a few
minutes to spare so he can tell you about the joy that will be yours if you
unlock your heart and let his love come in." I breathe sheer relief—they
take this as a "yes" and turn up their zeal volume even higher. "Your heart
seems no stranger to trouble, my friend. We are here with the Church of
Jesus Christ of Latter-day Saints—perhaps you've heard of our mission-
ary work?"

"No, no. I haven't, actually." Another stupid thing to say. When I
finally close the door—these Mormons' smiles are ironed on—holding a
brochure called "Truth" and get back to the living room, nobody is there.
I open the balcony doors, surprised. Did I imagine my grim visitor?
"Mrs. Yamaya?" The crow is gone too. Nothing but the layered buzzes
and summer creaks and hisses. A butterfly with gold-digger eyes mistakes me for a bush. I watch it, and moments telescope into minutes.
When I go back in I notice what I missed at first—a brown envelope,
lying on the sofa where Mrs. Yamaya had sat. Any brief hope that she left
me the file folder on my father is snuffed out right away—the envelope
is labeled "Tokyo Evening Mail—Correspondence Box 333." Inside is a
letter, addressed to me in the handwriting of a very old person. I sit
down and slit it open.

♌

Where mossy drapes hung so thickly that Goatwriter could hardly
advance, his feet sploshed in a babbling brook. The tea-colored stream
was clattery underhoof with dinner plates. Goatwriter lapped up a
mouthful and immediately his head cleared and spirits revived. "A
stream of consciousness!" he reJoyced. "I m-must be in the D-Darjeeling

foothills." As Goatwriter paddled upstream the moss thinned, lantern orchids lit the noon gloom, opal hummingbirds probed bleeding figs, and, far above, the forest canopy was chalk-dusted with daylight. It seemed to Goatwriter that they formed characters and words. "All m-my life," he mused, "I searched for the truly untold tale in sealed caves, in lost books of learning. Could it be that, instead, profundity is concealed in the obvious? Does the truest originality hide itself within the d-dullest cliche?" The stream led him into a glade misty with sunlight. A swinging girl with flaxen hair sang a melody with no name and no end. Goatwriter recognized her soft voice: it was that of the whisperings, heard by the old goat nightly since midsummer. "You wish to find the truly untold tale?" She swung up.

"Yes," replied Goatwriter.

"The untold tales hide in the highlands." Ursa Minor rose above the horizon.

"How m-might I find these highlands?" Orion descended to its sword.

"Around the bend, to the sacred pool, up the wall, and over the wall." The girl with the flaxen hair swung up. "Are you prepared to pay?"

"I have been paying all m-my life."

"Ah, but Goatwriter—you have not paid everything yet."

"What can be left to pay, pray?"

When the swing fell again it was empty.

Goatwriter arrived at the sacred pool, and removed his glasses to wipe away the waterfall spray, but to his surprise he could see better without them. So he left them on the rock and pondered the peculiar pool. The waterfall did not fall from the precipice high above but ascended in a giddied, foaming, lurching—and silent—torrent. Up the sheer face of the rock, Goatwriter saw no path. For a moment, he considered turning back. Mrs. Comb would be distraught if he failed to return. He thought to himself: "I'm not a kid anymore. Pithecanthropus will take care of her. I am getting too old for symbolic quests." The writer within the animal sighed, and jumped from the marble rock. The pool was as cold and sudden as death itself will doubtless be.

♦

Wednesday, September 20
Tokyo

Dear Eiji Miyake,

I hope you will forgive the sudden and possibly intrusive nature of this letter. Quite possibly, moreover, you and its intended recipient are not the same person, which would cause considerable embarrassment. Nonetheless, I feel it is a risk worth taking. Permit me to explain.

I am writing in response to an advertisement that appeared in the personal column of the *Tokyo Evening Mail* of September 14. The advertisement was brought to my attention only this morning by a visiting acquaintance. I should perhaps explain I am recovering from an operation to the valves in my heart. You appealed for any relatives of Eiji Miyake to respond. I believe I may be your paternal grandfather.

Two decades ago my son sired a pair of illegitimate twins—a boy and a girl. He broke relations with their mother, a woman of lowly occupation, and, as far as I know, never saw his twins again. I do not know where the children were brought up, nor by whom—the mother's people, one can only presume. The girl apparently drowned in her eleventh year, but the boy would now be twenty. I never knew their mother's name, nor did I see a picture of my illegitimate grandchildren. Relations with my son have never been as cordial as one would wish, and since his marriage we have corresponded ever less. I did, however, discover the names of the twins he fathered: hence this letter. The girl's name was Anju, and the boy's name is Eiji, written not in the commonplace manner (the kanji for "intelligent" plus "two" or "govern"), but with highly unusual kanji for "incant" and "world." I see your name is formed from the same kanji. Hence this letter.

I shall be brief for the reason that the "evidence" of the kanji remains inconclusive. A face-to-face meeting, I believe, will clarify this ambiguity. If we are related, I believe points of physical resemblance will be self-evident. I shall be at Amadeus Coffee Shop, on the ninth floor of the Righa Royal Hotel (opposite Harajuku Station), on Monday, September 25, at a table reserved in my name. Please present yourself at 10 A.M., with any evidence, documentary or otherwise, of your parentage that you may possess.

I trust you appreciate the sensitive nature of this matter, and will understand my reluctance to provide you with contact details at this time. Should you be another Eiji Miyake with identical kanji, please accept my sincerest apologies for raising your hopes unnecessarily. Should you be the same Eiji Miyake who I earnestly hope you are, we have many matters to discuss.

Yours faithfully,
Takara Tsukiyama

I feel clean and clear and happy. My grandfather wrote a letter to me. Imagine, meeting my grandfather as well as my father. "We have many matters to discuss"! Here I was, despairing at the impossibility of it all, when contacting my father really was as straightforward as I always hoped. Monday—only two days away! My grandfather writes with an educated, authoritative language—surely he holds more sway over family politics than my paranoid stepmother. I make myself a green tea and take it into the garden to smoke a Kent, Buntaro's brand of choice now that all the Marlboros are gone. Tsukiyama—cool name—is written with the kanji for "moon" and "mountain." The garden is all beauty, rightness, and life. I wish Monday could start in fifteen minutes. What is the real time? I go back in and check the clock that Mrs. Sasaki brought me midweek. Still three hours until Buntaro gets here. My absentee host in her seashell frame catches my eye. "So, your luck has turned, at last. Call Ai Imajo. It was her idea to place the personal ad, remember? Go on. Shyness at the break of day is attractive in a way, but shyness buried in its shell will never serve you very well."

"Was that supposed to rhyme?"

"Stop changing the subject! You are worse than your sister some-times. Go out and find a telephone."

Supermarket row is no different since my last visit, but I am. The world is an ordered flowchart of subplots, after all. Look at all these cars—driving past and never colliding. The order is difficult to see, but it is here, under the chaos. So, I lived through twelve hellish hours—so? People live through twelve hellish years and live to tell the tale. Life goes on. Luckily for us. I find a phone booth under the emergency stairs in a Uniqlo. As cell phones take over the world these old-fashioned booths will become as rare as gaslights. I pick up the receiver—but I am sud-denly frozen by the dread that all the conversations I have had with her in my imagination will now, right now, be proved to be the self-delusions of a boy from a muddy island so backward we still—as my trendy Money cousins joke—buy brides with barrels of daikon pickles. I replace the receiver. You coward, Miyake! I decide to get a haircut before I talk with Ai. You spineless worm, Miyake! I walk up the steps to Genji the Barber's. It has one of those red, white, and blue stripy poles—Anju despaired of ever getting me to understand where the stripes unwound from and wound to. It was crystal clear to her. Genji's shop is a poky joint, wintry with air-con—I am the only customer—and was last painted when Japan surrendered. A silent TV shows horse racing. Soft-porn magazines are piled high. The air is so thick with hairspray and tonic fumes that if you lit a match the whole building would probably go up in a fireball. Genji himself is an old man sprouting nasal hair, sweep-ing the floor with shaky hands. "C'mon in, son, c'mon in." He gestures toward the empty chair. I sit down and he flourishes a tablecloth over my shoulders. In the mirror my head seems amputated from the rest of me. I flinch as I remember Valhalla bowling alley. Genji switches on his electric clippers, but nothing happens so he whacks the thing against the counter. It buzzes into life, and he begins a stand-up comedy rou-tine about a luckless customer who came in the other day. I stop listen-ing somewhere after the customer sneezed and his glass eyeball shot out with such force that it broke his boss's nose. Genji must repeat these tired gags ninety times a day, refining them slightly each time. Or not. Certainly he does not notice that my attention has floated away. I begin rehearsing various opening lines I can use to impress Ai Imajo. I form the thought that reality is an unedited script performed once; that the truly untold tale is life itself. This seems extremely profound for about ninety seconds. Genji holds a mirror behind my head and I see myself from a new angle. "How d'you like it, son? Bit o' fresh air around the ears, eh?" I look as if I have been violently expelled from a monastery. "Thanks," I say, and ask for plenty of hundred-yen coins for the telephone.

♌

Meanwhile, back in the forest of moss, Pithecanthropus scratched his head and grunted doubtfully. Mrs. Comb perched on a fungi-feathered tree stump. "It must be way past Sir's mid-morning snack now . . . if only he'd said he'd be off gallivanting, I would have rustled him up something . . ."

A man crashed through the thick vegetation, tripped, and sprawled at their feet. Pithecanthropus bounded over to protect Mrs. Comb, but the man seemed to offer no threat. He climbed to his feet, brushed leaf mold off the leather elbow pads on his tweed jacket, and adjusted his Band-Aid-repaired horn-rimmed glasses. He registered no surprise at encountering a sentient hen and a long-extinct ancestor of *Homo sapiens* in this primeval forest. "Have they passed this way?"

Mrs. Comb was not impressed. "Have who passed this way?"

"The word hounds, of course."

"Not those slavering great beasts we saw in the margins?"

"That would be them!" He pressed a finger to his lips and stared at Pithecanthropus. "Hear anything?" Pithecanthropus grunted a "No." The writer slid a thorn from his crown. "You see, many years ago I wrote a novel. I never imagined anybody would want to publish it, but I took their money, and the more I wished every copy would turn to dust, the more the lamentable thing sold. Oh, its errors, its posturing, its arrogance! I offered to sell my soul to Lucifer in return for having the entire run eradicated, but the duplicitous devil never got back to me. The words I unloosed in that accursed book have dogged me ever since."

Mrs. Comb preened her feathers. "Why not retire, then?" The writer shrugged: "I tried! I hid in schools of thought, in mixed metaphors, in the airport lounges of unrecognized states, but sooner or later I always hear a distant baying and I know my words are on my trail." Abruptly, his face changed from doleful weariness to acute suspicion. "What are *you* doing here?" Mrs. Comb folded her wings. "My employer took it into his head to come gallivanting—have you seen him? Horns, a beard, hooves?" The writer shook his head. "Only writers, lunatics, or the Devil himself ever stray this deep into the forest of their own accord. Shhhhhhhhh!" The writer's eyes glazed with dread. "A baying! Don't you hear that baying?" Pithecanthropus grunted softly and shook his head. "Liars!" hissed the writer, and his eyes changed. "Liars! You're in league with the word hounds! I know your little game! They're in the trees! They're coming!" With that, the unhappy man crashed off through the undergrowth. Pithecanthropus grunted curiously. "Aye," agreed Mrs. Comb, "as bonkers as a balmy balaclava. But look . . . what's through this hole in the moss he made." A tea-tinted stream without sound.

"Hurry up, slowcoach!" Mrs. Comb fluttered from rock to rock, while Pithecanthropus had to wade against the current of consciousness. So it was that Mrs. Comb reached the sacred pool first. A second later she noticed Goatwriter's spectacles lying on the marble rock. Third, she saw the body of her best and dearest floating in the water. "Sir! Sir! What-ever's to do!" She flew forth across the pool without noticing the upward waterfall. On her fifth flap she reached Goatwriter's head. Pithecan-thropus's sixth sense told him the sacred pool was death, and roared a warning—but no sound carried, and he could only watch in despair as his beloved slipped, dipped a tip of her wing, and slapped lifeless into the water alongside Goatwriter. In seven bounds Pithecanthropus was atop the marble rock, where his body tore with eight howls of mute grief. He pounded the rock until his fists bled. And suddenly, our early ances-tor was calm. He picked the sticky burrs from his hair, and climbed the rock face until the overhang browed. He counted to nine, which was as high as Goatwriter could teach him, and dived for the spot between the floating bodies. A beautiful dive, a perfect ten. No thought bothered his head as Pithecanthropus entered the sacred pool. Serenity was never a word he would have comprehended, but perfect serenity was what he felt.

◆

"Good afternoon, Jupiter Cafe. Nagamimi here."

Donkey. I think. "Uh, hello. Can I speak to Miss Imajo, please?"

"Sorry, but she isn't working today, see."

"Oh. Could you tell me when her next shift is, then, please?"

"Sorry, but I can't do that."

"Oh. For, uh, security reasons?"

Donkey hee-haws. "No, not that. Miss Imajo's last shift was Sunday, see."

"Oh . . ."

"She's a music student, and her college term is starting again, so she had to quit her part-time job here to concentrate on her studies, see."

"I see. I was hoping to get in touch with her. I'm just a friend."

"Yeah, I can understand that, if you're her friend and all . . ."

"So, might you have her telephone number? On a form or in her record?"

"Miss Imajo was only here for a month, see." Donkey hums as she thinks. "We don't keep files and stuff like that here, see, 'cause of space. Even our cloakroom, it's got less room than one of those boxes that magicians put swords through. It isn't fair. At the Yoyogi branch, see, they have this cloakroom big enough to—"

"Thanks anyway, Miss Nagamimi, but . . ."

"Wait! Wait! Miss Imajo *did* leave me her number, but only if some-one called Eiji Miyake phoned."

I stop myself kicking the wall because it will hurt. "My name is Eiji Miyake."

"Really?" Donkey hee-haws.

"Really."

"Well, really! Isn't that a funny coincidence?"

"Isn't it just."

"Miss Imajo said, only if somebody called Eiji Miyake calls. And you call, and your name is Eiji Miyake! I remember you, you know. You hit that nasty man with your head. Did it hurt? It must have hurt. When I—"

"Miss Nagamimi, give me Miss Imajo's number. Now."

"Right, hang on a moment, where did I put it, I wonder?"

Ai Imajo's number is ten digits long. I get to the ninth before a paralysis reaches my hand. What if my call embarrasses her? What if she thinks I'm some slimeball who wants to hassle her every night? What if her boyfriend answers? Her father? What if she answers? What do I say? I look around Uniqlo. Shoppers, sweaters, space. My index finger presses the final digit. The number connects. A telephone in a distant apartment begins to ring. Somebody is getting up, maybe pausing the video, maybe putting down their chopsticks, cursing this interruption—

"Hello?" Her.

"Uh . . ." I try to speak but a sort of dry, spastic noise comes out.

"Hello?"

I should have planned this better.

"Hello? Do I get to know who you are?"

My voice comes back all on its own. "Hello, is this Ai Imajo?" Stupid question. I know this is Ai Imajo. "I, uh, my, uh . . ."

She sounds sort of pleased. "My knight in shining armor."

"How do you know?"

"A mysterious midnight vision warned me you would call."

"Really?"

"I recognized your voice, genius! How did you get my number?"

I blush. "Miss Nagamimi at Jupiter Cafe told me. Eventually. If this isn't a convenient time to call, I can, uh . . ."

"This is perfectly convenient. I tried to track you down at the Ueno lost-property office, where you said you worked, but they told me you suddenly left town."

"Yeah, uh, Mrs. Sasaki told me."

"Was it to do with your relative?"

"Sort of. I mean, no. In a way, yes."

"Well, that's that sorted out, anyway. Where did you disappear to at Xanadu the other weekend?"

"I figured lots of, uh, organizer people would want to talk with you."

"Exactly! I needed your headbutt to ward them off. How is your head, by the way? No lasting brain damage?"

"No, my brain is normal, thanks. Sort of normal." Ai Imajo finds this funny. We both begin talking at the same moment. "After you," I say.

"No, after you," she says.

"I, uh"—the electric chair must be more pleasant than this—"wonder if, I mean I completely understand if not, you know"—never commit your army without a clear path of retreat—"but if, uh, it's okay for me to, uh . . ."

"To . . . ?"

"Call you."

A pause.

"Help me. This call is to ask if it is okay to call, right?"

I really should have planned this better.

♌

Walking was a joy since Goatwriter sloughed off his body, and its rheumatism, in the sacred pool. The bamboo swayed sideways to let him pass, and whippoorwills wavered quarter-quavers. He paused to admire the view—highlands, lowlands, rainforests, slums, palaces, islands, plains, the nine corners of the compass. Peace rained. Up ahead, he saw a house in a meadow. It was a strange building to encounter in the Lapsang Souchong Plateau. A piebald rabbit disappeared amid a rhomboid rhubarb riot. Beneath the gable was an open triangular window. Whisperings swarmed through the air. Goatwriter took the path to the front door. Its lockless knob twirled uselessly, the door swung open, and Goatwriter climbed the stairs to the attic. The air grew lighter step by step. "Good afternoon," said the writing bureau. "About time," said the brush of Lady Shonagon.

"But I left you in the Venerable Bus!" exclaimed Goatwriter.

"We travel anywhere you go," explained the bureau.

"And since when did you learn to speak?"

"Since *you* learned to unblock your ears, you impertinent creature!" answered Sei Shonagon's brush. "Don't mind her," reassured the writing bureau, "she inherited her attitude from her illustrious mistress, but she will serve you well. Now. Shall we make a start? Mrs. Comb and Pithecanthropus will be along in a little while." Goatwriter sat down and looked through the previous chapter headings. "The All-Consuming Hunger Witch Shrouds the Study of Tales." Goatwriter sat at the writing bureau with a fresh sheet of paper, and for a moment the page is perfect.

six

♎

Kaiten

I found the Righa Royal Hotel immediately, which left over an hour to kill in Harajuku. Dreamy shopgirls cleaned boutique windows in the morning cool, and florists hosed down sidewalks. I read magazines in 7-Eleven, keeping a nervous eye on the clock, until it was time to report to the Amadeus Tea Room. It is a wedding-cake world with pasteled, fluted walls with tasteful little floral displays on every carefully spaced table. Aunt Yen would award it her highest decoration: "Rapturous!" I want to spray-paint its creamy carpets, milky walls, and buttery upholstery. I poke the ice in my water. My grandfather is due here in fifteen minutes. *Grandfather.* The word will acquire a new meaning for me. Weird, how words slip meanings on and off. Until last week, *grandfather* meant the man in the grainy photo on my grandmother's family altar. "The sea took him off" was all she ever told us about her long-dead husband. Yakushima folklore remembers him as a thief and a boozer who disappeared off the end of the harbor quay one windy night, which explains a lot about my grandmother's attitudes to men in general. Amadeus Tea Room is posh enough to support a butler. He stands behind a sort of pedestal at the pearly gates, examines the reservations book, lords it over the waitresses, and pedals his fingers. Do butlers go to butler school? How much are they paid? I practice pedaling my fingers, and at that very moment the butler looks straight at me. I drop my hands and look out the window, acutely embarrassed. At neighboring tables prosperous housewives discuss the secrets of their trade. Businessmen peruse spreadsheets and tap sparrow-size laptop keyboards. Wolfgang Amadeus Mozart looks down from his ceiling fresco, surrounded by margarine cherubs blasting trumpets. He looks puffy and pasty—little wonder he died young. I badly want to smoke one of my Clarks. Mozart has a great view through the panoramic window. Tokyo Tower, PanOpticon, Yoyogi Park—where the dirty old men hang out with telephoto lenses. On a soaring chrome block a giant crane builds a scale model of itself. Water tanks, antennas, rooftops. The weather is stained brown today. A silver teaspoon is struck against a bone china teacup—no, it is the carriage clock on the mantelpiece announcing the arrival of ten o'clock. Butler bows, and guides an elderly man this way.

Him!

My grandfather looks at me—I stand up, flustered, suddenly underrehearsed—and he gives me that "Yes, it *is* me" look you get when you turn up for an appointment with a stranger. I cannot say he looks like me, but I cannot say there is no resemblance either. My grandfather walks with a cane, wears a navy cotton suit and a bootlace tie with a clasp. Butler zips ahead and prepares a chair. My grandfather purses his lips. His skin is sickly gray and mottled, and he fails to hide how much effort walking costs him. "Eiji Miyake, one presumes?" I give a serious eight-eighths bow, searching for the right thing to say. My grandfather gives an amused one-eighth. "Mr. Miyake, I must inform you at the outset that I am not your grandfather."

I unbow. "Oh."

Butler withdraws, and the stranger sits down, leaving me marooned on my feet. "But, I am here at your grandfather's behest to discuss matters pertinent to the Tsukiyama family. Be seated, boy." He watches my every motion—his eyebrows are sunken, but the eyes inside are laser-guided. "The name is Raizo. Your grandfather and I go back many decades. I know about you, Miyake. In fact, it was I who brought your advertisement in the personals column to my friend's attention. As you are aware, your grandfather has been convalescent, in the wake of major heart surgery. His doctors' original forecasts were overly optimistic, and, regrettably, he is obliged to remain in the hospital for another three days. Hence I am here, in his stead. Questions?"

"Well . . . can I visit him?"

Mr. Raizo shakes his head. "Your stepmother is helping to nurse him in the ward, and—how can I express this?"

"She thinks I am a leech who wants to suck money from the Tsukiyamas."

"Precisely. Just for the record: is that your intention?"

"No, Mr. Raizo. All I want is to meet my father." If I insist on this often enough, will people finally begin to believe me?

Mr. Raizo is giving nothing away. "Your grandfather believes that secrecy is the wisest strategy to belay your stepmother's misgivings, at this point. Young lady!" Mr. Raizo crooks his finger at a passing waitress. "One of my giant cognacs, if you please. Your poison, Miyake?"

"Uh, green tea, please."

The waitress gives me a well-trained smile. "We have eighteen varieties—"

"Oh, just bring the boy a pot of tea, dammit!"

The waitress bows, her smile undented. "Yes, Admiral."

Admiral? How many of those are there? "*Admiral* Raizo?"

"All that was long before you were born. 'Mr.' is fine."

"Mr. Raizo. Do you actually know my father?"

"Blunt questions earn blunt answers. Well. I make no secret of the fact that I despise the man. I have assiduously avoided his company for nine years, since the day I learned he sold the Tsukiyama sword."

"A sword?"

"It had been in his—your—family for over five centuries, Miyake. Five hundred years! The snub that your father dealt five centuries of Tsukiyamas—not to mention the Tsukiyamas yet to be born—is immeasurable. Immeasurable! Your grandfather, Takara Tsukiyama, is a man who believes in bloodlines. Your father is a man who believes in joint stock ventures in Formosa. Do you know where the Tsukiyama sword presently resides?" The admiral rasps. "It resides in the boardroom of a pesticide factory in Nebraska! What do you think of that, Miyake?"

"It seems a shame, Mr. Raizo, but—"

"It is a crime, Miyake! Your father is a man devoid of honor! When he separated from your mother he would happily have cut her adrift without a thought for her future! It was your grandfather who ensured her financial survival." This is news to me. "There are codes of honor, even when dealing with concubines. Flesh and blood have meaning, Miyake! Bloodlines are the stuff of life, of identity. Knowing where you are from is a requisite of self-knowledge." The waitress arrives with a silver tray, and places our drinks on lace place mats.

"I agree that bloodlines are important, Mr. Raizo. This is why I am here."

The admiral sniffs his cognac moodily. I sip my soapy tea. "Y'know, Miyake, my doctors told me to lay off this stuff. But I meet more geriatric sailors than I do geriatric doctors." He drains half the glass in a single gulp, tips his head back, and savors every molecule. "Your half-sisters are dead losses, of course. A pair of screeching vulgarities, at some no-name college for half-wits. They rise at eleven o'clock in the morning. They wear white lipstick, astronaut boots, cowboy hats, Ukrainian peasant scarfs. They dye their hair the color of effluence. It is your grandfather's hope that his grandson—you—have principles loftier than those espoused in the latest pop hit."

"Mr. Raizo—forgive me if—I mean, I hope my grandfather doesn't see me as any kind of, uh, future heir. When I say I have no intention of muscling my way into the Tsukiyama family tree, I mean it. I hope my grandfather will see that."

Mr. Raizo rumbles. "Who—meant—what—where—when—why—whose . . . Look, your grandfather wants you to read this." He places a package on the table, wrapped in black cloth. "A loan, not a gift. This journal is his most treasured possession. Guard it with your life, literally if necessary, and bring it when you rendezvous with your grandfather seven days from now. Here. Same time—ten hundred hours—same table. Questions?"

"We've never met—is it wise to trust me with something so—"

"Brazen folly, I say. Make a copy, I told the stubborn fool. Don't entrust some boy you've never even met with the original. But he insisted. A copy would dilute its soul, its uniqueness. His words, not mine."

"I, uh"—I look at the black package—"I am honored."

"Indeed you are. Your father has never read these pages. He would probably auction them to the highest bidder, on his 'Inter Net.'"

"Mr. Raizo: could you tell me what my grandfather wants?"

"Another blunt question." The admiral downs the rest of his cognac. The jewel in his tie-clasp glimmers ocean-abyss blue. "I will tell you this. Growing old is an unwinnable campaign. During this war we witness the ugliest metamorphoses. Faith becomes cynical transactions between liars. Sacrifices turn out to be needless excesses. In a single generation, we saw enemy squadrons become tourist coachloads. You ask what your grandfather wants? I shall tell you. He wants what you want. No more, no less."

A coven of wives blowholes wild laughter.

"Uh, which is?"

Admiral Raizo stands. Butler is already here with his cane. "Meaning."

♎

August 1, 1944

Morning, cloudy. Afternoon, light rain. I am on the train from Nagasaki. My journey to Tokuyama in Yamaguchi Prefecture will take several more hours, and I will not reach Otsushima, the island of my destination, until tomorrow morning. Over the last weekend, Takara, I was torn between two promises. One promise was to you: to tell you every detail about my training in the Imperial Navy. My second promise was to my country and the Emperor: to keep every detail regarding my special-attack-forces training an absolute secret. The purpose of this journal is to resolve my dilemma. These words are for you. My silence is for the Emperor.

By the time you read these words, Mother will have already received a telegram informing you of my death and posthumous promotion. Perhaps you, Mother, and Yaeko are in mourning. Perhaps you wonder what my death means. Perhaps you regret you have no ash, no bones, to place in our family tomb. This journal is my solace, my meaning, and my body. The sea is a fine tomb. Do not mourn immoderately.

Let me begin. The war situation is deteriorating rapidly. The Emperor's forces have suffered severe losses in the Solomon Islands. The Americans are set to invade the Philippines with the clear aim of possessing the Ryukyu chain. To prevent the destruction of the home islands extraordinary measures are called for. This is why the Imperial Navy has authorized the kaiten program.

A kaiten is a modified mark-93 torpedo: the finest torpedo in the world, with a cockpit for a pilot. A kaiten can be steered, aligned, and rammed into an enemy vessel below the waterline. Destruction of the target is a theoretical certainty. You are fond of technical data, Takara, so here goes. A kaiten measures 14.75 meters in length. It is propelled by a 550 hp engine, and fueled by liquid oxygen, which leaves no wake of air bubbles on the surface, thereby allowing an invisible strike. A kaiten can cruise at 56 kph for 25 minutes, thus outpacing capital target vessels. A kaiten is tipped with a 1.55-ton TNT warhead that detonates on impact. Four kaitens will be mounted on I-class submarines. The submarines will sortie to within strike range of enemy anchorages, where the kaitens will be released. This new, deadly weapon will not only reverse the recent losses in the Great East Asian Co-Prosperity Sphere, but will dismay and decimate the American navy.

From the naval air bases at Nara and Tsuchiura, 1,375 volunteers offered their lives for the kaiten program. Only 160 passed the stringent selection procedures. You can see, my brother, how the Tsukiyama name shall be honored and remembered.

August 2

Hazy morning; a hot, cloudless afternoon. I awoke with other kaiten trainees in cells at the military police barracks in Tokuyama—regular billets were destroyed in bombing raids last month. A bomb struck the fuel depot, and in the ensuing destruction the port and large districts of the town were razed. From this wreckage a launch took us to Otsushima. The short voyage takes only thirty minutes, but the contrast could not be more complete. Otsushima is a body and head of peaceful wooded hills, terraced with rice fields. The kaiten base and torpedo works lie on the low-lying "neck" of the island.

Sub. Lt. Hiroshi Kuroki and Ens. Sekio Nishina, the two co-inventors of the kaiten, paid us the inestimable honor of meeting our launch. These men are living legends, Takara. Initially, Naval High Command was reluctant to sanction the use of special attack forces, and rejected the kaiten proposals submitted by Sub. Lt. Kuroki and Ens. Nishina. To convince High Command of their utmost sincerity, they resubmitted their proposals, written in the ink of their own blood. For all this, they are cheerful, unassuming fellows. They showed us to our quarters, joking about the "Otsushima Hotel." They led the technical briefings that took up the rest of the day, and postponed the tour of the base until tomorrow.

August 3

Conditions, windy. Sea, choppy. The perimeter fence of the kaiten base encloses an area of approximately six baseball grounds, and accommodates between 500 and 600 men. Security is tight—even the islanders are unaware of the true purpose of the Otsushima installation. The base includes a barracks, refectory, three torpedo factories, a machine shop to convert the mark-93 torpedoes to kaitens, an exercise yard, a ceremony square, administrative buildings, and the harbor. From the machine shop, a narrow-gauge railway enters a tunnel blasted through 400 meters of rock to the kaiten launch pier, where training began tonight. I jankenned with Takashi Higuchi, a classmate from Nara, for the privilege of the first kaiten run co-piloted with Sub. Lt. Kuroki. His stone beat my scissors! I must not be overly disappointed. My turn will come tomorrow.

August 4

Sultry, humid, hot weather. Tragedy has struck so soon. Last night, Sub. Lt. Kuroki and Lt. Higuchi failed to return from their run around the northern body of Otsushima. Frogmen spent the night searching for their kaiten. It was finally found shortly after dawn, a mere 300 meters from the launch pier, embedded in the sea-floor silt, sixteen hours after launching. Although kaitens have two escape hatches, these may only be opened above water. Underwater, the water pressure clamps them closed. A kaiten contains enough air for about ten hours—with two pilots, this time was halved. They ensured their sacrifices were not in vain by writing 2,000 kana of technical data and observations, pertinent to the fatal malfunction. When their paper was used up, they scratched words on the cockpit wall with a screwdriver. We just returned from their cremation ceremony. Ens. Nishina has sworn to carry the ashes of Kuroki aboard his kaiten when he meets his glory. The atmosphere on the base is one of mourning, obviously, but tempered with a determination that the lives of our brothers shall not be lost in vain. My own heart was burdened with guilt. I begged a private audience with Commandant Ujina and told him about how I felt a special responsibility to Higuchi's soul. Cmdt. Ujina promised to consider my request that I be included in the first sortie of kaiten attacks.

August 9

Weather extremely hot. Forgive the long silence, Takara. Training has swung into full gear, and finding even ten minutes to sit down with my journal during the day has been impossible. At night, I am asleep as my head touches my pillow. I have wonderful news. During the morning roll call, the names for the first wave of kaiten attacks were announced and Tsukiyama was among them! Kikusui is our unit emblem. This is the floating chrysanthemum crest of Masashige Kusunoki, champion of Emperor Godaigo. Kusunoki's 700 warriors withstood an onslaught of 35,000 Ashikaga traitors at the Battle of Minatogawa, and only after sustaining eleven terrible wounds did he commit seppuku with his brother,

Masasue. We are the 700. Our devotion to our beloved Emperor is ultimate.

Four fleet subs will each transport four kaitens. *I-47*, captained by *the* Lt. Cdr. Zenji Orita, will carry Ens. Nishina, Sato, and Watanabe, and Lt. Fukuda. *I-36* will carry Lt. Yoshimoto and Ens. Toyozumi, Imanishi, and Kudo. Aboard *I-37* will be Lt. Kamibeppu and Murakami, and Ens. Utsunomiya and Kondo. *I-333*, captained by Cpt. Yokota, will transport Lt. Abe and Goto, and Ens. Kusakabe and Tsukiyama Subaru. After the announcement we were re-allocated dorms, so members of the same sortie can sleep in the same room. We in *I-333* are on the second floor, at the end, overlooking the rice terraces. At night the croaking of frogs drowns out the foundries and I recall my old room in Nagasaki, which is yours, now.

August 12

Weather, cool and calm. Sea as smooth as Nakajima River, where we sailed our model yachts. Today I will write about our training. After breakfast we divide into Chrysanthemums and Drys. Because there are only six kaitens available for training, we are given priority practice privileges. At 0830 we proceed through the tunnel to the kaiten pier. After boarding, a crane lowers us into the sea. Usually we sail two to a cockpit. Of course, we have no room, but this doubling-up helps to save fuel, and "a drop of gasoline is as precious as a drop of blood." Our instructor knocks on the hull, and we knock back to show we are ready to embark. First we run through a series of descents. Then we solve a navigation problem, using a stopwatch and gyrocompass. We locate a target ship, and simulate a hit by passing under the bow. One must be careful not to clip the upper hatch on the keel—two kaiten pilots died in Base P this way. We also dread being stuck in silt, like Cdr. Lt. Kuroki and Lt. Higuchi. (It is hoped their posthumous promotions will comfort their grieving families.) If this misfortune occurs, one is supposed to blast compressed air into the warhead (filled with seawater rather than TNT), which should, in principle, buoy the kaiten to the surface. None of us is eager to test this flotation theory. What we dread most, however, is surviving the loss of a training kaiten. This occurred to a hapless cadet from Yokohama five days ago. He was dismissed, and his name is never mentioned. After returning to the pier or the base harbor, depending on our course, we attend briefing sessions to share our observations with the Drys. After the worst of the afternoon heat is over, we practice sumo wrestling, kendo fencing, athletics. Kaiten pilots must be in prime physical condition. Remember our father's words, Takara: the body is the outermost layer of the mind.

August 14

Weather: fine at first, clouding over by midday. As my training session was canceled today due to engine failure, I have a spare hour to write to you about my I-333 brothers. Yutaka Abe is our leader, aged 24, of old Tokyo stock and a graduate of Peers. His father was aboard the *Shimantogawa* at the glorious Battle of Tsushima thirty-nine years ago. Abe is a superhuman who excels in every field. Rowing, navigation, composing haiku. He let it slip that he has won every chess match he has played for the last nine years. The motto on his kaiten is to be "Unerring Arrow of the Emperor." Shigenobu Goto, aged 22, is from a merchant family in Osaka. He is a comedian. He gets love letters nearly every day from different girls, and complains about the lack of women on the base. Abe responds with a single word: *purity*. Goto can impersonate anybody and anything. He even takes requests: Chinaman attacked by snake in privy; Tohoku fishwife being blown through tuba. He uses his voices to distract Abe when they play chess. Abe wins anyway. The message on Goto's kaiten is to read: "Medicine for Yankees." Our third member is Issa Kusakabe. Kusakabe is a year older than me, quiet, and reads every word that comes his way. Technical manuals, novels, poetry, old magazines from before the war. Mrs. Oshige (our "mother" on Otsushima, who believes we are testing a new type of submarine) arranged for a boy to bring Kusakabe books from the school library every week. He even has a volume of Shakespeare. Abe questioned whether the works of an effete westerner were appropriate for a Japanese warrior. Kusakabe explained that Shakespeare is English kabuki. Abe said Shakespeare contained corrupting influences. Kusakabe asked which plays Abe was thinking of. Abe let it drop. After all, Kusakabe would not have volunteered to be a kaiten pilot if his ethics were in any way questionable. He is inscribing not a slogan but a line of verse on his kaiten. "The foe may raise ten thousand shouts—we conquer without a single word." I must not neglect Slick, our unit chief engineer. His nickname is derived from his hands, which are always oily and black. Slick is one of the oldest men on the base. He is vague about his age, but he is old enough to be our father. Goto jokes that he probably is our father. Slick's real children are his kaitens. I have elected to leave my kaiten without a motto. My sacrifice shall be its motto and its meaning.

◆

I put the journal under the counter of Shooting Star to rest my eyes—the pages have been professionally laminated, but the pencil marks are fading away to ghost lines. Plus, many of the kanji are obscure, so I often have to stop and refer to a dictionary. I open a can of Diet Pepsi and survey my new empire: video racks, stacks, shelves. Mucous aliens, shiny gladiators, squeaky idols. Soft rock pumps away. In my week away the old shoe repair next to FUJIFILM has been turned into a Kentucky Fried Chicken outlet. A life-size statue of Colonel Sanders stands outside, under a limp "Opening Fayre" banner. He is as fat and grinny as a statue of Ebisu in a temple. Does KFC make you that fat?

Buntaro and Machiko will be on their JAL airplane now, somewhere over the Pacific. My landlord was in a near-frenzy when I got back from my meeting with Mr. Raizo, even though he had ninety minutes before the taxi came. What would happen if the computer crashed? If the monitor broke down? When Machiko hauled him into the taxi, he was still hypothesizing disaster scenarios. When Kodai is born the nurses will have to sedate the father. I mean it. I can watch anything on the monitor, but there are too many films to choose, so I leave the same Tom Hanks movie running all day. Nobody will notice. Between two and five, business is pretty quiet; once offices and schools start winding up I get much busier. The regulars gape when they see me—they straightaway assume that Machiko has suffered a miscarriage. When I tell them the Ogisos are on vacation, they act as if I said Buntaro and his wife turned into teapots and flew to Tibet. The question of who I am is a trifle delicate—my scuzzy landlord sublets my capsule without troubling the tax office. Schoolkids cluster around horror, office ladies rent Hollywood movies with blond stars, salarymen rent titles such as *Pam the Clam from Amsterdam* and *Hot Dog Academy*. Several customers bring videos back late—you always have to check the dates. Mrs. Sasaki arrives at seven-thirty—I dash upstairs to feed Cat, and dash across to KFC to feed myself. Colonel Sanders's chicken tastes like sawdust. Mrs. Sasaki tells me about my replacement at Ueno, which makes me sort of nostalgic for the place. She leaves me the *Tokyo Evening Mail*—Monday has the jobs pages. If I want a career in kitchen portering, telesales, shelf stocking or mailbox stuffing then Tokyo is heaven on Earth. Cat appears on the stairs—during my week in hiding she learned how to open my capsule door. I tell her to go back but she ignores me, and after replacing a stack of returned videos I find her settled on the counter chair, so I have to make do with a wobbly stool. FUJIFILM says 22:26. Business drops off.

♎

September 2

Hot weather, but cooler in the evenings now. I received your letter today, Takara, and the parcel from Mother and Yaeko containing the thousand-stitch belt. Given the special attack nature of my mission, the five-sen coins sewn into the belt will not avert death, but I shall wrap it around my middle every time I climb aboard my kaiten. Abe, Goto, Kusakabe, and I read aloud our letters from home, and I was as proud as

Tengu when I told them my younger brother is already a junior squadron leader at the bullet factory. Your games resemble authentic military training—charging at Roosevelts and Churchills with bamboo bayonets. My thoughts are also with Yaeko at the parachute factory. Her stitches may save the lives of my former classmates at Nara Naval Air Academy. It must pain Mother to trade Tsukiyama family treasures for rice, but I know Father and our ancestors understand. War changes rules. It is wise of you to tape Xs over the windows. If the enemy's bombers get as far as Nagasaki, they will doubtless target the shipyards rather than our side of town, so your precautions are unlikely to be battle-tested. Be that as it may, a good soldier considers all possible contingencies.

I will reply to your letter very soon. By now, you will understand why my reply fails to provide answers to all the questions you asked.

September 9

Weather: warm, mild, balmy. I am 20 years old today. To celebrate my birthday in a time of national emergency is inappropriate, so after a warhead study session I snuck away before supper. I gratefully accepted the sunset as my birthday present. Inland Sea sunsets are special. Tonight's was the color of Yaeko's plum pickles. Do you remember the story of Urashima Taro? About how he saved the giant turtle, and stayed in the undersea palace for three days, but upon his return three generations had come and gone? I wondered about how this place will look in ninety years. The war will be a hazy memory then. Bring your children to Otsushima when the war is won. The local sea bream is delicious, as are the Inland Sea oysters. I was about to return to the mess hall when Abe, Goto, and Kusakabe found me. Somehow Abe had found out about my birthday and told Mrs. Oshige, who managed to prepare chicken kushiyaki. Kusakabe built a fire and we had supper on the seashore, and some homebrew sake that Goto appropriated from a canteen assistant. The drink was rough enough to paralyze our faces, but no meal ever tasted better. With the exception of Mother's, of course.

September 13

A warm morning, a muggy afternoon. An attack of flu has been around the base. I myself have been in the sick bay for 24 hours with a temperature of 39 degrees. I am recovering now. I suffered from strange dreams. One was particularly shameful, and makes me worry about my patriotism. I was in my kaiten cruising around the Solomon Islands in search of an enemy aircraft carrier. Everything was so blue. I felt indestructible, like a shark. Suddenly Mrs. Shiomi's son, the boy who threw himself under a Russian tank with a bomb at Nomonhan, was in my kaiten. "Did nobody tell you?" he said. "The war is over." I asked who won, and I saw Shiomi's eyes were missing. "The Emperor entertains the Americans with duck shoots in the palace grounds. In this way he hopes to save his skin." I decided I should sail into Tokyo harbor and sink at least one enemy vessel, and pointed my kaiten north. The acceleration slouched my body back, and when I woke I felt I was remembering being born, or perhaps dying, the last time or the next time. Kusakabe and Goto visited me later, to share notes they had taken in our navigation class, but I said nothing about my dream.

October 2

Drizzle all day. The Kikusui target sites were announced at a secret meeting this afternoon. *I-47* and *I-36* will head for Ulithi, a vast lagoon in the Carolines captured by the Americans only ten days ago. *I-37* and *I-333* will simultaneously attack Kossol Passage anchorage in the Palau Islands. The purpose of a dual-site attack is to ensure maximum damage to enemy morale. Find the Palau Islands in Father's atlas, Takara. You can see how vividly blue the seas are. When you wonder where I am, remember: your brother is the blue of the sea.

Disharmony grows between Abe and Kusakabe. Our unit leader challenged Kusakabe to a game of chess. He declined. Abe (apparently) teased him: "Are you afraid of losing?" Kusakabe made a strange reply: "No, I am afraid of winning." Abe retained his smile, but his irritation was plain. Brothers who shall die together should not quarrel in this way.

October 10

Weather clear. Dew on the grass this morning. Slick, his ground crew, and I were hauling our kaiten through the tunnel to the launch pier this afternoon when the air raid siren sounded. No drill had been scheduled. The tunnel filled up with men from the launch pier while the commandant shouted orders over the loudspeakers. TNT was secured in the deep bunker, the submarines maneuvered out of the bay, and we waited anxiously for the sound of B-29s. If a bomb scores a direct hit on the machine shops, the project could be delayed crucial weeks. Slick wondered aloud if an attack on the mainland means the Americans are attacking Okinawa already. We hear so many rumors but reliable news is scant. After a nervous forty minutes the all-clear siren sounded. Maybe a jumpy lookout post mistook our own Zeros for enemy planes.

October 13

Pleasant afternoon sun. Clouds by evening. Re-reading this journal, I notice that I have failed to describe the atmosphere of the base. It is unique, in my experience. Engineers, instructors, pilots, and trainees all work together toward the same end. I have never felt so alive as in these weeks. The meaning of my life is to defend the Motherland. Discipline is not lax. We undergo the same drills and inspections as any military base. But the excesses of ordinary camps, where green recruits are hazed and where soldiers are hung upside down and beaten, are unknown on Otsushima. We receive regular rations of cigarettes and candy, and real white rice. My one regret is that I cannot share my meals with you, Mother, and Yaeko. I am stockpiling my candy for you, however, and refuse to gamble with it like Goto and most of my co-trainees.

October 18

Steady rain all day. The *Zuikaku* is still afloat and Father is therefore almost certainly alive! Abe arranged for me to use military channels to dispatch a telegram to Mother immediately. I received the news from Cpt. Tsuyoshi Yokota of *I-333*, which docked in Otsushima today. Cpt. Yokota had himself spoken to Admiral Kurita aboard the *Atago* only seven days previously while on patrol in the Leyte Gulf. The news that Father is still well and thinking of us heartens me beyond words. One day he may hold this very journal in his hands! Cpt. Yokota says that the *Zuikaku* is regarded as a charmed ship since Pearl Harbor. Remember that civilian mail to the South Seas is a very low priority, so do not be discouraged if you hear nothing. I received some more good news this evening. A four-day leave was announced for the Kikusui Group men, before we depart for the target zone.

October 20

Clear day, refreshing breezes. Good fortune begets good fortune. During dinner, Cmdt. Ujina broadcasted the evening news over the camp speakers, and we heard of the extraordinary kamikaze successes in the Philippines yesterday. Five American aircraft carriers and six destroyers sunk! In a single wave! Surely even the American savages will realize the hopelessness of invading the home islands. Lt. Kamibeppu stood on his bench and proposed a toast to the souls of the brave aviators who had given their lives to our beloved Emperor Hirohito. Rarely have I heard such a moving speech. "Pure spirit, or metal? Which is the stronger? Spirit will buckle metal, and blacken it, and shred it! But metal can no more damage pure spirit than scissors can cut a rope of smoke!" I am embarrassed by my vanity, but I imagined the day when similar toasts shall be drunk to our souls.

October 28

Light rain today. The new *I-333* kaitens became operational today. They are much more responsive than the training kaitens. After a longer-than-expected test session, I ran back through the rain across the exercise ground and nearly collided with Kusakabe, who was leaning against the supply shed, staring intently at the ground. I asked him what had caught his attention so. Kusakabe pointed at a puddle, and spoke softly. "Circles are born, while circles born a second ago live. Circles live, while circles living a second ago die. Circles die, while new circles are born." A very Kusakabe comment. I told him he should have been born a wandering poet-priest. He said maybe he was, once. We watched the puddles for a while.

November 2

The dying heat of 1944. I just returned from Nagasaki for the final time. Those memories are yours, too, so I have no need to describe them here. I can still taste Mother's yokan and Yaeko's pumpkin tempura. The train journey took a long time because the engine constantly broke down. The military carriage was commandeered by a high-ranking party of officers, so I traveled with a carriage full of refugees from Manchukuo. Their stories of the Soviets' cruelty and their Chinese servants' treachery were terrible. How grateful I am that Father never joined the colonists. One girl younger than you was traveling alone to find an aunt in Tokyo. This was her first time in Japan. Around her neck was an urn. It contained the ashes of her father who died in Mukden, her mother who died in Karafuto, and her sister who died in Sasebo. She was afraid she would fall asleep and miss Tokyo, which she imagined was a small place like her frontier town. She believed she could find her aunt by asking people. At Tokuyama I gave her half my money, wrapped in a handkerchief, and left before she could refuse. I fear for her. I fear for all of them.

♦

"Golems," I explain, lying showered and naked in postmidnight capsule darkness with Ai on the other end of the phone, "are not the same as zombies. Sure, they are both undead, but you mold golems from graveyard mud in the image of the dead man buried below, and then you inscribe his rune on the torso. You can kill golems only by erasing the rune. Zombies you can easily decapitate, or set alight with a flamethrower. You make them from body parts, usually stolen from a morgue, or else you simply reanimate semirotten corpses."

"Is necrophilia a compulsory subject in Kyushu high schools?"

"I work in a video store now. I have to know these things."

"Change the subject."

"Okay. What to?"

"I asked you first."

"Well, I was always curious about the meaning of life."

"Easy. Eating macadamia ice cream and listening to Debussy."

"Be serious."

"Well," Ai shifts, "your question is wrong."

I imagine her lying here. "What should my question be, then?"

"It should be 'What is my meaning of life.' I mean, look at *The Well-Tempered Clavier*. To me, it means molecular harmony. To my father, it means a broken sewing machine. To Bach, it means an experiment in writing for every available key. To Bach's wife, it means money to pay his wig maker. Who is right? Individually, we all are. Generally, none of us are."

"I keep thinking about my great-uncle. What he wanted—his meaning—seemed so valid."

"To him, yes. To me, sacrificing your life for the vainglory of a military clique isn't my idea of 'valid,' but to your great-uncle, aspiring to be a concert pianist might not have seemed worth disobeying his father for." Cat patters in at this point. "Maybe the meaning of life lies in looking for it." Cat laps water in the thirsty moonlight.

◆

"So much space!" Buntaro yells into a telephone on a windy morning. "What do you do with all this space? Why did I never come here years ago? The plane took less time than my dentist. Do you know when I last took a vacation outside Tokyo?"

"Nope." I stifle a yawn.

"Me neither, kid. I arrived in Tokyo when I was twenty-two. My company made transformers, and it sent me up for training. I get off the train at Tokyo Station, and twenty minutes later I find the exit. 'Would I ever *hate* to spend my life living in this hellhole!' I think. Twenty years on, look at what I did. Be careful of vacations in paradise. You think too much about all the things you never did and never will do."

"Does everyone in paradise get up so early?"

"My wife was up before me. Strolling on the beach, under the palm trees. Why is the ocean so . . . y'know . . . blue? You can hear the waves crash from our balcony. My wife found a starfish washed up. A real, live starfish."

"That's the sea for you. Is there, uh, anything specific you wanted to talk to me about?"

"Oh, yeah. I thought I'd run through your problems."

"My problems? Which ones, uh, did you have in mind?"

"Your problems with the store, of course."

"Shooting Star? None I know of."

"None?"

"Not one."

"Oh."

"Get back to paradise, Buntaro."

I try to get back to sleep—I was talking with Ai until after three A.M.—but my mind is moving up its gears. FUJIFILM says 07:45. Cat laps water and leaves for work. I doodle blues chords for some time, smoke my last three Lucky Strikes, eat yogurt—after spooning out a mold colony—and listen to *Milk and Honey*. My favorite track on this one has always been "Borrowed Time." A kite of sunlight settles on Anju.

For two days she was classed as missing, but nobody was cruel enough to tell me not to give up hope. True, tourists go missing on Yakushima all the time, and often turn up—or get rescued—a day or two later. But locals are never so stupid, not even local eleven-year-olds—we all knew Anju had drowned. No goodbye, just gone. My grandmother aged ten years by the following morning, and looked at me as if she scarcely knew me. There was no big scene when I left that day. I remember her at the kitchen table. Her face was twisted in a new way. She told me that if I hadn't gone to Kagoshima, her granddaughter would still be alive. Which I thought—and still think—is only too true. It was not the bitter change in my grandmother that made me leave, however, but Anju's clothes and toys and books. The pain was unbearable. I walked to Uncle Orange's farmhouse and my aunt cleared a corner for me to sleep in. Officer Kuma called round the evening after to tell me the search for Anju's body had been called off. My Orange cousins are all older girls, and they decided I needed nursing through my grief—they kept saying it was okay to cry, that they understood how I felt, that Anju dying wasn't my fault, that I had always been a good brother. Sympathy was also unbearable. I had swapped my sister for a never-to-be-repeated goal. So I ran away. Running away on Yakushima is simple—you leave before the old women stir and the fog goes back to the sea, tread quietly through the weatherboarded alleyways, cross the coast road, skirt the tea fields and orange orchards, set a farm dog barking, enter the forest, and start climbing.

After the head of the thunder god vanishes into the ocean, I skirt the ridge above my grandmother's house. No light is on. An autumn morning, when rain is always ten minutes away. I climb. Waterfalls without names, waxy leaves, berries in jade pools. I climb. Boughs sag, ferns fan, roots trip. I climb. I eat peanuts and oranges, to make sure I can get high and deep enough before I disappear. Leech on my leg, creeping silence, day clots into gray afternoon, no sense of time. I climb. A graveyard of trees, a womb of trees, a war of trees. Sweat cools. I climb. Way up here, everything is covered in moss. Moss vivid as grief, muffling as snow. Sleep here, and moss covers you, too. My legs stiffen and wobble so I sit down, and here comes the foggy moon through a forest skylight. I am cold, and huddle in my blanket, niched in an ancient shipwreck of a cedar. I am not afraid. You have to value yourself to be afraid. Yet for the first time in three days, I want something. I want the forest lord to turn me into a cedar. The very oldest islanders—crones, who always outlive their husbands—say that if you are in the interior mountains on the night when the forest lord counts his trees, he includes you in the number and turns you into a tree. Animals call, darkness swarms, cold nips my toes. I remember Anju. Despite the cold, I fall asleep. Despite my tiredness, I wake up. A white fox picks its way along a fallen trunk. It stops, turns its head, and recognizes me with more-than-human eyes. Mist hangs in the spaces between my boughs, and birds nest in what was my ear. I want to thank the forest lord, but I have no mouth now. Never mind. Never mind anything, ever again. I wake, stiff, not a tree but a snot-dribbling boy again, throat tight with a cold. I sob and sob and sob and sob and sob and sob. *Milk and Honey* ends with Yoko singing "How do I tell you? You're the one, you're the one, you're the one . . ." and my Discman hums to a stop. The kite of sunlight has slid to my junk shelf, where Cockroach watches me. Its feelers twitch. I leap up, grab the bug killer, but Cockroach escapes down the gap between the floor and the wall—I zap in about a third of the can. And here I stand, in mammoth hunter pose, empty of everything. I ran away into the interior to understand why Anju had grown with me, cell by cell, day by day, if she was going to die before her twelfth birthday. I never did discover the answer. I made the descent without mishap the following day—the Orange house was having collective hysterics about me—but, looking back, did I ever really leave the interior? Is what Eiji Miyake means still rooted on Yakushima, magicked into a cedar on a mist-forgotten mountain flank, and my search for my father just a vague . . . passing . . . nothing? FUJIFILM says I have to get Shooting Star ready for business. Another day too busy to worry about what it all means. Luckily for me.

Ω

November 7

Mild weather, fish-scale clouds. I am in our dorm after our predeparture banquet. I am fat with fish, white rice, dried seaweed, victory chestnuts, canned fruit, and sake, which was presented by the Emperor himself. Because the weather was fine today, the Kikusui graduation ceremony was held outside, in the exercise yard. Everyone on the base was in attendance, from Cmdr. Ujina down to the lowliest kitchen boy. The rising-sun flags on the base, the ships, and the submarines were all raised in unison. A brass band performed the Kimigayo. We wore uniforms especially tailored for the kaiten division: black, cobalt trimmings, with green chrysanthemums embroidered on the left breast. Vice Admiral Miwa of the Sixth Fleet gave us the honor of a personal address. He is a fine orator as well as an unequaled naval tactician, and his words inscribed themselves on our hearts. "You are avengers, at last face-to-face with those who would murder your fathers and violate your mothers. Peace will never be yours if you fail! Death is lighter than a feather, but duty is heavier than a mountain! *Kai* and *ten* signify 'turn' and 'heaven'—therefore, I exhort you, turn the heavens so light shines anew on the land of the gods!" One by one, we ascended the podium, and the vice admiral presented each of us with a *hachimaki* to tie around our heads like the samurai of old, and a seppuku sword to remind us that our lives are His Imperial Majesty's possessions and to avert the indignity of surrender should disaster prevent us from striking our targets. During the closing Kimigayo we bowed before the portrait of the Emperor. A priest then led us to a shrine to pray for glory.

Abe, Goto, and Kusakabe are writing letters to their families, so I will do the same, and clip off some hair and nails for cremation. I shall write my final orders to you in this letter, but I shall reiterate them here: Takara, you are the acting head of the Tsukiyama family until Father returns. Whatever trials lie ahead, preserve the sword. Impress upon your sons, and their sons, the integrity and purity of the Tsukiyama bloodline. After deification my soul will reside at Yasukuni Shrine, with my myriad brothers who also gave their lives to the Emperor. Come to pray, bring our sword, and let the light dance on the blade. I shall be waiting.

November 8

Weather: fair, hazy. The first maple leaves are flaming scarlet. I-333 departed from Otsushima. The departure ceremony was held on the dock at 0900. A camera crew was present to make a newsreel of our departure. I waved at the camera as I passed, Takara, in case you and your friends see me at the cinema in Nagasaki. Lt. Kamibeppu gave a speech on behalf of the Kikusui Group, thanking our trainers, apologizing for our blunders, and promising that every kaiten pilot will do his utmost to make our country proud of us. After this, we thanked Mrs. Oshige individually. She was choked with emotion and unable to speak, but words may sully the message of the heart. The officers toasted us with an omiki libation, and we boarded the submarines to cries of "Banzai." We stood atop our kaitens, and waved back at our classmates on shore, until we rounded the western head of Otsushima. A small flotilla of fishing boats and training canoes saw us into the open sea. Goto looked at the fishermen's daughters through Kusakabe's binoculars. Abe has just announced that our maintenance check has been brought forward an hour, so I'll wait until tomorrow to tell you about *I-333*.

November 9

Weather: rain in the morning; a clear afternoon with swelling waves. Goto describes life in a submarine as being "corked into a tin flask and thrown into a flood." Into this tin flask is fitted the forward torpedo room, officers' qtrs., forward battery, pump room, conning tower, control room, mess, crew qtrs. for 60 men, fore/aft engine rooms, aft torpedoes. Slick likens *I-333* to an iron whale. I marvel at the crew: they have been on active duty since the war began with only ten days' shore leave! After one day, I am already aching to run, or throw a baseball. I miss our futons on Otsushima—on *I-333* we sleep on narrow shelves, with sides to stop us falling out. The air is stale and the light is sepia. I must emulate the endurance of the crew. Even walking requires contortion, especially at the beginning of a voyage when the gangways are used for food storage. There are only two places one can be alone. One is the kaitens, which can be accessed from the inside of the submarine via specially adapted tubes between the submarine deck and the kaiten lower hatch. The other is the toilet. (Submarine toilets are not conducive to meditation.) However, we have Cpt. Yokota's permission to use the bridge when conditions permit. Of course, I must inform the duty officer when I go abovedecks, so I can be accounted for if we have to make an emergency dive. After our evening calisthenics session I joined the ensign on lookout duty, starboard of the conning tower. At night the control room is "rigged for dark"—only red lights are permitted, so Cpt. or observers may move above- and belowdecks without loss of night vision. I watched the white spray on the bow and the foam wake to the rear. On moonlit nights these are telltale signs for bombers. He told me the coastline to the west was Cape Sata, in Kagoshima Prefecture. The end of Japan was lost in scarlet clouds.

◆

"EjjjMyake!" Masanobu Suga bumper-cars into Shooting Star from the neon night, trips over, and whacks the floor with his forehead. He noses the ground, and grins at me—he is so drunk that his brain cannot understand how much his body hurts. Suga wobbles up to a one-leg kneel, as if he is about to ask for my hand in marriage. I dive around from the counter to pick up his glasses before he grinds them to splinters. Suga thinks I am trying to help him up, and elbows me away with a "grfffme!" He stands up, stable as a newborn giraffe, and falls backward into a rack of war movies. The rack topples and a hundred video boxes cascade. A customer—only one, luckily—stares death rays at us through her half-moon glasses. Suga glares at the fallen video rack. "Poltygeists liv'nn heeer, Miyake. Needta leanov'r theeer a mo, mo-mo, justamo . . ." He tightrope-walks to the counter, lifting his head toward the monitor. "*Cassyblanca.*" The movie is actually *Blade Runner*. I right the rack and collect the video boxes. Suga dangles his head, broken-puppet style. "M'yake."

"Suga. Nice to, uh . . ."

Suga loses spittle control. I intercept the saliva stalactite with the *Tokyo Post*. "Notdrunk, n'vergetdrunk, notme. Happy, hap-py, he-he-hep-py, yes, mebbe, butnotnever out-of-cont. Roll." He sinks to his knees, his knuckles gripping the edge of the cliff. Even Uncle Pachinko on a whiskey bender is not this hopeless. "Wentaseeya, Mishish Shashashaki sedya quit. ByebyeUenobyebye, badvibes, bad, badbad-badvibes in Ueno, where allverlostnf'gottn orphans ended after the war, did did y'knowthat? Died like flies, poorlittlpoorlittl . . ." Tears blossom in Suga's eyes and one runs down his pocked cheek. Death-Ray Woman has a rape-alarm-in-a-library shrill: "Too much! The way you youngsters behave today makes me vomit out my own lungs!" She leaves before I can begin an apology. For a moment I wish Suga would pass out—I could pretend not to know him and maybe an ambulance would take him away. "Suga! You need to get home! You drank too much!"

Suga sniffs and focuses on me with puffy dogfish eyes. "I'm curshed."

"Have you got enough money for a taxi?"

"Curshed."

"Can you tell me your address?"

He clenches his eyes and deliberately slams his head back on the front of the counter as hard as he can, which luckily is not too hard as his neck control functions are offline, but even so his face is bright with pain. I hold his head and he pushes me away. "I'm curshed, Miyake! Dontchoogettitt? Curshed! One doughnut! For one fcknmeashly *dough-nut!* Littlkid, kindygartn littlkid, waiting jushinside th'bakery doordoor, hewuzcryin'seyes out . . ." The tears begin again and Suga trembles. A scared-dog sort of shiver.

"Suga, my room is upstairs, I'm going to—"

"*One*"—whack!—"*meashly*"—whack!—"*doughnut.* I opnd the door, littlkid runs out, fastazafastaza." Suga's eyes screw up in pain. "Bat-man'n'Robn on his T-shirt, littlkid, straight inta the middlvthe . . . road . . ." Suga blubbers and his breathing is chopped and sliced. "Wtchy'think I did, Miyake? Swoooooopd t'th'rescue, d'y'think? Nope, Miyake, nope nope nope rootd, rootd, I's rootd. T'th'spot, Miyake. Saw. Heard. Audiovshl. Car. Brakes. Littlkid. Wham, wham, wham. Flew, littlkid, flew like a baggagroceries, *ber-lattt,* bowlingball, bloodon-theroad, markerpen . . ." Suga's fingers claw for a ripcord on his face to pull—I grip his hands in my fists. Suga is losing his will to resist. "Mom, she . . . pushpass-pusspashme, wailing right . . . *AaarrrAaarrr! Aaaaaarrrrrr* . . . I ran. Ran ran ran . . . Ran, Miyake, nverstppd never,

run, Suga run, you *mur-der-rer* . . . Suga the mudderer." Suga swallows a
stone of grief. "Betchawishdyr poisoned th'pineapple now, doncha?
Howdjathink I got this this pizza cheezgraterskin? Curshed.
Icrossaroad, Isee Littlkid. Iseeanuvva Littlkid, Isee Littlkid. Curshed.
Curshed." His eyes ease themselves shut.

I see.

I take the key from the cash register, and manhandle the sack of
Suga upstairs. "Toilet. If you piss my futon I'll blowtorch your computers, okay? Suga? You hear me?" Suga nods, bleared and mumbly beyond
grammar. "I'll be downstairs." Down at the register a girl in a cow-print
T-shirt stands holding every Brad Pitt video in the shop. She studies her
watch and emits a sigh of pain. "Sorry to keep you waiting," I say. She
ignores me. I hear Suga barf. Barf one, Cowgirl looks puzzled. Barf two,
Cowgirl breaks her vow of noninteraction and stares at me questioningly. Barf three, Cowgirl says, "Can you hear anything?" I look at her as
if she is an utter lunatic. "Nothing. Why?" She leaves and I rearrange the
fallen video cases on the rack. My toilet flushes, which is sort of encouraging. A flurry of customers follows. I have lost track of who is human
and who is a replicant in *Blade Runner*. I wonder how many years Suga
has been carrying his curse around with him. I forget that other people
in the world have broken parts too. Eleven o'clock swings around, and
the night shows no sign of cooling. I hear a thump or two upstairs: at
least I don't have a dead body on the premises to explain to Buntaro. I
hear the drumming of water, and for a moment think the heat has
turned to rain—then I realize that no, to answer the last question he
asked me three weeks ago, Suga cannot piss straight when he whizzes.
Another treat in store tomorrow morning. I crank up the air-con a
notch, and retrieve my grandfather's journal and the kanji dictionary
from under the counter. The warmth between Subaru and Takara, his
younger brother, is in stark contrast to the cold between my father and
Takara, my grandfather. Admiral Raizo's mention of a "feud" makes me
uneasy. The Yakushima aunts happily used me as ammo in their endless
polite battles, and I cannot shake the feeling I am on the edge of another
war zone.

Ω

November 10, 1944

Conditions too poor to permit access to bridge. Abe reminds us we are irreplaceable components of our kaitens. Moreover, *I-333* rolls about too much to allow maintenance checks on our kaitens. We have sensed a certain reserve between ourselves and *I-333*'s crew. A certain distance is natural, but at times their conduct borders on coldness. For example, I discovered that Radioman First Class Hosokawa in communications grew up in Nagasaki, and when we passed in the corridor after dinner I addressed him in our local dialect. He looked startled, and replied using rigid, formal speech. When Abe suggested that the kaiten pilots contribute to the cleaning docket, Cpt. Yokota replied with terseness that our offer was generous but unthinkable. Abe believes the men regard us as incumbent gods, and are merely suffering from excess veneration. Goto pointed out that three and a half years of dodging depth charges would put a strain on anyone's mental state. Kusakabe speculated that the men may consider us insane. This angered Abe. Kusakabe calmly observed that submariners spend their lives slipping away from the jaws of death, while we seek to meet it head-on. Abe pulled rank and ordered Kusakabe—and Goto—never to voice such thoughts again, because he was demeaning the dedication and patriotism of our hosts. I said nothing for the sake of harmony, but inwardly I sympathized with Goto. Even the youngest crew members have the eyes of old men.

November 11

Fine conditions prevail. The mercury in the thermometer climbs as the sea warms. It is impossible to re-mount the kaitens on the submarine deck once released, so we are unable to make test runs in our vessels. We must, however, spend time in our kaitens checking that the engines and other systems are in perfect working order. Watching the sea rush by through the kaiten periscopes is most enjoyable, especially when *I-333* is submerged. As we proceed south, I notice changes in the animal kingdom. For example, today I saw a manatee. It swam the way a cow might swim. We passed through a school of tropical fish, brightly colored with marigolds, snow, and lilac. Two dolphins appeared this afternoon, swimming alongside us. The creatures appeared to be laughing at such a peculiar fish. May fortune similarly smile on our mission. Goto made a joke. "If a Chinese bandit, an American imperialist, and a British general jumped off a building at the same time, who would hit the ground first?" Nobody knew, so Goto gave the punchline. "Who cares?" The crew laughed heartily, and re-told the joke until everyone aboard had heard it.

November 12

Weather thundery, but no rain, yet. Cpt. Yokota is outspoken in his criticism of the Tokyo government, to say the least. If a civilian spoke in such a manner he would surely be arrested by the secret service. At dinner tonight, the captain opened a bottle of rum. I had never experienced the drink outside pirate tales of my boyhood. It certainly loosens the tongue. Abe drank least, being a weak drinker, but Cpt. Yokota can knock it back like cool tea on a hot day. Cpt. Yokota first savaged the Admiralty for failing to learn from the Midway fiasco, instead of suppressing news of the defeat and turning the very word into a taboo. "The sole strategy of our navy," according to Cpt. Yokota, "is to lure the enemy into a 'Decisive Naval Engagement' like the Battle of Tsushima against the Russians. But it isn't going to happen in this war. The Americans are not so stupid." Minister Tojo is "an army idiot of the highest magnitude" for ordering the invasion of uninhabited Alaskan islands: "For what? To liberate seabirds from Anglo-Saxon tyranny?" Prince Higashikuni is "so stupid he couldn't pour piss out of a boot if the instructions were written on the heel." Goto laughed, Kusakabe smiled, and Abe turned a polite pink. I was unsure of the appropriate response. Cpt. Yokota maintains the East Indies oilfields would still be in Japanese territory if the wings of the military had fought as one rather than against one another, and if radar technology had been developed with the same earnestness as our torpedoes, from the earliest stages. Now we must resort to begging the Germans for radar sets. He accuses the Imperial Army of operating subs undeclared to high command as "wheelbarrows," to support troops stranded on Rabaul and islands the enemy has bypassed. Most worrying of all is the Cpt.'s firm conviction that our secret codes have been cracked. Abe, perhaps rashly, observed that the codes were invented by a Tokyo Imperial University cryptologist to be undecipherable to the occidental brain. Cpt. Yokota retorted that no Tokyo Imperial University cryptologist was ever ambushed on the high seas by a pack of destroyers that had uncannily pinpointed his vessel's precise position and heading. We must all pray that Cpt. Yokota's pessimism is misplaced.

◆

"But what if"—I unpick loops in my phone cord—"you are right, and, uh, allocating meaning is one more job that our minds do, how come different people have different meanings of life? How come some people have no meaning? Or forget the meaning they started with?"

"Experiences, influences, diseases, divorces. What *is* that noise?"

"Suga snoring."

"I never imagined a cat could snore that loudly."

"Suga is human. Sort of."

"And is Suga a he or a she?"

I hunt in vain for traces of jealousy. "He. Very much so. A drunk friend crash-landed far from home. I let him sleep on my floor but he took my futon."

"Oh. Want to hear something private, about myself?"

I sit up. "Sure I do."

"I am a diabetic. A full-blown one. Every evening, for the last thirteen years, I have injected insulin into my arm. I conform to a meal regimen. If I neglect this, I may go into insulin shock. If my hypoglycemia is severe enough, I may, quite possibly, die. I have to carry a chocolate cookie around with me twenty-four hours a day. The basic meaning of my life is to balance death and sugar. People without time bombs built into their genes are not likely to have the same meaning. Maybe the truest difference between people is exactly this: why we think we are here."

Suga growls in his sleep. My cigarette glows. "Mmm."

"What's the matter with you tonight, Miyake?"

I tap my cigarette into a beer-can ashtray. "Meeting my father has been my meaning. Now I am about to—what do I do after I meet him?"

"Why worry about it now?"

"I dunno. I worry about things and I can never stop."

"Eiji Miyake, I want to sleep with you right now."

I choke on a lungful of smoke. *"What?"*

"Only a joke. I just wanted to prove that it isn't as difficult to stop worrying as you think. Debussy never worried about his meaning of life. He just got on with doing what he loved."

"Debussy—you mentioned him the other night. What band was he in?"

"Claude Debussy. Tell me you are joking."

"Claude Debussy . . . drummer in the Jimi Hendrix Experience, right?"

Ai does not have a gullible bone in her body. "Eagles will peck out your liver, blasphemer. I'm playing him for my tone piece in tomorrow's audition. Want to hear?"

"Sure." This is a first.

I hear her clunk and shuffle about. "Lie back and gaze at the stars."

"This is Kita Senju, not Tahiti. The sky is all murk."

"Then I'll play you 'Et la lune descend sur le temple qui fut.'"

"Help."

"It means . . . 'And the moon sets o'er the temple that was.' Near enough."

"You speak French as well as everything else?"

"I've been planning to run away to France since I was six, remember."

"France. What an elegant meaning of life."

"Shush, or you won't hear the stars."

♦

The oil in the frying pan spits. I botch the second egg, crush shell fragments between my fingers, and the spermy mess drops in. I love the way the clear part skins over white. I rescue the toast, nearly in time, and scrape the charcoal into the sink. The pile on my futon stirs— "Uuuoooeeeaaaiii." Suga—this unclodded lungfish—winches his head and surveys my capsule. I stub out my Philip Morris in an eggshell, draw the curtains, and the unwashed morning streams in over three days of dishes and a major spillage of socks and papers. Suga is not pretty. His neck is boiled-octopus pink and a volcanic island chain of mosquito bites trails over his face. He blinks. "Miyake? What are you doing here?"

"I live here."

"Oh. What am I doing here?"

"This is where you died last night."

"I gotta do a dinosaur piss. Which is the john?" I point with a nod. Suga gets up and goes. He comes out sighing, zipping up his fly. "Your toilet smells as bad as Ueno. Deep chemistry. Smells like serious upchuck."

"How about a nice fried egg for breakfast, swimming in tasty oil?"

". . . Did *I* puke last night?"

"You kindly got most of it down the toilet. Come anytime."

"I need to drink a swimming pool."

I fill a beer mug with tapwater. Suga downs it in a marathon gulp. "Thanks. Any chance of coffee?" I give Suga mine and start another pan of water boiling. Suga bunches the futon into a log, sits at the table, drinks his coffee, goes "aaaaaah," and rolls down his shirtsleeves to hide his eczema. "I never knew you play the guitar. Is that kid on the swing your little sister?" Near enough. "Yes." I tip the eggs onto the toast, clear junk, and sit down to eat. "Then the man in the funny sunglasses is your father?" My yolk bleeds yellow. "Not quite. John Lennon." Suga plies his temples with his thumbs. "I heard of him. October comes earlier every year. So where am I exactly?"

"Above a video store in Kita Senju."

"When did I get here?"

"About eleven last night."

"You live above your workplace? The commuting must be a bitch."

"Be grateful I had somewhere nearby to drag your carcass, otherwise a dog would be pissing on you in the gutter right now. How did you get here last night? Did you get a taxi from the station? You were in no condition to walk far."

Suga shakes his head blankly. "I really can't remember."

The eggs are good. "And why did you come to visit me?"

Suga shrugs. "Miyake, when I was blotto last night . . . I don't suppose I blabbed any stupid stories or anything? I spout utter drivel when I drink. If I said anything, there wasn't, y'know, a word of truth in it. Pure bull. Everything I said. Or may have said."

"Fair enough."

"But I didn't actually say any, y'know, crazy stuff, did I?"

I weigh things up. "No, Suga. Nothing."

Suga nods. "Yeah, I thought as much. Me and alcohol. Pfff." In strolls Cat and immediately recognizes Suga as a soft touch. "Hello, beautiful!" Suga pets Cat while Cat checks out the food situation. "What are you doing shacking up with this dubious character, then?"

"Your gratitude overwhelms me."

"Why did you leave Ueno after only two weeks of a life sentence?"

"Family stuff. So, do you have, uh, seminars today?"

Suga shrugs. "What day are we on?"

"Thursday."

"I don't know where I'll go today."

"Not questing for Holy Grail?"

"Pointless." Suga takes off his glasses and pinches the bridge of his nose. The gesture makes him look sixty-something. "Deep timewaste. I quit hacking."

"Am I hearing this right?"

"I backdoored the Pentagon two weeks ago. Guess what?"

"No Holy Grail?"

Suga combs his hair with his fingers. "Nine billion Holy Grails. I looked inside one. I found another nine Holy Grails. And in each of them?"

"Nine billion Holy Grails?" I have to get ready for work.

"It adds up to . . . no offense, but you don't have the math." Suga sighs. "The whole thing was just some government nerd practical joke. Every hour I spent hacking—and it adds up to years—I could have spent more profitably with my finger up my fat one. All that time, gone. Even looking at a computer makes me ill."

"So what do you do at the university?"

"I don't. I—walk around the streets. At night. I sleep in the day."

"Why not just find another site to hack?" I fetch a clean T-shirt from my curtain rail. It is dry but crumpled, so I plug in my iron.

"For hackers," Suga sighs, "well, for the best ones, Holy Grail is the ultimate *meaning* of hacking, right? Nonhackers couldn't understand this. Imagine if you suddenly discovered, say, your father isn't who you thought he was. I don't even have the heart to post the news to my newsgroup. They would never believe me, anyway. They'd think I'd gone over to the other side. I would have."

I add my plate to my sink collection and try to find two socks that match, sort of. "Nine billion Holy Grails filled with nine billion Holy Grails." I flick out the legs of my ironing board and set it upright. "What a great hiding place for a Holy Grail." It was an off-the-cuff comment, and Suga opens his mouth to answer, but changes his mind. He strokes Cat, who cruises at ninety purrs per minute. My iron breathes steam. Suga opens his mouth. "No," he says. "I ran a mylo-P search as a matter of course, and checked thousands of sample grail files, from all over the document field. Holy Grail is just an exercise in infinity. In meaninglessness."

♎

November 13

> Weather, unknown at present. We are silent running. Ten minutes ago the lookout sounded the alarm—a squadron of Lightnings heading straight this way. Rehearsed pandemonium ensued as the crew prepared the *I-333* for diving before we were spotted. "Lookouts below! Dive! Dive!" Abe, Goto, Kusakabe, and I returned to our bunks. "Hatches secured!"

Seawater filled the ballast tank. A high-pitched wail was air forced out through the topside vents. *I-333* tipped at 10 degrees. Light bulbs exploded. Dull pain rings in my ears. Our lives are in the hands of the crew now. We are down to a maximum of 80 meters. The hull of *I-333* groans like nothing I ever heard. Nobody dares make a sound. Cpt. Yokota has told us of rumors about buoys dropped by the enemy that emit sonar, and allow acoustic-guided missiles to locate and destroy submarines. Maybe Cpt. Yokota is right: courage is the highest quality for a soldier, but technology is a fine substitute. I keep thinking about all the water above us. What I detest most about *I-333* is the smell: it assaults my senses whenever I return from the bridge. Sweat, excrement, rotting food, and men. Men, men, men. Ashore, surprises are often welcome. They break dull routine and bring excitement. Aboard a sub, surprises can prove lethal. I am writing these words to distract my mind. Abe is meditating. Goto is praying. Kusakabe is reading. A kaiten pilot is the most dangerous agent of destruction in maritime history, but how vulnerable I feel now.

November 14

Weather deteriorating. *I-333* is about halfway to our destination. Relations between Abe and Kusakabe have worsened. Yesterday evening Abe challenged him to chess, and when Kusakabe declined, said, "Seems strange for a kaiten pilot to be afraid of losing a game." The accusation was dressed up as a joke, but jokes are usually other things in disguise. I think Abe is jealous of the territory Kusakabe refuses to share. Without a word Kusakabe put his book down and set up the chessboard. He destroyed Abe like you would destroy a six-year-old. He took about ten seconds per move. Abe took longer to move, his face grew grimmer, but he could not bring himself to resign. Kusakabe promoted a pawn to a queen three times while Abe's king waited in a corner for the inevitable. When Abe knocked his king over, he joked: "I only hope your final mission is as great a success as your chess playing." Kusakabe replied, "The Americans are formidable opponents, Lieutenant." Goto and I were afraid these insults could only lead to violence, but Abe calmly put the chessmen away. "The Americans are an effete race of cowards. Without his gun, the Yankee is nothing." Kusakabe folded the board. "We have lost this war by swallowing our own propaganda. It poisons our faculties." Abe lost control, grabbed the chess-board, and flung it across our cabin. "Then exactly why are you here, kaiten pilot?" Kusakabe stared back defiantly at our superior officer. "The meaning of my sacrifice is to help Tokyo negotiate a less humiliating surrender." Abe hissed with rage. "Surrender? That word is anathema to the Yamato-damashii spirit! We liberated Malaya in ten weeks! We bombed Darwin! We blasted the British from the Bay of Bengal! Our crusade created a co-prosperity sphere unrivaled in the east since Genghis Khan! Eight corners united under one roof!" Kusakabe was neither angry nor bowed. "A great pity the Yamato-damashii spirit never figured out how to stop the roof from collapsing in on us." Abe shouted hoarsely. "Your words disgrace the insignia on your uniform! They insult your squadron! If we were on Otsushima I would report you for seditious thought! We are talking about good and evil! The divine will made manifest!" Kusakabe glared back. "We are talking about bomb tonnage. I wish to sink an enemy car-rier, but not for you, Lieutenant, not for the regiment, not for the bluebloods or the clowns in Tokyo, but because the fewer planes the Americans have raining bombs on Japan, the greater the chances my sisters will survive this stupid bloody war." Abe struck Kusakabe's face with his right hand, twice, hard, then hooked him with his left. Kusakabe staggered but did not fall, and said, "An excellent line of reasoning, if I may say so, Lieutenant." Goto got between them, although Kusakabe made no sign of striking his superior. I was too shocked to move. Abe spat at Kusakabe and stormed out, but there are not many places to storm to on a submarine. I got a damp cloth to bathe the bruise, but Kusakabe picked up his book as if nothing had happened. So calm, I almost suspect him of provoking Abe in order to be left in peace.

November 15

Weather: rain and wind, tail of a typhoon. I am suffering mildly from diarrhea, but sick bay dispensed some effective medicine. We have lost contact with *I-37,* our sister submarine on this mission. An all-systems kaiten service took up most of the day. Following yesterday's incident, Abe avoided speaking unless he had to. Kusakabe addresses him with a politeness that is almost aggressive. His left eye is half-closed by a bruise. Goto told the crew that Kusakabe fell out of his bunk. I doubt the crew believed him. I asked Kusakabe if his offer to lend me his book of English kabuki was still open, and Kusakabe said sure, and recommended a play about the greatest soldier in Rome. Listen: "Let me have war, say I; it exceeds peace as far as day does night; it's spritely, waking, audible, and full of vent. Peace is a very apoplexy, lethargy; mulled, deaf, sleepy, insensible; a getter of more bastard children than war's a destroyer of men." Even when Abe came into our cabin I carried on reading it. Western military values are perplexing, however. The soldier, Coriolanus, talks about honor, but when he feels betrayed by the Romans, instead of registering his disapproval by hara-kiri, he deserts and fights for the enemy! Where is the honor in that? This afternoon an unescorted American freighter was sighted, but Cpt. Yokota is under strictest orders not to fire a conventional torpedo until the kaiten mission is completed. Goto swore he for one would never breathe a word to Admiralty HQ if Cpt. Yokota ignored this directive, which I only realized later was a black joke. *I-47* sent a communiqué warning of two enemy destroyers SSE 20 km, so we let the freighter escape. Later, Goto and I fabricated a model warship from stiff card, and practiced kaiten approach angles with a mock periscope. Then, as casually as a comment on the weather, Goto said,

"Tsukiyama, I want to introduce you to my wife." For once, he was quite serious. He wedded her on our final weekend leave. "If she wants to remarry after my death," he said, more to himself than to me, "she has my blessing. She may have more than one husband, but I will only ever have one wife." Goto then asked me why I volunteered for special attack forces. It may strike you as odd that we never discussed this topic at Otsushima or even Nara, but our minds were too involved in the "how" to see the "why." My answer was, and is, that I believe the kaiten project is the reason I was born.

♦

Suga lumbers downstairs. "Hey."

"Hey." I close the journal. "How are you feeling?"

"A ten-megaton headache."

"My boss keeps a first aid box somewhere—"

"I have a unique immunity to painkillers. I cleaned your toilet. I never cleaned one before. I hope I used the right cloths and stuff."

"Thank you."

Suga sniffs and watches the screen for a while. It is an American movie—most of them are—I chose at random called *An Officer and a Gentleman*. From the box I thought it might be about the Pacific War and the navy my great-uncle fought, but I was wrong. The star—he has a pained-rodent face—is stuck in boot camp in the 1980s. "Well," says Suga, "I see why you quit in Ueno. Is this all you do? Sit on your butt and watch movies all day?"

"Same as sitting on your butt and watching computer screens."

Suga inspects the new releases rack. "Living on borrowed time, these video stores. Pretty soon people will download all their videos via the net, right? DCDI format. The technology is already here, just waiting for marketing to catch up. I meant to ask: what happened with that Korean babe you were chasing?"

"Uh, mistaken identity."

A kryptonite green Jeep, throbbing with time-travel music, mounts the sidewalk. Lolita, sitting in the passenger seat, eats cherries the same color as her lips, while Dalai Lama darts in, nursing a fluffy white ferret—it sports a pink-and-lime bow tie—in one arm and three videos in the other. "*Jason and the Argonauts* thrilled us, *Sinbad* chilled us, *Titanic* killed us. Myths are no longer what they used to be." I check the return-by dates and thank him. Dalai Lama moonwalks out and waves the ferret's paw at us. The ferret yawns. The Jeep jets off, redshifting drum-and-bass music into a thudding hiss. Suga watches through the door. "I wish I had a friend like that. I could phone him up every time I feel like a misfit, right, just to remind myself how normal I actually am." Suga yawns, cleans his glasses on his T-shirt, and steps outside to consult the sky. "So. Another day."

"Audition hall waiting rooms are nurseries for lunatics," says Ai, the noise of the wind a hazy crackle of static, "or psychological warfare students. Musicians are worse than those chess grandmasters who kick each other under the table. One boy from Toho music school is eating garlic yogurt and reading French slang from a phrase book. Aloud. Another is chanting Buddhist scriptures with his mother. Two girls are discussing best-loved music-academy suicides who couldn't take the pressure."

"If your music sounds half as good to the judges as it did to me last night, you should breeze through it."

"I think you may be biased, Miyake. No points are awarded for neck contours. Anyway, nobody breezes into a Paris Conservatoire scholarship. You drag yourself there by your fingernails, over the corpses of slaughtered hopefuls. Like the Roman gladiators, except when you lose you have to simper politely and congratulate your nemesis. Playing over the phone to you is not the same as performing for a panel of dug-up A-class war criminal look-alikes who control my future and my meaning as a human being. If I blow this audition, it will be private lessons to Hello Kitty daughters until the day I die."

"There will be other auditions in the future," I point out.

"Nice try, but that is the wrong thing to say."

"When are the results announced?"

"Five o'clock today, after the final candidate has performed—the judges fly back to France tomorrow. Hang on—someone's coming"—

I get an earful of static swish and covered mumble—"that was my on-in-two-minutes call."

Say something powerful, encouraging, and witty, Miyake. "Uh, good luck."

Her breathing changes as she walks. "I was thinking earlier . . ."

"About?"

"I changed my mind about the meaning of life again."

"Yeah?"

"You look for your meaning. You find it, and at that moment, your meaning changes, and you have to start all over again."

"But that means that you never actually—Ai?"

Her footsteps echo and static blows, then the line is broken.

Customers come, customers go. A steady stream of movies about the end of the world is rented—must be something in the air. I wonder how Ai is doing in her audition. She sounds like a fine musician to me. I thought my guitar playing was okay, but compared to her I am a no-fingered amateur. A hassled mother comes in and asks me to recommend a video that will shut her kids up for an hour. I resist the temptation to slip her *Pam the Clam from Amsterdam*—"Well, madam, it *did* shut them up, didn't it?"—and suggest *Sky Castle Laputa*. I go to the door—the sky is one of those refracted marmalade sunsets. A Harley-Davidson growls by, a strolling lion. Its chromework is cometary, and its driver is a kid with leather pants, a designer-gashed T-shirt saying DAMN I'M GOOD, and an army outrider helmet with a cartoon duck stenciled on. The girlfriend, her perfect arms disappearing into the T-shirt, blond hair catching amber sunlight, is none other than Velvet. Love Hotel Velvet! Same pout, same time-zone straddling legs. I half-hide behind a Ken Takakura poster and watch the motorbike weave through the clogged traffic. Definitely Velvet—or her clone. Now I am not so certain. Velvet has millions of clones in Tokyo. I sit down and open my grandfather's journal. What would Subaru Tsukiyama say about Japan today? Was it worth dying for? Maybe he would reply that *this* Japan is not the Japan he did die for. The Japan he died for never came into being. It was a possible future, auditioned by the present but rejected with other dreams.

Maybe it is a mercy he cannot see the Japan that was chosen. I wonder what angle to take when I meet my grandfather next Monday. I wish I could do angles as skillfully as Daimon. I wish Admiral Raizo had given me a clue. Should I applaud the samurai spirit stuff? Does it matter? All I want is for my grandfather to introduce me to my father. Nothing more. I wonder how I would have fared in the war. Could I have calmly stayed in an iron whale cruising toward my death? I am the same age as my great-uncle when he died. I guess I would not have been "I." I would have been another "I." A weird thought, that—I am not made by me, or my parents, but by the Japan that did come into being. Subaru Tsukiyama was made by a Japan that died with surrender. It must be tough being made by both, like Takara Tsukiyama.

♎

November 18

Weather: tropical heat, blinding sunshine. This morning I spent thirty minutes on the lookout platform fore of the periscopes. The lookout lent me his binoculars. Our position is 60 kilometers west of Ulithi atoll. A high-altitude recon-naissance plane from Truk reported 200 enemy vessels, including four carriers. Enemy radio transmissions grow ever busier. Cpt. Yokota made the decision not to wait for *I-37*, as five days have passed since our last contact. Hailing her on VLF radio would be hazardous so close to an enemy strong-hold. I hope she has only been delayed. Being sunk so close to the target area would be a cruel irony for the kaiten pilots. We wished *I-36* and *I-47* good hunting and turned west toward the Palau Islands. *I-333* approached Peleliu around 1800 hours. The archipelago is as beautiful as places from old stories, but as outlandish as the landscapes I used to doo-dle on my copybook. I saw coral islets, twisted outcrops, gorges, peaks, swamps, and sandbars. Recent battle damage was much in evidence. The 14th Division of the Kwantung Army will have made the enemy pay dearly for the invasion of these islands. The bases and airfields were among the most battle-ready in the war, because the Palaus had been Japanese territory since the League of Nations mandate. But the enemy cannot guess the true price of anchoring in the Kossol Passage. The lookout spotted an enemy scout plane and we dived. As tonight's meal will, in all probability, be our final one, Cpt. Yokota produced his wind-up gramophone and two records. I instantly recognized a tune that Father used to play, before jazz was banned because of its corrupting influence. The musician's name is Jyu Keringuton. How strange to be listening to American jazz before setting out to kill Americans.

November 19

Weather: fine, calm conditions prevailing. A quiet last night. I-333 conducting submerged periscope watch. Slick has promised to visit Nagasaki and hand this journal to you personally, Takara. My co-Kikusui pilots are composing their final letters. Kusakabe asked Abe's advice regarding an obscure kanji for a haiku he was composing. Abe answered without rancor. I have little talent for poetry. Slick is presently servicing our kaitens for the final time, and the kaiten release mechanisms are being tested. Cpt. Yokota is approaching the mouth of Kossol Passage in a slow curve. We prayed at the special shrine and left incense as gifts to the god of the shrine. Goto burned his cardboard aircraft carrier and offered the ashes. We studied a cartographical chart of the target zone, with depth soundings. At our final supper we thanked the crew for bringing us here safely. We drank banzai toasts to the success of our mission and to the Emperor. I went up to the bridge one final time to see the moon and stars, and shared a cigarette with the ensign on duty. The moon was full and bright. It reminded me of the mirror Yaeko and Mother use to apply cosmetics. This moon will allow me to choose my target in under three hours from now. Three hours. This is all my lifeline has to run, if all goes well. My thoughts are now occupied with how I can best utilize my training to be sure of making a lethal hit. I will now entrust this journal to Slick.

Live my life for me, Takara, and I will die your death for you.

Live long, little brother.

◆

I had never heard Ai sound miserable. I hadn't thought misery was in her repertoire. I stroke the fluffy part below Cat's throat. "Your father knows how much the Conservatoire means to you?"

"That man knows exactly how much it means."

"And he knows how few scholarships get awarded?"

"Yes."

"Why has he forbidden you to go? Why isn't he brimming over with pride?"

"Niigata was good enough for him, so Niigata will be good enough for me. He refuses to use the word *music*. He says 'tinkling' instead."

"What does your mother think?"

"My mother? 'Think'? Not since her honeymoon. What she says is 'Obey your father!' Over and over. She let him finish her sentences for her for so long that now he starts them too. She actually apologizes to my father for making him yell at her. My sister and I used to be close, but she married the owner of the biggest concrete works on the Japan Sea coast because our father told her to. It was a dynastic alliance. Now she is turning into my mother. It's creepy. My mother heard they have big ozone holes over Austria, so—"

"Austria? Doesn't she mean Australia?"

"See what I'm up against? Their knowledge of the world outside Japan extends only as far as they can swim offshore. Sorry if I sound bitter. Then my brother was called over. He runs That Man's branch office, so you can imagine how sympathetic he was. I am wrecking the family harmony, he said. French food will make my diabetes worse—as if *he* ever cared about my diabetes—and the sheer worry will cause my mother's blood pressure to rise, and she may actually explode. Then I will be guilty of blowing up Mother as well as disobeying That Man. What's making that noise? Not Suga again?"

"Cat, this time. She feels sorry for you, but doesn't know what to say that wouldn't sound feeble. She hopes it will all work out okay."

"Thank her. At times like this I wish I smoked."

"Hold your mouth to the receiver—I'll blow smoke down the line."

"Don't. Diabetics have enough to worry about. My flatmate's magazine says that over 90 percent of teenagers fantasize that their parents are not their real parents. After this evening I can see the appeal. Truth is, That Man hates the idea of me not needing him. He wants to hire and fire the world as he sees fit. He is afraid of his employees finding out he can't control his daughter. What . . . a family of sand fleas I come from! I swear, sometimes I think I would be better off as an orphan. Oh. Oh . . . sorry, that was a stupid thing to say . . ."

"Hey, don't worry."

"Today has blown my tact chip. I should switch myself off and leave you in peace. I've done nothing but whine for thirty minutes."

"You can whine all night. Isn't that right, Cat?"

Cat, bless her, meooows right on cue.

"See? So whine."

"You look five years younger," I tell Buntaro when he gets back from Okinawa on Sunday evening, and he really does. "So if I go on four vacations in a row do I get to look like you?" He presents me with a keyring of Zizzi Hikaru—like most idols, Zizzi is Okinawan—who sheds her clothes when you breathe on the plastic casing. "Hey, thanks," I say, "this will be a family heirloom. Good to be back?"

"Ye-es." Buntaro looks around Shooting Star. "No. Yes. Don't know."

"Right. Did Machiko-san enjoy herself?"

"Way too much. She wants to move there. Tomorrow afternoon." Buntaro scratches his head. "Kodai being born soon . . . it changes the way you see things. Would you want to be brought up in Tokyo?"

I remember my mother's first letter, the balcony one. "Maybe not."

Buntaro checks his watch. "You must have a thousand things you want to do, kid." I don't, but I can see he wants to catch up on paperwork, so I climb up to my capsule and round up dirty laundry. I try calling Ai, but nobody answers. Netherworld noises vibrate down the apartment building tonight. Husband bawling, baby screaming, washing machine spinning. Tomorrow is Monday—grandfather day. I lie on my futon and begin decoding the final three pages of the journal. These are written on different paper, in cramped letters that get harder and harder to read. Across the top of the paper is stamped in red ink, in English: "SCAP"—which is not in my dictionary—and "Military Censor." These half-obscure a pencil inscription in Japanese: ". . . these words. . . . moral property . . . Takara Tsukiyama. . . ." An address in Nagasaki is illegible to me.

♎

November 20

> Weather—unknown. Dead but still alive. Alone in kaiten. Last 6 hours. At 0245 Cpt. Yokota came to cabin— announced the kaiten attack to commence in 15 mins. Stood in a circle and tied hachimaki of brother before us. Goto: "Just another training run, boys." Abe to Kusakabe: "You are a demon chess player, Ensign." Kusakabe: "Your right hook is the demon, Lieutenant." Toured *I-333*—thanked crew for bringing us here safely. Saluted, man by man. Shook hands before entering kaitens via chutes. Slick sealed the hatches behind us. His face last I saw. *I-333* dived for final approach. Radioman First Class Hosokawa maintained telephone link until release, providing last-minute orientation. Abe released 0315. Heard clamps fall loose. Goto released 0320. Kusakabe floated free 0335. Next 5 mins I thought many things, focus difficult. Hosokawa in Nagasaki dialect: "I'll be thinking of you. Glory is yours." Final human words. Foreclasps released. Started engine. Rears released. Floated free. Thrust sharp left avoid conning tower/periscope shears. Proceeded ESE heading, holding depth 5 meters. Surfaced 0342 confirm position with visual fix. Enemy fleet clearly silhouetted harbor lights. Troop carriers, transport ships, fuel tankers, at least 3 battleships, 3 destroyers, 2 heavy cruisers. No carriers, many fat targets. Eating, asleep, shitting, smoking, drink-

ing, talking Americans. I, their executioner. Strange sensation. At strategy meeting on *I-333* agreed first kaitens should target distant vessels—guesswork required. Used children's choosing chant: *Do-re-ni-shi-ma-sho-ka? Ka-mi-sa-ma-no-iu-to*-explosion. Shock waves rocked kaiten. Steadied periscope, saw fuel tanker, plum-blossom fire, smoke already obscuring stars. Secondary explosion. Orange. Beautiful, terrible, could not tear eyes away. Flares climbed, lit Passage brighter than day. Hunted, I dived. Waking dream. Being, not doing. Chose nearest large naval ship and maneuvered to appropriate angle. Klaxons, engines, chaos. Another major explosion—kaiten, nearby depth charge, no knowing. Patrol boat? Vibrations nearer, nearer, nearer—dived to 8 meters—passed over. Sizeable explosion to starboard. Loneliness—afraid brothers leave me here among hostile strangers not my race. Slowed to 2 kph, surfaced for position check. Fires/smoke/afterexplosions 2 locations. Chose large outline due west—light cruiser? 150 meters. Eyes dazzled by searchlight, but cloaked by chaos onshore. Dived to 6–7 meters. Throttled to 18 kph. Flying, strange air. Cut to dead halt. Surfaced, final check. Cruiser filled the night. 80 meters. Saw figures streaming. Ants. Fireflies. Dived 5 meters. Primed warhead. One thought: "This is my final thought." Opened throttle lever to maximum velocity. Acceleration shoved me back, hard . . . 70 meters closing, 60, 50, 40, 30, 20, impact next moment, impact now.

Clang like temple bell. Wild spinning—up = down, down = up, drilling, flung left right up down, loose objects flying, me too. Lungs empty. So this death, I think, then I think, Can dead think? Pain rings from head erased further thought. Lurching crunch > hung downward > judder halt. Engines howling, rudder control dead and free in hand, scream noise from engines, heat climbing, burning-oil smell—same moment I realize not dead and must cut engines, engines die.

Failure. Warhead did not detonate. Kaiten glanced off hull = bamboo spear off metal helmet. Periscope sights slashed face, broke nose. Sat, listened to noises from surface. Tried to ignite TNT manually, strike casing with wrench. Tore off fingernail in attempt. Impact broke chronometer. Minutes or hours, cannot tell. Periscope blackness > blueness now. Flask of whiskey. Will drink, put these pages into flask. Takara. Message in bottle in dead shark. Learn this song, Takara?

Corpses adrift and corpses swollen,
Corpses abed in the swollen sea,
Corpses adream in the mountain grasslands,
We shall die, we shall die, we shall die for the Emperor,
and we shall never look back.

Abed in the swollen sea. Air thinner. Or imagine air thinner. Now? Divers may discover me—typhoon shakes me loose, beaches me—remain here end of time. Kaiten was not way to glorious death. Kaiten is urn. Sea is tomb. Do not blame us who die so long before noon.

◆

"No hope," answers the woman who is not Ai. It is after midnight but she sounds more amused than angry. She has a brick-thick Osaka accent. "Sorry."

"Oh. Can I ask when, uh, Miss Imajo is expected back?"

"Feel free to ask, but whether I answer is another Q."

"When is Miss Imajo due back? Please?"

"And tonight's top news story: the rebel chieftainess Ai Imajo is summoned to the ancestral seat in Niigata in a last-ditch attempt to break the diplomatic deadlock. When reporters asked the defiant music student guerrilla how long the summit would last, we were told: 'As long as it takes.' Stay tuned!"

"Days, then?"

"My turn. Are you the karate kid?"

"No. The headbutt kid."

"Same kid. Nice to meet your disembodied voice at last, karate kid. Ai calls you headbutt kid, but I think karate kid sounds much wittier."

"Uh, for sure. When Ai gets back could you—"

"I inherited my granny's psychic powers. I knew it was you calling. Don't you want to know who I am?"

"Are you Ai's shy, retiring roommate, by any chance?"

"Hole in one! So. Is Ai dating a human being, or are you another psycho gremlin?"

"Not exactly dating . . ." I take the bait. "'Psycho gremlin'?"

"Fact. Eighty percent of Ai's admirers go on to successful careers in the horror movie industry. The last one was the Creature from the Black Lagoon. Webby, floppy, water-resistant, caught bluebottles with his tongue. Phoned at midnight and croaked until dawn. Drove a Volvo, wore blazers, gave out CDs of himself singing madrigals, and confided his fantasies—quite unsolicited—when Ai begged me to say she was out. He and Ai would marry at Tokyo Disneyland, tour Athens, Montreal, and Paris with their three sons, Delius, Sibelius, and Yoyo. One time his mother called—she wanted Ai's parents' number in Niigata so she could start marriage negotiations directly with the manufacturer. Ai and I had to concoct an ex-boxer boyfriend in prison who half-strangled Ai's last admirer."

"I can promise, right now, my mother will never call you. But—"

"Ever worked in a pizza kitchen, karate kid?"

"A pizza kitchen? Why?"

"Ai says you need a job as of tomorrow."

"True, but I never worked in a kitchen before."

"No worries. Chimpanzees could do the job. In fact, we have hired lots of hairy primates in the past. The hours are lousy—midnight to eight A.M.—the kitchen is hotter than the core of the sun but on the graveyard shift the money is good. Central location—the Nero's opposite Jupiter Cafe, site of legendary headbutt. Plus, you get to work with me. Has Ai mentioned my name?"

"Uh . . ."

"Obviously I am the last thing on her mind. Sachiko Sera. As in
'*Que sera, sera, whatever li-lah, li-lah.*' Can you start tomorrow evening?
Monday?"

"I don't want to talk you out of giving me a job I need so badly, Ms.
Sera, but, uh, don't you want to meet me first?"

Sachiko Sera does a beyond-the-tomb voice. "Eiji Miyake, native
son of Yakushima . . . I know *everything* about you . . ."

"Mr. Miyake?" At Amadeus Tea Room, Butler stops drumming his fingers. Arched eyebrows: butlership is all in the eyebrows. "Please follow
me. The Tsukiyamas are waiting for you." Tsukiyamas? Could my grandfather have persuaded my father to come too? I search the faces. The
place is busier than last week—a funeral party is meeting here, many of
the customers are in black—and I have trouble trying to locate an elderly man and a middle-aged one who looks like me. So when Butler pulls
a chair out at a table where a woman and a girl my age are seated, I
assume he has made a mistake. His eyebrows tell me there is no mistake, so I gawk, while they assess me. "Will you require an additional
cup, madam?" asks Butler. The woman dismisses him with a quarter-
smile and a "Most certainly not." The girl stares at me—a "Will the turd
fit around the U-bend?" sort of stare—while my memory grapples with a
similarity . . . Anju! A chubby, crinkle-cut, scowly Anju. We have the
same feather eyebrows. "Eiji Miyake," she says, and I nod as if it were a
question. "I knew it was you because you have that 'Do you like me?'
look you'd expect to see on an orphan. You are one sorry, shameless
creep, Eiji Miyake." All at once, I understand. She is my half-sister. My
stepmother fingers the bronze torque around her neck—thick enough to
halt an ax swing—and sighs. "Let us try to keep this meeting as brief and
painless as possible. Sit down, Mr. Miyake."

I sit down. Amadeus Tea Room continues in the background, as if
on a video screen. "Mrs. Tsukiyama"—I grope around for pleasantries—
"thank you for your letter last month."

Fake surprise. "'Thank you'? Irony is your opening move, Mr. Miyake?"

"No." I look around. "Uh . . . actually, I was expecting my grandfather . . ."

"Yes, we know all about that. Your little rendezvous was recorded in his diary. Regrettably, my father-in-law is unable to attend."

"Oh . . . I see." Have you locked him in a closet?

Half-sister has a slappy voice. "Grandpapa passed away three days ago."

Slap.

A waitress passes with a tray of raspberry cheesecake slices.

Stepmother does not bother to conceal her disdain either. "I am frankly astonished that you failed to see how sick he was last Monday. Running around at your beck and call, plotting conspiracies. I only hope you are proud of yourself."

This makes no sense. "I didn't meet him last Monday."

"Liar!" slaps Half-sister. "Liar! Mother already told you—we have his appointment diary! Guess whose name we found for a meeting here one week ago!" I want to wrap her mouth in carpet tape.

"But my grandfather was still in the hospital last Monday."

Stepmother does a head-resting-on-hands pose. "Your lies are embarrassing, Mr. Miyake. We know my father-in-law left his hospice last Monday to meet you! He didn't ask for permission from the duty nurse, because he wouldn't have received it. He was far too sick."

"I am not lying! My grandfather was too sick to come, so he sent his friend."

"What friend?"

"Admiral Raizo."

Stepmother and Half-sister look at each other. Half-sister snickers a jerky laugh and Stepmother smiles so that her mouth shrinks to a lipsticked tip. Those lips kiss my father. "Then you did meet Grandpapa," slaps Half-sister, "but you were too dumb to recognize him!" My temper takes the strain. I look at Stepmother for an explanation. "My father-in-law's last practical joke."

"Why would my grandfather pretend to be this Admiral Raizo?"

Half-sister thumps the table. "He is *not* your 'grandfather'!" I ignore her. Stepmother's eyes glint with war. "Did he give you any documents to sign?"

"Why," I repeat, "would my grandfather pretend to be somebody else?"

"Did," she repeats, "he give you any documents to sign?"

This is going nowhere. I put my hands behind my head, lean back, and study the ceiling while I try to calm down. "Yes, my friend," observes Mozart, "you have a problem here. But it is your problem. Not mine." I badly want to smoke. "Mrs. Tsukiyama, is this bad blood necessary?"

"'Bad blood,'" mutters Half-sister. "Nice expression."

"What do I have to do to prove to you that all I want is to meet my father?"

Stepmother tilts her head. "Do calm down, Mr. Miyake—"

This makes me boil over. "No, Mrs. Tsukiyama, I am tired of calming down! I do not—"

"Mr. Miyake, you are making a—"

"Shut up and listen to me! I do not want your money! I do not want favors! And *blackmail*! How did you come up with the theory I wanted to *blackmail* you? I am so, so, so *tired* of scrubbing around this city trying to find my own father! You want to despise me, fine, I can live with that. Just let me meet him—just once—and if he tells me himself that he never wants to see me again, okay, I will vanish from your lives and start my own, properly. That is it. That is all. Is this too much to ask?"

I am so drained.

Half-sister is unsure of herself.

Stepmother has finally put away her unbearable sneer.

I think I got them to listen. And half the customers in Amadeus Tea Room.

"Actually, yes." Stepmother pours herself and her pouty, piggy daughter weak tea from an inoffensive no-drip teapot. "It is too much to ask. Let us concede that I accept you mean my family no malice, Mr. Miyake. Let us even concede that I feel some sympathy for your position. The basic situation still stands unchanged."

"The basic situation."

"There is no nice way to say it. My husband does not wish to meet you. I will say it again, for emphasis. My husband does not wish to meet you. You seem to believe in a dark conspiracy keeping you away from him—this is simply not true. We are not here to confuse your trail. We are here at the behest of my husband to ask you, *please,* to leave him in peace. He has paid for your upkeep not to maintain hopes of a future reunion, but to buy his right to privacy. Is this too much to ask?"

I want to cry. "Why won't he just tell me this himself?"

"In a word"—Stepmother sips her tea—"shame."

I have no defense lined up for this.

Stepmother says it again. "He is ashamed of you."

"But how can he be ashamed of somebody he refuses to meet?"

"My husband isn't ashamed of who you are. He doesn't really care who you are. He is ashamed of what you are. An illegitimate reminder of the worst mistake of his life."

At the far side a customer abruptly stands up, sliding his chair behind him.

"You are causing pain for him, for us, for yourself. Please stop."

The waitress walks into the chair. Teacups and raspberry cheesecakes slide off her tray, and fine bone china chimes to pieces in a ripple of "Ooooooooo"'s. Stepmother and Half-sister watch with me. Butler paraglides over to supervise the cleanup operation. Apologies, counterapologies, assurances, orders, carpet sponges, dustpans. Sixty seconds later no evidence remains of the great crisis. "Okay," I say.

Half-sister slides her cup away. "Okay what?"

I address the woman my father chose to marry. "Okay, you win." She did not expect this. Neither did I. She searches my face for a catch. There is none. "My father—just by never getting in touch himself—made his, uh, position clear a long time ago. I . . . I . . . dunno, I never wanted to believe it. But tell him"—an apricot carnation sits in a glass tear vase—"hello. Hello and goodbye."

Stepmother keeps her gaze steady.

I stand up to go.

"Did you get that from Grandpapa?" Half-sister has a way of prodding your ribs with words. She nods at the kaiten journal, wrapped in its black cloth. "Because if so, it is the legal property of the Tsukiyamas."

I look at this anti-Anju. "No." If she had asked nicely, I would have handed it over. "This is my lunch box. I have to go to work. It was really nice to meet you both. Thank you for your time." I take the journal and walk out of Amadeus Tea Room without looking back. Butler summons an elevator and bows—not so ironically that I could complain, but ironically enough to mock me—as the doors close. Who cares? I have the elevator to myself—the Muzak is "Top of the World" by the Carpenters, a tune that makes my teeth throb, but I am too drained to hate anything now. I think about the decision I just took. I am stunned by it. I watch the floor numbers descend. Do I mean it? My father never wants to meet me . . . So my search for him is . . . not valid? Finished? My meaning is canceled? I guess, yes, I do mean it. "First floor" says the elevator. The doors open and a crowd of very busy people surges in. I have to fight my way out before the doors close.

seven

Cards

Sachiko Sera, my third boss in four weeks, was not exaggerating: the Nero's kitchen is hot as hell and a monkey could do my pizza-by-numbers job. The kitchen is a rat run—it measures five paces by one, with a sort of cage at one end with lockers and chairs where the delivery bikers wait. Sachiko and Tomomi take the orders by telephone or from walk-in customers, and pass the orders through the hatch from the front counter. I dress the crusts in the correct toppings by matching the pizza name to the giant chart that takes up an entire wall, coded with colored icons for the benefit of monkeys who never learned to read. So, for example, in the big circle marked "Chicago Gunfight" are little pictures of tomato, meatballs, sausage, chili, red and yellow peppers, cheese; "Hawaii Honeymoon" is tomato, pineapple, tuna, coconut; "Neromaniac" is pepperoni, sour cream, capers, olives, and jumbo shrimp. Then you have the crust types: thick, crusty, herb, mozzarella-filled. The toppings live in a cave-size fridge—each container lid has a picture of the contents. Once the pizzas are dressed, you slide them into a two-lane gas-fired inferno. Rollers convey the pizzas through its geothermic innards at about ten centimeters per minute, although if the orders are piling up you can reach in with a pair of forceps and give the pizza a premature birth. "Timing is the trick," says Sachiko, tying back her hair. "Ideally, the pizza lands in its box—tape the order slip to the lid thusly—the same moment the biker lands from his last delivery." It is sort of fun, and the orders never stop, not even at one or two A.M., so unlike at Ueno lost property or Shooting Star I never have much time to get bored. Our customers include students, card sharks, businessmen working through the night—Shinjuku is a nocturnal jungle. I drink liters of water, sweat liters of water, and never need to piss once. There is an exhaust fan as loud as an engine room and a tinny radio that only picks up one local station trapped in the 1980s. There is a gunk-smattered world map to tantalize us slaves of the inferno with thoughts of all the countries in the world—and their many-tinted women—where we are not free to go. A clock drags the minutes past. Sachiko is how I imagined her on the telephone—loopy, organized, stable. Tomomi is an evil hag who has been at Nero's since Commodore Perry sailed into old Edo Bay and has no intention of upsetting her cozy life by ever getting promoted. She chats with her friends on the phone, flirts with privileged bikers, selects arts courses she will never actually apply for, and drops heavy hints about the affair she had with the owner of Nero's x years ago and the damage she could inflict on his marriage if her pleasant equilibrium were ever threatened. Her laugh is a loud, glittery fake. The delivery bikers come and go week by week—mostly they are students—but tonight they are Onizuka and Doi. Onizuka has a lip spike, custard yellow hair, and wears a death's-head biker's jacket instead of the Nero's Pizza uniform. When Sachiko introduces us, he says this: "Last guy before you, he fucked up the orders. Customers gave me shit. Don't you fuck up the orders." He comes from Tohoku and still has a northern accent as thick as crude oil—this worries me, in case I mistake a mortal threat for a weather remark. Doi is ancient, over forty, walks with a limp, and has a Jesus-being-crucified expression. Suffering, spaced-out screensaver eyes, not much hair on his head but loads on his chin. "Don't let Onizuka get you down, man," he tells me. "The man is mellow. Saw to my motor for free, man. Smoke pot?" When I say no, he shakes his head sadly. "Youth of today, man, you misspend the prime of your life, you'll repent at your leisure, man. Got friends who know how to party? Premium quality, discreet service." Tomomi enters the cage—she is a gifted eavesdropper. "Discreet? As discreet as a mile-wide UFO playing the *Mission: Impossible* music over the Imperial Palace." At three A.M. Sachiko brings me a mug of the thickest coffee known to chemistry—thick enough to stand pencils in, I mean it—which makes my body forget how tired it is. Onizuka waits in the staff cube at the end of my rat run, but never says another word to me. Twice I smoke a John Player Special outside the storefront. I have a prime view of PanOpticon. Antiaircraft lights blink on and off from dusk until dawn. Very Gotham City. Both times the inferno summons me back before I can finish the cigarette. While I am waiting for a Health Club—asparagus, sour cream, olives, potato wedges, garlic—to emerge from the inferno, Doi leans over the hatch. "You know how hungry I am, Miyake?"

"How hungry are you, Doi?"

"I am hungry enough to cut off my thumb and chew it."

"Really hungry, then."

"Pass me that knife, will you?"

I make a "Do I have to?" face.

"Pass me the knife, man, this is a hunger crisis."

"Be careful with that knife. Razor sharp."

"Why else would I want it, man?" Doi places his left thumb on my chopping board, places the blade over it, and thumps the handle with his right fist. The blade slices clean through the knuckle. Blood spills over the counter—Doi reins in his breath. "There, that wasn't so bad! He picks up his thumb with his right hand and dangles it in his mouth. Plop. I gargle dry air. Doi munches slowly, deciding if he likes the taste. "Gristly, man, but not bad." Doi spits out his thumb bone, sucked shiny and white. I drop whatever it was I was holding. Sachiko appears in the hatch—I point, and glug. "Doi!" scolds Sachiko. "You prima donna! You can't resist a captive audience, can you? Sorry, Miyake, I should have warned you about Doi's little hobby: magic school." Doi mimes a kung-fu retaliatory shuffle. "The Sacred Academy of Illusionists ain't no 'hobby,' chieftainess. One day there'll be lines outside the Budokan to see me perform." He waggles his two attached thumbs at me. "You can tell from his eyes, that Shiyake is one cat in sore need of the magic arts." "Miyake," corrects Sachiko. "Him, too," says Doi. I do not know how to respond—I am just relieved that the blood was tomato juice. At five A.M. morning comes in for landing. Sachiko asks me to prepare some mini-salads for the next shift, so I wash some lettuce and cherry tomatoes. The pizza orders thicken again—who eats pizzas for breakfast?—and before I know it Sachiko is back, doing a high-court voice. "Eiji Miyake, by the powers vested in me by Emperor Nero, and in view of your satis-factory behavior, I declare your life sentence suspended for the period of sixteen hours. You will present yourself at this correctional institu-tion at midnight, for a further eight hours' hard labor." I frown. "Huh?" Sachiko points at the clock—"Eight o'clock. Surely you have a home to go to?" The front door slides open. Sachiko glances around, and looks back at me with an "aha!" look. "The prisoner has a visitor waiting out-side the gates."

Ai says anywhere except Jupiter Cafe, so we walk toward Shinjuku to find a breakfast place. Talking is a bit awkward—we have not actually met since the day in Jupiter Cafe, even though we must have spent over twenty-four hours on the telephone last week. "If it was any more humid than this," I venture, "it would be raining." Ai tilts her face skyward. "Y'know, it is raining." She caught a bus back from Niigata yesterday evening, and looks travel-worn. I am sweaty and disheveled. "So how did it go with your father?" Ai hums. "Going back was a futile exercise. I knew it would be . . ." she begins. I make the right noises at the right times, but as usual when people discuss parental problems, I feel as if I am being told about a medical condition in an organ I lack. Still, I am booming with pleasure that Ai came to meet me for breakfast, and I have to work at not looking too happy. We pass a tiny shrine—Ai breaks off to look at the trees, torii gate, straw ropes, and twists of paper. A Jizo statue sits behind an orange, a bottle of Suntory whiskey, and a vase of chrysanthemums. An old man is having a good long pray. I wonder why. I must be an island gossip at heart too. "Are musicians supersti-tious?" I ask.

"Depends on the instrument. String players, technically including pianists, have the luxury of being able to practice until we get it right, and any mistakes we do make usually get swallowed up by the orchestra. Woodwind, and especially brass, have it tougher. However good you are, one unlucky blast and Bruckner's celestial ninth gets blasted open with a—well, my last conductor's metaphor—a shotgun fart. Most trumpet players I know have beta blockers instead of peanut cookies with their morning coffee. Are Yakushima pizza chefs superstitious?"

"The last time I went to a shrine it was to, uh, decapitate its god."

"With a lightning bolt?"

"I only had a junior-carpenter-set hacksaw."

She sees I am serious. "Didn't the god give you what you wanted?"

"The god gave me exactly what I wanted."

"Which is why you sawed his head off?"

"Yep."

"My, I must be careful about giving you what you want."

"Ai Imajo—I, Eiji Miyake, hereby swear I will never saw your head off."

"That comes as a relief. But isn't destroying religious artifacts a juvenile-court-size offense?"

"I never told anyone until this morning."

Ai gives me a look with ninety-nine possible meanings. McDonald's has an electronic signboard above the door that reports how many seats are vacant—it flits in and out of single figures. Detectors must be built into the seats, I guess. Ai tells me to go upstairs and find a table while she gets in line, and I am too exhausted to argue. McDonald's stinks of McDonald's but at least it will disguise the stink of Miyake the unshowered kitchen slave. Upstairs a flock of student nurses smokes, bitches, and shrieks into their cell phones. I add up the money I earned since midnight and I feel a little less tired. It is Europe Week in McDonald's—a video screen hangs on the wall, and scenes of Rome glide by while soporific music sucks you in. Ai appears at the top of the steps holding the tray, looking around for me. I could wave, but I enjoy looking at her as if I am seeing her for the first time. Black leggings, a sky blue T-shirt under a berry-juice silk shirt, and amber magma earrings. If Ai were a nurse I would break a major bone to get a bed in her ward. "They were out of chocolate shake," she says, "so I chose banana. I see you have a kinky fetish for nurse uniforms."

"They must have, uh, followed me in."

Ai sticks the straw through my lid. "In your dreams—anyway, you reek of cheese. Sachiko says a lot of your customers are nurses—they train across the road. That squat gray building across the road is Sensoji Hospital."

"I thought it was a prison. Are you only having green tea?"

"Green tea is all that my meal plan allows until lunch."

"Oh—I forgot again. Sorry."

"No need to be. Diabetes is a medical condition, not a sin."

"I didn't mean—"

"Relax, relax; I know. Eat."

A mighty river of drones flows below the window—civil servants rushing to get to their desks before their section chief is at his. "Once upon a time," says Ai, "people used to build Tokyo. But that changed somewhere down the line, and now Tokyo builds people."

I let a squirt of shake dissolve on my tongue. "Back to your father: he said if you ignore him and go to Paris, you can forget ever being welcome in Niigata."

"So I said he can have it his way."

"So you won't go to Paris?"

"I am going to Paris. But I am never going back to Niigata."

"Does your father mean what he said?"

"That was a threat aimed at my mother, not me. 'If *you* want to be looked after by your own daughter in your old age, *you* make her stay.' In fact, he left shortly after to go and play pachinko. My mother broke down in gales of tears, just as he knew she would. She kept asking how I could be so ungrateful. I am thinking: What century is this? You know, there are mountain villages in Niigata that import Filipina wives in wholesale groups, because as soon as the local girls come of age they are on board the fastest *shinkansen* out of there. The men wonder why."

"So you won. You can go to Paris."

"In disgrace, but I am going."

I light a JPS and say what I am thinking. "You are the toughest person I know, Ai." She shakes her head, unconvinced. "The gap between how other people see you and how you see yourself is . . . a mystery, for me. I think *you* are tough. I think *I* am as tough as your shake—which is nine parts pig lard, incidentally. I desperately want my parents to be proud of me. Real strength is not needing the approval of other people all the time." On a Roman balcony one slanting evening a girl puts sunflowers in a terra-cotta jar. She sees the cameraman, scowls, pouts, flicks her hair, and vanishes. Ai dangles her tea bag in and out of the hot water. "I honestly think they would have been happier if I had done a two-year course in applied cosmetics at a women's college, married the family dentist's son, and spawned a hive of babies. Music. You eat it, but it eats you, too." I swallow hash-brown-and-fries cud. "Cheer up. Compared to the Miyakes, your family are the Von Trapps in *The Sound of Music*." Ai spins her tea bag. "Von Tropps."

A little girl with gaps in her teeth comes up to our table and looks at Ai through enormous glasses. "Where do babies come from *before* they get into mommies' tummies?"

"You know what a stork is? The big white birds?"

"Yes."

"Storks bring the babies to the mommies."

The kid looks dubious. "So where do the storks get the babies, then?"

"Paris," I tell her, which forces a smile out of Ai.

"Where's Paris?"

"There." I point at the video screen. The girl's father appears at the top of the stairs carrying a tray of bright food and a baby mounted in a back harness, and calls his daughter over with an apologetic nod at us. He must be a fine father. Ai looks at me in a strange way. I see her face as a very old woman, and also as a very little girl. Slow seconds come and go. I have never looked at anyone this long, this close up, in silence, since my who-blinks-last-wins games with Anju. If this were a movie and not McDonald's we would kiss. I think. Maybe this is more intimate than kissing. Loyalty, grief, good news, bad days. "Okay," I finally say, and Ai does not say "okay what?" She rubs her thumbnail over a McTeriyakiburger scratch card. "Look. I won a baby robot turkey lunch box. Must be a good omen. Will you let me buy you a new baseball cap?"

"This one was a present from Anju," I reply before I change my mind.

Ai frowns. "Who?"

"My twin sister."

Ai's frown deepens. "You said you were an only child."

No going back now. "I want to untell the only lie I told you last week. I have a whole load of other stuff to tell you too: my grandfather contacted me—thanks to the personal ad you suggested—and my stepmother and half-sister met me. More of an ambush than a meeting, really. I also figured that trying to find someone who obviously doesn't want to meet me, even if he is my father, will only make me miserable, so I quit . . . what is it?" Ai is frying with exasperation. "That is so *you* of you, Miyake!" I try to understand. "What is?" Ai knocks on her forehead with her knuckles. "Okay, okay. Start with your twin sister. Then do the stepmother. Go."

I float back to Shooting Star around noon buoyant as a light particle. Ai has classes for the rest of today, but she is coming around to my capsule tomorrow—Wednesday; I have to stop to remember which day I am on. I am thinking about Ai about ninety times an hour. It was funny when we said goodbye at Shinjuku—we got hopelessly lost because I was following her while she was following me. The walk from Kita Senju Station is pleasant today—shrubs, autumn trees, kids in strollers—today they defeat the ugliness of Tokyo. "Good morning, Eiji-kun," says Machiko pleasantly, "you reek of cheese." She is watching a Takeshi Kitano movie set in Okinawa. I ask her if it is worth watching. "He can be a good director, but he gives himself the coolest roles. Only good actors dare take on uncool roles." Machiko shows me her vacation photos and gives me a picture I like of an orange orchard vanishing up a rain-hazed hillside. We talk about Nero's for a while. Machiko has this gift of making me feel I am interesting—and I nearly tell her about Ai but I am afraid I would sound slushy, and besides, there still is not much to tell, so I climb up to my capsule.

"Eiji-kun! I forgot to give you this. The mailman brought it this morning." I turn around, and go back down for the package—one of those padded envelopes, the smallest size they come in. The addressee is Mr. Fujin Yoda—who?—living in Hakodate up in Hokkaido. An INCORRECTLY ADDRESSED message has been stamped on the front. On the back is my name and address, printed under SENDER on a stick-on label. "Anything wrong?" asks Machiko.

I keep my wits about me and say, "Nothing." Something *is* wrong, however—I didn't mail it. Up in my capsule a shredded tea towel temporarily puts the mysterious package out of my mind—Cat, purely out of spite, because she slept alone last night. I hope she stops shredding before she starts on my shirts. I shower, tidy up the scraps of clawed cloth, and thrash out a Howlin' Wolf version of "All You Need Is Love" on my guitar. I should be dropping with tiredness, but I am immune to sleep. Then I remember the package. I must be more tired than I think. I slit the package open. Inside is a computer disk wrapped in a letter. I twist some ice from the ice tray into a glass and fill it with water. I love the sound the cubes make as fissures shoot through.

Tokyo, October 1

The name I went by was Kozue Yamaya. I was a freelance investigator. However unlikely or brutal this account of the last nine years of my life appears, I ask you to read it until the end. In your hands is my final testament. I shall ask you to be my legal executor.

Endings are simple, but every beginning is made by the beginning before. The one I shall choose is a night in the rainy season nine years ago. In those days my name was Makino Matani. She was a housewife with a two-year-old son, and married to the owner of a financial services company. She was a recent graduate in business studies from a respectable women's college in Kobe. Every New Year she exchanged greetings cards with her ex-classmates who were married to dentists, judges, and civil servants. An ordinary life. The rainy season came. I remember those last moments perfectly—my son was playing with a plastic train set, and I was cleaning the rainy-season mold in the shower cubicle. I could hear the television reporting flash floods and landslides.

The doorbell rang. I answered it, and three men barged in the door and snapped the chain my husband had trained me to use. They demanded to know where my husband was hiding. I demanded to know who they were. One slapped me hard enough to dislodge a tooth. "Your husband's case officers," he snarled, "and *we* ask the questions." He and another searched the house while the third watched me try to reassure my screaming son. He threatened to maim my son if I didn't tell him where my husband was. I called my husband at work and discovered he had phoned in sick that morning. I called my husband's cell phone and discovered the number had been disconnected. I called his pager—dead. I was nearly hysterical by now—the thug poured me a shot of my husband's whiskey, but I couldn't swallow it. My son watched with big scared eyes. The two other thugs returned with a box of my husband's personal effects and all of my jewelry. Then the bad news really began. I learned that my husband had run up debts of over fifty million yen with a yakuza-backed credit organization. Our life insurance policy had been doctored to name this organization as sole beneficiary in the event of his suicide. The house and contents were their property if my husband defaulted on repayments. "And that," said the most violent of the three, "includes you." My son was taken into the next room. I was told I was now responsible for my husband's debts. I was then beaten and raped. Photographs were taken "to guarantee my obedience." I had to endure this torment in silence, for the sake of my son. If I failed to obey their orders, the photographs would be sent to every name in my address book.

A month later I was living in a single windowless room in a *buraku* area of Osaka. I was indentured to a brothel, and I was not allowed to leave the building or have any contact with the outside world, beyond sex with my customers. You may doubt that sexual enslavement is practiced in twenty-first-century Japan. Your ignorance is enviable, but your disbelief is precisely why such enslavement can prosper unchecked. It happens; it happened to me. I myself would have doubted "respectable" women could be forced into the sex industry, but the owners are masters of control. I was dispossessed of every item from my old life that could have reminded me who I was—except my son. I was allowed to keep my son—this prevented me from escaping by suicide. My customers not only knew about my imprisonment, they derived pleasure from it, and would have been implicated in the crime had it become public. The final wall between me and the real world was perhaps the strongest: a phenomenon psychologists label "hostage syndrome"—the conviction that my fate was deserved and that no "crime" was being perpetrated. After all, I was a prostitute. What right did I have to bring shame to my old friends or even to my mother by appealing for help? Better that they carry on believing I had disappeared overseas with my bankrupt husband. Six other women, three with babies younger than my son, shared my floor. The man who raped me was our pimp—it was him we had to beg for food, medicine, even diapers for our children. He also supplied narcotics, in careful quantities. He administered them personally to ensure we couldn't overdose. False names were given to us, and we adopted them to hide behind. In time our old lives became detached from what we had become. All of us dreamed of killing our owner at some vague point in the future after our escape, but the more we dreamed, the weaker our will to shape our own reality became. We were required to take care of one another's children while their mothers were working. The pimp told us that after we had worked off the amounts the defaulting members of our families had embezzled we would be free to go, so the harder we worked to please our customers, the quicker we would be out of there. In autumn, a girl who had been working in the brothel for two years was released. So we thought.

My "release" came sooner, because over the following New Year my resilience exhausted itself and I suffered a nervous breakdown. The customers complained to the pimp that I was no longer trying. The pimp talked to me for a while. He could be gentle when he chose. It was one of his weapons. He said he had talked to my creditors and that I would be transferred with my son to another branch that night. We drank gin and tonic to celebrate.

I awoke wrapped in a blanket in a black, airless place. My head was groggy and drugged. My son was not with me. I was still in my brothel nightshirt. For a terrible moment I thought I had been buried alive, but groping around, I realized I was in the trunk of a stationary car. I found a jack, and finally forced an exit. I was in a garage. I saw the pimp's reflection in the side mirror and froze. He was asleep. Then I saw his nose was missing.

Someone had put a gun to his nostrils and pulled the trigger. There was no sign of my son. I ran—but before I had got out of the garage my senses began to return. I was lost, penniless, believed to have vanished by anyone who remembered me. My former owners would jump to the conclusion that I had been taken as a spoil of war. I hesitated—but I ran back, groped inside the pimp's jacket for his wallet. I found a travel bag strapped around his groin. The bag contained a pile of ten-thousand-yen notes inches thick. I had never seen so much money. When I found my way out of the garage I found myself in the vast Osaka central hospital, the only place in the city where a woman with a sick-as-death complexion in nightclothes could blend into the background.

I do not have time to tell you much about the years that followed. I lived for a year in women's refuges, cheap hotels. My bank accounts were in false names. The meaning of my life had become the search for my son. My ex-husband was now a ghost I never thought of. I hired a private detective to investigate the yakuza branch that had imprisoned me. The investigator returned my advance one week later—he was warned away. Out of sympathy and guilt, he ended up hiring me as a secretary-accountant. This was a smart business decision, because three quarters of his customers were women wanting their husbands tailed to fatten divorce settlements. They preferred discussing the sordid details with another woman. As with gynecology, so for marital infidelity. They recommended our agency to their friends, and business thrived. I began accompanying my boss on fieldwork. Women are virtually invisible, even to the most paranoid of men. (Furthermore, I discovered that the brothel organization had deleted every computer reference to me and my son. I enjoy the privileges of being a nonexistent woman.) My life in the brothel had hardened as well as scarred me. After three years my boss offered me a partnership, and when his cancer finally killed him I took over the business. All this time, I was hunting for the roots of the organization that had killed Makino Matani and her son, and created Kozue Yamaya. It is nameless and many-headed. It has no name. Its membership is in excess of six thousand. I swung introductions to its leaders, even invitations to the weddings of their children. I entered its employ as a freelance researcher. My status as a semi-insider gave me greater access to its secrets, and deflected suspicion.

My son was murdered in order to sell his organs to extremely rich, desperate parents of the elite in Japan. The home market is most lucrative, because the parents will pay for pure, home-grown stock, but the export market to Eastern Asia, North America, and Russia is also significant. This fate is shared by the children and eventually the women enslaved in the brothels. The disk I have enclosed in this package contains the names, digital images, and personal histories of the men who head this organization; the law enforcers who protect them; the surgeons who carry out the work; the politicians who blanket the operation; the businessmen who launder the money; the men and customs officers who freeze and smuggle the organs.

Why are you being told this? Tomorrow is the final day of September. It is the day I plan to go public. I shall hand my data over to my contacts in the police and the media. One of two things will happen: the media will scream, and Japanese public and political life will be hit by a vice scandal that will send shock waves from hospitals in Kyushu to the parliament building; or I shall be killed by those I seek to expose. If the latter comes to pass copies of this disk and letter will be distributed to an audience I have selected for widely differing reasons.

Understand this: you are holding a letter from a dead woman. I have been killed by my enemies, as foreseen by laws of probability and power. My death itself is of no importance to me. You can understand why, I am sure. What is important is that the information now in your possession is the only weapon that could destroy the harvesters. Act with your eyes open, as your conscience dictates. I cannot advise you—my best attempts have failed. The yakuza is a ninety-thousand-strong state within our state. If you approach regular police channels, you will achieve only the issue of your own death warrant. You are holding a high card for a very dangerous game into which you never asked to be dealt. But for the repose of the soul of my son Eiji Matani, who was killed by these people, and for countless others, past, present, and future, I implore you to act.

Please.

Kozue Yamaya

Why me? Her son and I share a name with the exact same kanji—*ei* for "incant," *ji* for "world." I have never encountered this combination in someone else before, but this alone cannot account for Kozue Yamaya putting me on her trustee list. I sift my memory of the time we met for clues, but find none.

I call downstairs. "Machiko-san? Any big stories in the paper today?"

"What?" says Machiko. "Don't tell me you haven't heard?"

"What?"

Machiko reads from the front page: "'Top Politician in Honesty Shocker—"I'm Not on the Take!" Integrity Revelation by Minister Stuns Colleagues!'"

I manage a smile, and close the door. So Kozue Yamaya is probably dead. I feel hollow with pity for that scarred person who visited me during my week at the study of tales. But I would be a fool to get involved in this. Keeping this disk is suicidally dangerous. I stow it in the most unused corner of my apartment—my condom box under my socks—until I figure out what to do. If no foolproof idea comes today or tomorrow, I should drop it in the river and hope another addressee is in a wiser, stronger position. Uneasily, I imagine us lined up in a row on the bridge, all dropping our disks in, acting on the same easiest-way-out impulse. I change the water for Cat, switch on my fan, unroll my futon, and try to sleep. Despite not having slept for twenty hours, I keep thinking of Mrs. Yamaya. I sense a weird week ahead, one with sharp teeth. My pulse thuds. An unbreakable spear striking an impenetrable shield.

I arrive at work at one minute to midnight. I change into my apron and white bandanna—I wear it to keep my hairs out of the food, not as a fashion accessory—and a big group of off-duty taxi drivers stops by to order an office-party quantity of pizzas. I am kept busy for ninety minutes. The radio is weird tonight—it keeps changing frequency at whim, swinging among Chinese-, Spanish-, and Other-speaking stations. "Tagalog, man," reckons Doi. "The stratospheric ether is hyperpure tonight, man, I can feel it in my sinuses." He waits for the inferno to deliver his pizza, smoking a cigarette of his own creation in the cage. He rubs his eye. "Miyake, I got something stuck in the corner here—pass me a toothpick, man?" I ignore my misgivings and pass him a toothpick. "Thanks." Doi uses it to pluck his eyelid down. "No good, would you mind looking? I think a tiny fly flew in." I walk over, and peer close. Doi suddenly sneezes, his head jerks down, and the toothpick punctures his eyeball. A jet of white fluid spatters my face. "Shit!" screams Doi. "Oh shit! I *hate* it when that happens!" I just stand there, unable to believe that reality is this grotesque. Sachiko appears in the hatch. I gibber— she shakes her head—I stop gibbering. "Falling for him once is cute, Miyake, but two strikes and you're Mr. Gullible. Doi, if you waste many more of those coffee whiteners you're going to force me to be Ms. Assistant Manager and dock your salary." Doi snickers. I realize I have been fooled again. "Hear and *ooo*bey, chieftainess." Sachiko glowers and addresses a supernatural agency above the inferno. "Is it my karmic destiny to oversee lunatic asylums, lifetime after lifetime, over and over, until I get it right? Miyake—one double Titanic, thick base, extra shark meat." I box up Doi's pizza. He leaves, bathed in victory. I cannot stop thinking about the package from Mrs. Yamaya. Tomomi slinks into the cage for one of her never-ending coffee breaks. She tells me how frantically busy her life is—*busy* is definitely her favorite word—and asks how I know Ai doesn't fake her orgasms when we have sex, because while she was having her affair with Mr. Nero she felt obliged to *busy* things up on a number of occasions, because men are so insecure about performance. Tomomi has a tarantula-in-underpants effect on me. She sharpens her fingernails while I try to work out what sort of denial would give her least gossip fuel. I am saved by a toy-helicopter-size wasp that flies in—Tomomi shrieks, "Kill it! Kill it!" and runs back through to the front. The hatch doors slam shut. The wasp buzzsaws around for a minute, warily checking me out in its multilens eyes, and lands on Laos. Hard to concentrate on the pizzas, but I prefer its company to Tomomi's. I stand on the counter and clap a plastic tub over Southeast Asia—the wasp strikes up a death-by-flugelhorn noise and tries to knock a hole through the side—I get unbearably itchy and, instead of making a portable wasp-release box, semipanic and shove the tub over the exhaust fan, which is flush to the wall. The flugelhorn stops with a nearly inaudible crackle. "Last of the action heroes," says Onizuka, fingering the spike in his lower lip. He always arrives in the cage quiet as a ghost, and he speaks so softly I have to semi-lip-read. He nods at the inferno, where a pizza is waiting to be boxed. "That my Eskimo Quinn for the KDD building? Customers give me shit if their pizzas get cold." The hatch opens a crack. "Is it dead?" asks Tomomi. "The wasp is fine," says Onizuka, "but Miyake got mushed trying to leave through the extractor." Tomomi performs an overture laugh to see if she can rile me. Onizuka departs with his pizza without another word. Doi arrives back a minute later—I could swear his *left* leg was limping yesterday, but today it is his right—and Tomomi tells him about the wasp. The drug pusher and the queen of all evil discuss whether I am guilty of the murder of a life-form. "It was only a wasp," I say, "there are plenty more where it came from." This is not good enough for Tomomi: "There are plenty more humans where we come from, so does that make homicide okay?" This is too stupid to argue about—especially as Tomomi was shrieking "Kill it! Kill it!"—so I watch pizzas inching through the inferno. When I tune in again Doi and Tomomi are talking about crows. "Say what you want," Tomomi says, "crows are cute." Doi shakes his head. "Crows are winged Nazis, man. The porter in our building, he chased one away with a broom. The next day, the same crow dive-bombed him and pecked his head hard enough to draw blood, man. A crow? Attacking a uniformed porter? Freaky, man. Kinda short-circuits nature." Tomomi sharpens her eyeliner pencil and snaps open her hand mirror. "I love nature. The weak are meat, the strong eat."

Ueno to Kita Senju is easy, even during rush hour, because outbound submarines are empty except for night-shift workers and eccentric billionaires. The subs heading the other way into Ueno are human freight wagons. Tokyo is a model of that serial big-bang theory of the universe. It explodes at five P.M. and people matter is hurled to the suburbs, but by five A.M. the people-matter gravity reasserts itself, and everything surges back toward the center, where mass densens for the next explosion. My commute is against the natural law of Tokyo. I feel dead beat. Giving up on my father is taking some getting used to. Ai is coming over to my capsule after her rehearsal, at about five in the afternoon. Her dinner is my breakfast. To my relief she asked if she could do the cooking— she prefers to choose what she eats because of her diabetes. To call my culinary repertoire "limited" would be boastful. Walking back from Kita Senju Station to Shooting Star, a weird cloud slides over half the sky. Cyclists, women with strollers, taxi drivers stop to stare up at it. Half the sky is clear October blue—the other half is a dark funnel of storm cloud. Plastic bags get caught in vortexes and fly up to heaven. Buntaro is in the store early to bring the accounts up to date after his week away. He looks up at me and sniffs. "I know," I say, "I know. Cheese." Buntaro shrugs, all innocence, and goes back to his calculator. I crawl upstairs. Cat bids me good morning before vanishing into her universe. I wash her bowl, change her water, shower, and decide to have a quick nap before cleaning up for Ai.

My face is melted out of position. My tongue is a pumice stone. Saliva, collected in my tongue-root gully, drools out onto my pillow. At my table, Ai chops carrots and apples. For a moment I think I have married Ai, and she is making dinner for our nine children—but then I smell the apple. Nutmeg, too. Cat is licking her paws, watching me. Buntaro lets Ai up, she knocks, I am too deeply asleep to wake up, Buntaro confirms I am definitely up here, Ai peers in, sees me, goes out and buys food for a salad. Life is crisp bliss when it wants to be. Ai must trust me, to be alone with me in my capsule while I am dressed—or not dressed—how I am. Being trusted makes me trustworthy. Carrot and apple go together great. She is chopping walnuts—I never much cared for walnuts until this moment—and raisins, and sprinkles them over lettuce. She is wearing old jeans and a faded yellow T-shirt lighter than her skin and her hair is up. Here is that mythical neck. She scrapes peelings into the garbage bag. She wears thick black-framed glasses that suit her in a quirky sort of way. Ai never ever tries to impress, and that impresses me *so* much. She has a silver pirate earring. "Hey, Kyushu Cannibal," she says—I realize all this time she knew I was watching her—and chords inside me change from A flat to loose-string D minor, I am that happy. "Why do you keep letters in your icebox?"

"Watch out," says Ai, "I think there may be fish in these bones."

"It tastes great."

"Do you live entirely on noodle cups?"

"I vary my diet with pizza, courtesy of Nero. Mind if I finish the salad?"

"Do, before you die of scurvy. You never told me about your view."

"That is no view. Yakushima has views."

"It beats the view Sachiko and I have at present. We used to overlook a low-security prison exercise yard. That was quite nice. I used to leave the windows open and play Chopin waltzes back-to-back. But then I got back from class one day to find a parking garage had sprung up since breakfast. Now we have a view of concrete six inches away. We want to move, but paying a deposit on a new place would wipe out our savings."

The telephone riiiiiiiiings. I answer: "Hello?"

"Miyake!"

"Suga? Where are you?"

"Downstairs."

"Downstairs, where?"

"Downstairs here. Mr. Ogiso tells me you have company in your chambers—but would you mind if I come up?"

I do, to be honest. "Sure. Come up."

When Suga enters my capsule I gape. He has apparently had a body transplant. His eczema has vanished. He has a contoured haircut that must have cost ten thousand yen. He is wearing the suit of a Milanese diamond robber, and *Revolver*-period Lennon electric-folksinger glasses. "Are you going for an interview?" I ask. Suga ignores me and bows shyly at Ai. "Hi, I'm Masanobu Suga. Are you Miyake's Korean girlfriend?"

Ai bites the head off a celery stick and looks at me quizzically.

"No, uh, no. Suga, this is Miss Imajo."

Ai looks thoughtful. "Suga the Snorer?"

Now Suga looks confused. "I—er—Miyake?"

"Uh . . . Some other time."

The only sound in this very awkward pause is celery being munched. Suga breaks it with some news. "There won't be another time for a long time—I came to say goodbye."

"Leaving Tokyo?" I chuck a cushion down for him. "Near or far?"

Suga slips out of his sandals and sits down. "Saratoga."

"Which prefecture is that in?"

Ai has heard of it. "Saratoga, eastern Texas?"

"Heart of the desert."

"Beautiful." Ai munches. "But wild."

I find a sort of clean cup. "Why are you going to a desert?"

"I'm not allowed to tell anyone exactly why."

I pour his tea. "Why not?"

"I'm not allowed to tell anyone that, either."

"Is any of this to do with your Holy Grail?"

"After I left here last week, I went to my research room and got my brain back in gear. So offensively obvious. Write a Waldrop search program, smuggle it into the file field, and get it to scan through the nine billion files to see if a real Holy Grail site had been hidden anywhere, right? My first attempt backfired. In megabyte terms it was like trying to squeeze China through the Sumida Tunnel. The Pentagon immune system recognizes the program as an alien body, zaps it, and launches a tracer program. I only just get out in time."

"*The* Pentagon?" Ai asks.

Suga twiddles his thumbs, modest and boastful. "So I sleep on the problem for a couple of days, then—deep genius busts the door down.

Dawn raid of inspiration. I break into the Pentagon immune system, softjack its own OS, muzzle its alarms with a *highly* localized Jassem-style virus, and get *it* to search the very files its job is to protect! Like retraining your enemy's sniffer dogs to show you his hidey-hole. I make it sound easy, I know, but first I had to boot my flight path through six different zombies across six different cell-phone networks, second I had to rewrite Jassem's bioform program, third—"

"You did it?"

Suga lets the details slide. "I did it. But the number of Holy Grails it had to check was, right, deeply cosmic. Think about it. Nine billion files, at the apex of nine billion pyramids, each one built of nine billion files—as far as I had dared to look. After turning loose my search program, I drowse off. Deep Sleep City. It is eleven in the morning by now, right—I worked at my computer since seven the evening before, and you know how low I was last week. My body decided to shut down until I was fully repaired. So. What next? I wake up to find three men searching my office. Late afternoon, deep shock. One guy—a hacker, I can tell—is downloading all my personal files onto a handheld drive I'd never even seen before. Second guy, an older headmaster type, is making an inventory of my hardware. The third is this fat, sunburned foreigner in a cowboy hat leafing through my Zax Omega mangas and drinking my beer. I was too amazed to be scared. The headmaster guy flashes some ID at me—Data Protection Agency, ever heard of that?—and tells me I have violated the Japan–United States Bilateral Defense Treaty and that I have the right to remain silent but that if I don't want to be tried for espionage under U.S. jurisprudence at the nearest military base, I had better get down on my knees and blab for dear life."

"Is all this true?" Ai asks me.

"Is all this true?" I ask Suga.

"I was wishing to hell that it wasn't. The buggery scenes in every prison movie I ever saw keep flashing before me. The headmaster gets out a matchbox-size recorder and starts firing questions at me. I'm expecting him to strap electrodes to my balls. How had I got into the Pentagon in the first place? How had I softjacked their antiviral OS? Was I working alone? Who had I spoken to since? Had I heard of any of the following organizations—I hadn't, I can't even remember them now.

They know what schools I went to, where I live, everything. Then the hacker guy talks technical data—I can see he is impressed with my zombie ring. Even so, it gets dark, and I don't know what they plan to do to me. Finally, the foreigner, who has been flicking through my photo albums and *MasterHacker,* speaks to the headmaster, in English. I realize he is the one in charge here. I ask if I can take a leak. The younger hacker accompanies me—I ask him for some more lowdown but he shakes his head. We get back to my office and headmaster offers me a job or prosecution under some obscure but terrifying-sounding law buried in the U.S.-Japan Defense Pact. He describes the job, and the money—serious Big Time! Artificial intelligence, missile shield systems"—Suga bites his lips. "Whoops. That's the only downer. I can't go around boasting to anyone about it."

"What about IBM and your university?"

"Yeah, that was my next question. Headmaster nods at the foreigner—the foreigner barks an order into his cell phone. 'Already taken care of, Mr. Suga,' the headmaster tells me. 'And we can arrange a Ph.D. if your parents are worried about qualifications. Would MIT be acceptable? Other details can be worked out later.' In fact, I fly out the day after tomorrow, so I have a million things to do. I brought you a present, Miyake. I considered tropical fruit, but this is a bit more personal. Here." He produces a square case, flips it open, and unclips a black flat thing. "This is my finest home-cultivated computer virus. For peacetime uses." For the second time in two days I am being given a computer disk. "Uh . . . thanks. Nobody ever gave me a virus before." Ai mutters something, and then speaks up: "If those things get into hospital systems they put lives at risk. Do you ever think about that?" Suga nods righteously, and slurps his tea. "For sure. Ethical cyberexplorers are responsible, yeah? We are friendly ghosts in the machine, not poltergeists or hooligans. We are a growing breed. Over sixty-five percent of top-flight systems explorers are ethical." Ai gives Suga a black look. "And over eighty-five percent of all statistics are made up on the spot." Suga soldiers on. "Take this virus—'Mailman,' I call it—it delivers your message to every addressee on the address book of whoever you send it to. Then it duplicates itself and delivers itself to all the addresses in those address books—and so on, for ninety-nine generations. It doesn't even need to be opened. Neat or what? Direct democracy, it is. Freedom of speech. Mailman can't be censored—it outperforms any antiviral software on the market. But it won't harm any system it enters." Ai looks unconvinced. "Spreading junk mail to tens of thousands of people doesn't strike me as especially ethical." Suga has a proud-father beam. "Not junk mail! Miyake can spread whatever message of joy and peace he wants to hundreds of thousands of users. It isn't the sort of thing I can take to Texas, Saratoga being a top-secret research installation, right, and it would be a shame to let it go to waste."

Suga leaves. I finish the salad and slice a melon for dessert. I take some down to Buntaro, who nods at the ceiling and waggles his little finger questioningly. I pretend not to understand. No way am I going to make a pass at Ai. There is a sort of not-yetness between us, I tell myself. She is clearing a space on the table. "Time for my insulin. Want to watch, or are you squeamish?"

"I want to watch," I lie.

Ai gets a medical box from her bag, prepares the syringe, disinfects her forearm, and calmly slips the needle in. I order myself not to flinch but I flinch. She is watching me watching her as the insulin shoots into her bloodstream. I suddenly feel humble. Making a pass at Ai would be as uncouth as yelling at a flower to hurry up. Plus, if she rejected me I would have to microwave myself out of existence. "So, Miyake," says Ai, as the needle slides out. "What's your next move?"

I swallow dryly. "Uh . . . what?"

She dabs a droplet of blood with sterilized cotton wool. "Are you going to stay in Tokyo now that you've changed your mind about tracking down your father?" I get up and wipe my fry pan. "I . . . dunno. I need money before I can do anything else, so I'll probably stay at Nero's until something better comes along. . . . I want to show you a couple of letters my mother wrote to me."

Ai shrugs. "Okay."

I brush the ice granules off the plastic—she reads the letters while I finish the dishes. She is still rereading them, so I wash my hair.

"Long shower."

"Uh . . . when I take a shower I feel I'm back on Yakushima. Warm rain." I nod at the letters. "What do you think?"

Ai folds them and puts them back into the envelope. "I'm thinking about what I think about them." FUJIFILM says ten o'clock. We have to leave—Ai wants to be home before the stalkers leave their bars, and I have to get to work before midnight. Downstairs, Buntaro munches cheese Pringles and watches a movie full of cyborgs, motorbikes, and welders. "Have a nice salad, young people?" he asks, so innocently I could kill him. I nod at the screen. "What are you watching?"

"I am testing the two laws of cinema."

"Which are?"

"The first law states: 'Any movie with a title ending in *-ator* is guaranteed to be drivel.'"

"The second?"

"The quality of any movie is in inverse proportion to the number of helicopters it features."

"In a way," Ai says as we arrive at Kita Senju Station, "I wish you hadn't shown me those letters from your mother."

"Why not?"

Ai jangles loose change. "I don't think you'll like hearing what I really think." The last moths of autumn swirl around a stuttering light.

"Hearing what you really think was the point of showing you."

Ai buys her ticket—I show my pass—and we walk down to the platform. "Your mother wants you in her life, and your life could be a whole lot richer with her in it. Your standoffishness isn't helping you or her. I think it's cruel of you to ignore them."

I feel jabbed. "If she wanted me to contact her, why didn't she give me her Nagano address?"

"She is afraid of giving you the power to reject her. Again." Ai hunts out my eyes. "Anyway, she did tell you where she is—Mount Hakuba."

"*Me* rejecting *her*? 'Mount Hakuba' is not an address."

Ai stops walking. "Miyake, for someone so bright"—sarcasm from the top university student—"you are a virtuoso self-delusionist. There can be no more than ten hotels at the foot of Mount Hakuba. Compared to finding a nameless man in Tokyo, finding your mother is simple. You could find her by tomorrow evening if you actually wanted to."

Now she is trespassing. I know I should say nothing or change the subject but I am too weak. "And why exactly do you think I don't want to?"

"I'm not your shrink." Ai shrugs. "You tell me. Anger? Blame?"

"You have no idea what you are talking about." I have already told her, apparently, in an angry voice. "She had eleven years to unabandon us, and another nine years to unabandon me."

Ai frowns. "Okay, but if you don't want to know what I really think about your issues, then talk about the weather instead of showing me personal letters. And—hell, Miyake—" I look at her. "What?" Now Ai semisnarls. "Do you *have* to smoke all the time?" I put away my MacArthur lighter and slide my Parliaments back into my shirt pocket. "I had no idea it bothered you so much." Once the words are out I know they are way too snide. Ai gives me a side glare. "How could it not bother me? Since I was nine my arm has been a pincushion, just so my pancreas doesn't kill me. My life is this balancing act of sugar intake. I endure hypoglycemia twice a year while you fill your lungs with cancer—and the lungs of everyone downwind—just so you can look like the Marlboro Man. Yes, Miyake, your smoking *really* bothers me."

I cannot think of a single thing to say.

The evening is in pieces.

The train arrives. We sit next to each other back to Ueno, but we may as well be sitting in different cities. I wish we were. The jolly citizens of Adland mock me with minty smiles. Ai says nothing. The moment something becomes good its doom is sealed. We get off at Ueno, which is as quiet as Ueno ever gets.

"Mind if I walk with you to your platform?" I ask, as a peace offering.

Ai shrugs, obviously refusing my peace offering. We walk down a corridor as vast as the suspended-animation chamber in a space ark. A rhythmic, fierce whacking noise starts up from ahead—a man in orange is pounding something with a sort of rubber mallet. Whatever—whoever—is being pounded is hidden behind a column. We both alter our course to give the man a wide berth—we have to walk past him to get to Ai's platform. I seriously think he is beating somebody to death. But it is only a paving tile the man is trying to coerce into a hole too small for it. *Whack! Whack! Whack!* "That," says Ai, probably to herself, "is life." What she means by that, I could not say. From the tunnel an approaching train wolfhowls and Ai's hair swims in its wind. I feel miserable. "Uh . . . Ai . . ." I begin, but Ai interrupts me with an irritated shake of her head. "I'll call you." Does that mean "It's okay, don't worry" or "Don't you dare call until I decide to forgive you"? Perfect ambiguity from the Paris Conservatoire Scholarship Student. The train comes, she gets on, sits down, folds her arms, and crosses her legs. Without thinking about it I wave goodbye with one hand, and with my other hand pull my Parliaments from my shirt pocket and lob them down the gap between the train and the platform. But Ai has already closed her eyes. The train pulls away, without her having seen.

Shit. *That,* I think to myself, *that* is life.

My Nero's rat run shrinks every evening. The inferno gets hotter. Sachiko says nothing about Ai. Thursday night is the busiest so far. One o'clock, two o'clock spin around. Emotions are so tiring. I guess this is why I avoid them. The moment anything becomes good, it is doomed. Doi sucks ice cubes, scratches inside his nostril with his finger, and shuffles his playing cards. "Take a card," he says, "any card." I shake my head—I am not in the mood. "Go on! This is ancient Sumerian enchantment with third-millennial twists, man. Take a card." Doi thrusts the fanned cards at me and looks away. So I take a card. "Memorize it, but don't say what it is." Nine of diamonds. "Okay? Replace and shuffle! Anyway, anyhow, anywhere, bury the mortal remains of your card . . ." I do so—no way could Doi have seen. Tomomi drapes herself in the hatch. "Miyake! Three Fat Mermaids, extra seaweed and squid. Doi—nosepicking doesn't suit a hippie of your years." Doi scratches outside his nose: "Muzzle the grizzly, man . . . ain't you had an intranasal zit before?" Tomomi stares at him. "I have an intranasal zit right now. Its name is Doi. That delivery to the spine doctor's wingding is due seven days ago—if they phone to complain I'm shoving the headset inside your ear and you can deal with their negative energy. Man." Doi does a whoah! gesture. "Lady, I am mid-trick here." Tomomi whistles inward. "Do you *want* me to tell Mr. Nero about the aromatic substances in your scooter box?" Doi returns his cards to their box and whispers to me as he leaves: "Fear not, man, this trick is to be continued . . ." The minutes jog up the down escalator. Onizuka takes a break after a long-distance delivery. He broods in the cage, ripping a grapefruit to bits. I box up the Chicken Tikka and minisalad for his next delivery. To hurry the night along I practice clock management: before checking the time I kid myself it is twenty minutes earlier than the time I truly believe it is, so I can pleasantly surprise myself. This clever strategy is not working tonight. Doi reappears in the cage, listening to a song on the radio in ecstasy—"'Riders on the Storm,' man . . ." He could be a songbird fancier in a deep wood. "Me on my pizza scooter." He drinks butter-vomit Tibetan tea from a flask and practices making cards appear from his ears. He has forgotten about the unfinished trick, and I don't remind him. "The human condition is a card game, man. Our hand is dealt in the womb. During infancy we lay a few cards down, pick up a few more. Puberty, man—more cards—jobs, flings, busts, marriage . . . cards come, cards go. Some days, you get a strong hand. Other days, your winning streaks end in bad gongs. You bet, call, bluff." Sachiko enters the cage for her break. "And how do you win this game?" Doi peacock-tails the cards and fans himself. "When you win, the rules change, and you find you've lost." Sachiko rests her feet on a box of Nero's ketchup packets. "Nice, straightforward metaphor, there, Doi. Not." Tomomi feeds through an order for a Satanica crisp-crust, triple capers. I lay out the base and imagine Ai, asleep, dreaming of Paris. Suga is dreaming of America. Cat is dreaming of cats. Pizzas come, pizzas leave. The stack of completed orders climbs up the spike. Another hot dawn glows in the real world outside. I peel cucumbers until eight o'clock brings the new chef, a slap on the back, and a nine-decibel "Miyake, go home!" Taking the Ginza Line submarine, I plug myself into my Discman. No music. Weird. I changed the batteries yesterday evening. I press EJECT—there is no CD inside, only a playing card. Nine of diamonds.

A message is waiting on my capsule answering machine. It is not from Ai. "Uh . . . well, hello Eiji. This is your father." Laughter. I freeze—the first time I've felt cold since March. "Hey, I said it. This is your father, Eiji." A deep breath. He is smoking. "Not so difficult. Well. What a mess. Where do I start?" A *phew* noise. "First—believe me—I did *not* know you had come to Tokyo to search for me. Akiko Kato dealt with my wife, not me—I've been in Canada on a series of conferences since August—I only got back to town last week." Deep sigh. "I always hoped this day would come, Eiji, but I never . . . dared make the first move. I never thought I had the right. If that makes sense. Second—about my wife. This is so embarrassing—Eiji—can I call you Eiji? Anything else seems wrong. My wife never breathed a word about the letter she wrote to warn you away, nor about meeting you earlier this week . . . I only found out when my daughter let it slip out an hour ago." Ruffle shuffle. "Well, I went ballistic and I only just calmed down enough to call you. How petty! How suspicious! What right did she have to keep you away from me? And on the heels of the death of my father, too . . . I shudder to think what kind of family you must think we are. Then again, you might be right. My wife and I—our marriage, it is not exactly . . . never mind." Pause. "Third. What is third? I'm losing track. That was the past. The future, Eiji. I want very badly to meet you, in case you were wondering. Right now, if possible. Today. We have so much to say, where do I start? Where do I stop?" Bemused laugh. "Come to my clinic today— I'm a cosmetic surgeon, incidentally, if your mother never told you. We won't be disturbed by my wife or any hostile parties—or we could go to a restaurant if you haven't eaten by the time you get this. . . . Look, I cleared my afternoon surgery. Can you make one o'clock? This is my office number." I scribble it down. "Get to Edogawabashi subway station, call, and Ms. Sarashina—my assistant, completely trustworthy— will come and meet you. Only a minute away. So. Until one o'clock this afternoon . . ." An amazed sort of coo noise. "I've been praying this day would come for years, and years, and years . . . every time I went to the shrine, I asked . . . I can hardly—" He laughs. "Enough of this, Eiji! One o'clock! Edogawabashi subway station!"

Life is sweet, rich, and fair.

I forget Ai Imajo, I forget Kozue Yamaya, I lie back, and I replay the message over until I have every word, every mannerism, by heart. I get out the picture of my father and animate his face so he speaks the words. An educated, warm, dry voice that inspires respect. Not so nasal as mine. I want to tell Buntaro and Machiko—no, I want to wait. Later today, I will walk calmly into Shooting Star with a mysterious gentleman behind me and let drop a "By the way, Buntaro, may I introduce you to my father?" Cat watches me from the closet—"Today is the day, Cat!" I iron my good shirt, shower, and then try to doze for an hour. No hope. I listen to John and Yoko's *Some Time in New York City,* and it is lucky I set my alarm clock, because the next thing I know it is eleven-thirty and the clock is ringingingingining inside my ears. I dress, fuss Cat, and dish up her dinner six hours early in case I have to go straight to work after my father. Luckily Buntaro is on the phone to a distributor so he cannot pry under my halo of joy.

Edogawabashi Station. I scan the midday crowds so intently that I miss her. "Excuse me? I'm guessing you're Eiji Miyake, from your baseball cap." I nod at the smartly dressed woman, not exactly young, not exactly old. She smiles with blackcurrant lips. "I'm Mari Sarashina, your father's assistant—we spoke on the phone just now. What a thrill it is to have you visit."

I bow. "Thank you for coming out to meet me, Ms. Sarashina."

"No trouble at all. The clinic is a stroll away. Well, this is a very special day for your father. Canceling an afternoon of appointments"—she shakes her head—"unprecedented in six years! I thought, 'Is the Emperor visiting?' Then he said his son had come to meet him!—his words, not mine—and I thought 'Aha! All is explained!' He meant to fetch you from the station himself, you know, but lost his nerve at the last minute—between you and me, he's afraid of emotional displays, et cetera. Enough gossip. Follow me." Ms. Sarashina walks and talks unswervingly. A cat-size dog crosses our path. Oncoming pedestrians and cyclists make way for her. She navigates side streets of labelless boutiques and art galleries. "Your father's clinic is a state-of-the-art establishment in the beautician sphere. We have a loyal word-of-mouth clientele, so we avoid ostentatious advertising, unlike the down-market clip-and-tuck shops." A mouse-size cat crosses our path. "Here we are— see, you could pass by none the wiser." It is a tall, anonymous building, sandwiched by flashier neighbors. The first floor is a jewelry business, viewing by appointment. Set down a short corridor is a steel door. Mari Sarashina points to a brass plaque. "This is us—Juno. Zeus turned her into a swan." Her fingers dance over a security keypad. "Or was it a bull?" A video camera watches us. "Rather draconian security, I know, but our client list includes television stars, et cetera. You would not believe"—Mari Sarashina glares at heaven—"what the grubbier paparazzi will do for a peek. Your father reviewed security after a reporter, disguised as a health ministry inspector, tried to bluff his way into our client files. Jackals, those people. Leeches. He had fake ID, business card, the works. Ms. Kato, your father's lawyer, bled them dry in court, naturally—although I gather she's not exactly flavor of the month, vis-à-vis yourself." An elevator arrives. Mari Sarashina presses 9. "A room with a view." She smiles reassuringly. "Apprehensive?"

I nod, hollow with nervous excitement. "A little."

She brushes fluff off her cuff. "Quite natural." She stage-whispers. "Your father is three times jumpier. But—relax." The doors open onto a gleaming white reception area decked with lilies. Perfumed antiseptic. Pinstriped sofas, slab-of-glass tables, a tapestry of swans on a lost river. The walls curve into the ceiling—whorled and delicate, bones inside an ear. Celtic harp music accompanies the air-conned hush. Ms. Sarashina jabs the intercom on her desk—"Dr. Tsukiyama? Congratulations, it's a boy!" She shows me her perfect teeth. "Shall I send him in?" I hear his voice crackle. Mari Sarashina laughs. "Fine, Doctor. Coming up." She sits down in front of her computer and gestures toward the steel door. "Go on, Eiji. Your father is waiting." I move, but real time is on PAUSE. "Thanks," I tell her. She makes a "don't mention it" face. One door away now—go! I turn the handle—the room beyond is airtight. The steel door opens with a kissing sound.

My arms are swung behind my back, my body is rammed against the wall, my feet are kicked away, and the cold floor slams into my ribs. One set of hands frisks me while another set holds my arms way past the angle they were designed to bend—the pain is record-breaking. Yakuza again. If I did have a concealed knife I would stick it into myself for being so stupid. Again. I consider volunteering to give up the Kozue Yamaya disk until a foot in the small of my back knocks the thought from my head. I am flipped over, and hauled to my feet. At first, I think I am standing on the TV set of a medical drama. A trolley of surgical equipment, a drug cabinet, an operating table. The edges are shadowy, with ten or eleven men whose faces I cannot make out. I smell sausages. A man is filming me with a Handycam, and on a large overhead screen I see myself. Two men with the bodies of Olympic shot-putters are holding an arm each. The camera zooms in, and captures my face from various angles. "Light!" comes an old man's voice, and whiteness fills my eyeballs. I am dragged forward a few paces, and sat down. When I can see again I find myself at a card table. Mama-san and three men. Near enough to touch is a smoked-glass screen taking up most of the wall. An intercom clicks on, and the voice of God fills the room. "This lamentable specimen is him?"

Mama-san looks at the smoked glass. "This is him."

"I had no idea," says God, "Morino had fallen on such hard times."

Now I really know I am in trouble. My "father" on the telephone was obviously an actor who saved them the trouble of collecting me. I want to whimper and cry but it would not help. I rub life back into my arms, and glance at the three men also sitting at the card table. From their postures and expressions, I can tell that they are also here against their will. A sweat-shiny fat-as-a-doughnut asthmatic, a man who keeps twitching as if his face is under attack, and an older guy who was once handsome but who has had scars gouged upward from the corners of his mouth that fix his face in a mockery of a smile. Mr. Doughnut, Twitcher, and Smiley all fix their eyes on the table.

"We are gathered here today," says God, "for you to pay your debts to me."

I cannot address a disembodied voice so I address Mama-san. "What debts?"

God replies first. "Major damage to Pluto Pachinko. Compensation for loss of trading time on the opening day. Two Cadillacs. Lost insurance premiums, cleaning bills, and general indemnities. Fifty-four million yen."

"But Morino caused that damage."

"And you," says Mama-san, "are the last living disciple of his faction."

I want to be sick. "You know I was no disciple."

God rattles his speakers. "We have your contract! Signed in your mixed blood! What faster-binding ink is there?"

I look at the smoked glass. "How about her?" I point at Mama-san. "She was Morino's accountant."

Mama-san is nearly smiling. "Child, I was a spy. Now shut up and listen or one of these bad, evil men will take a scalpel and slice your tongue in two." So I shut up and listen. "Mr. Tsuru has selected you four guests, his most hopeless debtors, to play a card game. A simple card game, with three winners and one loser. The winners will leave this chamber free men, owing not a single yen. The loser will donate organs to needy patients. A lung"—she stares at me—"a retina, and a kidney."

Everyone in the room behaves as if this is quite normal.

"I am supposed to say"—I have to start again because no voice came out the first time—"I am supposed to say 'Sure, fine, let's gamble with my body parts'?"

"You are free to decline."

"But?"

"But you will then be declared the loser."

"Decline, kid," jeers Twitcher, opposite me. "Stick to your principles."

I smell mustard and ketchup. I have no logic to combat any of this. "A game?"

Mama-san produces a pack of cards. "You shall cut to decide shuffling order. Aces high, highest shuffles first, the other players follow clockwise from the starter. Then we begin the game proper. In the same order, you shall turn over the top card until the queen of spades appears."

"Whoever she chooses," says God, "loses."

I feel how I felt back in the bowling alley.

"Is that voice him?" I ask Mama-san. My vocal cords are dry as sand. "Is that Mr. Tsuru?"

Twitcher gives me a round of sarcastic applause.

So, Tsuru is God. God is Tsuru. I try to buy time. "Even you," I say to Mama-san, "must think this is insane."

Mama-san's mouth becomes a tight slit. "I take my orders from the company president. So do you. Cut."

My hand feels as heavy as a brick. The jack of spades.

Mr. Doughnut draws the ten of diamonds.

Twitcher cuts the two of clubs.

Smiley turns over the nine of spades.

"The boy is the first to shuffle," says Tsuru from behind his smoked glass.

The players look at me.

I clumsily flicker-shuffle the pack. Up on the screen, hands many times the size of my own do the same. Nine times, for luck.

Mr. Doughnut wipes his hands on his shirt. The cards fly from hand to hand in gymnastic formation.

Twitcher makes a magical gesture with three fingers and cuts once.

Smiley shuffles in precise, circular motions.

Mama-san slides the pack to the center of the table. It sits there innocently. I look at it as I would a bomb, which is exactly what it is. I wait for an explosion, an earthquake, a gunshot, an "It's the cops!" But the only sound is sausages spitting on a grill. The slow breathing of men.

"Take the top card now," prompts Tsuru's voice gently, "or a guard will remove your eyelids, and you will never be able to close your eyes again, not even to blink."

I turn over the nine of diamonds.

Mr. Doughnut's breathing grates as his asthma worsens. He draws the ace of clubs.

Twitcher had a Buddhist education—he intones "*Namu amida butsu*" three times before his hand darts out and snatches the ace of spades. "Thank you," he says.

Smiley is the coolest of us all. He calmly turns over the seven of spades.

My turn again. I feel as if Miyake is operating Miyake by remote control. I look at myself on the screen. Myself stares back. I never knew I looked like that. My hand extends—

A narrow door in the smoked glass swings open and a waggy Labrador skitters out, chomping on a sausage and slipping on the polished marble. "Bring her back!" cries Tsuru, his real voice emerging from the entrance, only half picked up by the microphone and speakers. "She mustn't run on a full stomach! Her digestion is delicate!" Two of the guards eventually shepherd the dog back to its master.

"We," murmurs Smiley, "are just TV dinner for the mad old fuck."

All eyes in the room on me again.

Something alien is under my tongue.

I turn over the six of hearts.

I lick my forearm, taste salt, and see a tiny black insect.

Mr. Doughnut's arm leaves a sweat patch on the felt. The three of diamonds.

Twitcher prays to Buddha and flips over the joker. "Thank you."

Smiley sighs and turns over the five of clubs.

Twelve cards gone out of fifty-two, fifty-four including two jokers.

I look at the backing of the top card for a clue, and two trapezoid eyes stare straight back at me. I know those eyes.

What is life like without half your organs?

No, Tsuru would never let the loser walk away to tell the tale, with a torso of scars and holes to prove it. The silence of the lucky winners can be relied upon, but the loser would end up the same way as Kozue Yamaya's son.

How did I get here?

I look at the screen Miyake. He has no answers either.

Mama-san opens her mouth to threaten me—

I turn over the card, and the black queen looks into my eyes.

The room slants from side to side.

Apparently I have lost.

"Fuck," says Twitcher, "I thought the kid found the bitch, not her sister."

"So," says Smiley, "does the kid."

What are they talking about?

Smiley nods at my death notice on the table. "Look closer."

It is the queen of clubs, not spades. Clubs.

Mr. Doughnut says, "I need my inhaler. Can I take it out of my jacket pocket?" Mama-san nods, and he fishes the plastic tube from his jacket. He holds his head back, breathes in a blast, holds it, and breathes out. Then he turns over the queen of spades.

Nobody says anything.

The screen Mr. Doughnut is sweating worse than a man dying of plague.

My head is swelling with relief and guilt and pity. It really hurts.

Mama-san clears her throat. "Your queen has appeared, Mr. Tsuru."

The speakers stay silent.

"Mr. Tsuru?" Mama-san frowns at the smoked glass. "Your queen has spoken."

No response.

Mama-san leans over and knocks on the glass. "Mr. Tsuru?"

A guard wrinkles his nose. "What meat is he cooking?"

Another guard frowns. "Well, it ain't sausages . . ."

The guard nearest the door in the glass pushes it open and peers in. "Mr. Tsuru?" He breathes sharply, as if karate-kicked in his stomach. "Mr. Tsuru!" He stays where he is, and turns around to face us, blankly.

"Well?" demands Mama-san.

His jaw moves but nothing comes out.

"What?"

He swallows. "Mr. Tsuru has grilled his face to the hot plate."

A riot of improvised theater breaks out. All I can do is close my eyes.

"Mr. Tsuru Mr. Tsuru Mr. Tsuru! Can you hear me?"

"Scrape his head off!"

"Turn the gas off!"

"His lip has fused to the metal!"

"Ambulance ambulance ambulance someone call—"

"Fuck! His eyeball just popped!"

"Wipe it off on your own shirt!"

"Get that fucking dog out of here!"

Someone vomits.

The dog barks joyfully.

Casually, Mama-san scrapes a metallic object down the smoked glass. The screech is unbearable, and the chamber falls silent. Her composure is perfect, as though she scripted this moment many years ago and has rehearsed it regularly. "Mr. Tsuru's entertainment has been overtaken by a deus ex machina. The facts, gentlemen, suggest that the excitement triggered a second stroke, and since our dear leader chose his barbecue to fall on, it no longer matters particularly when that ambulance gets here." She now addresses the older two or three men. "I am appointing myself the acting head of this organization. You shall obey me, or oppose me. Make your intentions known. Now."

The moment is dense with calculations.

The men look at us. "What will we do with them, Mama-san?"

Their deferral is her coronation. "Card games are no longer company policy. Show them the door."

I dare not trust this new development, not until I am outside and running. Mama-san addresses us. "If any of you go to the police and somehow convince a recently graduated detective that you are not a lunatic, three things will occur, in this order. One: you will be taken into protective custody. Two: a bullet will be put through your head within six hours. Three: your debts to us will be transferred to your next of kin and, I give you my word, I will personally ensure that their lives are destroyed. This is not a threat, this is standard procedure. You will now indicate that you understand."

We nod.

"We have been in business for thirty years. Draw your own conclusions about our ability to protect our interests. Now get out of here."

The cinema is full. Couples, students, drones. The only free seats are in the front, where the screen looms over your head. Everything in Tokyo is nearly full, full, or too full. There was no trace of Mari Sarashina in the reception area outside the chamber. "Hey, if I was you guys," said the guard as the elevator doors closed, "I'd buy a fucking lottery ticket." In the seat next to me is a girl—her boyfriend's hand has been edging closer over the back of her seat. The elevator began its long, slow descent. Mr. Doughnut dropped his cigarettes. We watched them lying where they fell. Mr. Doughnut began shaking, but with laughter or fear or what, none of us knew. Smiley closed his eyes and tilted his head back. I kept my eye on the descending floor numbers. Twitcher picked up a cigarette and lit it. This movie is brutal and cheap and fake. If people who dream up violent scripts ever came into contact with real violence, they would be too sickened to write such scenes. When the elevator doors opened we plunged into the afternoon crowds without a word. The sunny weather was a sick prank. I came to a place where street performers twisted balloons into crocodiles and giraffes, and had to dig my fingernails into my arm to stop myself crying. The movie finishes and the audience files out. I stay and watch the credits. The key grips, the animal trainers, the caterers. A new audience files in. I rewatch the movie until my brain starts to melt. After the balloon man, I wandered wherever the crowds looked thickest. I cursed myself for not leaving Tokyo after Morino. I should have known. In the cinema foyer I call Ai and quickly hang up when she answers. I get on a Yamanote circle line submarine, and sit with the drones. I wish I was a common drone. I hope their normality will seep into me. The stations roll by, and by, and by, and repeat themselves. I am too full of fear-pollution to ever sleep again.

A conductor gently shakes me awake. "You've gone around six times, kid, I thought I should wake you up." His eyes are kind and I envy his son.

"Is it night or are we underground?"

"Quarter to eleven, Thursday the fifth. Know what year we are in?"

"Yeah, I know that."

"You should get home while the trains are still running."

I wish. "I have to get to work."

"What are you, a grave robber?"

"Nothing so exotic . . . thanks for waking me up."

"Anytime."

The conductor moves down the compartment. Above the seats opposite, behind the swaying hand rings, is an ad for an internet advertising company. An apple tree grows from a computer chip, and from this apple tree grow more computer chips, and from these computer chips grow more apple trees. The forest grows out of the frame and invades the advertising spaces on either side. I was unaware that any part of my brain was thinking about the Kozue Yamaya disk, but an enormous idea occurs to me. I am wide, wide awake.

My mind is not here, but I never need my mind in Nero's. When I arrive on the last stroke of Thursday, I get a weird look from Sachiko—she knows about my argument with Ai—but it is hard to care. I think about the twenty-four-hours-ago Eiji Miyake, chicken-cooping up and down these same three-by-one square meters of Tokyo giving birth to his pizzas. Lucky, blind, cursed idiot. I wish I could warn him. I knock back a health drink to ward off sleeplessness and start work on the backed-up orders. "You got a nine of diamonds for me, man?" asks Doi when he returns. I forgot it. "No. Tomorrow." Doi congratulates himself. "Magic is the manipulation of coincidence, man. You can only rely on coincidences." I wash my hands and face. Every time the door buzzes, I am afraid it could be a Tsuru thug. Every time the telephone rings, I am afraid Sachiko or Tomomi will appear in the hatch and pass the handset through, saying: "A call for you, Miyake. No name." Doi is supercommunicative tonight—he tells me how he got dismissed from his last job. He was a night watchman in a multistory cemetery where the ashes of the dead are stored in hives of tiny locker-shrines. He was fired for substituting his own music for the tapes of Buddhist funerary mantras. "I figured, man, if *I* were stuck in a box for all eternity, which would I prefer? Priests making opening-seriously-larger-than-expected-phone-bill moans, or the golden age of rock 'n' roll? No contest! I could *feel* the vibes in the place change, man, whenever I put on my Grateful Dead tapes." Doi slashes his throat with his forefinger. I hear Doi without listening. His pizza comes through for delivery. I box it and off he goes. The radio plays "I Heard It Through the Grapevine"—a scheming song of paranoia. Sachiko leans through the hatch—"You have a mystery caller on line three!"

"Ai?"

"Nooo . . . She prefers not to give her name."

Sachiko leans through to the kitchen wall phone, presses a button, and passes me the reciever.

No name? Then it must be Mama-san.

"Hello?"

The caller does not respond.

Fear makes my voice sharp. "Hello?"

"Is two A.M. good morning or good night, Eiji? I'm not very sure." A middle-aged woman, not Mama-san. She is as nervous as I am, I think.

"Look, would you just tell me who you are?"

"Me, Eiji, your mother."

I lean against the counter.

Tomomi is studying me through the crack in the hatch. I close it gently.

"This is, uh, a surprise."

"Did you get my letters? Your uncle said he forwarded them to you. He said you're living in Tokyo now."

"Yeah."

Yeah, I got your letters. But therapy that closes wounds in you just opens wounds in me.

She takes a deep breath. "A man has asked me to be his wife."

The words sink in. "Oh." Tomomi inches open the doors. I bang them shut savagely. "Well." Hope I broke the bitch's nose. "Congratulations."

"Yes. The hotelier in Nagano I told you about in my last letter."

A hotelier, huh? Nice catch. Especially with your history.

Why are you telling me this now?

You never bothered telling us about your life before.

You never cared what we thought. Not remotely.

You want me to be happy for you? To say "Sure, Mom, great news!"?

I very nearly put us both out of our misery and hang up.

"Where are you calling from?" I end up saying.

"I'm back at the clinic in Miyazaki. The . . . drinking, you know, I was poorly for a very long time. That's why . . . But now, he—the hotelier, his name is Mr. Ota, by the way—he says after we marry my problems are his problems too, and so . . . I want to get better. So I came back here."

"I see. Good. Good luck." Doubtless he is bankrolling her. "Mrs. Ota." Ordinary, married, respectable. RESET. A new patron, a new set of bank cards, a new wardrobe. Nice. But answer my question: why are you telling me this now? I see. Mr. Ota doesn't know about us. You never told him. You want to make sure I won't fuck things up when I hear the news.

"He'd love to meet you, Eiji."

So I was wrong. Mr. Ota would love to meet me. But tell me this, Mother: why would I want to meet this owner of fat hotels? Twenty years is a little late to start playing the dutiful mother, Mother. Fact is, you only ever make me unhappy. You are making me unhappy now.

So fine. Get over your drinking problem, get married, live happily ever after and leave me alone. You neurotic, grasping, betraying witch.

The hatch opens—a pen with a white flag waves—Sachiko's untouchable Doraemon mug appears on the shelf, emitting coffee particles. The hatch closes.

"Eiji?"

The DJ cuts "I Heard It Through the Grapevine" short.

Why I say what I say now, I could never explain, not even to myself.

"Mom, can I, uh . . . I'd, uh, like to come and see you in Miyazaki tomorrow."

When I finish explaining Sachiko nods. "Not the sort of humanitarian mission I could stand in the way of, is it? But my last order as your superior officer in the great army of Nero is this: phone my roommate before you leave Tokyo."

"Did she, uh, say anything?"

"I can tell her mood by her piano playing. While you were calling her last week? Ai played nice stuff. Yesterday evening, I had to get ready for work to those blocky-cocky Erik Satie pieces he wrote to evict his neighbors."

"I, uh, sort of messed up, Sachiko."

"Ai is no Miss Twenty-four-hour Sunshine. Life is short, Miyake. Call her."

"I dunno . . ."

"No. 'Dunno' is not acceptable. Say: 'I hear and obey, Miss Sera.'"

"I really—"

"Say it, or I invent the Miyake Pizza. If you think I'm joking, try me."

"I hear and obey, Miss Sera."

"Tomomi tells me some heavy vibes are going down, man . . ." Doi appears in the cage with a mini–food blender. "Know what I do to subdue all those spiked-up feelings, man?"

I turn away. "Doi, this is my last shift. Have mercy."

"No tricks, man! Just a magic antistress cocktail . . ." Would he put me through this if he knew I had come within one card and a burst artery of having half my organs removed this afternoon? Probably, yes. "First, strawberries!" Doi empties a pint of them into the blender. He pulls a black velvet hood over the blender and liquidizes them. He removes hood and lid. "Then, tomatoes!" He drops three overripe tomatoes in. "Red food massages away stress waves. Green aggravates. That's why rabbits and veggies are so uptight. . . . What next? Raspberry juice . . . raw tuna . . . azuki beans . . . all the major food groups." Doi replaces the lid, the hood, and blends. "And last of all, the crucial ingredient—" With a flourish he produces a pink parakeet from a handkerchief. It flaps, blinks, and tweets. "In you go, little guy!" He gently lowers it into the bright red liquid mush, and replaces the lid and hood. I know it is a stupid trick, so I refuse to look shocked—but I have to watch. He lowers the blender behind the ledge between the cage and my rat run—where he switches blenders, perhaps?—and then shakes the blender jug, bartender-style, to the Hawaiian slide guitar music on the radio.

"Doi!" Sachiko comes into the cage with her clipboard.

Doi jumps and guiltily puts down what he is holding.

"I hate to inconvenience you with this annoying 'work' business, but . . ."

"Still on my break, chieftainess! Three more minutes! I'm showing Miyake my peace potion . . ." He picks up the blender jug, still in its black hood, and liquidizes the contents for thirty seconds. Sachiko, defeated, sits down. Doi removes the hood and lid and drinks the soupy liquid straight back. "Deeelicious."

"Wow . . ." Sachiko stands up, putting blender B—I knew it—on the ledge, minus velvet hood. "Did you make this imitation parakeet? It's so realistic. What's it made of?" She is genuinely impressed.

"Lady boss! You gave my trick away!"

"Then don't leave your props lying around the kitchen!"

"Don't call my Chiko-chan a prop! Parakeets have feelings too, diggit?"

"Chiko-chan doesn't look very animated for a live parakeet." Sachiko extracts the bird from the red goop. Its head detaches in a shower of white powder.

"Doi," I say, "please tell me this is part of the trick."

Doi's eyes bulge in pure panic. "Oh, man . . . ."

After the ambulance takes Doi to the hospital for a stomach pump and a course of injections, I offer to do the scooter deliveries. Sachiko says she will because she knows the area better, and leaves Tomomi to handle the phones alone. I prepare and box up three El Gringos—thick base, gorgonzola, spicy salami, tomato and basil crust—by the time Onizuka gets back. Tomomi tells him what happened to Doi—for a moment I think Onizuka may abandon his principles and smile, but the danger passes and he reverts to his sullen self. Business slackens a little. By 07:30 I have already memorized the breakfast news roundup. Trade talks, summits, visiting dignitaries. This is how to control entire populations—don't suppress news, but make it so dumb and dull that nobody has any interest in it. The weather on Friday, October 12 will start cloudy, with a 60 percent chance of rain by midafternoon, and a 90 percent chance of rain by evening. I scour down the counters, hoping that no more orders come in during the next thirty minutes. I need to work out the cheapest way to get to Miyazaki. I peer into the inferno—six pizzas inching onward, glowing karmalike. The radio plays a song called "I Feel the Earth Move Under My Feet." Radios and cats both go about their business if anyone is there or not. Unlike a guitar, which sort of stops being a guitar when you close its case. Sachiko lays an envelope on the counter of my rat run. "I fiddled petty cash, but this is what Nero owes you."

"Thanks, Sachiko. Sorry to leave you in the lurch."

"Well, the Nippon Index will plummet once the news breaks, but somehow we'll pull through. I may even don the chef's apron myself, if head office can't send anyone. It has been known. Call me, when and if you come back to Tokyo—I can't promise to keep your job open in this branch, but I can get you in anywhere there's a vacancy."

"I appreciate it."

"Any idea how long you'll be away?"

"Depends on . . . lots of things. If I can help my mother get well." I fold the envelope into my starved wallet.

"Phone Ai. I don't want to be the one to tell her that you've skipped town."

"I, uh, don't think I'm friend of the month at the moment."

"Ai has no friends of the month, you idiot. *Phone* her."

Tomomi slouches in the hatch. "If you can spare the energy to prepare another pizza before your glorious reunion, the Osugi Bosugi man has ordered his weekly Kamikaze." She slaps the order dupe on the ledge and disappears. I frown at Sachiko, feeling as if my feet are sliding away. "Osugi and Bosugi? PanOpticon?"

"A regular order since time began. 'Kamikaze' is a pizza not on the wall chart—we should get around to putting it up, only nobody else in Tokyo could stomach it. Mozzarella crust, banana, quail eggs, scallops, octopus ink."

"Unchopped chilis."

"One of the other chefs mentioned it?"

This is a mystery to me. "I guess . . ."

"It is an unforgettable creation. Speaking of which, I have to go and write Doi's accident report"—so she doesn't see my face when I look at the order slip. Tomomi's handwriting is clear as malice. *Tsukiyama, Osugi & Bosugi, PanOpticon.*

First, I laugh in disbelief.

Then, I think: Another trap.

Then, I think: No trap. Apart from the fact that nobody knows I know my father's name, since Tsuru died nobody wants to trap me. Mama-san let me go once already. This is no trap but a card trick that Tokyo has performed. How is it done? Look at it stage by stage. I know "Kamikaze" because . . . here it is. I remember. Weeks ago, that night when Cat came back from the dead, a man misdialed, called my capsule thinking I was a pizza restaurant, and ordered this same pizza. Only he hadn't misdialed. That man was my father.

The rest is simple. My father is not Akiko Kato's client—he is her colleague.

Akiko Kato is why I watched PanOpticon from Jupiter Cafe.

Jupiter Cafe is why I met Ai Imajo.

Ai is why I met Sachiko Sera.

Sachiko Sera is why I am standing in Nero's, preparing a pizza for my father. No more misdirections, jumped conclusions, lies. To my father, I was a sixty-second amusement. Then I was a zero. Now I am an embarrassment. I feel so, so . . . stupid. I dress his pizza. It looks as disgusting as it sounds. I feed it into the inferno, watch the black glow orange. Why "stupid"? How about "angry"? Since I wrote to Akiko Kato my father has known how to contact me. Morino, Tsuru, everything . . . if only he had just told me to go away two months ago. I would have honored his wish. I even stopped looking—but Tokyo found him. This time, I decide what happens. I don't know what I will do when I confront him, but I am going to see him. No chance will ever come along again. I open the hatch. No sign of Tomomi. Sachiko gnaws a pen. "If I say that a wild parakeet flew into the blender of its own accord, d'you think head office will believe me?"

"Only if they want to."

"Lot of use you are."

"But I could deliver this Kamikaze for you."

Sachiko checks her watch. "Your shift ends in two minutes."

"PanOpticon is on my way to the station."

"You are an angel sent from heaven, Miyake."

The door to PanOpticon revolves in perpetual motion. Palm trees sit in bronze urns. Gaudy, people-eating orchids watch me pass. Nine identical leather armchairs wait for occupiers. A one-legged man crutches across the polished floor. Rubber squeaks, metal clinks. Behind the desk is the chubby security guard who threw me out when I tried to see Akiko Kato two months ago. A smear of shaving foam is under one ear. He puts down his sports paper and yawns as I approach. "Yeah, son?"

"I have a pizza for Mr. Tsukiyama in Osugi and Bosugi."

"Do you?"

I hold my box up.

"'Never fear-o, it's a Nero.' No explosives in there now, are there? You international terrorists always smuggle weapons into buildings using pizza boxes." He thinks this is very amusing indeed.

"Put it through a scanner, if you want."

He waves a night stick at the elevators. "East elevator, ninth floor."

The Osugi & Bosugi reception area appears deserted. A console piled with files, plants dying of sun starvation, a monitor on screensaver mode—a computer face drifts from anger to surprise to jealousy to joy to grief back to anger. A single corridor runs to a pane of morning. A photocopier intones. Where do I go? A human head rises up from a swamp of sleep. "Yes?"

"Morning. Pizza for Mr. Tsukiyama."

"Fine. One moment." She drags herself to a higher plane of consciousness, clips a headphone over her ear, and presses a button on her console. She lights a cigarette while waiting. "Mr. Tsukiyama, Momoe here. Pizza boy with breakfast. Shall I send him along or are you still projecting possible positions with your client?" She suctions in her cheeks while my father replies. "Received and understood, Mr. Tsukiyama." She jerks a thumb up the corridor and removes her headphone. "All the way, turn right at the end, Mr. Tsukiyama is dead ahead. And knock first."

The carpet is worn, the air-con is old, the walls need repainting. A door ahead opens and—right on cue—Akiko Kato appears, carrying a wire basket of shuttlecocks. Her silver sea-urchin earrings dangle. She is older and more lined than in the picture I got from Morino. Akiko Kato catches me sneaking my glance at her as I catch her looking at me. I say nothing—what could I say?—and keep walking, reminding myself that I am doing nothing illegal. I reach the end of the corridor, turn the corner, and nearly collide with another woman adjusting her shoe. She is my age, with sexier legs than Zizzi Hikaru. I smell perfume and wine. She regains her balance and walks the way I came. Ahead is a single door, ajar—DAISUKE TSUKIYAMA, PARTNER. *Daisuke.* I never liked that name. Inside, a man—my father, I guess—is on the telephone. I eavesdrop. "Darling, I *know*! You're overreacting—you—just—darling—LISTEN TO ME! Are you listening? Thank you. I *had* to spend the night here because if I give this one to the underlings they'll fuck it up and then I'll have to spend even more nights here sorting out the mess and my client will be pissed off too and take his account somewhere swankier, so my bonus gets slashed and then how am I supposed to pay for the fucking pony in the first fucking place? Stop—stop it, darling—yeah, I know her friends all have ponies, but all her friends' daddies are judges with more money than fucking Switzerland . . . You think I *like* doing this overtime-slave shift? You think I *like*—what? *WHAT*? Oh, oh, oh, *this* is what we're really talking about it, is it? Paranoia strikes back! Ever occurred to you, *darling* . . ." He is now shouting. "*WHAT*? You didn't! No. Tell me you didn't. You did. Well, this is your morning bombshell. A private investigator. You stupid little woman. *Of course* private investigators feed you bullshit! Why? Because they want repeat business! I am too outraged to continue this conversation. I have a company to run. And if you have cash to throw away on your detective games, why all the hurry to sell off the shares the old man left? Yeah, you have a nice day too. *Darling.*" He hangs up. "And throw yourself off the balcony, *darling.*"

I take a deep breath—

He may recognize me—

He may not recognize me, and I may tell him—

He may not recognize me, and I may not tell him—

I knock.

A pause. Then a cheerful "Come!"

I recognize my father from the photograph I got from Morino. He lies on a vast sofa, wearing a dressing gown. "Pizza boy! You overhear my telephone call?"

"I did my best not to." My first words to my father.

"Let it be a lesson to you."

"I'm sorry, I—"

"Remember: it costs more to keep a pony in straw than a whore in fur."

"I can't imagine ever needing to remember that."

My father grins—a grin that is used to getting what it wants—and beckons me over. There is a great view of skyscrapers in the background, but I drink in every detail. The too-black hair. The racks of shoes in his closet. The photo of Half-sister on his desk as a ballerina swan. The shape of his hands. The way he swivels upright. His body seems to be in better shape than his company—I guess he works out at a gym. "You're not Onizuka, and you're not Doi."

No, I am your son by your first mistress. "No."

"So?" My father waits. "You are?"

"The chef."

"Oho! So *you* make my delectable Kamikazes."

Don't just see me, look at me. "Only this week. I'm temporary."

"My creation must have come as quite a surprise."

You really don't know who I am, do you? "It's an unusual combination."

"Unusual? Unique!"

I smell perfume and wine.

"Are you all right?"

I tell you now, or I go away forever.

He grins. "You look like your night was almost as long and hard as mine."

How you love yourself. "Goodbye."

Mock-offended surprise. "You don't want me to sign anywhere?"

"Oh. Yeah. Here, please—"

My father scribbles on the receipt.

I want to smash your skull with your golfing trophy.

I want to shout and I think I want to cry.

I want you to know. Your consequences, your damage, your dead. I want to drag you down to the seabed between foot rock and whalestone.

"Hell-o-oo-ooo!" My father waves his hand. "I said, 'Is Doi back next week?'"

I swallow and nod and leave this man. How is it that I feel nothing, when, for so long, meeting him was everything. I doubt I will ever meet him again, so I look back once—his eyes close as his jaws sink into black stodge.

Outside PanOpticon, I buy a pack of Hopes, sit on a post, and watch the traffic stop and start. Twenty years translated to two minutes. I smoke one, two, three. The cloud atlas turns its pages over. Crows dissect a pile of trash. Tokyo is the color of a dirty eraser. Summer left without notice or ceremony. Drones in Jupiter Cafe tuck into their breakfasts. I want to stop a passerby, and tell the story of the last seven weeks, from PanOpticon stakeout up until this moment. How do I feel? Oh, I cannot begin. But hey, Anju, I kept my promise. I wish Ai were working at the Jupiter Cafe today. I would ride in on my Harley-Davidson like Richard Gere in *An Officer and a Gentleman*, our argument would be forgotten, she would climb on, and we would vanish down the narrow road to the deep north. I watch the pedestrians crossing en masse when the green man says so. I join them. I cross Kita Street—I feel disappointment that our father turned out exactly as all the evidence said he would. I wait for the man to turn green. I cross over Omekaido Avenue—I feel shame that his blood runs in my veins—and I wait for the man to turn green. Then I cross back over Kita Street—I feel sad that I found what I searched for, but no longer want what I found. I wait, and cross back over Omekaido Avenue. I feel release. I complete one, two, three circuits. A scooter beeps. Release. I can go now. The scooter beeps again and I hear my name. Onizuka has pulled up on his Nero's scooter. I am immune to surprise, now and maybe forever. I don't know what he wants, but I rule out walking away from Onizuka in case he knifes me in the kidneys. "C'm here." He clears his throat and spits. "Been looking for you."

"You found me."

"Been watching you walking in circles."

"Squares. Not circles."

He toys with his lip stud. "Want to ask you something."

I go up to him.

He thumbs toward Nero's. "Mouth says you're going to Miyazaki."

"Tomomi?"

"Mouth."

I half-snigger against my will. "Yes, Mouth is right."

"Your mom's ill?"

"She is, yeah."

"Short of cash?"

Where is this going? "I'm not exactly the Bank of Japan, no."

"My stepdad runs a trucking business. I called him. Said one of his drivers'll get you to Osaka, then fix you up with a rig for Fukuoka."

Onizuka never jokes, and he hasn't started now. He hands me a slip of paper. "Map, address, phone number. Be there by noon."

I'm too surprised—too grateful—to say anything.

Onizuka drives off even before I properly thank him.

"You want to visit your mother in Miyazaki, but you can't be sure when you'll be back," Buntaro announces before I can utter a word. My landlord folds his *Okinawa Property Weekly*. "As if I could say no, kid! My own mother would murder me. Yes, my wife will take care of the cat. Like old times. Your rent is covered until the end of October, and your deposit can take care of November, unless you need me to return it, in which case I'll pay it into your bank account, box your stuff, and put it into storage. Call me from Miyazaki when you know what your plans are. Shooting Star isn't going anywhere. My wife has made you a lunch box." He rubs his gold tooth, and I realize that this tooth is Buntaro's lucky amulet. "Go on then, kid," he says. "Pack!" My capsule is exactly as I left it twenty hours ago. Socks, yogurt cartons, scrunched pillows. Weird. Cat is out, but Cockroach waits on the window ledge. I get the death spray, creep up on it, and—Cockroach is motionless. Daydreaming? I prod him with a sheet of junk mail. Cockroach is a dead husk.

Onizuka TransJapan Ltd. is near Takashimadaira Station out on the Toei Mita Line. Through the gates is a walled yard with a loading bay and three medium-size trucks. It is still eleven. I walk back toward the station, where a giant electronics store is opening. Inside is cold as predawn February. Two identical receptionists at the help desk chime "Good morning" in such angelic harmony that I am unsure which to speak to. "Uh, on which floor are the computers, please?"

"Basement, third level," answers Miss Left.

"Mind if I leave my backpack with you?"

"No problem at all, sir," answers Miss Right.

I float on the down escalator. Souls of shoppers float with me. Everywhere is draped with tinselly maple leaves to proclaim the coming of autumn. Miniature TVs, spherical stereos, intelligent microwaves, digital cameras, cell phones, ionizing freezers, dehumidifying heaters, hot rugs, massage chairs, heated dish racks, 256-color printers. The escalator announcement warns me not to stand on the yellow lines, to assist children and old people at all times, and to enjoy quality shopping. Goods sit on their shelves, watching us browse—anglers on a riverbank. Not a single window. In the computer section I am accosted by a tame Suga in a clip-on tie. His skin has a shrink-wrap gleam. I wonder if they have Vitamin B–emitting fluorescent lights down here to compensate for the total absence of natural light. "You look like a man with his mind made up, sir!"

"Yes, I'm thinking of upgrading one of my PCs."

"Well, I promise we can spoil you for choice. What's your budget?"

"Uh . . . I've got a research grant to burn through. My modem's from the twenty-fifth century, now all I need is the hardware to match it."

"No problem. What's your modem?"

I overdid it. "Uh . . . a very fast one indeed."

"Yes, sir, but which make?"

"Uh, a Suga modem. Saratoga Instruments."

He bluffs. "Verrrrrrrrry nice machines. Which university are you at?"

"Uh, Waseda."

I have used a magic word. His face shines; he produces his card and bows low enough to lick my shoes. "Fujimoto—at your service. We do operate an academic discount scheme. Well. I'll let you play—you just call me if I can assist."

"I will."

I pretend to read the specifications on a few machines, gather a sheaf of brochures, and choose a machine to sit at. I click onto the internet, and find the e-mail address of the Tokyo Metropolitan Police. I write it on my hand. I glance around, hoping no hidden video cameras are watching. I load Suga's disk. A hearty welcome to the Mailman virus! Suga made his virus more user-friendly than he ever made himself. Do you want to enter your message to the masses via keyboard or load it from disk? I press D. Okay. Load your disk and hit ENTER. I eject the Suga disk, insert the Kozue Yamaya one, and press ENTER. The virus program takes over. The drive buzzes and blinks. Okay. Now enter address of lucky recipient. I type in the police address from my hand. Hit ENTER to lick stamp! The cursor pulses, my finger hovers—the consequences of pressing this key swarm—click. Too late to change my mind now. Mailman is delivering your letter to primary addressee . . . Flash. Mailman is forwarding your letter to second-generation addressees . . . Short pause. Third-generation addressees . . . Long pause. Fourth-generation . . . (Yawn.) The screen clears. Mailman will continue to generation 99. The message scrolls offscreen. Log off now/leave the crime scene/run like hell. Beep. Bye-bye. Bye-bye, Suga. I eject the Yamaya disk and put it into my shirt pocket. I am a plague spreader. Only this plague might cure something. "Hey! You! Yes, you!" An older salesman strides over. I think about running, but then every security guard would assume I was a shoplifter. The salesman blocks off my escape route, anyway. "I saw you! What did you just put into our computer?" I grope for a plausible lie but fail completely. "Well, uh, a dead woman placed me under a moral obligation to, uh, release information about a nameless yakuza network that steals people, cuts them up, and, uh, sells the body parts to the highest bidders. I was afraid that if I used a computer in a private apartment or somewhere, they might be able to trace it back, so using the computer here seemed to be the safest way. I hope that was okay? It didn't do any harm to your equipment." The salesman thinks this over, wondering where I am on the basically harmless to moon-barking spectrum of lunacy. Finally his face softens. "In that case, sir, I'm very glad we could help. Perhaps you could let me know beforehand, next time, or even use a terminal at the public library." I promise to do so, and we thank each other, bow deeply, and I let the escalator whisk me away. I retrieve my backpack from the help desk and walk out into the warm traffic fumes. I drop the two disks down the nearest storm drain. From a phone booth near Onizuka TransJapan I try calling Ai at home, then on her cell phone, but nothing doing. Quarter to noon. I had better find Onizuka's stepfather and introduce myself. I am so tired nothing seems real.

eight

♦

The Language
of Mountains Is Rain

Balletjellyfish waft down from the roof of the shopping mall. Watch their faerie lights for too long and you lose yourself. They form a clear, gelatinous sludge that slurps shin-high. Walking is wading and progress is slow, but I have to push deeper into enemy territory by nightfall. Claude Debussy hisses from a doorway, twirling his pedophile mustache: "The enemy have learned their lessons from the Battle of Midway. They have radar. They know you are here." Genji the barber asks me to vote for him, but he is hardly a viable candidate, dripping in jellyfish juice. Shooting Star was abandoned years ago. Tatty "Forthcoming Releases" posters hang from rusty pins. I push the door open. "Buntaro? Machiko?" Inside it looks as if an earthquake hit. "It did." The young man inside sitting behind the counter smiles. "I'm only looking after the place for a few days." I feel a surge of unease— "Machiko—is she okay? The baby, I mean?" The young man smiles as if I am making a joke several degrees of wit higher than I am, in fact, capable of. I realize I am talking to Kodai. So I pretend I was joking, too, and mumble something about how fast he has grown. "Dad's scared of aftershocks," Kodai explains. "Well. I expect you'll be wanting to get upstairs. They are waiting." I remember I am late, but cannot quite recall what I am late for. I climb up to my capsule. Weird, I never noticed how my capsule is in fact my old school gym where we played five-a-side soccer when it rained. Debris is everywhere. Here is the goal. My team and the enemy line the box, waiting for me to take the crucial penalty shot.

Nakamori and Nakamura are here. I know that if I score this goal all the damage will be undone. The booming bell will draw its chime back into itself and the god of thunder will sleep on. Anju will swim to the whale-stone and back again, and be at Wheatie's when I return with my man-of-the-match trophy. I see the goalkeeper making a date with a cheerleader. I run up to the ball and boot it. The ball scuds and wobbles toward the goal line, slowing down. Desperately, I follow it—"No second kick allowed!" warns my stepmother—and crawl on my hands and knees, blowing the ball over the gravel. The track winds up the valley through the Neck. My right knee is shaking. "What are you d-doing, child?" asks Goatwriter. "You scored m-miles ago. D-d-didn't you notice?" I did? When? Is this hope I am feeling?

◆

An ogre shakes my right knee with his left hand. His right grips the steering wheel. "Hey! You're dreaming, son. Mumbling, you were." I take in my new surroundings. The cab of a truck, festooned with amulets from shrines the length and breadth of Japan. Traffic crawls into the gray middle distance. The driver is a sad ogre. His pool-ball eyes look in different directions and his face ends at his lower lip. "Mumbling, you were," he repeats, "but what you were mumbling about, I got no idea." In a microsecond all the information that constitutes Eiji Miyake and the last twenty-four hours—and the last seven weeks—downloads. I think the ogre said his name was Honda, but it would be rude to check now. I wonder how I can trick him into repeating his name. Fine rain flies, and every ten seconds or so the wipers drag themselves across the big windshield. I feel a weird lightness. What was I dreaming about? I met Kodai, already grown—I must tell Buntaro and Machiko how cool he looked—but what else was there? I met my father this morning. So. The postfather epoch of Eiji Miyake's life is under way. I feel both anti-climactic loss and a sort of triumph. And now, in a perfect reversal of my semilaid plans, I am headed to Miyazaki, back to Kyushu to see my mother. At about five kilometers per hour in four lanes of traffic. So how come I feel so hopeful? The dashboard clock blinks 16:47. I have been asleep for over three hours. I feel gritty and stretched, but have paid back a chunk of my overdraft at the Miyake Bank of Sleep. I locate some gum in my shirt pocket—BlackBlack gum, my favorite since I quit smoking—and offer Ogre a stick. "No, son. Never touch the stuff." I unglue the paper from the gum and start chewing. I am forgetting something else, something important. The Mailman virus! If Suga's boast was truthful, Kozue Yamaya's file has already spread to every contact on every address book of every contact on every address book . . . et cetera . . . for ninety-nine generations. That adds up to . . . more computers than there are in Japan, I guess. I imagine the program hurtling outward, the same way shock waves expand from the epicenter of a detonated atom bomb. Will antivirus software stop it? No idea. Suga would have made his Mailman as dogged and devious as himself, I guess. Will it take nanoseconds or hours to run through all ninety-nine generations? No idea, again. But any high-level cover-up should now be impossible, surely. Too many people will find it in their inboxes tomorrow. I guess. Anyway, it is all out of my hands. "Going nowhere at the speed of light, we are," murmurs Ogre. "Traffic news said a rig overturned, 'bout ten clicks downstream from here. Milk rig, it was. Driver taken to the hospital, 'nother driver suffering shock, but nobody killed. Could've been worse." Rented-by-the-square-meter Tokyo has turned into zones of rice fields, houses, industrial units. The landscape itself looks like its map. "On a fine day," says Ogre, "you can see Mount Fuji over there, you can." Rain stars go nova on the glass, and Ogre speeds up the wipers. They squelch. The radio burbles away. Tires hiss on the wet Tomei Expressway. A minibus of kids from a school for the disabled passes on the inside. A pair in the back row wave. Ogre flashes his headlights and the whole bus goes wild. I wave too. I still cannot say why I feel so at peace with the world. I am suspicious of this feeling—when it leaves you feel hollower than before. Ogre is chuckling. "Who knows what makes kids tick? Not me. Alien species, kids are nowadays, if you ask me." Row upon row of polyethylene hothouses troop past. I feel I should stoke the conversation to pay for my fare, but when I begin a sentence a yawn splits my face in two. So I ask Ogre if he has any kids himself.

Ogre takes his time answering. "Nah, not me. No kids. Me and marriage, marriage and me, it was not to be. Loads of truckers have wives in every port. At least, according to truckers." I can tell Ogre has a tale, but it would be rude to probe. "Cigarette?" He offers me a box of Cabins, and I get as far as taking one out before I remember. "Sorry, I promised a friend I would give it up." I light Ogre's, and try to smoke my craving instead of its object. "Important things to keep, promises," mutters Ogre. "If a man keeps his promises or not, that is what that man is worth. You with me?" I nod. Traffic nudges, stops and starts. Ogre inhales, rests his elbows on the big-as-a-hoop steering wheel, and inhales. "I was your age too, once, believe it or not, I was. Got a job at Showa-Shell driving their gianormous oil tankers. How gianormous? So gianormous that the freight division had its own one-month training program, it did. Those babies are not your regular boxes-on-wheels, get the picture? So me and twelve other trainees, we stayed in dorms outside Yamagata. Ex-barracks, they were. Bleak spot, even in March, it was. Sleet and frost and icicles, there was. One long corridor, we were put in, twelve guys, with a partition for a bit of privacy." Ogre taps ash into the tray. I pry a minute dagger of crusted sleep from the corner of my eye. "Now, I never sleepwalked in my life. Not never, I didn't. But on my third night in Yamagata, I started. Not just walking, neither. I did stuff. Stuff tied in with what I was dreaming about, you with me? So, say I dream a dream about walking 'round Kure—my hometown, is Kure—then I sleepwalk up and down the corridor saying, 'Afternoon. Nice spot of weather we're having,' to all the other trainees in their beds. Or say I dream of being Picasso or someone: in the morning we wake up and find I've drawn stuff on the mirrors with toothpaste and stuff. At first, I thought they were winding me up, the other trainees, I mean. But they weren't. It was me who was doing it, all right. They took a picture to prove it. Spooky picture, that was, I can tell you. By the third night, it was a bit of a laugh. I cleaned up my own mess. It was, 'Well, what's Honda going to get up to tonight?' You with me? After a week we were used to it, we were. They never woke me up. Everyone knows you never wake up a sleepwalker, not never, you don't." We sidle past the minibus of kids again. They press their faces against the glass and do chimpanzees. I wave again, but I think of submariners dying, and Ogre Honda does not notice them this time. The radio whips and spikes. Ogre tries to retune it, but gives up and switches it off. "On the ninth night, I remember, I was dreaming of strolling around a shady market in China. Hot day, it was, a hot noon. Next moment, I find myself pinned to the ground, four guys kneeling on my arms, grappling with my fingers. I'm not a small man, I'm not, and I wallop my attacker with my right fist. Well, lucky thing I missed, it was. I was holding a cleaver. "Honda!" they shouted. "Honda!" Stolen the cleaver from the canteen in my sleep, I had. One of those lethal fuck-off blades. Type that butchers chop up frozen cows with, it was." The traffic slows further as four lanes merge into two. Ambulance lights pulse in the soggy dusk. A silver container truck lies on one side. Its cabin is crushed. Cones, and traffic controllers with glowing batons and reflective vests. Two firemen are hosing the road. Ogre strokes an amulet from Ise. "Rock solid, you believe the world is, see? Then you open your eyes and find it's all melted away, it has." The truck—or rig, as I am learning to call it—squeezes through the traffic cones, and finally we speed up. Ogre is looking for something—I wonder if the story is over. "Light me another cigarette, son? Thanks. My dream. That night. Baking hot day in China, it was, like I said. In the market I came to the watermelon stalls. Row of them. Big, green, juicy, chilled watermelons, they had. My mom whispers in my ear: 'Watch out for the Chinamen, they'll try to sell you rotten fruit, the rogues!' And she puts the cleaver in my hand, she did. I walked from fruit to fruit, tapping each watermelon with the edge of my blade, I did, judging if it was ripe or rotten by the feel of the blade. First decent fruit I got to, I would—*wham!*—whack it in half, eat it up, there and then, I would." Ogre climbs through the gears. "That's what woke the trainees up, me tapping their heads. Medication stops the sleepwalking, and the dreaming. I take a pill in the morning to keep me awake until I take a pill at night to knock me out. Out cold, I am, when I get to sleep. But to stay in the union I have to have it on my license. Them big rigs were out. A wife? Kids? Too afraid of what I might do if I dream of wringing out washing, or swatting cockroaches, or shelling peanuts. Not a small man, see?" Ogre inhales all the life from his cigarette in one go. "Just be careful what you dream, son, see? Be very careful."

"Medical researchers call it the Ai Imajo Effect." Her voice is clear as a bell. She could be in the next room. "The brightest minds in psychology have given this strange enigma the best research years of their lives, but mainstream science is still baffled. Why, oh why, whenever I fix a meal for a man, does he jump on the first truck out of Tokyo?"

I was not expecting humor. "I did try calling this morning."

"It would be useful to blame my mood swings on my old pal diabetes, but to be fair I have to blame my mood swings on my old pal me. Sorry for being such a bitch last time."

"No way, Ai, I was completely—"

"Shut up. It was my fault."

"Shut up yourself. It was my fault."

"You will hear my apology, Miyake, or our blossoming friendship is off."

"But—"

"Shut—"

"But—"

"Up!"

"Look—"

"Silence! Shut up! Okay?"

She is scary sometimes, even when she is being funny. "Okay."

"So I'm sorry for mouthing off about you and your mother, okay?"

"Okay, okay."

Pause. "So you're saying it was all my fault now, are you, you belligerent Yakushima yokel?" I have never heard her do a Kagoshima accent before. She does it with uncanny talent, the same way she does most things. I retaliate, feebly: "Us Niigata peasant farmers have no idea how to behave in polite society, see."

"That was supposed to be a Niigata accent?"

"Uh, maybe."

"Pathetic."

"I, uh, have some explaining to do. My mother called me from Miyazaki."

"I know, I know, Sachiko woke me up to tell me this morning. I had the phone machine on sleep mode. Why didn't you leave a message?"

"Us yokels don't understand these newfangled machines."

"Miyake the Brave. I was glad you threw your cigarettes away, by the way."

"You saw?"

"I have eyes everywhere. Have you smoked since?"

"No."

"Good boy. So, where are you now?"

"Uh . . . being eaten alive by insects in a phone booth outside a truckers' cafe called Okachan's."

"There must be ten thousand truckers' cafes called Okachan's."

"This one is between . . . uh, nowhere and nowhere."

"Must be in Gifu Prefecture."

"Actually, I think you're right. The last truck driver—Mr. Honda— dropped me off here, after radioing his friend—a man called Monk- fish—to ask him to pick me up when he passes by on his way down to Fukuoka. But Okachan just told me Monkfish is going to be held up. Fistfight, hunchback gas station owner, that sort of stuff."

"Pray Monkfish wins unconcussed. Poor Miyake. Sounds like you're stuck in a Nikkatsu trucker film."

"Not the fastest way to Miyazaki, but it is the cheapest. I have news."

"More news? Is it going to make me botch my toenail varnishing?"

"For sure."

Ai senses I want to be serious. "Okay . . . ready."

"Yesterday was . . ." Where do I begin? "The weirdest day of my life. I know, people say that all the time, but it really was. I—" Should I tell her about the organ harvesters? No. Not yet, anyway, not for a long time. "I met him."

A short pause. "Who?"

"My dad."

A long pause this time. "I'll call you back. Give me the number."

◆

"Eiji!" Bamboo shadows sway over the tatami mats and faded *fusuma* screens. I get up and walk through dental-floss cobwebs to the window. My grandmother must have moved to Ueno Park. Everyone has gone home. There is Anju, kneeling before an ancient, shipwrecked cedar. Yes, I scored the winning goal, and she is alive again, but her kite of sun- light is tangled in the most inaccessible branches. It shines dark gold. My sister is in despair. "Set it free, bro, please!" Delighted as I am to see her again, this puzzles me. "You're better than me at climbing, sis, why don't you set it free yourself?" Anju airs her recently acquired sigh. "Diabetes, remember?" Her legs are half bioborg—syringes, drips, instruments of torture. "Set it free for me, Eiji." So I begin climbing. Cedars have reptilian bark. Sheep bleat in a far valley. Socks, dirty beyond hope. Dark winds bay, and crows come looking for beautiful necks to plunge their spiky beaks into. I am afraid the sunlit kite will rip and shred before I can get to it. Where in this sea of leaves can it be? I find my father on the top branch, trying to unknot his shoelaces. "You didn't fool me, you know. I knew who you were all along." This no longer matters to me, and I ask him if he has seen a kite. He gives his aching digits a rest. "Chasing kites is more important than looking after your own sister?" Suddenly I remember I have left Anju alone—how many days has it been?—in our grandmother's house without food or water. Who will open her canned dinner? The house has decayed since my last visit. The lockless knob twirls uselessly. When I knock, the doorframe falls in. Cat shadows slide behind rafters. Inside my guitar case I hear Anju scrabbling—she cannot open the escape hatches, she is running out of air—I fumble, my fingernails come off, but the clasps are so rusted up—

◆

"Then I woke up," cackled Monkfish, "and it was all a dream." Croaky laughter, one, two, three. I had meant to ask him about his nickname, but one look at his face and there is really no need. His eyes have migrated to either temple and he has the rubberiest lips I have ever seen on anyone, ever. I mean it. I make a groaning, lip-smacking postsnooze noise, and mumble, "Weird dream." We are traveling down the Meishin Expressway through a hyperspace of rain. A road sign flies by at light speed—OTSU EXIT 9 KM. The dashboard clock glows 21:09. "What was it about?" I try to reassemble the jigsaw, but the pieces have blown away in the last few seconds. "Dunno . . . about my guitar, and my sister." Monkfish wipes his brow on his mesh undershirt. His rig is more modern than Ogre's, but everything is more ingrained with dirt. Uncle Tarmac says vehicles always resemble their owners, and likes advising my female cousins to judge whether boyfriends will make decent husbands or not by observing how they treat or mistreat their cars. "Dreams are funny things," says Monkfish. "I suppose Honda told you his sleepwalking story? Yeah? Knew it. He tells everyone. Load of bullshit. Just a spooky excuse for never getting laid. If you were a lady—just if, right, just if, I'm not saying nothing else, right—just if you were a lady, would you lay Honda? Pa! 'Course not. Dreams. I read up on dreams. Tell you something. Nobody knows what dreams are. Not really. Scientists say they do, but they don't. Gave a lift to a student last month. Psychology. Interesting guy. Not stuck up or anything. He said dreams are made by your hippocampus. Hippocampus, it was. It shuffles through memories in the left side of your brain. Left or right? Couldn't rightly say. Let's say left. So you have all these random memories. Then the right side of your brain dreams up a story to link all these memories together. Abracadabra. That's your dream." Monkfish does not expect me to reply—I guess he would be having this same conversation with his dangling Zizzi Hikaru doll if I were not here. KYOTO EXIT 18 KM. "I say to this student guy, I say: 'Same as a long-distance trucking job. Different customers. You got your locations. You plan your route.' He says, 'Yeah. Or scriptwriting.'" A hairy fly strolls across the inside of the windshield. I guess Monkfish is keeping the hairy fly awake too. "Ever tell you my dream story? No? Want to hear it? Tell you what, I'll tell it to you now. No time like the present. We all have a dream story. You heard Honda's. This is mine. I was your age. Head over heels in love. Or mentally ill. Same difference. Whatever. Girl by the name of Kirara. She was one of those pampered daughters-in-a-box. We went to the same swimming club. Quite a body I had in those days. Shaved my pecs. Not like now. Gone to pot, now, I have. Whatever. Kirara's daddy was the mastermind of some right-wing group. What was it?" Monkfish frowns, trying to remember. "The Emperor Party?" I suggest. "Nope, I remember now. The Ministry of Education. Which meant Kirara was way, way above the likes of me. My old man was a bricklayer. Died when I was fifteen. Not soon enough, the miserable old alkie. That's another story. This is a few years later. I was at junior college, doing auto mechanics. Kirara was at husband-netting college, doing languages and cooking. I was obsessed with Kirara. I copied out a love poem from a library book, and gave it to her one day after swimming. Swimming clubs are great. You get to see the goods before you buy. I digress. I started walking Kirara home. There was an underpass. I got a kiss! Well, hey! I have a goaty appeal to the

fairer sex. Often remarked upon, that is. Kirara fell for my charms too. I
borrowed my brother's car. We counted the stars. I counted her birth-
marks. Never knew bliss like that. Never will again. Whatever. But then
her daddy got wind of me. Checked me out, realized from my address
that I was not prince material for his princess. Told Kirara to drop me.
Kirara compared my credit rating to her daddy's and dropped me like a
scabby corpse. Stopped going to the swimming club. Went to a million-
yen-a-year health club pool instead. Now, for Kirara, I was just a dish of
peanuts to nibble with her entree. For me, Kirara was the entire menu at
the Viking feast of love. I was gutted. Distraught. Insane. I sent her
more poems. Kirara ignored them. I stopped eating. Drinking. Sleeping.
I sent her flowers. Never heard a thing. Decided to prove my devotion
by killing myself. Stupid? Yes. Young? Same difference. My mom's
brother had—still has, far as I know—a cabin in the Sea of Trees. Know
that? Not a Tokyo kid, are you? I can tell by the funny way you speak.
The Sea of Trees is at the foot of Mount Fuji. Where all the suicides go.
Anyway. I wrote a goodbye letter to Kirara, saying where I had hanged
myself, and why. 'That'll show her I loved her!' I thought. Posted the letter. Registered. Took the first train out the next morning. Imagined the
tragedy of it all. Got off at a deserted country station and started hiking.
The weather was moody and changeable, but not me. I was never so
sure. I was going to die for Kirara. Found my uncle's cabin. Nobody
around. Nice quiet glade. Guess what I see next, up in the air?"

"Uh . . . a bird?"

"No. I saw Kirara."

"What?"

"Kirara. My Kirara. With a noose around her neck. She had gotten
the same idea. Couldn't be with me, so she killed herself. To prove
her love. For me. Give her old man the finger. Did I think, 'Oh, my darling, let us be united in death!'? Did I hell. Not with her feet doing the
clockwise-anticlockwise biz. Bloated neck. Shitted thighs. Crows and
maggots already at work. I was terrified. I thought I had a moral duty to
hang myself, too, only I didn't want to anymore. Not after I'd seen what
it looked like. Death is never beautiful. Never. Lots of other things, but
beautiful? Never."

"What did you do next?"

"Woke up groaning. I was still on the early train out to Mount Fuji. Talk about an eye opener! Got off at the next station. Caught the first train going back to Tokyo. Got home. Mom and her boyfriend were still in bed. Brother came in with the dog, handed me a letter. My suicide note. Kirara had written 'Return to Sender' on it. That was that." Monkfish changes lanes to let another rig pass. The driver waves across, and Monkfish grins. "Kajiwaki! An oily dick if I ever knew one! Crafty sod still owes me fifty thousand yen." The speedometer says 100 kph, but I get the illusion we are standing still. The rig pulls forward and we enter a tunnel of echoes and air. "Saw Kirara one more time. Years later. Swear it was her. I was on my honeymoon. Narita Airport. Saw her buying perfume in duty-free. Fat-cat husband. Gold jangly things. Brat in a stroller. Guess what flashed through my head? Go on. Guess."

"You were glad you hadn't hanged yourself?"

"No. Go on. Guess again."

"Uh . . . jealousy?"

"Nothing. Nothing flashed through my head. I was ready to hang myself for her, but I never even loved her. Only thought I did. But that 'thought I loved her' was stronger than my grip on life. Took a dream to scare me back to my senses. At Narita Airport that time, I said nothing. I just watched her. She signed for the designer crap she'd bought. Husband's gold card, no doubt. Then she walked off to her departure lounge to get on her plane. My wife, she asked if something was wrong. 'No,' I told her. 'Everything is all right, love.' We had a lovely honeymoon. Dreams tell you stuff. You should listen to them."

More tunnels, valley bridges, service stations. The truck judders down the Chugoku Expressway toward a still-distant dawn. Monkfish lets me sleep. He has a tape of opera highlights that plays nonstop. He said he hates classical music, but opera keeps him awake. Grime and sweat have glued my butt to the inside of my jeans. I think of how many weeks this journey would have taken wandering poets in earlier centuries. I can hang on two or three more hours. Half-rain in quarter-light. Shapes get their names back, and names their shapes. An island in an estuary, more an ambitious sandbank. Herons fishing on flood defenses.

Lavender bulldozers leveling hills that are in the way. Bricked-up tunnels. A beer-crate depot. I imagine my mother waking up, looking at the ceiling. Is she thinking, "I wonder where Eiji is now? I wonder what time he'll get here?" I still do not completely understand how this visit is happening, how I just invited myself like I did. I was still angry with her when I asked if we could meet, so why did I say it? Sort of rude of me to corner her like that. But when she gave me her address, she seemed genuinely happy. It was in her voice. That, and I think she was nervous I was playing a sick trick on her. But this is no trick. As soon as I had invited myself, I felt it was right. I was happy she was happy. I cannot remember ever making her happy. OKAYAMA EXIT. Smoke unravels from factory stacks. Monkfish sings "tra-la-la"s to an aria the same way Yoko Ono does on "I'm Your Angel" on the *Double Fantasy* album. Vehicles rule the highways, not their drivers, I decide. Trucks change drivers as easily as men dump hostess girls. Those visits my mom used to make to Yakushima were excruciating. Between the time she left us with Wheatie and the day Anju drowned she would turn up about once a year, usually for a single afternoon. FUKUYAMA EXIT. Flame licks the corner of a mist field. Land cleared of trees in a week, asphalted in an afternoon, and forgotten ever since some committee of Mr. Aoyamas somewhere was disbanded. Weeds and saplings grow back. Pollen and spores are tougher than you think, given rain and years. Lines and wires sag and tauten from pole to pole. Wheatie refused to see her after a certain point—that must have been after the ring-tempura incident. Our grandmother brews bitterness for personal consumption later. We are good at sulking, us Miyakes, this much I do know: we could sulk for Japan. Sulking, and its deadlier mature equivalents. Anju and I would be taken to Uncle Pachinko's old house in Miyanoura—the main port—the night before. We wore our school uniforms, even though it was Sunday. Aunt Pachinko took us to the barber's the night before. Everybody knew our mother was coming, of course. She took a taxi from the wharf, even though it would have taken her less than ten minutes to walk. She would be shown into the best room, and return my aunt's small talk with a savage attention to pointless detail. HIROSHIMA EXIT. Monkfish switches off the wipers. A big sign on a mountainside advertises a bank that crashed many months ago. I remember the president of the com-

pany, weeping in front of the TV cameras as a penance. It made me sick
to see the old fart do that: "Forget the bonuses I snuck away abroad,
everyone, look at how real my tears are!" I am sure the tears were gen-
uine: no more bonuses. Maybe my grandfather was right. Maybe the old
and young are different species, and that is how the world marches on,
for better or worse, who knows? But always marching on. Mountains
march back years to the Sea of Japan. The view reminds me of the
map/progress screen between stages of a kung-fu video game. Monkfish's rig passes through uncolored-in suburbs of rerun cities. Uncle Tarmac told me years, and beers, later that Uncle Pachinko had forced our
mother to visit, as a condition of the allowance he sent her. I guess he
meant well, but it was wrong to bribe or force people to be together,
even—especially—a mother. She asked us questions. Anju and I answered them. Always the same ones, ducking hazardous topics: What
subjects do you like best? Really? How about the subjects you like least?
I see. Soccer? Nice. Any other hobbies? An interview with an anonymous orphanage inspector would have had more glimmers of fondness.
Packing me off to an orphanage would have brought such shame on the
family, though, nobody ever discussed it. TOKUYAMA EXIT. This is a familiar place-name. This is where Subaru Tsukiyama, my great-uncle, spent
his final weeks in Japan. He could not begin to recognize Yamaguchi
Prefecture today. A golf range has been hacked out of a mountain,
shrouded in green netting. Early rising microgolfers swing, and tiny
white pellets inscribe arcs. I reremember the Mailman virus for some
reason, and resolve to reforget it, but I think about it for a while. Police
officers e-mail bureaucrats, bureaucrats e-mail journalists, journalists
e-mail politicians. Most results of most actions are invisible to the prime
doer. Calm down, Miyake, I tell myself, but I cannot calm down. I say it
again in Ai's voice, "Calm down, Miyake," and this time it works. A dirty
rag of bleached blue sky—the rainy-day forecast is forgotten, the instan-
taneous way a distracted child forgets she was crying. Anju would have
been a lot chattier with Mom, I think, if I had not shot her such fierce
looks for being nice. I throttled moments that could have turned into
memories to keep Mom warm, even now. That was wrong of me. Our
mother chain-smoked. Every image I have of those memories is dim
with cigarette smoke. We never asked questions. Aunt Pachinko served

those gaudy sweets that old people imagine kids to like, and stoked the stalling conversation with recipe discussions, and our mother played along to kill more minutes as humanely as possible. Even island gossip was shaky ground—it reminded everyone that our mother had once lived on Yakushima, and, by extension, should be there now. All we knew about Mom's life, we overheard later. At night, behind partitions, through thin walls. Finally, our mother would take the early evening jet-foil back to Kagoshima, and everyone would breathe a sigh of relief. She didn't kiss us. It would have been too . . . too too. YAMAGUCHI EXIT. A tree—I wish I knew tree names—seems to dance by itself on a ridge. The mountains level out into a rockier tableland. Our mother did not come to Yakushima for Anju's funeral. Far more than dumping us there in the first place, that entered her name on the Island Book of Infamy. Gossip, the island blood-sport, reported that my mother had flown to Guam for "work" the day before Anju went missing, and had left no contact number. Other, even less sympathetic stories did the rounds. I don't know when or how she found out. Uncle Tarmac, I assume. I don't think I cared by then. The last time we met I was fourteen or fifteen. This time we were in Kagoshima, at Uncle Yen's. My mother was too ashamed, or wise, to set foot on Yakushima again. She wore dark glasses. Her hair was short and her jewelry not flashy but obviously expensive. I shambled into the room, *Homo adolescentus.* "You've grown, Eiji," was her crisp opening gambit. "You haven't," was my witty reply. "Yes," said Uncle Yen hurriedly, "Eiji's rocketed up over the last six months. Like a giraffe! And his music teacher says he's a guitar natural! Such a pity you didn't bring your guitar, Eiji. You could have played a tune or something for your mother." The rocketing giraffe scowled at the bridge of his visitor's glasses. "'Mother'? I don't have one of those, Uncle. She died before Anju died. I do have a father, somewhere, but no mother. You know that, Uncle."

I think the most powerful poison is the malicious word. Its effects may last a lifetime and there is no serum. Forgiveness may soothe the inflammation later, sure, but there is no actual serum. My mother lit a cigarette. I was already smoking by that age and I wanted one, but not one of *hers,* so I got one of mine out. That made Uncle Yen angry, I could tell. He didn't know that I smoked until then, and it put him in a bad light, since he was one of my guardians. His jaw was clenched as he poured tea for Mom, himself, and me, a little at a time in each cup, in rotation. "Your mother has traveled a long way to see you, Eiji. I want you to show her courtesy. She will think we have brought you up to be a lout. You can start by putting out that cigarette and apologizing." Before I could blurt out something like "She obviously doesn't care how I am brought up!" my mother had stubbed out her cigarette and stood up. "No apology is necessary." She spoke to her brother: she never looked at me again. "He said nothing I wish to take issue with. What I take issue with are these 'discussion sessions' that you put us through. I know you act out of niceness, but this niceness is crueler than nastiness. There is an express train leaving Kagoshima Station"—she looked at her sleek watch—"in fifty minutes, and I shall be on it. Give my regards to your wife." Maybe the passing years have rewritten the script a little, but this is the gist of what was said. Maybe I added her dark glasses, too, but even now, I have no memory of my mother's eyes.

Monkfish opens a can of coffee, switches off the opera, and tunes in to Radio Kitakyushu. The sun switches on as we cross the Shimonoseki Bridge. So much distance and height compared to that hot iron lung the world knows as Tokyo. Cargo ships and ferries to Pusan and Shanghai line up in the port. I am back on Kyushu soil and maybe this is why I am smiling. Broken fences, wildflower breakouts, unplotted spaces. Kyushu is the run-wild underworld of Japan. All myths slithered, galloped, and swam from this part of the country. The farther south you go, the more people think for themselves. Governments in Kyoto and Tokyo forget this at their peril. The expressway ends, and Monkfish slows for the toll-gate. "As my dear old granny used to say, every single morning, 'Rise early. The hour before dawn is a gift from paradise.' That was when she died. Hour before dawn."

◆

My hand falls off and I have to screw it back on. "Stationmaster! How are you? Please accept my sincerest condolences on your, uh, untimely death." Mr. Aoyama lowers his binoculars. He is still wearing his JR uniform, but he looks much more distinguished than during his life at Ueno. "Death is not so bad, Miyake. It is much the same as being paid.

Did you find your sister's kite?" I cannot make any sense of the last remark, so I just stand there wondering what you say to a dead person. Mr. Aoyama fiddles with the focusing. "I must apologize, incidentally," he continues, "for accusing you of espionage." I smile. "You were under loads of stress. Obviously." Mr. Aoyama touches his upper lip. "See? I shaved off my mustache." I tell him that major life shifts should be commemorated, somehow. "And you don't get more major than death," he agrees. This reminds me that I, too, must be dead. "May I ask how I died, Stationmaster?" He frowns at his binoculars. "Oh, no no no, Miyake, you aren't dead. Your body is on the expressway bus to Miyazaki, in fine condition except for a fungal growth about to break out between your toes. You are dreaming." This does not bring me the relief you might expect. "I've never had such an . . . undreamlike dream before." Mr. Aoyama finally looks through the binoculars. "Your own dead can calibrate your dreams. The contrast/brightness/color controls. Come with me." I realize we are flying. Mr. Aoyama is floating along freestyle, I have a Zax Omega jetpack strapped to my back. "So, are you my dead, Mr. Aoyama?" I ask. "We hired each other," Aoyama replies, "although I never hired you to spit in my teapot." Below us the majesty of creation unspools. "No offense, Stationmaster, but how come Anju never visits me? If anyone is my own dead, she is." Mr. Aoyama checks his watch. "Your sister is not exactly dead." I hit a pocket of turbulence. Aoyama dives below the cloud and points. There is the secret beach, there is the foot rock, there is the whalestone. If I could only see Anju, maybe I could pick her out of the water in time. "What is keeping her from being dead?" I ask. The last thing Mr. Aoyama says is "You." Suddenly my jetpack fails, and I am falling from a ninth-floor balcony, a playground is spinning nearer and nearer and if you don't wake up before you hit the ground you—

♦

"Gaaaaaa!" or a noise like it stuck in my throat wakes me up. I am on the backseat of a bus. Some passengers—old women, mostly—look at me. I hear somebody say "Drugs!" and tut in my direction. The doors hiss shut and the bus lurches forward. I sit up, blinking. Yes, I remember the coach. Monkfish offered to ask around some truckers' hangouts for me, but Mom is expecting me in a few hours and I can hardly be late after a six-year gap. An old lady has joined me on the back row since I fell asleep. Weird. There are plenty of unoccupied seats. She knits. Her knitting needles click very softly. Her face is oval and chipped as an aging moon. She must do aromatherapy—I can smell a herb called . . . no name comes. Between us is a bag full of ripe persimmons—not the watery Tokyo persimmons, but ripe, sticky, scarlet-flavored persimmons spirited away from the wrath of enchantresses. I drool. I have eaten crap and crap only for two days. "I propose we barter," says Mrs. Persimmon. "I give you a fruit. You give me the dream you just had."

"I never remember my dreams."

"Do you flush banknotes down the toilet?"

"No."

"Then you should train yourself to remember your dreams. We can start with the older man in uniform."

She means Mr. Aoyama! I feel cold. "How did you know?"

"Nothing sinister about that. Most dreams have an authority figure, just as most ghost stories have a ghost." From this starting point I reconstruct the dream as best I can, and I think I do a reasonable job. I leave out the detail about Anju being my sister because it may lead to all the usual embarrassing questions—I just say she was a girl in my class. She counts the stitches on her needles. "No, I will not be shortchanged, young man. What did you omit?" So I have to admit that Anju is my twin sister. Mrs. Persimmon considers. "When did she leave, this unfortunate?"

"Leave where?"

"This side, of course."

"This side of . . ."

"Life." No, her knitting needles make the sound of a blind person's stick.

"Nine years ago. How did you know that?"

"I shall be eighty-one a week from Thursday." Her mind is wandering, or mine is plodding. She yawns. Tiny, white teeth. I think of Cat. She unpicks a stitch. Have I offended her? I ask her what she thinks my dream means. "Dreams are shores where the ocean of spirit meets the land of matter. Dreams are beaches where the yet-to-be, the once-were, the will-never-be may walk awhile with the still-are. You believe I am an old woman hoary with superstition, and possibly deranged to boot." I could not have put it that well. "If I were not deranged, how else could I know what I know? Here. You have, at last, earned your persimmon."

Miyazaki is toy town after Tokyo. At the bus station I go to the tourist information office to find out about the clinic my mother is staying at. Nobody has heard of it, but when I tell her the address I am told I will need to get on a local bus headed for Kirishima. The next one is not for over an hour, so I go to the station bathroom and clean my teeth. Next I find a pharmacist, buy some athlete's foot powder, empty a quarter of it into a pair of relatively clean socks, and change into them. I sit down in the waiting room drinking a can of cold coffee, watching the buses and passengers come and go. Miyazaki people amble. The clouds are in no hurry and a fountain makes rainbows under palm trees. A retired dog with cloudy eyes comes to sniff hello. A very pregnant mother tries to control a clutch of floppy, spring-heeled children. I remember my persimmon—my grandmother says pregnant women must never eat persimmons—and peel it with my penknife. I get sticky fingers, but the fruit is sweet, pearly, perfect. I spit out shiny stones. One of the boys has just learned to whistle but he can only do one tune. The mother watches the kids leap along the plastic seats. I wonder where their father is. Only when they start playing with a fire extinguisher does she say anything: "If you touch that, the bus men will be angry!" I go for a walk. In a gift shop still with its unsold 1950s stock I find a bowl of faded plastic fruit with smiley faces. I buy it for Buntaro to get back at him for my Zizzi key holder. At a Lawson's I buy a tube of champagne bombs and read magazines until the bus arrives. I should be nervous, I guess, but I lack the energy. I cannot remember what day it is, even.

I expect a smartish institution with car parks and wheelchair ramps on the outskirts of town—instead, the bus follows a lane deeper and deeper into the countryside. Over a thousand yen later, a farmer on the bus points down a country road with a daikon and tells me to walk until the road becomes a track and to go on until the track runs out. "Can't miss it," he insists, which usually spells disaster. A hillside of pines sheers up on one side: on the other, early rice is being harvested and hung out to dry. I find a big, flat, round stone on the track. Grasshoppers trill and ratchet. I put the stone in my backpack. Cosmos flowers sway, all mauve, magenta, and white. All this space. All this air. I walk, and walk. What is the word that means a fear of open spaces? I begin to worry—after twenty minutes I can see the end of the lane, but there is still no clinic in sight. Comic-horror scarecrows leer. Big heads, bony necks. Agoraphobia? The road runs out of tarmac, and I can see the track dies altogether at a group of old farm buildings at the foot of an early autumn mountain. Sweat pools in the small of my back—I must smell none too fresh. Did the bus driver let me off at the wrong stop? I decide to ask at the farmhouse. A skylark stops singing and the silence is loud. Vegetable plots, sunflowers, blue sheets hanging in the sun. A teahouse stands on a small rise in a rockery. I am already past the gate when I see the hand-painted sign: MIYAZAKI MOUNTAIN CLINIC. Despite the signs of life, I cannot actually see a soul. I feel uneasy—I am an intruder here. My mother is in this building! I very nearly lose my nerve and backtrack. I see no bell or buzzer near the front door, so I just open the door and enter a cool reception room where a woman—a maid?—in a white uniform is organizing mountains of files into hills. It is a losing battle. I wonder how to attract her attention without scaring her. She sees me, and stops what she is doing. "Hi."

"Hello. Can I, uh, speak to the nurse in charge, please?"

"You can speak with me, if you like. Suzuki. Doctor. You are?"

"Uh, Eiji Miyake. I'm here to meet my mother—a patient. Mariko Miyake."

Dr. Suzuki makes an ahaaaaaaaa! noise. "A very welcome guest you are too, Eiji Miyake. Yes, our prodigal returnee has been on tenterhooks all morning. We prefer the word *members* to *patients,* if that doesn't sound too cultish. We were expecting you to call from Miyazaki. Did you have any trouble finding us? I'm afraid we are rather a long way out. Of course, a measure of solitude assists treatment. In the cities we Japanese force ourselves to live in, the question should not be 'Why do so many of us suffer from mental illness?' but 'Why do any of us not suffer from mental illness?'" The doctor watches me working out whether she expects to hear an answer, and smiles. "Put your bag down. Have you eaten? Our members are having lunch in the refectory."

"I had a rice ball on the bus . . ."

"Then you must still be hungry."

"It came with pickles."

Dr. Suzuki correctly reads my nervousness at meeting my mother in front of a party of onlookers. "Why don't you wait in the teahouse, then? We are rather proud of it—one of our members was a tea master, and will be again, if I have any say in the matter. He modeled it on Senno Rikyu's teahouse and the groundsman helped him build it. It really is quite something. A crafts journal did a piece on it. I'll go tell your mother her visitor is here."

"Doctor—"

Dr. Suzuki swivels around on one foot. "Yes?"

"Nothing."

I think she smiles, almost. "Just be who you are."

I take off my shoes and sit in the shady, four-and-a-half-mat hut. Yes, I am nervous, but acoustic-strumming nervous, not death-metal-megawatt nervous. I watch the humming garden. Bees, runner beans, lavender. I drink some barley tea—warm now, and frothed up—from the bottle I bought in Miyazaki. I can smell pine resin, straw thatch, fungal infection powder. Kneeling on the ceiling, a papyrus butterfly folds its wings. I lie back and close my eyes to compose myself, just for a moment.

♦

New York billows snows and gray crows. I know the blond driver of my big yellow taxi, but her name escapes while I look for it. I fight past journalists and bug-eyed lenses outside the recording studio, where John Lennon is swigging his barley tea. "Eiji! Your guitar had given up all hope." Since I was twelve years old, I have wanted to meet this man of genius. My dream has come true, and my English is a hundred times better than I dared hope, but all I can think of to say is "Sorry I'm late, Mr. Lennon." The great man shrugs, exactly like Yuzu Daimon. "After nine years of learning my songs you can call me John. Call me anything. Except Paul." This strikes us as very funny. "Let me introduce you to the rest of the band. Yoko you already met at Karuizawa one summer, on our bicycles—" Yoko Ono has shrink-wrapped her head and is dressed like the queen of spades. "It's all right, Sean," she says, "Mummy's only looking for her hand in the snow." I appreciate the filial reference. John-san points to the bass guitarist. "Klaus Voorman, the unsour Kraut." I shake hands with the reliable German. "And on keyboards, ladies and genitals, may I introduce our old friend Misterrrrrrrr Claude Debussy." The composer sneezes and a tooth flies out, which causes a new round of laughter—yet more teeth fall out, causing yet more laughter. "My pianist friend, Ai Imajo," I tell Debussy, "worships your work. She won a scholarship for the Paris Conservatoire, but her father says she isn't allowed to go." Hey, my French is perfect too, and I've never even studied it! "Then her father is a boar with pox," says Debussy, on his knees to gather up his teeth, "and Ms. Imajo is a woman of distinction. Give her my address! I always had a love for the Orient!" We step outside into Ueno Park, among the bushes and tents where the homeless people live. "John-san—what is 'Tomorrow Never Knows' actually about?" John pulls a philosopher pose. "I never knew." We giggle helplessly. "But you wrote it!" He dabs his tears away. "No, Eiji, it wrote me." Doi lifts the tent flap. The pizza box contains cannabis compost. Picture Lady—it seems we are her guests—produces a cake knife with a polished stoat-skull handle. We are each served a thin slice—it tastes of green tea. "Which is your favorite song by John, Eiji-kun?" I realize that Picture Lady is in fact Kozue Yamaya working undercover, but her secret is safe with me. "Simple. '#9 Dream,'" I answer. "It should be considered a masterpiece." John is delighted with this answer, and mimes an Indian deity, singing "Ah, bowakama pousse pousse." Even the Perspex whale outside the science museum giggles. My lungs fill up with laughter and I am having serious trouble breathing. "Truth is," John continues, "and I know you have waited patiently for this explanation, '#9 Dream' is a son of 'Norwegian Wood.' Both are ghost stories. 'She' in 'Norwegian Wood' curses the listener with loneliness. The 'Two spirits dancing so strange' in '#9 Dream' bless the listener with harmony. But people prefer loneliness to harmony. That's why you hear 'Norwegian Wood' played in elevators."

What an honor to have a conversation like this with my virtual father. "John-san," I say, "I don't know if I'll get another chance to say this, but your songs help me understand my life." John shrugs. "You're welcome. I wrote them for me and Yoko, but if other people get a kick out of them, great." "Power to the people," I answer, inspired. "Power to the people, right on!" He giggles. I have one last question. "What does the actual title of '#9 Dream' mean?" John-san thinks. "The meaning of the ninth dream begins after all meanings appear to be dead and gone . . ." We are interrupted by a furious guru. "Your meaning is too vague, Mr. Lennon! Your wanton imagination has run wild again! Why are you quitting your search for enlightenment?" John scoffs. "If you're so bloody cosmic, you'll know why!" I am laughing so hard.

◆

"I was laughing so hard," I tell Ai, "I woke up."

I hear Ai flumf onto her sofa. "And?"

"And there was Mom, standing in the doorway."

"What must she have thought?"

"Well, first she thought I was drunk. Then she thought I was having a seizure. She was about to run for Dr. Suzuki."

Ai selects one question from the crowd. "What were the first things you both said?"

"I . . . dunno. I guess I said, 'Don't worry, I was only dreaming,' or something just as forgettable. I remember what she said, though. She told me that Anju used to giggle in her sleep too. Weird. I think it got us off to a good start. I mean, I could hardly get all defensive and sulky after she found me rolling with laughter and unconscious at the same time, even if I had wanted to."

"How long did you talk for?"

"Oh . . . three hours. Dr. Suzuki brought some tea out."

"Three hours!"

"We kind of cut a deal. We—what do lawyers say—we dropped charges. She is my mother, and I am her son, yes, but we sort of pretended not to be. That way we could get on and talk."

"'(Just Like) Starting Over.'"

"Hey! You listened to *Double Fantasy*?"

"Mmm, of course. So where are you left now, you and your mother, I mean?"

"Well, I don't want to pretend this was a summer-of-love festival. I mean, yes, we had the first real conversation I think we have ever had. I asked a question. Then she asked a question. We took it in turns, like that, and talked about a lot, but neither of us wanted to push the other too hard, and really get into the minefield stuff, y'know, 'Did you ever stop to think about what it would do to us?,' 'Did you mean it that time you said you didn't have a mother?,' that degree of stuff. One day we probably will have to do all that. But the teahouse was just too summery. I did say that I wish I hadn't stopped Anju from talking with her on her visits, and she told me I didn't have to apologize because I was so young at the time, and I said I wanted to apologize for my own peace of mind, not hers, and she nodded and left it at that. I sort of liked her. She can be very funny. She was telling me how they all cheat at dominoes. Apparently Dr. Suzuki is the biggest cheat of them all. I realized she is a real person. Mom, I mean."

"I could have told you that."

"I always thought of her as a magazine cutout who did *this* and did *this* but who never actually felt anything. Today, I saw her as a woman in her forties who has not had as easy a life as the rumor mill on Yakushima reckons. When she talks, she is sort of in her words. She told me about alcoholism, about what it does to you. Not blaming it or anything, just like a scientist analyzing a disease. An alcoholic, she says, is three things: a wounded person who desperately needs love and support; a person controlled by a parasite that lives in that person but is not that person; and a wounded person who will devour love and support until nobody and nothing remain. I am talking a lot."

"Talk, Miyake, talk."

"And guess what—my guitar? It turns out it was my mother's—all these years, my guitar was her guitar, and I never even knew she could play."

"Was the hotelier from Nagano there?"

"He visits every other weekend: not today. I said I'd go back next Saturday."

"Good. Ensure his intentions are honorable. And your real father?"

"Ah, yes. That was one of the minefield issues. She didn't mention him once. And what could I say? 'Yeah, incidentally, I tracked down my father. Yes, still married, yes, still porking any gullible woman he can dazzle with gleaming bullshit and later bribe with luxury crap.' I was enjoying the conversation too much to screw things up. She asked how I liked Tokyo, and if I had any friends. I boasted about my one friend, the genius pianist bound for the world-famous Paris Conservatoire."

"One friend. What an elite club. Where are you staying tonight?"

"Dr. Suzuki offered to find a futon in a corner somewhere, but I'm catching a train down to Kagoshima to stay with my uncle—"

"Uncle Yen, right? And tomorrow morning you board the Yakushima ferry and visit Anju's grave. And the day after tomorrow, you decide tomorrow."

I am lost for words. Ai is so cool sometimes. "How did you know?"

Urgent clouds stream across a cinema sky. I know Ai's face has its "so what?" expression on. "I have perfect pitch," she says.

The bored horizon yawns down the coast south from Miyazaki. Only the swaying carriages tell you that the train is even moving. These tidal mud flats belong to the Hyuga Nada Sea, south of the Bungo Strait, where my great-uncle sailed on his first and last mission aboard *I-333*. If binoculars were powerful enough to bring the last year of the war into focus, we could see each other across these waters. I wonder if I will meet him in a dream one of these nights. Time may be what stops everything happening at once, but rules are different asleep. I smell autumn fruit. "What a small world it is," says Mrs. Persimmon, without a flicker of surprise. "This seat is free?"

"Sure." I dump my backpack on the rack.

She sits as if she is easily bruiseable. "Did you enjoy my fruit?"

"Uh, delicious, thanks. How was my dream?"

"Not particularly flavorsome, I am sorry to say." She pulls her knitting out.

"What do you do with the dreams you, uh, acquire?"

"What do you do with persimmons?"

"I eat them."

"You think old ladies do not require a little nourishment too?"

I wait for an explanation, but Mrs. Persimmon gives none. I am about to ask, "Are you saying that you eat dreams?" but stop myself. Too stupid a question. I look out of the window instead. An atomic power plant, a frigate, a lone windsurfer. I feel pressure to make polite conversation. "Are you going to Kagoshima?"

"Between here and there."

"Seeing relatives?"

"A conference."

I wait for further explanation. Flower arranging? Needlework? Chairlifts? But she concentrates on her knitting. It appears to be a pair of gloves, but she has made way too many fingers. "Are you a dream interpreter?"

"A less stupid guess than usual. My younger sister, who handles the business side of things, describes our profession as 'channeling.'"

I assume I mishear. "You collect Chanel accessories?"

"What a ridiculous notion. Do I look like I do?"

"Sorry . . . 'Channeling.' Is that, uh, the same as irrigation?"

Mrs. Persimmon holds up a thumb to silence me while she counts a row of stitches. "Waterless irrigation. I rather like that. But you prove my point. This word-meddling confuses people. I told my sister, 'We are witches, plain and simple, and witches are what we should call ourselves. Why be ashamed of our true nature?' How annoying. I dropped a stitch. I shall have to begin this line again or my grandmother will belittle me."

"Excuse me—did you say 'witch'?"

"Semiretired. I believe in making room for the young ones."

Why me? "I, uh, would never have guessed."

"Of course not. Not in a world lit by television, threaded by satellites, cemented by science. The idea of elderly women fueling their life spans in perpetuity by absorbing energy released in dreams is insane, is it not?" I hunt for something appropriate to say, and fail. "Disbelief is good for business. We can get on unhindered. When the age of reason reached these shores it was us witches who breathed the most heartfelt sigh of relief."

A girl in a JR uniform wheels a refreshments cart past. I want help, not tea or coffee. "So, uh, how do you eat a dream?"

"I never said I did. I said 'absorb.' A dream is a fusion of spirit and matter. Fusions release energy, which is why sleep invigorates. If you do not dream you will not hold on to your mind. Channelers, witches, what you will, are able to absorb the dreams of healthy youngsters such as yourself. The way sunflowers draw strength from the sun."

"Is it wise to go around telling people this?"

She grins at me nastily. "Anyone insisting it was true would be locked up."

I regret eating that persimmon. "I, uh . . . need to use the bathroom." Walking to the toilets I try to piece together an elaborate no-offense escape plan: I should say goodbye and leave our compartment at the next station, and then sprint up the platform to a carriage farther back before the doors close again. Coming back, I am made giddy by the illusion that the train is quite stationary but I am strolling over the landscape at Zax Omega speeds. When I reach my seat I find she has vanished.

◆

Red plague eradicated all human life except Ai and myself, who survive thanks to natural immunity. We have made ourselves a home in the Amadeus Tea Room. We go on long walks through the parks and stores of postapocalypse Tokyo. The end of the world has improved the city. She performs a Debussy arabesque at the empty Budokan, although it sounds similar to "Strawberry Fields Forever." I run through my Lennon repertoire on the finest guitars stocked by the music store near Suga's university. Ai makes delicious salads and serves them in TV satellite dishes. We live as brother and sister for a long time until we hear a meeeeeeeeep noise from the balcony. We peer out, through the half-open window. A hideous bird strolls along the railing toward us. Pig-big, turkey-necked, condor-shaggy. Its beak is a hacksaw. Its eyes are alcoholic and snotty. "Quick!" cries Ai. "Close the window! It wants to get inside!" She is right, but I am scared of that beak and I hesitate. Too late! The bird thing hops onto the window frame, onto a chair, and rolls on the carpet. Ai and I are still afraid but also curious. Great evil may follow, but also great good. The bird peers at the decor with the eye of a potential buyer. It finally roosts on the wedding cake and speaks. "The cat in the wig on the ceiling will have to go."

◆

Ai answers on the third ring. "You again."

"Yeah. I want to be your prank caller."

"I saw on the news, Kagoshima has a typhoon warning. Are you there already?"

"Not yet. I have to change trains here."

"Where is here?"

I read the peeling sign. "Miyakonojo."

"Never heard of it."

"Only train drivers and the people who live here have. Am I interrupting anything more interesting than waiting around on a deserted platform?"

"Me? I've been floozying around with Scarlatti."

"You loose woman. First Debussy, now . . . Who?"

"Domenico Scarlatti. He wrote five hundred and fifty-five harpsichord exercises. The more he felt death breathing down his neck, the faster and more magnificently he wrote his sonatas. I find geriatric prodigies much more interesting than child prodigies. What kicked his creative booster rockets into life? Kirkpatrick, his biographer and the finest American harpsichordist in history, suspects Scarlatti's patron extorted the sonatas from him in return for paying his gambling debts. A fabulous story, if it's true. All this miraculous music gets bequeathed to humanity just because its creator was lousy at poker."

I would rather avoid talk about card games. "I dreamed about you on the train just now. There was you, and this scabby turkey thing."

"Eiji Miyake and his killer charm."

"I love you."

What?

Ai actually splutters. "*What?*"

What?

I am hurled clean out of the ring by the sumo wrestler of embarrassment. "Uh . . . I didn't mean to say that. Oh. Uh, I am so sorry, I didn't plan it or anything, it just came out all on its own. I am so sorry. I haven't known you long enough, Ai, I mean, we haven't even, uh . . . done anything. No, I didn't mean you have to do, uh, anything to feel what I just

said, I know, before, I mean. But. Uh . . . I don't understand myself
sometimes. I really don't. I can hang up if you want. How can I—"

"Calm down, Miyake." I cannot calm down but I do shut up. I can
hear distant traffic in Tokyo coming down the line. "Did you mean what
you just said?"

"What part?"

Is she smiling? "You know what part."

"Uh . . . what do you think?"

"Oooh, no. You're the man. You take *your* dignity to the pawnbroker."

"That's so unfair."

"Unfair? Try being a woman sometime."

I take a deep breath. I am gambling with my only friendship. "I
dunno, Ai. Really. It just slipped out, just then."

"Let me try again. Did you mean what you just said?"

"Well, I know I can't say I didn't mean it."

"That must be one of the most romantic affirmations I ever heard."
Ai's irony is sort of therapeutic. "And to think it all began with a dream
of a putrid chicken."

"Scabby turkey. And it was a cute scabby turkey. Sort of." I think she
is smiling, and I begin to feel sure of myself for the first time since . . .
who knows? "So say something back, Miss Imajo."

"Okay." Her piano lid clunks open. "This is Scarlatti's K. 8 in
G minor. Allegro." Ai performs until my phone card dies. I think she
likes me.

The crowded train pulls into Kagoshima JR station under an end-of-the-
world sky. Ghosts of K. 8 in G minor tango in the atmosphere. I should
be thinking about Mom, or even my anticlimax father, but the truth is,
right now, nothing can remove Ai. Sometimes the thought of her burns
even brighter and my heart sort of squid-propels itself toward the sun. I
can remember her perfume. How she looked that first rainy day I saw
her washing up. So this is why love changes the course of history. Love.
Love? Love! The conductor announces that due to typhoon eighteen all
train services are canceled until further notice. That means tomorrow
morning, at the earliest, and half the passengers moan in unison. The

conductor adds that all bus and streetcar services have been suspended, which gets the other half of the passengers groaning. So I have an immediate problem that not even love can fix, because Uncle Yen lives over the ridge of hills to the northeast of Kagoshima, way past the university, and it takes two hours on foot. At the station I call him, hoping to cadge a lift, but the line is busy. I guess I should walk to the port and camp out in the ferry terminal. They have a cheap noodle joint and a cleanish bathroom. Powerful gusts of wind kickbox across the bus square. Palm trees take up the strain, banners flap stiff, cardboard boxes cartwheel. People run as if a bomb is about to drop, and businesses are closing up early. Turning the corner into Harbor Road, I nearly get picked up and half-volleyed to Nagasaki. The wind god is driving a juggernaut this evening. I have to lean to walk. Sakurajima, the volcano island, is there across the bay but not quite real. The dark sea is crazed with waves. A hundred meters later I see my problem is worse than I thought—the entire harbor is closed because of possible tsunamis. Right, what now? There are no taxis running. I could stay in a hotel, and then not be able to pay in the morning. I could find shelter in a doorway? Not much shelter, not tonight. Beg mercy at a police station? When I remember that yesterday morning I anonymously informed on a massive organ-extraction and smuggling syndicate undoubtedly involving the participation of high-ranking law enforcers, I decide to give police stations a miss. Just sometimes, I wish I was as rich as Yuzu Daimon. Right now, for example. I decide to brave the walk to Uncle Yen's, hoping—against my better judgment—that we are in injury time of the typhoon as opposed to shortly after kickoff. I take a shortcut across the school soccer field where I scored the only goal of my cut-short career, nine years ago. Nine years! It seems only . . . nine years. Time has so many gears. I walk back past the JR station and push on down the coastal road, but walking is wading and progress is slow. This feels as if I dreamed it. I have the road to myself, or I might try to hitch, even though mainlanders rarely pick you up. Nonaerodynamic objects soar gracefully past my head—car shrouds, beer crates, tricycles. The wind assaults and batters, the sea banzai-charges the defenses, lashing up spray to slap my face. I walk past a bus shelter without a roof. I seriously consider stopping at any of these houses and asking if I can sleep in the entrance hall. I walk past a tree with a bus-shelter roof embedded in its trunk. Then I hear a whooooooooosh a meter from my head. I crouch on reflex, and it was lucky I did. A screaming pterodactyl—no, an enormous tire with a diameter wider than I am tall—bounces off the road and leaps over the seawall. It might have fallen off a Chinook helicopter. Now I am afraid of winding up as roadkill. I draw level with Iso Garden, where I had intended to turn inland, but the typhoon is growing so I decide to jump over the wall and find shelter inside. I was brought here on school outings and remember some brick buildings with protected alcoves. The wind flips me over the wall, and I land in thrashing bougainvillea. The peaceful Japanese garden I remember is now a demonic-possession movie. A madwoman is banging doors over and over. Over there— I scramble through stinging twiggy nails—up a steep slope, and I trip into the gardener's hut. Compost, tarpaulin, twine. The latch is smashed, but I drag a sack of soil and succeed in wedging shut the door. I am alone with spades, trowels, rakes. A narrow partition runs down one wall, too dark to see behind. First, I straighten out chaos caused by the typhoon's forced entry. Second, I arrange a makeshift bed from the tarpaulin. Third, I finish the bottle of Java tea I bought in Miyakonowherever. Fourth, I listen to the typhoon rhino-whip this old crate of a shed and worry about tsunamis and a certain scene from that old movie Anju loved, *The Wizard of Oz*. Fifth, I stop worrying and try to single out voices in this symphony of roaring.

◆

My bladder sags painfully from my navel. Liverpool is much as I imagined. Those minicars with surprised headlamps, haircuts like Julian Lennon's, although the PanOpticon comes as a surprise. In the entrance lobby Lao Tzu is grinning on one leg. "Need the toilet, Captain?" I nod. "Fifty thousand yen." The price is exorbitant, but my bladder is puffing up, balloonlike, so I pay, complaining that I already paid at the unfinished airport. Lao Tzu crawls ahead on his belly because the stalactites hang down so low. Water drips down. I have to proceed on my back to avoid rupturing my bladder, which wails "Are we nearly there yet?" with the voice of a marine mammal being dragged inland. "Here," says Lao Tzu, occupying the only unoccupied urinal in a row of nine. I wait, but the men appear to have calcified. Careworn Mrs. Marui bobs an apology and withdraws. "Colonel Sanders!" General MacArthur claps my shoulder. "One of these goddamn yellow monkeys stole my platinum lighter. Heard anything?" I shake my head, which is difficult in this asbestos-molded fat Kentuckyman costume. "I see. Heard anything about a top-secret project called Kaiten?" Now I have a dilemma. "No, General." That wasn't so difficult. He leads me up shelves that are not shelves, but steep stairs. A knotted rope hangs down to help you haul yourself up. I find myself in the ferry building in Kagoshima, which I had mistakenly thought closed due to a typhoon. The place has been renovated. Where is the toilet? All the signs are in braille. I imagine my aunts reading the headline "Local Boy Miyake Forgets Toilet Training in Tokyo!" My bladder is now a child-shaped wobbling mass of urine that clings around my middle. "Over there, Daddy!" it squeals. I follow its erect finger and find myself in a men's room as big as a soccer field. The only other patron is a speck in the distance. I unzip my jeans, aim my single-mindedly asexual Godzilla at the urinal, and—the patron whistles the whistling part from "Jealous Guy" in my ear. I hadn't felt him move this near! His voice crackles with hatred. "So where is she now, hey? Up her tree? On the whalestone? In the guitar case? How do you sleep? How do you sleep at night?" He is trying his best to make me afraid, but suddenly *I* am the one crackling with hatred. "Oh, fuck off!"

◆

I wake up with an aching bladder to a hideous shipwreck noise, very near. The typhoon shoulder-barges the door open when I shift the sack of soil. I piss through the crack, wedging the door between my feet very very carefully indeed. My piss is unthreaded by the wind and probably reaches Singapore. I wonder if the Singapore police will trace it back and fine me. I return to my tarpaulin nest, but going back to sleep is made difficult by the violence in the sky. I wonder if the teahouse at Miyazaki Mountain Clinic is still standing. I hope so. If not, I will help the tea master repair it next weekend. I remember every detail of my last dream. I seem to be in one of my dream binges. When I began my serial uncle visits after Anju drowned, I imagined there lived somewhere the Real Eiji Miyake, in an Adland house with the Real Anju of course, not the one who drowned. This Real Eiji Miyake dreamed me, every night. My waking life was his dream. The typhoon catches its breath, and renews its assault as a gale. I roll over on something hard, and find a medium-size, flat, round stone. I put it in my backpack. The potting shed is not going to blow away, not tonight. The gale catches its breath, and renews its assault as a high wind. It is then that I hear a person, snoring! Inside the potting shed! Amazed, I get up and look behind the narrow partition. My eyes must have adjusted to the darkness, because I can see a woman, asleep. She does not look like a gardener. She must be a visitor who got trapped by the typhoon, and snuck in here for shelter, the same as me. Do I wake her? Or would that scare her? Her eyes open. "Don't be afraid," I begin, although I am the one who is afraid. "I was wondering when you would wake up." She springs up and her kimono swings open. I am too startled to squeak. For a very weird moment, I mistake her for the mother of Yuki Chiyo, the little lost-property girl at Ueno. It cannot be her. Can it? She dabs Godzilla with her thumb, and dabs my nipples with her wet thumb. Her other hand explores my boxer shorts. I begin to realize this is very wrong, that Ai and I are not yet lovers but we are no longer single, but her lips slide open and a million tiny silver fish change direction with one accord. I cannot fight this, or look away, or respond. So I come.

Over the shoulder of Yuki Chiyo's mother I see Mrs. Persimmon. She perches on the sack of soil and sucks pulp from her favorite fruit. Shiny stones slide from between her wrinkled lips and fall to earth, ever so slowly.

The bright garden lies trashed by an orgy of gods. Spilt juices from green veins scent the air. Ripped blooms, torn branches, uprooted shrubs. I find a small, flat, round stone. I put it in my backpack. I would love to stay awhile and watch the pond, but I want to avoid the potting-shed owner, and anyway the Yakushima ferry leaves in ninety minutes. I wade through the ripped bougainvillea and clamber over the wall, in time to surprise a schoolgirl on a passing bus—she grabs the attention of her classmate, but the bus has already moved on. My only witness. Back among the houses, neighbors are already up, discussing the mending of fences. I stop at a Lawson's and buy a bottle of Minute Maid grapefruit juice and a cup of ramen—kimchi flavor—and ask the girl to add hot water. I eat it on the seawall. Sakurajima belches ash into the spotless sky, and handkerchief waves fold blue to white. Typhoons wreck worlds but the following morning clean worlds up. I phone Uncle Yen to say I am still alive—I tell him I spent the night with friends in Kagoshima, otherwise he will probably insist I pay Iso Garden the entrance fee, he is that sort of man—then I walk the rest of the way to the port. The ferry is waiting—cars and trucks are already being herded on by harbormen with flags and whistles. I fill in my boarding card, pay my fare, wash, brush my teeth. I need a shower, and I need to clean my boxer shorts. I look for a telephone.

"Typhoon eighteen was on the news," said Ai, "but it didn't get much attention because of the pigeons."

"Pigeons are grabbing headlines now?"

"All day yesterday, all over Tokyo, pigeons were flying into buildings, colliding with cars. Like some freaky disaster movie. You can imagine the rumors, theories, and experts cramming the TV stations. Secret government tests, avian flu, Aum cultists, magnetic wave shifts. Then the moon last night had its brightest halo for nineteen years. How ice crystals in the atmosphere could affect pigeons nobody knows, but it adds to the spookiness. And this morning, I went to buy some coffee for breakfast, and the camphor tree in front of the prison was black with crows! What a noise! Worse than a brass orchestra warming up! Seriously, it was as if the prince of darkness was due any moment."

"So much for my measly typhoon."

"Let me change the subject before your coins run out. I spoke with Sachiko before she went to work yesterday evening. If you need anywhere to stay when you get back to Tokyo, you can crash here. On the sofa. When I say so, which will depend on how I feel. You have to clean up and cook every third day. And you mustn't answer the phone in case Sachiko's grandmother calls and assumes you are her live-in lover, or worse still, in case my mother calls and assumes your accent is not Yakushima but French."

"Hey . . ." I like the sound of "when I say so." "Thanks."
"No need to decide yet. Mull it over."

Several islanders spot me as I board the ferry. Schoolmates' mothers, cousins' friends, a sugar cane and fruit wholesaler who does business with Uncle Orange. They ask about life in Tokyo, more out of politeness than interest. I say I am back to collect my winter clothes before the weather changes. Talk is of typhoon eighteen, and how much damage repair will cost, and who is likely to pay for what. I hide in the second-class area, and make a sort of barrier with my backpack to doze behind. A Kansai ladies' ramblers' club takes up the rest of the floor around me. They are decked out in flannel shirts, bodywarmers, multiweather trousers, silly hats, and sensible footwear. They unfold maps and plot routes. You can tell the islanders apart easily—they look bored. Because there was no sailing yesterday afternoon the boat continues to fill with passengers. I shuffle up for a man with a greyhound jawline and cheekbones who asks me what time the ferry arrives at Miyanoura. He pays for this information in unshelled peanuts. I accept a few because it would be rude not to, but in fact I really enjoy them. We munch our way through most of the bag, piling up a mound of husks. Greyhound is a publisher in the Ochiai area of Tokyo and knows Ueno lost-property office—he met Mrs. Sasaki's sister at a literary dinner once. The engines grooooaaarrrrrrrrr into life, the hiking ladies wooooooooo! and the porthole view rotates and slides away. The nine o'clock news bulletin is about the expected resignation of another prime minister following a coalition collapse. "Nothing is older than this morning's news," says Greyhound, "and nothing is newer than Pericles." Pretty soon the offshore reception turns the news to hiss, and the Kirishima-Yaku National Park video clicks on. All islanders know the script by heart. It lullabies us on these crossings.

◆

All Japan has been concreted over. The last forests are now discarded chopsticks, the Inland Sea is covered and declared a national parking lot, and where mountains once stood apartment buildings vanish into the clouds. When people reach the age of twenty their legs are amputated and their torsos are fitted with interfaces that plug directly into sophisticated skateboards for use in the home or office. My twentieth birthday was back in September, so I am long overdue for this rite-of-passage operation. But I want to keep my legs attached, so I have joined the resistance movement. I am taken to be introduced to our three leaders, who live in Miyakonojo, the rebel hideout. Their bodies are amputated too, for extra camouflage. Their heads sit in a row, drying in the sun. Their necks are trussed to the edge of a bowling alley, and I realize I have been brought before Gunzo, Nabe, and Kakizaki. I hope they don't recognize me—they could have me executed as a double agent. Fortunately, when they see me they blink—"Messiah! Messiah! Messiah!" This perplexes me. "Are you quite sure?" They seem to be. "The message shall be revealed to you! You alone shall reverse the meteoric dive of humanity into endless suffering!" That sounds great. "How?" Kakizaki smiles tenderly. "Pull out the plug." Between my feet is a bath plug, with a shining chain. I pull. Underneath is earth—since the asphalting laws, earth is forbidden. It stirs, and a worm wriggles upward and out of the hole. Another follows, and another, another. The last Japanese worms. They wriggle their way to a preordained position on a nine-by-nine grid. Each position on this grid is a kanji or kana, written in worm bodies instead of brushstrokes. These words form the true scripture. It is also death for the worms—the tarmac hot-plates their tender bodies. As they sizzle, they smell of tuna and mayonnaise. But their sacrifice is not in vain. In the eighty-one characters I read truth—naked, pure, golden. The secrets of hearts and minds, quarks and love, peace and time. The truth glows in blazing jade on my memory's retina. I shall impart this wisdom to my thirsty species, and the arid desert of humanity will bloom again.

♦

"Miyake! Miyake, you mongrel! Wake up!"

The upside-down face of Mr. Ikeda, my ex–sports teacher. A half-eaten tuna and mayonnaise sandwich wilts in his hand. I jerk up, groaning with annoyance. Mr. Ikeda assumes I am just sleepy. I have to remember something, and look away, but Mr. Ikeda buzzes back into my field of vision. . . . "I saw you in the ferry terminal, but then I said to myself, 'No, Miyake is in distant Edo!' What are you doing back so soon? The big city too much to handle, hey?"

I am forgetting something. What is it? "Not really, sir. Actually, I—"

"Ah, to be young in Tokyo. I could almost envy you if I wasn't already me. I spent the first two Great Primes of my life in Tokyo. I waltzed into *the* top sports university—you wouldn't have heard of it—and a wild young thing I was, too. The days I had! The nights I had! My nickname among the ladies gives you the full story. Ace. Ace Ikeda. Then in my first teaching post I put together one of the finest high school soccer teams Japan ever saw. Could have gone all the way to the national cup qualifiers, if the referee hadn't been a geriatric, blind, crippled, corrupt, menstruating, dribbling sack of slug shit. Me and my boys—our nickname? The Invincibles! Not like"—Mr. Ikeda waves his hand in disgust at the students in their YAKUSHIMA JUNIOR HIGH tracksuit tops—"this pack of mongrels."

"Are you coming back from a friendly game, sir?"

"Nothing friendly about that bloated faggot tapeworm Kagoshima coach. During the typhoon last night I was praying a truckload of Agent Orange would crash into his house."

Whatever I had been charged to remember, it has slipped away. "So, what was the score, sir?"

Mr. Ikeda grimaces. "Kagoshima Tosspots—twenty. Yakushima Mongrels—one."

This knife I cannot resist twisting. "One goal? A hopeful sign, sir."

"Kagoshima Tosspots scored an own goal. Well, doubtless I'll be seeing you around." Mr. Ikeda skulks off. The tourist video clicks off—we must be within broadcasting range of Yakushima. I look through the window and see the island, sliding over the horizon. The prime minister promises that under his guidance the country will become a lifestyle superpower. Greyhound cracks open a peanut. "Politicians and sports coaches both need to be smart enough to master the game, but dumb enough to think it matters."

I remember my dream.

"Are you unwell?" asks Greyhound.

"I . . . dreamed I was a sort of Sanzohoshi carrying the Buddhist scriptures from India. I was shown the divine knowledge necessary to save humanity from itself."

"I'll give you six percent on the first ten thousand copies sold, nine percent thereafter."

"But I can only remember one word."

"Which is?"

"*Mumps.*"

"As in . . ."

"Yeah, the illness that makes your neck swell up."

"*Mumps* . . . what?"

"Mumps . . . nothing."

"Deal's off." Greyhound shakes the bag. "Sorry. I ate the last peanut."

Yakushima increases in size every time I take my eyes off it. One of the hiking-club ladies' hats flies away over the sea, and I turn away from the coos and consternation to hide my laugh. I can see the jetfoil in Miyanoura harbor . . . the new tourist center . . . the taxi stand. Mitsui's father still drives his taxi. Leaving a place is weird, returning is weirder. In eight weeks nothing has changed on the island, it seems, but nothing is the same. The bridge, the crushed-velvet mountains, the prison gray escarpments. A book you finish reading is not the same book it was before you read it. Girls are the same, too, perhaps, in the morning. Not that I would really know. Here comes the quay—one of the cable throwers shouts, "Hey, Miyake!," waves, and spits into the swell—one of Uncle Tarmac's mah-jongg drinking crowd. The gangplank is lowered, and I join the big group of disembarking passengers. I should go and pay my respects to the head of the family here in Kamiyaku, Uncle Pachinko, or at the very least give Aunt Tarmac a call to say I need to stay over tonight. Problem is, once word of my homecoming is out I will have a spontaneous celebration to fend off, and I won't make it to Anbo until the day after tomorrow. The point of this visit is to pay my respects to Anju. I am still dithering outside the ferry ticket office when a van pulls up and the wholesaler offers me a lift. "Going as far as Anbo?" I ask. "Jump in," he replies, and we drive off. "Warm day," I say. "Rain soon," he answers, and I nod. Rain is always a safe bet on Yakushima. The wholesaler is a silent man, so there are no embarrassing silences or sly questions. He gestures to me to help myself to a sack of

ponkan oranges, the island's chief export and easily the best fruit product in Japan, if not eastern Asia. I must have eaten ten thousand of them
in my life. Cut me open, you get ponkan juice. I watch the forgotten
details of my home. Rusty oil drums by the vacation homes, the tiny
airstrip—I used to think it was huge—and the dying sawmill. I am so far
southwest that I have caught up with the shabby summer leaves. We
pass a cluster of sleek racing cyclists in tropical-fish colors. Over the
bridge, the waterfall. "Anbo village," says the quiet wholesaler, slowing
to let a tanuki cross the road ahead. "Welcome back, Eiji."

The cemetery hammers and saws with the empire of insects. The trees
shimmer and stir. The afternoon simmers, as the ancient October recipe
suggests. The Miyake corner is one of the best-tended corners of the
enclosure—my grandmother still comes every morning to clean, weed,
sweep, and change the wildflowers. I heard she was making money by
doing the same for the graves of islanders who have left for Osaka and
Tokyo, who cannot get back for the Obon week of the dead in August. I
bow before the main family stone, and walk around the side to the
smaller one that was erected just for Anju. It is inscribed with the death
name the priest chose for her, but I never bothered learning the kanji
because I think it is just a way for temples to palm more money from
mourners. Anju is Anju. I pour the afternoon's dust off her with mineral
water, and arrange the flowers I picked walking down from the road.
Clusters of white stars, pink comet tails, crimson semiquaver berries. I
make an offering of a champagne bomb, and unwrap one for myself, too.
Then I light the incense. "This is a present from Mom. From Miyazaki.
She says hello, and she'll come and see you properly one day after she
gets married. I found our father, eventually, but I also found he's a prize
jerk, and we were best off without him, believe me." I take out my three
flat, round stones and build Anju a pyramid. I sit on the step and press
my ear against the tombstone to see if I can hear anything. The sea
breathes peacefully beyond the edge where the land falls away. I want to
kiss the tombstone, so I do. It is hot against my dry lips. A dark bird with
rose eyes is the only witness. I lean back in the sun and think about
nothing in particular until my champagne bomb explodes. So little lasts.

Mountains, classic songs, friendships, perhaps, and not much else. Maybe I doze for a while, because suddenly the glossy sky is turning matte, and mist is flanking down Mount Miyanoura. The sea is beery. I brought our great-uncle's kaiten journal to read parts to Anju, because they both died in the ocean, but I think if Anju can hear me here she can hear me anywhere, and this afternoon I think being here is louder than saying anything. Ants have discovered Anju's champagne bomb. I make another unplanned break with recent Miyake tradition. "Hey, sis, guess who I'm going to see now?"

I half-expect to meet my eleven-year-old self retrieving his sports bag from behind the lichen-disfigured stone lions in the Neck. I never went back to the thunder god shrine. His beheading made the Kyushu newspapers. Nobody assumed a local would vandalize our own heritage. A famous craftsman was brought from Kyoto to replace the missing head. You can see the head in the tourist brochures. Even so, the forest has all but reclaimed the dead-kid path. Every winter the thunder god's believers become fewer. Gods die, the same as pop idols and sisters. The hanging bridge no longer looks so safe. The sun has gone in. A nightingale sings about another world. A monkey curses his luck in this one. The river is hurrying and swollen with typhoon rain. Over half the farms in the valley have fallen into disuse since Anju and I lived here. Old farmers die too, and their sons move away to mainland cities, do very well for themselves, and never come back, like Uncle Yen has done. I realize that I have left Yakushima too, without ever meaning to. Life never labels the last time you do something. Rice-field terraces and old storehouses are allowed to collapse, typhoons doing the job at a better price than demolition companies. The valley is between rain and not rain. I kick stones. The roof of my grandmother's house reminds me of Buntaro's unkempt beard. Shrubs sprout from the eaves. I watch the old place, and think of all the family dramas that have happened in its rooms. Shuttlecocks trapped in drainpipes, broken greenhouse panes, Anju's complex burglar traps. Mist is already gathering on the lower slopes of the valley. My grandmother is a sour old lady but she loved Anju, too, in her fierce way. Leaving a picture lets you see the things in it. What is there to lose? The worst that could happen is that she throws a rolling pin at me and screams at me to go away, but after some of the people I have met in the last eight weeks that would amount to a polite refusal.

"Gran?"

I wade through the grass in the courtyard, and think of the old tale of a spinning-wheel sorceress awaiting her adulterous lover's return. Years pass, and the house goes to rot and ruin, but she never ages a day. In this mist I could be in a tale. Behind mossy stones I see a pearly movement—a snake! Its head and tail are invisible but its coil must be as thick as my arm. Did Anju say something about a pale snake, once? Or was it one of the Goatwriter stories? Or was it my grandmother who said how every house in olden times had its own snake that appeared to announce an imminent death, and that she had seen one in this house just before her father died? The animal vanishes behind a rusting cultivator. Just an old superstition—snakes never live for seventy years. I knock on the frame, and force open the stubborn door. I hear the radio. "Are you home, Gran? Wheatie? It's Eiji."

Nothing. She was deaf when we lived with her, though, and my aunts say her hearing has gotten worse over recent years. I slide the insect screen aside, step into the cool, and slip out of my sneakers without undoing the laces. I breathe in deeply. Cooking sake, damp wood, chemical toilet. Incense from the tatami room. That particular old-person odor—I guess they can detect a particular young-person odor too. A mouse disappears. The radio means my gran is probably not at home—she was in the habit of leaving it on for the dog, and after the dog died she left it on for the house. "Gran?" In the tatami room I feel that somebody I know has died—caused by seeing that pale snake, no doubt. My grandmother is fine, or the silent wholesaler would have said something. A feather duster is propped up against the foot of the family altar. Hanging scrolls of autumn scenes, a vase of flowers, a cabinet filled with trinkets and baubles of an island lifetime. My grandmother has never even crossed the water to Kagoshima. Raindrops, barely heavy enough to fall, splash through the mosquito netting, so I draw the window shut. The respect I felt for this room and its visiting spirits verged on fear when I was a small boy. Not so for Anju, of course. She used to hide outside and burst in to catch the ghostly Miyake ancestors munching the cherries our grandmother left out for them. I look at the black-and-white dead and the Fujifilm deceased in the lacquer cabinet. Dressed in oilskins, suits, uniforms, flying goggles, costumes rented from the photographer in Kamiyaku. Here is Anju, toothy on her first day at elementary school. I go into the kitchen and help myself to a glass of water. I even recognize this glass. I sit down on the sofa that Anju and I tried to levitate and fly to Tahiti—why there, I do not know. She blamed our failure on my puny ESP powers. I believed her for years. The sofa, which is as old as my gran, boingggs, but after two long, sleep-starved days it is comfortable, way too comfortable . . .

♦

I dream everyone in the world is asleep, dreaming. I dream frost patterns on a temple bell. I dream bright water dripping from the spear of Izanagi, and the alchemy that transforms these drips into the land we call Japan. I dream the Pleiades, and flying fish, and speckled eggs in nests. I dream of skin flakes in keyboard gullies. I dream cities and the ovaries they issue from. I dream lovers who glimpse each other long before they become lovers, and I dream the songs they fall in love to, and I dream the songwriters who find the songs. I dream a mind in eight parts, and a compass rose. I dream of a girl, drowning, resigned to her fate now that she knows there is no possibility of being saved by her brother. Her willowy body is passed from current to current, tide to tide, until it has dissolved into pure blue, and I am sorry, but she knows I am sorry, and she wants me to let her go because she does not want me to drown too, which I will, if I spend the rest of my life looking for her. I dream of a stone whale, of barnacles on the whale, watching it all. When my dream falters, all the world questions its own substance, so it is no surprise that I also dream the message bubbling from the stone whale's blowhole. "This is the National Seismology Bureau, interrupting this program to bring you an emergency news flash . . .

♦

. . . a major earthquake has struck the Tokyo region within the last thirty seconds. It measured 7.3 on the Richter scale. I repeat, 7.3. This magnitude represents an earthquake with a greater destructive power than the Great Kansai Earthquake of 1995. Widespread structural damage must be expected throughout the Kanto plain. Imminent aftershocks are likely, and the public in the affected area is advised to evacuate buildings immediately and proceed to an open space if possible, and away from the danger of falling masonry. Do not use elevators, turn off gas and electricity, stay away from windows, and leave personal belongings behind. Due to the scale of the earthquake, all programs on this channel are canceled until the dangers are more fully assessed. People living in coastal areas on the Pacific coast north of Wakayama are advised to prepare for tsunamis, and to move to higher ground if possible. We will be updating nonstop as we receive more news. . . . I repeat, a massive earthquake has hit the Tokyo Bay area . . ." Cold and shaking, I turn the radio down and lift the receiver of my grandmother's antique telephone. I dial three times, but Ai and Sachiko's number is dead. Same with Shooting Star. I cannot get through to Nero's. I try Ueno: even here, I am not connected. In desperation I try the Tokyo operator. Nothing. I would sell my soul for this to be a dream. I feel strangled by helplessness. Are the cables and airwaves jammed because of the volume of traffic trying to place calls to the capital? Or because . . . the images start, and I cannot stop them. Windows exploding an inch from Ai's face. All the capsules above Shooting Star collapsing into the first floor. Ten thousand pans of boiling oil in ten thousand kitchens overspilling. Pizza ovens tipping over. Girders crashing through pianos and beds. Shelves shooting their contents across rooms. Overpass pillars turning to sand, underpasses caving in. The subway system . . . Rush hour has started . . . All those people in tunnels . . . Here on Yakushima, centuries of quiet rain are falling among the pine needles. What now? What now? I cannot think straight, so my body takes over. I fly down the polished hallway, scrunch my feet into my sneakers, fight with the knots, scrape open the door, and begin running.

nine

About the Author

DAVID MITCHELL is thirty-three years old and lives in
Hiroshima. He is the author of the novel *Ghostwritten*.

About the Type

This book was set in Fairfield, the first typeface from the hand of the distinguished American artist and engraver Rudolph Ruzicka (1883–1978). In its structure Fairfield displays the sober and sane qualities of the master craftsman whose talent has long been dedicated to clarity. It is this trait that accounts for the trim grace and vigor, the spirited design and sensitive balance, of this original typeface.

Rudolph Ruzicka was born in Bohemia and came to America in 1894. He set up his own shop, devoted to wood engraving and printing, in New York in 1913 after a varied career working as a wood engraver, in photoengraving and banknote printing plants, and as an art director and freelance artist. He designed and illustrated many books, and was the creator of a considerable list of individual prints—wood engravings, line engravings on copper, and aquatints.